KAREN HARPER

The Falls

KAREN HARPER

The Falls

MIRA®

ISBN 0-7394-3502-7

THE FALLS

Copyright © 2003 by Karen Harper.

Printed in U.S.A.

For Meg Ruley
Who knows a good story when she sees one.
Thanks for ten years
of advice and friendship.

And, as ever, to Don
For twenty-seven years and those yet to come.

1

September 5, 2000
Portfalls, Washington

Though Claire Malvern was a sound sleeper, something woke her. Except for the constant, distant roar of the waterfall, their fishing lodge lay silent. She couldn't even hear her husband's usual deep and steady breathing.

She reached across the king-size bed. The sheets on his side were cold. Still groggy, she pushed herself up on her elbows. The muted red glow of the digital clock on his side of the bed illuminated no shoulder, no silhouette. The numbers read 3:13 a.m.

She flopped back down, then held her breath, straining to listen, but the rush of river mingled with the falls shrouded other sounds. Once comprising a central dining hall and a series of separate cabins, their rebuilt fishing lodge sprawled along a heavily treed crest overlooking the volatile Bloodroot River, which ran with rain and snowmelt from the Cascades to Puget Sound.

Claire fought her exhaustion. They had both been working too hard. Yesterday had been Labor Day, and labor they had, on this big, old place into which they'd sunk their assets, toiling toward their dream of opening The Falls Bed and Breakfast as soon as possible. Keith had been a bit edgy lately; he'd probably just had a bad dream or couldn't sleep. Or maybe the anchovy pizza had given him heartburn.

Their attached bathroom was dark, and the door wide-open. Perhaps he was downstairs, just wandering, planning, envisioning the future. Their move from Seattle to the small town of Portfalls, in rural, rugged Washington, had been his idea. She loved the beauty here, too, but they had left good careers in their mid-thirties for this great escape, as he called it.

Adrenaline pumped through her. She sat up. The room seemed chilly, but she felt flushed with distress.

"Keith?"

The sharp sound of her voice startled her. "Keith?" she repeated louder.

Claire got up, shoved her feet into her slippers and tugged on her terry-cloth robe. In the cold moonlight that threw itself through the tall, new windows, she could see quite clearly. Knotting her belt, she looked over the banister at the hulking shadows cast by the big pieces of furniture in the high-ceilinged great room below.

"Keith? Where are you? Are you okay?"

In both the bedroom and loft, she began to turn on lights, even though it meant anyone on the river would be able to look in on her through the span of windows, as if this were a lighted aquarium. But surely no one was out there at three-thirteen in the morning. Besides, if Keith had stepped out on the deck for some reason, the lights would draw him back. So what if he'd surprised her with a late-night walk, however unusual?

Claire hit the recessed ceiling lights for the great room and hurried down the curved wooden staircase, blinking at the brightness. She sensed, somehow, that Keith wasn't in the house, but she kept looking. She checked that the doors were still locked, the bolts shot, too, then realized he could have gone out and relocked everything. She rushed through the kitchen to the garage, where their SUV and truck sat. Then, hoping he had just walked to one of the three bedrooms in the wing they'd been renovating for future guests, she snapped on more lights. In each room, Claire looked out onto the deck that ran the entire length of the lodge above the river.

No sign of Keith.

She began to panic. Claire considered herself a down-to-earth person, but she had a fanciful bent, too, or she would never have been a successful interior designer and painter. Her serious nature began to do battle with her imagination. Her husband had gone for a walk and had been sitting on the deck stairs, staring at the beauty of the moonlit woods and the rapids of the foaming salmon river, when he tumbled off the step and hurt his ankle. Maybe he'd been calling for her outside and she hadn't heard him. Or he'd gone out to the old fish-cleaning shed to putter.

But none of that was like him.

Her heart pounding, she tore back upstairs, taking the steps two at a time, and yanked off her robe and nightgown. Shivering, she pulled on underpants, jeans and a sweatshirt, and shoved her feet into her old, paint-splattered loafers. She was angry with him now. Why had he left without waking her? This wasn't like him. In ten years of marriage, he'd never done anything like this.

She took his pistol from the bedside table drawer. The Smith & Wesson .38 revolver was ice-cold to the touch; she grabbed a jacket just to have a pocket to carry it. Though only nine inches long and one pound in weight, it felt huge and heavy. She hated guns and rarely touched the thing. But outsiders might be camped nearby, especially during these big salmon runs on the river. It was common for fishermen to walk under their windows, hopping across the boulders below, or to park along River Road and access the river through their driveway, even though their sign said Private—No Parking or Stopping.

Downstairs again, with a flashlight in one hand and cell phone in the other, Claire went outside and checked the back deck. She thudded down the stairs, circling the lodge and looking in the outbuildings, then moved away from the lights. She decided she'd have to shout for him, even if it attracted someone else. Fishermen were mostly a helpful lot, caught up in the excitement and camaraderie of chasing the silvers, pinks and sockeyes driven here by desperate instinct to spawn.

For once she cursed the Bloodroot River and the falls, wishing for silence so she could hear Keith's voice. Her flashlight trained on the ground, she started down the path that ran along the river.

"Keith?" she shouted, her voice breaking. "Answer me!"

"I can't believe it's this late—or early," Nick Braden told the two other men chowing down at the counter of D.B. Café at the tiny Portfalls airport.

"It's four a.m., I'm on duty at eight, and need some shut-eye. I haven't done the graveyard shift for years—thank God. Even with this food, I'm starting to feel like a zombie."

"You make out the schedules," said Jackson, the Native American counter cook. "Give yourself a coupla days off for once."

"You the man!" Herb Black agreed, his mouth half-full. "So how in the Sam Hill you gonna get the graveyard shift when you're doing the sched'ling?"

All three customers, hunched over the cedar counter, were polishing off plates of bacon, eggs and hash browns smothered in ketchup. Jackson kept the coffee cups full. Nick sat around the corner from the other two, where he could observe them and the entire room—habit from years as a military policeman and then as an officer for various rural Washington police departments.

"Yeah, you got you a real hotbed of crime to keep an eye on 'round here, Sheriff," Herb kidded him. Herb was a pilot who flew fishermen or tourists out to the San Juan islands. "Piece o' cake—that's what you oughta be eatin'."

On Herb's other side, Pete Simpson, who was shiny-head bald, snorted a laugh as he wiped his plate with a piece of toast. "Hell, show some respect here. The man's got three deputies to cover three islands, on top a big, bad Portfalls. He's not exactly Sheriff Andy Taylor of Mayberry anymore. I'll bet his officers got more than one bullet in their guns, too. With the growth 'round here, it's more like *NYPD Blue* these days."

"You got that right," Nick said, going along with

their ribbing. He was used to masculine kidding from the military and the sheriff's office, and always gave as good as he got. "Juvies with too many beers in them, domestic spats—I could tell tales that would curl your hair, me hearties." He rose from his stool and dropped a folded five on the counter, though the bill only came to $2.99.

"Not to mention," he added under his breath, "drugs, thefts and the big biz in search and rescue for jumpers."

Beyond banter now, the others nodded. Citizens were concerned about crime creeping north from Seattle as the population of tourists and citizens climbed. It was common knowledge that the old railroad bridge had been a favorite site for local or drive-in suicides for years.

The derelict bridge offered a scenic view of swift water fed by the mesmerizing falls, but there were few observers. Only the occasional fisherman hiked up the river that far; once in a while, Nick's deputies on random patrol checked the river path. Unfortunately, during the overlapping salmon runs, something especially luring and elemental seemed to beckon as a person looked down into the rushing river with fish leaping, fighting hard against the pristine but powerful current.

On his way out, Nick nodded to Jackson, who sent him a two-fingers salute on his baseball cap for the good tip. More than once, the cook had given Nick a heads-up when he suspected something strange going down around here. Just last month, Nick had busted a so-called sportsman flying cocaine in from Canada, in a clever reversal of the usual south-to-north route.

Nick walked through the otherwise empty café, which was built like a big Quonset hut. He stopped part way, looking out the windows that faced the short, blue-light-edged runway where small planes landed from the various islands and towns up and down this part of the coast. His only luxury in life, the beloved purple-and-white Cessna 206 Amphib, sat anchored near the single hangar, sitting high on her wheels and floats. He often flew the *Susan* to the small outer islands included in his jurisdiction. Despite the heckling he took, his duties as small-town, rural county sheriff were many and demanding, so he rarely used the plane just to get away anymore.

He started out of the café again, glancing as he always did at the framed, yellowed FBI poster hanging by the front door. MOST WANTED, the big print read. Twenty-some years ago, the now-notorious D. B. Cooper had hijacked a Boeing 727, then bailed out nearby at ten thousand feet with $200,000. Some of the money had been found, but never the man himself—who would be in his seventies by now. The guy had simply disappeared, and many, including Nick, had spent far too much time trying to figure out how.

Capturing such a high-profile criminal was the stuff that law enforcement officers' dreams were made of. Nick's ambition had been to be sheriff here, so he'd worked hard and spent too much money for his campaign last November. His landslide election had been worth it, but being sheriff was a double-edged sword.

It meant more Rotary Club speeches, more PR work and even media interviews, more hand-holding of distraught victims before turning the case over to his staff—and, in this day and age, more attempts to stay politically correct and not get sued. It meant less time for the hands-on solving of cases that had once excited and challenged him. But it kept him damn busy, and he needed that. He'd lost his wife, Susan, five years ago this week, but somehow he had never quite moved on emotionally from her death.

The moment he unlocked the door of his unmarked Ford, he heard his radio crackle with the night dispatcher's voice. The static of his portable radio had bugged him while he was eating; at this late hour, since he wasn't technically on duty, he'd turned it off for once.

"Nine-one-one emergency, code 2, 302 River Road, the old fishing lodge just west of the falls," the night dispatcher, Peggy, was saying. "Raven, do you copy or are you still at that domestic?"

If his night deputy was on a domestic disturbance call, he could cover, Nick thought. Ordinarily he'd used his cell phone so he could call in directly to the dispatcher. Too many people could monitor their frequencies these days, so his department tried to keep things private, using a minimum of coded messages on the radio. But it was late at night, and he wanted to intervene before Mike Woods, alias Raven, was drawn away from the domestic.

"Eagle One," he told Peggy, using his call sign. "What's the nature of the 911?"

"The woman says her husband's missing. She's been looking inside and out, and sounds really shook. Name of Claire Malvern, husband Keith Malvern. You at home, Sheriff? I heard you went to Cedar Island."

"I'm at our airport. Leave Raven on the domestic,

and I'm en route. I know that old place from years ago. You know how these MIA things go with wandering husbands, especially during the last hurrah of the summer, when the beer is flowing.''

"Affirmative. Don't you go falling in that wild water out there!''

Though she was expecting the police, Claire jumped at the three strong raps on her kitchen door. "Keith,'' she whispered, praying it would be him as she rushed to answer. She'd finally come back inside after searching and shouting in the forest around the lodge, both before and after she'd called 911. The only living thing she'd seen was an owl.

"Mrs. Malvern?'' the man who stood outside called to her. "Sheriff Nicholas Braden. You called in that your husband's missing?''

His voice was deep and clear. Sheriff Braden was not in uniform, but she recognized him from photos in the local paper and on his campaign posters. He looked like a logger in his flannel shirt, jeans and jacket. Behind him sat a car without any logo or bar lights. Perhaps he realized he didn't look official, because he held up his badge in a sort of leather wallet, then pocketed it when she pulled the bolt to let him in.

"I was out early this morning, so I took the 911,'' he explained. "Mr. Malvern hasn't returned?''

"No, and I'm not even certain when he left. I just discovered at about three-fifteen he was gone.''

He followed her in and closed the door behind himself. "Three-fifteen a.m.?''

"Of course, a.m.!''

"Ma'am, sometimes we get calls like this hours after the person disappears."

"I didn't mean to snap at you. I don't care what other people do, this isn't like him. His car's here—both the SUV and truck. And he always sleeps soundly." She started to pace, her arms wrapped around herself as if she were chilled instead of perspiring.

"Okay, fine. Let's go over a few other things," he said, but his voice had gone suddenly gruff.

For one moment, when he'd first looked at her in good light, he'd startled and almost gaped. She was certain they'd never met, but he'd reacted as if he'd seen a ghost. Maybe he was shocked at the way she must look, with her face tear-streaked and her hair wild.

"What is it?" she asked, wiping her cheeks with both palms.

"No problem. Let's just go over a few things," he said, clearing his throat. He sat at the kitchen table after she indicated he should, then flipped open a small, spiral notebook. "It's significant that the vehicles are here. Has he taken anything else?"

"You mean his wallet or a suitcase?" Raking her fingers through her hair, she sank into the chair across the big pine table from him.

"Right. Keys, too."

"I'm so out of it I didn't check. I just ran everywhere looking for him, including outside. But I can go upstairs and see. He must have had his keys to relock the dead bolt from the outside."

"You'll need to check for such personal items."

"Yes, yes, of course." He was obviously used to distraught people. His voice and demeanor remained calm, controlled and politely commanding, though he kept darting looks at her.

"How old is your husband, Mrs. Malvern?"

"He's thirty-six."

"Height? Weight?" He wrote with a ballpoint pen, hardly looking at his notebook and focusing on her instead.

"Five-nine, almost five-ten. Light brown hair, pale blue eyes. He's a jogger, so he's thin, about 170, I guess...I really don't know how much he weighs. I guess he lost some weight before we moved here."

"From?"

"From jogging, from all the physical labor around here, I don't know."

"I mean, where did you move here from?"

"Oh, Seattle, last year."

"Does he have family ties there?"

"No. We're both from San Diego, but he has no immediate family anymore."

"How many years married?"

"Why does that matter?" she cried. She wanted to scream at him to stop chatting and start a search. Then, realizing he had to do things his own way, she added, "Ten. Almost ten years."

"Any children or other parties living in the home?"

"No."

"Had Keith been drinking?"

"Drinking? Two beers with a pizza, hours ago. Keith hardly drinks at all, since getting out of the corporate rat race."

Nodding, he went on. "Back to jogging. Does he ever do it at night?"

"No, never."

"Never?"

"Not since we moved here, at least. In Seattle, he used to get home late and then he would."

"Does he jog along River Road? Those turns can be treacherous."

"Yes, but not at night! He jogs the river path sometimes, but again, *not* at night."

"Okay. I'd like to see a photo of him. If he left his wallet, his driver's license will do. With your permission, I'd like to do a little walk-through of the house."

"Fine, though I swear I've looked everywhere in here." Claire noted that while Nick Braden scanned the room, he was also watching her like a hawk. "I can show you around the house, anything to help," she added. "I know it's pitch-dark outside, but I have lanterns we could take, too."

"If we decide to do a wide search, it will be when daylight—"

"*If?* And who is the *we* who will decide?" she exploded, jumping to her feet.

"Technically, I'll decide," he admitted, standing.

For the first time, Claire realized that he was much taller than Keith. It seemed so strange to have him in her kitchen, where she kept picturing her husband, wanting to see her husband.

"But I do have precedents and procedures to follow," he went on, "especially if I can ascertain there is no reasonable explanation for his disappearance. Of course, if there's any hint of foul play—"

"Impossible. I'm not claiming he was abducted from our bed or spirited off by aliens, Sheriff. There has to be some…some accident or something. What do you mean by 'precedent'?"

"Adults missing for thirty or more days—"

"Thirty days? A whole month?"

"The good news is that most people reported missing turn up alive and well within a couple of days. Some have just walked away for a while."

"Not Keith. He's been busy, looking forward to the opening of this place."

"He's seemed happy? You've both been getting along?"

"Of course," she blurted defensively, but she suddenly wasn't sure of that. He must have been happy, and they'd always gotten along. It seemed they'd known each other forever; they had started dating in high school. It was a friendship that became a marriage and partnership. Though this new life was his idea, his dream, she had tried hard to make it hers. Sheriff Braden was still scrutinizing her, when he should be starting a search.

"Mrs. Malvern," he said as he walked slowly toward her, "it looks to me like you've got a firearm secreted on your person. You want to take it out slowly and put it on the counter for me?"

For a moment she just gaped at him. It was like the man could see right through her clothes. So that's why he'd been watching her so closely. "I—it's Keith's, not mine. I forgot. I just thought I should carry it when I went outside."

She took it out and put it down, holding the handle with her thumb and index finger as if it would burn her. To her chagrin, he took a paper napkin from the counter, picked up the pistol and sniffed at it. Did he think she had fired it? At Keith?

"He has a license for that," she said.

"Fine, good. It's significant that he didn't take it

with him. But if you don't usually handle it—and it looks like you don't—just carrying it could be more dangerous for you than going unarmed.''

He squinted to see if it was loaded, while she bit her lip and glared at him. He shook six bullets to the kitchen counter. Both embarrassed and angry, she resented his lecture and his attitude. He should be doing everything he could to find Keith.

"Why don't we both look around inside again. You can give me a sort of tour,'' he said, rising and placing the gun on the counter, a good distance from the bullets.

"Fine with me. Time's wasting, Sheriff. What if he's lying injured outside somewhere? What if he's even fallen in the river? What if...''

Her voice trailed off as, for the first time, she let herself think—fear—he could even be dead. What if he'd gone down to walk the river in the moonlight? Those boulders could be slick and the rock-strewn current was strong. Worse, less than half a mile away, overlooking Bloodroot Falls, that railroad trestle bridge spanned the river. She'd heard the county had tried to get it torn down for years, but the railroad refused to fund its demolition and the county never had enough money. Of course, the bridge might have nothing to do with Keith, but Claire knew he thought the view from it was thrilling.

"Mrs. Malvern?'' The sheriff was waiting for her to take him around the lodge. "I said, let's be sure your doors and windows are all locked from the inside. If we can determine if he let himself out—''

"He must have. I didn't, and no one's been in here. We were just working so hard today on one of the guest rooms,'' she insisted helplessly, flinging gestures. "We didn't even leave the property, just sent out for pizza."

"Did he ever walk in his sleep?"

"No, he slept like a dead ma—like a rock," she corrected herself before she exploded in tears.

The sheriff quickly came closer. Stiff-armed, he cupped her shoulders in his big hands to prop her up against the kitchen door. To keep from collapsing, she seized his wrists hard in both hands and sobbed.

2

"Sorry...I'm all right," Claire choked out, as Nick watched her fight back an attack of hysteria. They stared into each other's eyes at close range, as he half propped her up, half held her against the door. "I know this isn't helping."

It was helping him to assess her. Nick didn't tell her that the spouse was of almost as much immediate interest as the missing partner. When he'd first returned to the States after the Gulf War, he'd worked a missing persons case where a couple was in cahoots and faked the husband's death for a big insurance policy. He knew of another case in which a spouse murdered her mate. But experience and gut instinct told him this woman, though strong-willed and volatile, was not hiding something dire—unless that was just wishful thinking on his part.

Because his problem with Claire Malvern was partly a personal one: though her coloring was not like his dead wife's, she was the same size and build as Susan. Something about the way she tilted her head, the graceful way she gestured, rocked him. Claire's deceptive fragility coupled with her inner strength, obvious even under stress, made him feel more protective than he should. All that had been part of Susan's allure. He had never believed in love at first sight until he met Susan.

He shook his head to clear it. Though it was second nature for him to stay in control of situations, Claire Malvern somehow pushed his emotional buttons. Maybe it was just because Susan had died exactly five years ago this week, or because, alone in this sprawling, masculine lodge, Claire seemed so vulnerable. He hoped this rush of desire to help her came from the fact that he so seldom experienced the challenge of hands-on interrogation and investigation anymore.

Claire pulled away, stepping out from between him and the kitchen door. She swiped at her tears, and he offered her a tissue from the box of them on the kitchen counter.

"If Keith's done this, something unexpected and strange," she said, dabbing under her eyes, "it's just so unlike him."

Nick noted she was talking in circles now, but as she shoved her hair back from her face with both hands, she seemed to regain control of herself.

"I understand." He forced himself to give the pat answer he used when someone distressed—or someone suspect—was emoting.

"You don't! You can't!" she challenged. "How can you possibly understand suddenly losing my husband into thin air?"

"Then, maybe you can help me understand it. I'd like to look around."

"Yes, all right," she said with a sniff. "Any more questions, just ask."

The place was ablaze with lights, which suggested she'd already searched every nook and cranny. He almost told her he'd been to this once bare-boned place with his grandfather years ago, but she hardly needed to hear his happy memories right now. The Malverns had done a great job, gutting, rebuilding and decorating the place.

Though the lodge reeked of virility, he noted softer touches, no doubt her doing. In the high-ceilinged common area, three overstuffed, blue-green tartan chairs sporting plump pillows faced a dark green leather sofa, across a huge coffee table. Braided area rugs looked like water-washed pebbles on the shiny cedar floor. One wall was all glass windows. Facing that, the mantel over the stone hearth displayed two tall oriental vases in vibrant cobalt blue and white. The other two walls looked totally different: both were paneled, but one seemed weighed down by four large, mounted salmon, frozen in the midst of eternal leaps. The other was graced by four small oil paintings of local scenes.

She led him up the corkscrew staircase to the second floor. They had evidently added it on to the main part of the lodge, because he didn't recall the staircase or the height of this ceiling.

"The loft area could be an extra bedroom someday, but we've been using it as an office," she explained, gesturing toward the first door.

He looked inside and around, even under the desk. It held a computer and monitor with a screen saver of colorful fish constantly swimming back and forth, as if in a fishbowl. If Keith Malvern stayed missing awhile, Nick would ask her permission or get a search warrant for a tech consultant to check the hard drive for clues. He slid open the doors to the closet. It held cartons marked Books and X-tra Linens. Nick hesitated at the door of the master bedroom, then followed her in. He'd coldly assessed and searched numerous other bedrooms, but this beamed room seemed not only personal, but intimate. Once again, framed paintings of local scenes, including the falls and the trestle bridge, caught his eye.

In place of a headboard, a huge navy, white and yellow quilt hung on the wall above the mussed king-size bed. "Yes," Claire said, standing at the dresser, "his driver's license is still in his wallet—credit cards and cash, too—but his keys are gone." She extended the license to him, so he walked over to take it, then went closer to the bed to tilt and read it by the light of the bedside lamp.

Keith Malvern, handsome in a fading, blond, boyish-good-looks kind of way, stood staring blankly at the camera in a picture that was as bad as a mug shot. Nick's quick scan of the room revealed the ubiquitous smiling wedding photo and two more stunning oriental vases. Someone must collect those expensive-looking pieces. The covers of the big bed showed they had been sleeping far apart; the sheets were barely ruffled on his side while her side looked churned to waves.

"I guess you can tell that's his side, his bedside table."

"How about his clothes?" he asked, shifting away from the bed to glance into their adjoining bathroom, then behind their door and even into the frosted-glass shower stall, though he could tell no one was in there. It looked neatly scrubbed and smelled faintly of some sweet scent. He raised his voice slightly to call out to her. "Can you tell what he might have been wearing, or do you think he went out in his pajamas, or whatever?"

"Oh, no. Because he slept without any—without

anything,'' she said as he stepped back into the bedroom. He watched as she dropped to her knees by
the walk-in closet, evidently open on Keith's side,
and looked through shoes neatly aligned in three
rows on the floor. ''His loafers are gone, I think. Yes,
I didn't see them anywhere else. They're comfortable, scuffed, old ones with paint on them, just like
mine.''

''Which would have been easy to slip into,'' he
said, looking at her shoes as she stood. ''And his
clothes?''

She glanced into his closet, raising her hands as
if bewildered. Once again, Nick noted Keith's half
of the closet looked orderly, while hers, which he
could barely glimpse, was more haphazard. He was
never any good at guessing women's dress sizes, but
he pegged her to be about five foot six, as she came
to just over his shoulder. Slender yet shapely, she
was no doubt mid-thirties. Her curly auburn hair was
chin-length, disheveled as if she still slept in the big
bed. She had a natural, old-fashioned kind of beauty,
like the Victorian Valentine's Day card his grand-
mother had framed. There was something compel-
ling about the way her features were arranged in her
heart-shaped face. Lush brown lashes, clumped together by tears she kept blotting, framed her green
eyes.

Whoa, man, he told himself. Keep your mind on
the facts, on business here. The appearance of the
missing man's wife is of absolutely no relevance,
except that she looks like the kind of woman a man
would never run out on.

''I can go through all his drawers and this closet
with a fine-tooth comb,'' she was saying, ''but it

would take a while. I can't say I'd recall every sweatshirt and pair of jeans, but I'll try.''

''Why don't you show me the rest of the house, Mrs. Malvern, then just sit by the phone while I take a quick look outside?'' He followed her out onto the long upstairs landing, guarded by a banister.

''Please, call me Claire. But what if you don't find him, or any trace?'' she asked, turning to face him.

''I'm going to level with you, Claire. Considering that you live practically on top of the river, I think we should mount some sort of search if he doesn't show up when daylight comes.''

''Oh, thank you. Thank you for all your help, for coming in person. I just know we'll find him. Maybe he'll have a twisted ankle or broken leg, but we'll find him safe!''

Nick nodded. A happy ending was possible, of course. A lot of guys just wandered back after some sort of booze or babes binge. But one way or the other, this poor woman was facing much more grief.

Dawn permeated the darkness, only to reveal a shroud of fog. With his single, powerful flashlight beam, Claire saw Nick Braden climb back up to the deck after being outside for what seemed to her a very long time. She looked at the clock: dawn had been at six-thirty, and he had been gone only twenty minutes.

''I walked the path as far as the next residence to the west,'' he told her, shaking the mist from his jacket and hair as she opened the sliding deck door for him. ''Sam Twoclaws's place, isn't it? It's early, but we should phone him, especially before I walk the other way toward the bridge or consider a search and rescue.''

Their nearest neighbor, Sam Twoclaws, was pure Sammamish Native American and proud of it. His tribe, one of the local historic Nootkan confedera- tion, had once been plentiful in this area, but their numbers were so low they didn't have a reservation like other tribes along Puget Sound. Sam was at least seventy, but he often roamed the area, sometimes at night. He could know something of Keith's where- abouts.

''I should have thought of Sam,'' Claire said, hit- ting her palm to her forehead. ''Not that Keith ever goes over there at night, but they've fished together, and he said sometimes Sam just knows things. I can call him.''

''I'll do it. You have his number here? That coffee smells good.''

Straining to hear as Nick made the call, she went into the kitchen to cut a thick slice of cranberry bread and pour him a mug of coffee. Somehow she was certain he took it black.

''Okay. I see. Right,'' was all she could overhear as he spoke on his cell phone in the great room.

''Sam hasn't seen him,'' Nick reported, ''though Keith phoned him yesterday about ordering more mounted salmon for your guest rooms.''

''Another dead end,'' she said, before she pressed her lips tight and shook her head at what she'd just said. Since this nightmare had begun, so many sim- ple, innocent things seemed to take on new and frightening meanings. Her legs were so weak she sank on the couch.

She was amazed Nick Braden could drink the hot

coffee straight down, but he didn't so much as blink. She sipped some for the warmth and stimulant power, but she couldn't bear to take a bite of bread. Her stomach, as well as her mind, was in knots.

"Despite the fog, I'm going to walk the path the other way, then if I don't find anything, I'll call for an SAR team," he told her, putting his mug down but taking his piece of bread with him.

"I'm going, too!" she insisted, jumping up. "I can take my cell phone in case Keith calls."

"And if someone comes to the house with information?" he pointed out. "Or he comes back without calling first, and you're not here?"

"I'll call Sam and ask him to come over. I can't bear just sitting here waiting, as if there will be some ransom call. I'm sure he must have gone out and fallen. That has to be it. I'm going with you," she repeated.

She thought he was going to order her to stay put, but he didn't. Instead, he waited while she called Sam, who appeared so fast it amazed both of them. He seemed barely out of breath, his leathery copper face pearlized by the fog. His skin always reminded her of the gnarly, twisted Garry oaks the Native Americans had supposedly brought to this area. It seemed to Claire that emotions never altered Sam's face, but could be seen in the depths of his dark eyes.

"Not like him to wander at night," Sam said. He spoke in a distinctive way, giving equal emphasis to every syllable. "Night walking—I never seen him out then."

Claire pulled on her slicker, realizing for the first time she hadn't even put on a bra under her sweatshirt. Well, no one would know or care.

She got the smaller of the lodge's two first-aid kits and one of their large, battery-operated lanterns and followed Nick Braden toward the bridge and the falls.

The watcher shifted slowly, carefully, from tree to tree, just above the river. Foggy or not, it would be no good if the lights from the lodge caught a foreign form out here. Hopefully, there weren't bears around, fishing the salmon at night, let alone fishermen.

The forest and river in the misty moonlight made the scene very romantic, except when the occasional whiff of dead salmon, caught on the rocks, wafted upward on the stiff breeze. The stink of death made the watcher's hand shake while adjusting the long-distance lens on the camera.

If only other places were this easy to observe and photograph. Just peering past the drooping Douglas firs allowed quite a view through the huge-paned windows of the lodge, as if the entire back wall were cut away. Since the building was lit from within, it was like viewing a movie screen, especially now that the fog was lifting.

And in this film, you might know the woman had called the cops. Damn the sheriff for coming himself. Worse, he'd gone upstairs with her. That was obvious enough, even through shifting layers of fog. They'd been up there, beyond view, for over ten minutes, obviously unaware that every move must be noted and recorded.

Again, here he came, down the deck steps—no, both of them this time! The nearby thick foliage was better than the tree trunks, and the remaining tatters of mist were now a blessing. Even a sheriff trained to find criminals, bodies—and stalkers—would never suspect this one.

Originally a deer or Native trail, the path followed the contour of the river. Frequent use kept it clear of most leaves and needles from the trees hunched over it, but sword and club moss still brushed wet against their legs or grabbed at their elbows as they passed. The rush of the river and the voice of the waterfall roared even louder here.

"This fog didn't come in until almost daybreak," Claire called to Nick, "so Keith could have gone a ways. I was this far before. Shouldn't we shout for him or something?"

He began to yell, "Keith! Keith Malvern!" every minute or so. Between times, she called out. A search party could cover more area than this path, Claire thought. She could not believe any of this was happening. Surely she would awake from the nightmare and find herself and Keith back in bed. She caught a terrifying glimpse of losing her best friend. And along with that, she'd lose her stability, her well-plotted future, the reality of who they were together. For years, she had not felt like a separate person. But she was starting to now. She felt flushed, but she was trembling hard enough that her teeth began to chatter.

"The fog's so thick we won't even be able to see the old bridge," the sheriff said, stopping so abruptly she bumped into him.

The air seemed silvered by the sun's smothered face trying to burn through. He turned to her. Again, as whenever he looked at her, and even when it seemed he did not, she felt his searching gaze.

"I saw paintings of this scene in the lodge," he said, gesturing toward the bridge and falls shrouded by fog. "Does Keith like this place?"

"Yes, he loves it here. So do I. When I painted those, sometimes he'd sit on the old trestles just looking at the falls, but there's no way he'd do that in the middle of the night. No sane person would. I can't even stand to go out on the bridge in broad daylight, so I'd sit over there—see, on that big boulder—or more often in this opening where fishermen sometimes had a fire..." Her voice trailed off. "Don't look at me that way," she challenged. "I know what you're thinking."

"Which is?"

"It's a suicide bridge. I'm sure it's your job to worry about that and deal with it. But there's no way—not Keith, never!"

She shouldn't have come with or trusted this man. All his questions had presumed Keith was guilty of something, and that maybe she was, too. Her control was slipping again, just when she needed to be strong. She felt exhausted, almost dizzy, floating...

Back in hot San Diego, more than twenty years ago, she had come into the house after that normal day of high school and called her mother's name. When no one answered, Claire walked upstairs. She heard the old record player, caught at the end of the song "Do You Know the Way to San Jose?"

"Mom?" she called again. "Mom!" And then she went into her parents' bedroom and found her, her wrists pouring a river of blood.

"Claire, I'm not assuming anything." Nick's

voice pulled her back from the dreadful memory. "But when I first arrived, you refused to believe Keith would so much as leave the house. Sometimes people, even those we know best, surprise us. And, unfortunately, life-shattering, spur-of-the-moment decisions and accidents do happen."

However true that was, she wanted to argue with him again. She was so grateful when her phone beeped. *Thank you, Lord,* she thought as she grabbed for it in the pocket of her slicker. Surely it was Keith, and he'd explain everything. But she was doubly wrong; it was the sheriff's phone that had rung, and he was walking away to take the call.

Her surge of elation ebbed. It was probably just regular police business.

"Eagle One here," she heard him say. "Affirmative. Copy that. Tell me."

It seemed he mumbled. As he nodded and whispered, she could make out nothing else. She began to breathe easier. The message was private, surely nothing about Keith.

But she feared the look on his face when he turned back to her. His expression seemed stony, stoic. No, it was more like he, too, was in pain.

"Let's head back," he told her curtly. "As I said earlier, I'm going to call for an SAR team."

He took her by the arm, nearly propelling her along before the twisting path narrowed again and they had to walk single file. The fog was lifting slightly, breaking into floating blankets of puffy down. In the river, the boils of foaming water and the dark blue pools between those rapids were growing more distinct. Occasionally, she could see the flash of silver salmon as they leaped rocks or crested currents.

When the lodge came into sight, they clicked off their lights. As she started to climb the wooden steps to the deck ahead of him, he took her lantern, turned her to him and sat her down on the third step.

"That call was from my night dispatcher," he said, "the same woman who took your 911 earlier. She took an anonymous phone call from a guy claiming to be a fisherman. He says he was drinking near the bridge tonight."

"And he saw Keith walk by?"

"No. Now, I don't like anonymous calls, but in police work, they can pan out as often as not."

"What did she say?" Claire demanded, as dread, thick as fog, enveloped her.

Nick Braden put one foot up on the step where she sat and leaned forward to brace her shoulders as he had earlier when she'd nearly collapsed. She stared at his taut mouth as it moved to form more words.

"The fisherman said that at about two a.m., he went off into the bushes to relieve himself. He looked up and saw a guy, who had been sitting on the old railroad bridge, stand and jump off it."

"No!" she shouted so loud that Sam Twoclaws came out onto the deck. His shadow blotted out the light as he bent over the railing. "No, it could not be Keith, and I'll tell you why." She tried to hit Nick's hands away, but he wasn't budging. "He knows my mother killed herself," she plunged on, "and I found her. He would never, never do that to himself or me!"

Claire heard a woman's voice become an awful

shriek, so shrill she covered her ears. But that just trapped the sound inside her head, echoing like her mother's favorite song over and over on the road to San Jose, the red river running to the sea...

"Claire. Claire! Do you have someone I can call, a friend to be with you during the search?" a man's voice was asking from far away.

Suddenly, she was surprised to find herself stretched out on the couch in the lodge. The cedar ceiling beams looked like bars on a cage above her, pressing down, down. Sam stood over her, holding out a glass of water. And the other man—the sheriff—was holding her hand and bending over her.

"The man who jumped wasn't Keith," she said, sounding so reasonable to herself.

"Stay with her a minute, Sam," Nick said, moving away.

She realized he'd carried her up here and that he had been holding her hands, rubbing her wrists. They still tingled. Now he was using his cell phone again. This time, with the scream of the falls more muted, she could hear what he said, even from across the room.

"Peggy, Eagle here. Assemble the SAR team and tell them we need an underwater K-9. Yeah, I'm afraid so."

Claire sat up, gripping her head in her hands. *I'm afraid so,* he'd said. She was finally, completely afraid, too. So afraid.

3

By noon Claire Malvern's lodge and life had been turned upside down. The mobile command center—a stripped-down, refurbished RV—sat in her driveway, swarming with the SAR team. Though she had thought that abbreviation stood for Search and Rescue, she'd overheard someone call it a Search and Recovery, which made her feel as nauseated as she was furious. She'd had the dry heaves twice already.

Fifteen people came and went from the RV to walk the length of the river downstream from the falls. Several were adjunct police called in from nearby jurisdictions, two officers were Nick Braden's, the others were trained volunteers. Nick himself had left for several hours but was back again, talking to the only man in uniform, his deputy, Aaron Curtis, whom he'd put in charge.

Occasionally, Claire could hear the team planning strategy. She knew some of them had worked other searches on this stretch of river—four alone had occurred since she and Keith had moved here. She kept telling herself that, phone tip or not, they weren't going to find Keith in the water, unless he had merely slipped and fallen.

"At least the current's not as bad as in full snowmelt," one man said, his voice drifting through the screened kitchen window as he left the RV.

"The Bloodroot's always deceptive, with the rocks making rapids and whirlpools," the other man said. "We'll do this side of the river first, since the big bend moves the water faster over the gravel bottom. Then we'll go across. A body's more likely to wedge in the rocks on this side. The dog and handler here yet?"

"Yeah, just arrived."

Several months ago, during a previous search on the river, Claire had briefly met Jillian Carmichael, a big-boned woman from Seattle, and Scout, her German shepherd. Today, Nick had called Scout a search K-9, but Claire had overheard someone else call him "a cadaver dog."

"I can't believe this is happening," Claire told Anne Cunningham as they watched the action from the back deck of the lodge. When Nick had insisted Claire have someone with her besides Sam, Claire had phoned Anne. She had been their real estate agent, their first contact in Portfalls, and she remained close to both Claire and Keith. She would often visit to see the progress they were making with the lodge, usually arriving with little gourmet treats or boutique gifts she bought on trips into Seattle.

Anne was a striking forty-something, tall and slender. Her black leather miniskirt and azure blouse seemed molded to her shapely body, accented with a huge Navajo silver belt, dangling earrings and tooled boots. Short, white-blond hair cupped Anne's head and framed her fabulous face, highlighting her blue eyes. Since her arrival, Anne had been crying silently, dabbing at her eyes, though her mascara never ran. It made Claire feel both guilty that she was dry-eyed now and annoyed at Anne for coming here and then depressing the hell out of her—not that she wasn't already in the depths of despair.

Claire had wanted to do something to assist the team, but they already had coffee and doughnuts in the RV, and Nick had, politely, told her to stay out of the way. Instead, she ended up just watching and praying. The minister from the community church they attended had phoned and offered to come over, but she'd told him she had a friend here. He'd assured her he'd already put her and Keith—who had attended church for a few weeks, then stopped going with her—on the prayer chain.

Prayer chain. The words echoed in Claire's mind. She felt chained and weighed down by grief and fear.

"Are you sure you want to watch all this?" Anne's words broke into her silent agonizing.

"Sheriff Braden asked the same. Yes, I do. If I didn't think he'd probably have me cuffed to a tree to keep me out of everyone's way, I'd be down there with the team and that dog. I can't stand being cooped up right now, even with all the windows to look out. I have to know what's going on."

"I heard them say it can take days," her friend protested, dabbing at her eyes again.

"One other time they were on the river, we let them use our driveway for access. And that same lady dog handler down there," she said, pointing, "told me that a drowned body is usually recovered within a mile downstream of where it's lost from the PMS or something—"

"PLS," a deep voice corrected from the steps below as Nick Braden came up to join them.

For the first time, since last night had been such a blur, Claire took in his appearance. Nick's short, quasi–military-cut hair was black with slight silvering around the temples. His mustache was immaculately trimmed as if to make up for his unruly eyebrows. Little frown lines etched his face, perhaps because he squinted into the sun to see her. In this bright light, paler circles around his eyes showed he usually wore sunglasses.

"PLS—the Point Last Seen, in this case the railroad bridge," he said. "Claire, if you could give us something Keith's worn recently, we'll put Scout on his scent on the banks and in the water."

It hit her again what the dog was really here to do. Since Scout was a water search dog, his primary purpose was not to follow Keith's scent on dry ground, but to locate his submerged body. She'd read in the paper that overwater dogs could find decaying corpses that had been under water for many days.

"But won't a body float?" she blurted.

"Not for about two weeks."

"Why that long?"

"Claire, just get something of his, will you?" Nick countered, sounding angry now.

Claire stopped herself from responding. After all, she thought, he'd been up all night too, and she needed him to be on her side so he could find out what had really happened, especially when they didn't find Keith's body.

She started inside, but as she glimpsed her reflection in the expanse of glass, she felt everything pressing in again. It was as if she were gasping for air, trapped by the weight of rushing water, being pushed and dragged along, deafened by the booming falls. She feared she might faint again, but she couldn't, or Nick and Anne would never let her come

back out here to watch. She'd always felt protective
of Keith, even though he liked to think of himself
as the man of the house. And now, there was nothing
she could do to protect him. She had failed to help
her mother, and her father, too, when he'd shut her
out of his life.

When she opened the deck door, she held on to it
for a moment until she could quell her panic. Sum-
moning the remnants of her strength and sanity, she
stepped inside.

"Anne, you want to go with her?" she heard Nick
say.

Claire spun back to face them. "I'm fine to just
go upstairs. And to help on the river, if you'd let
me."

"I won't let you," he said, "and not just because
you'd get in the way of the experts and possibly even
confuse the dog if you have Keith's scent on you.
This could take a long time, and I wish you'd go lie
down. Anne could phone your doctor and get some
sedatives. Besides, I'll bet the Seattle media will be
here soon with cameras, and however much I try to
keep them back, they've got their telephoto lenses.
Think about it."

"I can't think about anything right now. I still
don't believe he jumped. That anonymous caller
could have made it up."

Before he could argue again, she went inside with
Anne trailing her. Upstairs she looked for the sweatshirt Keith had worn when they'd painted yesterday,
black with the scarlet San Diego State emblem and
the words *Go Aztecs!* printed on it. It wasn't in the
wicker clothes hamper in their bathroom, where she
was sure he'd thrown it when he took a shower. He

must have been wearing it when he went out last night, along with the paint-splattered jeans from yesterday. He'd evidently pulled them both out of the hamper rather than risk noise from sliding open a drawer or his closet door for fresh clothes. Either he'd been in a hurry, or he didn't want to wake her— or figured it didn't matter what he wore.

"Claire, you all right in there?" Anne called from the upstairs hall just outside the bedroom.

The question seemed so silly and stupid that Claire almost told Anne to leave. But she got hold of herself again. Anne was kind to be here. Claire grabbed a rumpled T-shirt from the hamper and hurried downstairs with Anne behind her. Did Nick Braden think she needed a watchdog sniffing after her, too? She wished she'd never told him about her mother's suicide. Sometimes that ran in families: Claire had a heritage of it, but Keith had nothing like that in his past. No, Keith could not have killed himself.

"Sheriff," she said as she handed him the shirt, "I think I know what Keith was wearing."

"White or bright colors, I hope," he said, alternately studying her and scanning the busy scene on the river below.

"Unfortunately not, but that may prove that caller was lying. I think he was in jeans and a black sweatshirt. We're supposed to believe some anonymous tipster who'd been drinking could see him?" she demanded, pointing and gesturing. "We're supposed to believe that some fisherman stumbling around after dark in the bushes to 'relieve himself,' as you put it, could look up from the riverbank and see a man all in dark colors jump?"

"The moon was bright before the fog set in,

Claire. And from the observer's angle, Keith might have been silhouetted against the white falls. Why would a caller make that up or even know a man was out there if he didn't see him?''

''The question is, why didn't the caller give his name?'' she countered, hands on her hips.

''Maybe because he'd been drinking, or littered, or didn't have a fishing license. More likely, he felt guilty he didn't call out to Keith to stop him. Or because he just took off and didn't search for him. Claire, you'll drive yourself crazy with *whys* and *what ifs*. Now, I've got to get this shirt down to the dog handler. I'll tell the team Keith might have been in dark colors. Just leave this to the experts, all right?''

It wasn't all right, but she decided to shut up for now. They might be experts in searching this river, but she was the only expert in knowing Keith. He had been a thoughtful, kind husband, at least as long as things were going his way, which they usually were. He'd been ambitious enough for both of them, whatever task they tackled, but that was all right, she thought defensively, as if she were still arguing with Nick Braden. But the *whys* and *what ifs* Nick told her to leave alone were already driving her crazy.

About one o'clock, while Anne was inside fixing something for them to eat because Claire wouldn't budge from her self-appointed post on the deck, she saw a new person on the scene. The young blonde seemed out of place; she looked overweight and awkward among the athletic, surefooted officers and rescue team members clambering over the river rocks. Her pink linen skirt and suit jacket were too tight and stood out in contrast to her plain, pale face, despite the bright blue mascara and crimson lipstick she wore. Huge fold marks crisscrossed her skirt from sitting too long. She wore high heels, despite how she wobbled on the grass and down the path.

Claire watched as the woman, who was maybe in her early twenties, picked her way straight for Nick. The sheriff was standing on a big boulder, watching the dog work its way around a river pool where the salmon rested before fighting and leaping up and onward.

It appeared Nick knew her. He nodded and smiled in a flash of white teeth as he jumped down to join her; Claire had never seen him smile. The girl tossed her long, straight hair and briefly touched his arm before handing him something. He helped her to the path, and she trudged back up it, then looked up at Claire on the deck.

"Mrs. Malvern?" she called, shading her eyes and coming closer. "We're all so sorry. I'm DeeDee Duncan, the weekday dispatcher at the SO."

"The SO?"

"Sheriff's office. Your 911 came in to Peggy, the night dispatcher, but if there's anything I can do, please let me know."

DeeDee had freckles and wore braces, not that adults didn't sometimes these days. Above all else, Claire would have described her as bouncy. She must have overexerted herself, because she was flushed and out of breath.

"I appreciate that, DeeDee."

"I just dropped by on my lunchtime to give the sheriff his sunglasses. He left them at the office. Hey, I'm serious now. If you need anything at the SO, just feel free to call our regular number. I answer that as well as the 911s. By the way, I know this is not a good time, but your place looks really pretty—gorgeous.''

"You're welcome to come in and look around," Claire offered.

"Oh, I'd love to, but I'd better not right now. I got to be getting back or the place will fall apart without me, 'specially with everyone out here today. Well...God bless, and all that.''

But moments after DeeDee disappeared around the side of the lodge, she was back, hustling along. "Mrs. Malvern! A Seattle TV station's here, so if you don't want to be bugged for comments, you'd better go inside. I know how these people can be, because I screen all the sheriff's calls for interviews, and you'll be a sitting duck if you're out here!''

DeeDee was already walking back toward the river, evidently to tell the sheriff. Claire finally went inside. It annoyed her that the media was here to probe, but it bothered her even more that Nick Braden had correctly predicted they would come.

When the doorbell kept ringing, Claire sent Anne out to refuse any interviews for her. Then, through the window, she watched Nick talk to the TV people. The side of their camera read "BREAKING NEWS."

Breaking news, that was a good one, Claire thought. She felt her entire life was breaking apart while she waited for news of Keith. As for whether there were any breaks in her marriage, as Nick had tried to discern last night, Keith had never given her a moment's worry about other women, even when

he traveled a lot. Granted, she'd seen him be atten-
tive to other women, smile and tease a bit, even
with Anne.

But he would never be one of those men who just
took off with someone else, who suddenly just said
they didn't love their wives anymore, or who went
through "male menopause" and turned rebel. His
sudden retirement from his company and move here
had been his only break from the expected. Keith
had been thrilled with their new life at the lodge. It
was true that she wouldn't exactly call their relationship thrilling anymore. But their marriage was comfortable and solid, as deeply rooted as these trees
clutching the rocks that withstood the river current—
wasn't it?

When the reporter and cameraman kept getting in
the way of the recovery efforts, Nick came up to the
house to get her permission to ask them to leave.
Still, they hovered just off the property line as Scout
and her handler searched back and forth. Because
Keith had been down the path and perhaps to the
edge of the river, the dog kept alerting by barking,
even though there obviously was no body.

The afternoon dragged on as the SAR team
worked up and down the river, sometimes out of
sight, sometimes near, occasionally right under the
lodge, where several pools of water lay between the
rockier rapids.

At three p.m., Claire heard strange, hollow rattling
sounds from the back of the house. When she investigated, she was surprised to see that Sam Twoclaws
had suddenly appeared on her back deck, at the end
closest to the search. He sat on the deck boards with
his legs folded, hunched over something. Still not

wanting to be part of the six o'clock *Breaking News,* Claire walked down the hall that led to the guest bedrooms and opened the window to talk to Sam through the screen.

"Sam, what are you doing? Do you want to come in?"

"I have to be out here," he muttered after a moment; she thought at first he hadn't heard her.

He went back to mumbling in some unfamiliar tongue that she assumed was Sammamish. His long hair was pulled back in such a tight ponytail that his features looked distorted, painted on a leather skull. And the strange sound she'd heard appeared to be deer hoofs, strung along the bottom of a fur vest he wore.

Although Sam supported himself by taxidermy and carving, he had told Keith stories of his ancestors' past as hereditary shamans of the tribe. With his unusual ways, most people in these parts knew Sam, although most avoided him, too.

Claire knelt at the window, watching him, gesturing for Anne to stay back when the sound drew her down the hall. Finally, Claire couldn't stand not knowing what, exactly, he was doing.

"Sam?" she whispered, realizing he might wrongly think she was kneeling as if to join in whatever this solemn, sacred chant and rite was.

"I am searching for his soul," he said, so low she wasn't sure she heard him right. "If it has taken a journey to the spirit world, this may bring him back. It will hover like a butterfly, his soul. But this is empty, and I can't find him."

She gaped at him, but he didn't so much as look at her. By shifting to another window, she could see he was huddled over a carved bone soul-catcher, like those she had seen in The Scrimshaw Shop in town. Unlike the webbed dream-catchers of the Plains Indians, this had two open ends. The pile of dark stuff beside it appeared to be cedar bark, which he was chopping finer and finer with a knife that glinted in the afternoon sun. Around his neck from a leather strap hung bone pendants carved with some sort of markings.

Though she knew Sam was talking about superstition, she said, "But how—and where—are you looking for Keith?"

"I didn't know if it would work for him, like for the people. So I came close to where he lives, to this land. But if the shaman tries to follow a lost soul, the guardian spirits send the shaman back, bleeding."

"Sam, you're not cutting yourself? Sam?"

She knew she could be in camera range, but she ran down the hall, out on the deck. He was not cutting himself, but continued to chop the cedar bark, then stuff it into one end of the bone while his pendant necklace and deer hoof rattles clicked in the wind. She had not seen Sam hurt himself, but when he turned to look up at her, she saw he was bleeding profusely from both nostrils, his blood strange, a thin, red-orange color.

"Anne," Claire called, "get a dishtowel or something. Sam has a bad nosebleed!"

"No, woman," he said, and despite his age, rose by merely crossing his feet and standing straight up with a half turn. "Your words—your presence here—that is what's wrong. This is bloodroot juice from down on the river, sacred paint of the people in this place.''

The bloodroot plant was toxic and grew prolifically in this area. It flowered prettily in the spring, but that was all Claire knew about it. Stunned by Sam's blaming her for meddling, she could only stare as he bent to gather his bone and bark and went down the deck stairs to walk the path toward his house.

''I always knew he was weird,'' Anne said, coming up behind her.

''Only sometimes,'' Claire told her. ''Keith says the pureblood Indian stuff only goes so far with Sam. The truth is, he's evidently got one of the best vintage baseball card collections in the country.''

''Good old American baseball? You're kidding. Is it true he likes rock music, too? I mean, Noah says it's all bone-flute music and drums when he's been to see him.''

''Keith made me promise not to tell.''

''What? That the old man's granddaughter is the lead singer for some rock band?'' Anne blurted, and then looked as if she regretted the outburst.

Claire wondered where Anne had learned that, because Keith had told her not to tell that Sam's granddaughter was often on the pop charts as Dark Sky, the lead singer of The Red Feathers Band. It seemed Sam could not come to terms with some of their anti-authoritarian and -elders lyrics.

Oh, hell, what did any of this matter now, she thought, despairing of ever coming to terms with life without Keith—if it came to that.

''I still say Twoclaws is strange,'' Anne said, crossing her arms with a shudder. ''I've heard he's got stuffed, dead animal bodies all over his place, though Noah Markwood makes a killing from his bone carvings."

"Let's just say he's different—and trying to help," Claire insisted, "even though I'm starting to think no one possibly can."

By five p.m. Nick was getting ready to call the search off until morning. Daggers of sun stabbed long shadows sideways through the trees. The early chill of evening crept in again.

Claire dreaded the thought of this night. She couldn't ask Anne to stay. The agent had already called clients to delay showings of property and had missed a meeting.

For the past hour, the search had been on the other bank, which the SAR team had accessed by rigging a series of ropes from tree to tree across a boulder-strewn section of river, so they had a double hand-hold against the current. About half the team members wore waders now; the other half, including Nick, were soaked to their hips in the cold water. And still the salmon, fighting to get home again, swam and leaped upstream.

From a distance, Claire heard Scout begin to bark, something the dog hadn't done since they'd moved him to the other bank. Excited voices carried to Claire: "That big branch might have acted as a strainer here...I think we've got something."

Despite Anne's hand on her arm and the fact the TV people still lurked, Claire ran outside and down the deck stairs. She tore along the path to the bank directly across from where they were working. The two men who'd worn hip-highs all day were standing in the swirl of shoreline water, steadied by others behind them. One held something that looked like a pair of big tongs.

"Claire, go back inside!" Nick called from across the river. "I'll come get you if you should be here."

"I should be here!" she told him, hugging herself hard to stop shaking. To her dismay, Nick came back across the ropes, walking from boulder to boulder in the middle but soaking himself again. He was in the same outfit he'd worn last night. His curved aviator sunglasses, flecked with spray, reflected trees and her. He pulled them off and stuffed them in his jacket pocket.

"I'm not going back in," she insisted, but he only took her arm and stood there, watching with her.

Like one of her oil paintings, an image forever frozen in memory, the scene imprinted itself on Claire's brain. It was like that moment when she found her mother on the bed with the sheets stained crimson. She saw the tall dog handler pulling the barking dog away and giving her a treat; the men leaning toward the half-protruding tree trunk; the one with the tongs, standing in the rush of water reaching down. He put his arm in clear up to the shoulder.

"Snagged," he called out, "but it's gotta be him!"

4

The men pulled Keith's body from the river. He was bare-chested and barefooted, so the river must have yanked off his sweatshirt and shoes. On the opposite bank, they zipped him into a black plastic body bag, while Nick held Claire where she was. When Anne reached them, Nick stepped away to notify the county coroner on his cell phone.

At this very time just yesterday, Claire thought, standing with Anne's trembling arm around her now instead of Nick's steady one, Keith had phoned his former boss, Ethan Nance, in Seattle to invite him and his wife to visit. The Nances had promised to help launch the lodge by promoting the project among all their contacts in Seattle...

As four men brought the body bag across the river, holding to the guide ropes they'd rigged earlier, everything blurred as if Claire stood beneath the crash of the falls. She pulled away from Anne and touched the plastic bag, then followed it down the path and up onto the sloped lawn, where they laid it.

In the circle of rescuers, oblivious to everything but shattering reality, Claire said to Nick, "I want to see it's really him."

Nick nodded to his deputy who had overseen the operations. Still in waders, Aaron dropped to his knees and unzipped the top of the bag. The hair alone, though wet and stuck and darker-looking from the water, told her it was Keith.

"Yes," she said.

She did not cry, for she did not feel anything but dead herself.

After the pizza and the phone call to the Nances, they'd gone back to painting the largest of the three guest rooms, the one for which they'd installed the antique, claw-foot iron bathtub they'd wanted for their own bedroom but had found was too heavy and unwieldy to take up the corkscrew stairs. Once—too long ago—after they'd got the plumbing completed, they'd stripped and tried out the tub together, splashing, laughing. Her hair had gotten wet; his, too.

Was that the last time they'd made love and really meant it? They were both so tired, sometimes too busy or distracted. Was that carefree, crazy time in the tub also the last time they'd just taken a break from the work and laughed? And right after that, instead of savoring the moment and holding each other tight, they'd had an argument about Keith's wanting to put more of Sam's mounted salmon on the walls. She had said it was starting to look like a tacky seafood display. How could she have been so mean? If she could only tell him she was sorry for that and for sometimes being unhappy with him.

The county coroner's van finally arrived. David Shaw was actually a dentist in town, as well as being the coroner. In his and Nick's presence, Claire formally identified Keith's bloated body. He looked as if he'd been beaten; and by the river and its rocks, he had been. But he had not been beaten by life, she vowed, and only that kind of person deliberately killed himself.

With great effort, Claire swam upward through her frozen feelings. "It had to be an accident," she told the coroner, a stout, middle-aged man with a buzz haircut. "He must have slipped off those old, rotten railroad ties. The so-called eyewitness said he jumped, but he could have thought a fall was a jump."

"Cause and manner of death are yet to be determined, Mrs. Malvern," he told her. "The body will be released to you after the autopsy."

"Autopsy? I—I don't want an autopsy."

"Standard procedure in a death investigation," Nick put in, "especially this kind."

"The coroner doesn't do the autopsy?" she asked David Shaw. She was going to lose control again. A gruesome vision of this dentist leaning over Keith's body with his drill and little pick flashed through her brain.

"No, ma'am. Just like Sheriff Braden here, I'm elected," David Shaw explained. "I just sign all the papers, oversee things, keep local records. It's done by a pathologist—a doctor—in Seattle."

"And I can't do anything to stop it? I don't want Keith—don't want him…cut."

She wavered on her feet, but Nick was quick to prop her up, one hand under her elbow, an arm around her shoulders.

"I'm very sorry for your loss, Mrs. Malvern," the coroner said as he rezipped the body bag and slid it easily onto a rolling gurney in the back of his little truck. "But like the sheriff says, in a sudden, unexpected and unobserved death—"

"The man who claimed to be a witness," Claire

interrupted him, "called in anonymously. He can't be trusted."

"I'm sorry, ma'am," he repeated. "It's a shock even when someone sees the danger signs."

Was he accusing her of missing signs of impending suicide? She'd never do that, not after her mother's loss—unless, she wondered, she'd built up barriers against ever accepting such a thing again. Should she have seen it coming? No, she was not going to let all these so-called experts convince her that Keith jumped.

"This is Tuesday," she said. "How long before…"

"I'd say you can expect a ruling and a release by Thursday," he told her, "so you can make plans and go ahead with things."

Release? Make plans and go ahead with things? How could she do that when her whole life had just taken a flying leap right along with Keith? Damn if she wasn't going to get Nick Braden to help her prove Keith hadn't killed himself.

That night, as Claire drifted between waking exhaustion and fitful sleep, she heard something rattle. Her eyes shot open and she sat straight up in bed. It was nearly three a.m., just twenty-four hours after this nightmare had begun. She strained to listen, haunted by the empty vastness of her bed as well as by the sound. What—where had it been?

She'd told Nick, Anne and her minister she would be fine alone, that she wanted to be alone. She'd called her father to inform him, but had insisted he not come—not that he would have, anyhow, and this way he didn't need to fumble for excuses. His newly diagnosed kidney disease required frequent dialysis, and he had his new family to help his wife keep an eye on. She needed to think, to mourn, and did not want someone watching her all the time, especially someone who had failed her when she'd lost her mother. He'd acted then almost as if it could be her fault. But now, despite all that, she wished she had him here.

The moon that had streamed in these windows last night was still calmly, coldly shining. Leaving the lights off, she padded barefoot to the window and looked out. Their bedroom faced the driveway. She saw nothing but silvered blackness, not even headlights passing this late on the twisting road.

Then a dark, tall form moved in the shadows, shoulders hunched. A bear? That was where she'd put the garbage cans to be collected tomorrow. Around here, everyone knew to close the galvanized tin cans securely and even chain or weight them closed, otherwise, marauding raccoons and bears could make a real mess. But she'd been certain hers were closed. She was strangely proud of herself for doing something that normal on this horrendous day.

She went downstairs and, still in the dark, leaned over the sink to peer out the kitchen windows and see if it was a bear. The sound that awakened her could have been the lid hitting the can or pavement.

Despite civilization encroaching on their habitat, bears preferred privacy. Yet they were sometimes sighted on the river, especially during the salmon runs, when their razor-sharp claws forked up fish for dinner. People were asked to report them if they began feeding away from the river.

Of course, she'd heard that Joel Markwood, the

local jokester who oversaw his family's cranberry bogs just outside of town, was always claiming he'd seen the beast named Sasquatch in the area. But then, Joel was the same guy who had joked about meeting D. B. Cooper's ghost in the woods, after Cooper had parachuted out of a plane and disappeared years ago.

Even when she finally flipped on the outside lights, she saw no bear, no marauding raccoon or any other kind of beast—just deep, dark night.

Late Thursday, Nick left a lot of paperwork and online business yet undone, got up from his cluttered desk and stretched. He'd been in and out of the office all day, still trying to catch up from the hours he'd spent on the river. But however hard he worked, he couldn't get Claire Malvern out of his mind.

She'd called this afternoon to ask about the autopsy report, and DeeDee had politely told her it wasn't in yet. He was irritated that DeeDee, who doubled as front office staff, hadn't put Claire's call through, but then, she evidently hadn't asked for him.

Yet he kept seeing her face and hearing her voice, and that annoyed him. Surely, it was mostly because she had initially reminded him of Susan. He wanted to call her, but he would not have done that with anyone else, though he would provide security and an escort for the funeral. At least Claire had her minister with her today, DeeDee said, and no doubt church people as well as Anne, maybe even stalwart old Sam Twoclaws.

"You done already, chief?" DeeDee asked, looking up from the front desk as he headed for the door.

"Wouldn't blame you for getting some extra shut-eye after pulling that all-nighter Monday night."

"Just going to walk down to Dr. Shaw's to check on that autopsy," he told her. "Tell Peggy when she comes on duty, I'll be here for a while tonight, catching up on that desk work." He pulled on his suit jacket as he went. Most days he came to the office dressed in business attire.

"I'm sure Dr. Shaw will call to let you know, so—" she called after him, but he closed the door and kept going.

Sometimes that girl was too much like a mother hen, even though she was almost young enough to be his daughter. She insisted on bringing him his coffee "just the way you like it," even though he'd told her she did not have to fetch things for him. She kept trying different kinds of doughnuts to entice him, even when he'd told her he was trying to lay off sweets. She knew more about his schedule—past, present and future—than he did. But she was great with attention to details and loyal to a fault. He needed and admired that, when so many young people were slipshod in their work ethic these days and seemed totally self-centered.

But DeeDee was right. He was dog tired and running on adrenaline. Still, though he dealt with deeply distressed people all the time, he wanted to do one last thing to help Claire Malvern. He was going to find out the cause of her husband's death from the autopsy, and urge her to accept it and go on with her life.

"Hello, Sheriff," Noah Markwood greeted him cheerily as Nick strode along the town square. He was just locking up The Scrimshaw Shop, one of several unique stores in town. Noah was a short, compact man, always nattily attired. He shaved his entire head, making his aquiline nose and dark eyes, under the slash of eyebrows that almost connected, stand out.

Noah Markwood was a local boy made good. He'd moved away, gone to art school and lived in Europe, then had returned home to get in on the ground floor of the blossoming tourist trade here. He also did big business in scrimshaw and Indian art sold online. His family, from which he seemed somewhat estranged, were hard-scrabble cranberry farmers who owned bogs just east of town. The bogs were now run by Noah's brother, Joel, who was about as earthy as Noah was ethereal. The independent and eccentric people were what Nick had always loved about little Portfalls, and he hoped it never got too homogenized or large. His grandfather would be proud of him, having come back to this place of happy memories to make his home.

"I hear via the grapevine," Noah said, falling into step with him, "the bridge's latest jumper was a local, that newcomer fixing up the old fishing lodge."

"Sad but true. Keith Malvern. You ever meet him?"

"As a matter of fact, I did," Noah said, checking to be sure the door of his antiques and crafts shop, Puget Treasures, was locked. Noah owned both shops, which had separate street doors but were connected within. That arrangement, Nick thought, was more or less the way Noah related to his family.

As was his habit, Nick kept a good eye on the area as they walked and talked: everything was familiar except one couple strolling across the square and two cars parked along the street. Despite some occasional drug traffic creeping in lately, Portfalls was hardly a high-crime area. Still, it was in his blood to know what was going on around him at all times. Noah, however, seemed to be staring into space—or into his own world—as they went along.

Both Nick and Noah were unmarried, but were day and night apart in interests and personalities. Still, Nick had talked Noah into helping out with several cancer fund benefits, including one in Seattle this weekend. Now Nick groaned inwardly just thinking about the format for that fundraiser. At least Noah would be there, too—misery loved company.

"Malvern's wife—widow—paints moody local landscapes," Noah said. "You should see the mauve haze she creates around the alder trees along the turbulent river, and the brilliant barks of the madronas clinging to the rock faces near the falls. Anyhow, not to wax too poetic, her husband wondered if I'd take a few to sell on commission. He actually hinted at a show for her, too."

"He came in, not her? She's not the shy type."

"He wanted it to be a special surprise for her, I take it. He was hoping I could provide the matting, framing and space for the showing, then take a cut of the profits. Her work is good—not totally mature, but good. I kept several of them to consider. I told him I'd think about it and get back to him, as I didn't want to start an onslaught of local crafters wanting display space. I'll have to call her when she gets through this. Her work grows on you, if you know what I mean."

"Yeah, I do." Nick was both surprised that he'd

said that and a bit annoyed, but Noah didn't seem to notice.

"She was an up-and-coming interior decorator in Seattle, you know."

"No, I didn't." Nick's gut instinct was to question Noah more about what Keith was like, but why? He hoped this case would be cut-and-dried enough to force Claire to accept reality.

He walked a while with Noah. Then after telling him he'd see him in Seattle on Sunday, he cut across the grassy square. Buildings lined it on two sides, for it was open to the cove where the Bloodroot flowed into deep blue Puget Sound. A forest of masts still bobbed from boats at anchor, though most owners would soon take them out of the water until spring. The town curled around the cove, with most of the commercial buildings on this side, including where he was headed.

David Shaw's dentist office, one of two in town, was a suite of rooms above the Three Whales in a Pod restaurant. In a former life, it had been a greasy spoon called Chips 'N' Chowder, but had gone pretty tony now. After nodding or stopping to talk to several others, Nick climbed the covered staircase to the carpeted reception area. The interior was ultramodern, a shock when the rest of the town tried to hang on to the aura of the quaint, rugged past.

"Hi, Jackie," he greeted David's longtime, white-haired receptionist. "The doctor busy?" he asked. He was probably here at a good time, since the waiting room was empty.

"Got a toothache?" she asked with a grin. She flashed a set of teeth so perfect that, at her age, Nick knew they were false.

"If I do, you're pretty cheery about it. No—the other business," he told her.

"Let me just tell him you're here."

Assuming she would have Keith's body back for burial on Saturday, Claire had further exhausted herself planning the funeral. She'd placed his obituary in the weekly *Portfalls Portfolio* and in both Seattle papers. They'd been gone from San Diego for a while, but they'd both grown up there and knew all the same people from way back, so she phoned to get the obit in the *Union Tribune*, too. Keith had been the only child of older parents who had died several years ago, and Claire felt some comfort that they were spared having to go through this.

She'd met with the minister, made arrangements with the local Dortmund Funeral Home, all the while fielding calls and refusing media interviews. She'd been horrified to see that the Seattle TV stations was covering Keith's death as, "yet another suicide from the notorious 'Jumpers' Bridge' at scenic Bloodroot Falls," as one reporter had put it.

If that didn't bring ghouls and gawkers to the river, on top of the usual fisherman, she didn't know what would. They'd all be staring at the falls, and maybe the lodge, too. For the first time, she wished the lodge didn't have such a panoramic view. The only thing that calmed her was a visit from Tess Markwood, a friend from church who carted in two baskets of food from her truck.

"Now, I know you're living alone, but you'll have a lot of visitors," Tess told her as she hefted the baskets to the counter. Tess was a big woman; she looked like Claire's idea of an old-fashioned farm wife. Salt-and-pepper hair, muscular arms—she was an earth mother in a long denim skirt and jacket, quite dressed up for Tess.

"I'm sure Pastor Snell will be by, and you can feed him up and anyone who's in from out of town for the funeral. And the Church Care Committee will provide a light meal at Fellowship Hall directly after the funeral, so don't you even consider getting that catered. The restaurants in town are getting too big for their britches anyway lately, kowtowing to all the invaders we've had—just like Noah's doing."

Tess was Noah Markwood's sister-in-law, and wife to Joel Markwood, from the branch of the family that owned the cranberry bogs outside town. Tess was always busy with church work, but Joel hardly ever attended services. Claire had heard Joel was the town clown, but she barely knew him.

"I can't thank all of you enough," Claire told Tess, as she helped her unload the baskets filled with casseroles, salads, pies and other treasures in Tupperware. Deeply touched, Claire had to keep blinking back tears. "We—I don't have family coming in, so would it be all right if I took some of this to the local people who helped with the search team?"

"Sure, but you keep this cranberry cake for yourself. Made it just for you, since you're such a good customer at the stand. You know, since you are a cranberry fan, you should come on out and Joel will give you a tour of the bogs someday. We'll be harvesting soon. It's always something to see."

"Thanks, Tess. I'd like that."

"Oh, and better keep this salmon dip refrigerated. I made that, too. Cranberries and salmon—don't know what I'd do without them."

"Living around here, you'll never have to find out."

"You never know," she said, helping Claire put several other covered dishes in the refrigerator. "Truth is, the cranberry business is really up and down, and lately it's pretty down. Joel says he's 'sleepless outside Seattle,' worrying about it."

"Is business down because people just think of cranberries at Thanksgiving?"

"The bottom line is that cranberries are tart and Americans have a terrible sweet tooth. The push is on to start growing a sweeter, white berry to compete with wines and drink coolers. Joel's furious about it, he won't change. I'm sorry, you don't need to hear our woes, not with all you got on your plate—well, I didn't mean it that way."

Tess gave a rueful laugh, and Claire managed a teary smile. They hugged in the cold blast of air from the open refrigerator door. The visit and the honesty—and the glimpse into someone else's troubles, however trivial they looked compared to hers—helped.

When Tess left, Claire noted that the newspaper that had lined one of the baskets was yesterday's *Seattle Times.* It was folded inward, but Claire opened it. A large article on the first page of the section, surrounded by articles on metro and rural accidents and fires, had been cut out.

The missing piece had to be about what the media was evidently accepting as Keith's suicide, and the Markwoods had cut it out either to spare her or save it. The missing piece...cut out...

Claire leaned against the kitchen counter, sobbing, the first time she'd lost control since she'd learned

Keith was dead. Her life was like that paper now, where events went on around her but there was a hole right in the middle.

Claire got hold of herself as frustration and fury rushed back. She was not going to just phone Nick Braden again; she was going into town to see him. She needed to know—dreaded to know—what the autopsy report said. And Nick needed to help her examine the area around and on the so-called suicide bridge. If he wouldn't help, she'd do it alone. She would look for broken railroad ties, for Keith's lost keys, for clues as to the identity of the fisherman who had made that anonymous call but hadn't tried to help Keith. Maybe that's why the coward had called without leaving his name: he was ashamed he hadn't helped a man who'd had an accident, so he'd said that Keith had jumped.

"The morgue just faxed the autopsy report to me, so I've hardly had time to read it myself," David Shaw told Nick as he sat across the desk from him in his back office and began to scan the pages. "Let me just go through it here with you. By the way, did Keith Malvern leave a note behind?"

"Not that the widow's found yet, or I assume I would have heard."

"Mrs. Malvern was pretty adamant he didn't kill himself," the doctor said with a shake of his head. "I mean, that's understandable, given the stigma and all, the blame and guilt that goes with suicide. It's not so much from others these days, but from within."

"Right," Nick said, remembering Claire's admission that her mother had killed herself. *Keith would not do that to himself and me,* she'd said. Nick couldn't imagine the guy even leaving her, unless he'd been really messed up. But Claire was bright and seemed very perceptive. Wouldn't she have sensed if her husband was suicidal?

Nick's own guilt flooded him, fierce and deep and cold. Susan had kept her illness from him until the last few months. He had been angry and hurt that she hadn't shared her diagnosis with him, that she didn't want him to go through it with her. It was as if she didn't believe he could help her in any way, so she had just pretended things were fine and shut him out.

"I wanted to protect you, to keep you happy as long as I could," Susan had said when she could no longer hide the ravages of the cancer on her young body.

Maybe Keith Malvern had had problems but wanted to keep them from Claire. It had such a sadly familiar ring...

"Nick, you listening? I said, there's a note here that the only item found on the body was his wedding ring."

Nick's head cleared. "No keys in the jeans pockets?"

"Nothing else, but you know how that river can rip things away. Remember the nine-pound sockeye I hooked there in July? Ah, let's see," he said, glancing back to the fax when he saw Nick was in no mood to trade fish stories. "I'll just read the facts off from the postmortem, then.

"Time of death from rigor mortis, which was adjusted for water temperature," he read, putting on his reading glasses, "was about two a.m., September

5. Needless to say, a large number of contusions and abrasions, four fractured ribs, and the standard diagrams to illustrate location on the corpse. And a broken neck—here's the vertebra the pathologist checked.''

Nick glanced at both diagrams. ''The thing about jumping thirty feet into a rough, rocky river,'' he said, ''is that any bruises or broken bones could be from the impact of hitting that water—''

''Like hitting a wall of concrete at forty m.p.h.''

''Or they could be from the rocks in the current.''

''Oh, he's got a note here that, as usual, the toxicology report will come later,'' Dr. Shaw went on. ''The SNOMED codes for injuries, et cetera, and photos from the post will be sent back tomorrow morning with the body.''

''I want to make sure you get them and not the widow, though she'll probably demand to see them.''

''Here's something else. Malvern had two ulcers so advanced they were ready to start hemorrhaging. He must have had digestive troubles and pain from them. She mention that?''

''No, but then, I never asked. Besides, most people with ulcers just get treatment and adjust their diets, they don't leap off bridges to their deaths.'' He thought again of Susan. What had been lacking in him that she hadn't shared a terminal illness with her own husband? ''So what does the pathologist list in his conclusions?'' Nick asked, anxious to stay on track.

''Cause of death, drowning,'' David told him, flipping pages and scanning. ''Immediate cause of death, asphyxia, including right pneumothorax, a collapsed lung. Manner—suicide.''

"Damn.''

"What else is he going to rule, Nick?''

"I know, I know. It's no surprise. I was expecting it.''

"But wanting it to be different for her sake?''

Nick only shrugged, but he had to admit that was exactly it.

"It's your eyewitness that confirms it,'' David went on. "He saw the guy take a dive off what everyone calls 'suicide bridge' in the middle of the night. Just tell the widow to go ahead and believe it was an accident if she wants. Or is it that the ruling can affect life insurance or something? Hey—you're not thinking foul play, like the eyewitness lied or got bought off, are you?'' he asked, sitting up straight in his swivel chair. "You don't mean you like her for it?''

"Hell, no!'' Nick insisted. "You've made two leaps of logic there, and neither is warranted. You've been watching too damn much police procedural TV.''

But the coroner's words had snagged his attention. Nick didn't suspect Claire of anything, but in the other sense of the coroner's word—and this annoyed him—he did *like her.* He only hoped he could get her to accept these findings without an argument.

But when he started out of Dr. Shaw's office and saw Claire climbing the stairs, one look told him that was not going to happen.

5

Claire looked bad, Nick thought, for such a beautiful woman, even considering she was in mourning. She seemed more drawn and delicate than he remembered. He'd bet she hadn't been eating or sleeping.

"Oh, it's you," she said as he thudded down the steps toward her. "I guess I wasn't expecting you to be in a business suit. I went to your office instead of calling, this time. DeeDee said I could wait for you there, but I finally got out of her where you went. She's very helpful."

"Meaning I'm not?" he asked, before he realized that sounded like he wanted to pick a fight. "Sorry. It's just, I've had too many jumpers from the bridge in the years I've been back here—it's four since I've been sheriff. In the end, the families have always accepted the facts, sadly, of course."

"Nick—Sheriff Braden—"

"You can call me Nick."

"Nick, the facts in this case are still undecided, as far as I'm concerned."

"No, they're not," he said, lifting the packet of photocopied autopsy papers the coroner had just made for him. They were still warm from the copier. "You want the facts, let's go back to my office and go over them."

But when he held the door at the bottom of the

stairs for her and she brushed by, he could see—almost feel—her trembling. She stubbed her toe on the threshold and nearly stumbled; he reached out to steady her. How could a woman be so shaken and yet remain so stubborn?

"Did you finally get some sleep?" he asked as he turned to face her. "I'll share all of this with you, but not if you're going to faint on me again."

"I won't faint. That other time was from shock. I slept some last night, but I woke up when a bear or something disturbed my garbage can. That got me nerved up, but I'm fine."

He studied her again. "You're fine?" he repeated, his voice edged with disbelief. "I told you to call the doctor for some sleeping pills, just for a while."

"I don't want pills, I don't take pills, all right?"

"Have you been eating?"

"Tess Markwood brought me food from the church women, which I want to ask you to distribute to the team who worked on the river, as my thanks—for you, too."

"But the food was for you, so did you eat anything?"

"Not yet."

"It's almost dinnertime, which means you probably haven't eaten for at least eight hours. Come on."

"Where? Your office is back that way."

Nick knew he should just make sure she got home, maybe send DeeDee with her or call Anne again to make certain she ate the food she had there, and get some sleep. But he didn't.

"We're going," he said, indicating the direction

of the water, "to get some carryout right here at Connie's, and then we'll go over the report."

To his amazement, she didn't argue. She sat on a bench overlooking the water while he knocked at the outside window boaters often used at the little cove-side restaurant. He ordered two cheeseburgers and two coffees, which he quickly changed to lemonades because he didn't want caffeine to keep her awake on top of her grief and nerves.

He joined her on the bench, with her back to the square, Nick angled so he could watch the cove and the town, and they ate silently. Overhead, seagulls sniped at each other, hoping for handouts. On the shore beneath them, bull kelp lay tangled and twisted like ropes, as if holding the sea-battered rocks in place.

"I heard from your minister the funeral's set for one p.m. Saturday," he said when they'd finished eating. "I'll be there to make sure everything goes smoothly, and Officer Curtis will lead the procession to the cemetery."

"Thank you. I appreciate anything you can do. Actually, I was hoping you'd be willing to help me search the old railroad bridge area with a fine-tooth comb."

"I'd like to make it off-limits, but people would only tear down the police tape or barriers. I've tried that before. Actually, I'd like to dynamite the bridge into oblivion, but if people want to jump into the river—or just admire the scenery from above—they'll find another way."

"In short, you're not about to help me search the area and you have decided Keith killed himself."

"Claire, what good would a search do?" he argued.

"I've been looking for a suicide note, but there is none—because he left none, because he *did not* kill himself!"

"A lot of suicides don't leave notes. Do you think he left a note nailed to the bridge or something? Is that what you want to look for?"

"I don't want to argue with you. I assure you I can take care of it myself."

He bit his lip hard to keep from ordering her to stay away from the bridge. He wanted to comfort her, but a vulnerable, beautiful widow was a web of trouble. Hell, two months ago he'd suspended Aaron Curtis from a case after he became too involved with an attractive victim, and he'd served on a police force where a detective had made a mess of things by having an affair with a suspect, no less.

"I know the funeral and burial is a big expense," he said, leaning closer in the increasing wind. "Did Keith have any life insurance to help cover things?"

"Neither of us did, not since we left Seattle. He redeemed his term life insurance to get more capital to rebuild the lodge."

"I know it may be too early to answer this, but will you stay there without him? I thought maybe you'd be heading back to Seattle, since the lodge seems like such a—"

"An albatross around my neck? A man thing?" she put in when he hesitated. "We decided to go into it together, but it was his dream. Right now, I want to see it through, open up in the spring and get some paying clientele in there, even though I won't be much help with fishing advice. Maybe I can hire

Sam for that. He already agreed to do whatever mounting our guests want for their trophies. Some fishermen would love a Native American guide, I suppose, and if anyone knows that river and the fish, it's Sam. After I've tried it for a while, I'll decide if I like it. I do love the area."

"Yeah, me, too. Good luck with the lodge," he added.

She wadded up her napkin and sandwich wrapper and stuck them in her empty cup. Turning toward him on the bench, she asked, "Will you let me see the autopsy now? I suppose that the pathologist, who never even met Keith, thinks he can say how he died."

"I've been to that morgue before. There's a traditional Latin saying over the entry that translates to something like, 'This place is where death gives answers to come to the aid of life.' In other words, autopsies can help find the truth, however upsetting. The finding is suicide," he told her, handing over the papers. "But there is nothing here that rules out the fact Keith could have walked out on that bridge at night for his own reasons and simply fallen."

"That's why we have to locate and question that anonymous caller," Claire insisted as she took the papers. The stiff wind rattled them in her hands. "Maybe, under interrogation, the caller would describe that what he saw was an accident—a fall, not a definite dive or leap. Can't you trace that call?"

"I already did. It was made from the public phone booth at a gas station on Route 9, just outside of town. I even talked to the night attendant. He doesn't recall anyone using the phone at all, but then, it's not in his line of vision."

"Oh," she said, looking crestfallen. "I thank you for looking into it. So you think there's something fishy, too—well, I didn't mean to put it that way."

He did not think something was fishy, but he didn't want to argue. She had lit up for a moment when she'd thanked him; despite the ravages of grief, her expression had turned briefly incandescent. He realized he'd never seen her smile, and wanted to. He watched her as she skimmed the autopsy report and studied the anatomical diagrams of vertebra and contusions. When she turned to the official conclusion of suicide, he waited for a protest or outburst.

"Two serious ulcers ready to hemorrhage?" she whispered, staring at the page.

"You didn't know that? He didn't tell you?"

"No. I—I didn't know—maybe I didn't know him at all, if he could sneak out at night like that without telling me. So what else was he not telling me?"

She thrust the papers at him and jumped up. She took a few quick strides away, then spun back as he rose to follow.

"I'm going home now," she told him, holding up both hands. "I have a lot to do. And I owe you for the burger—and for all your help. Once I start serving dinners at the lodge, you're invited to come for drinks and dinner. Fisherman that he was, Keith said we would call the traditional happy hour the liars' hour, so everyone could trade tall tales about the one that got away...."

With a single sob, Claire turned and rushed toward the town square. He wanted to run after her, but he stood rooted in duty and in his own despair, remembering Susan's liar's hours in his own marriage.

*   *   *

Claire was surprised and touched that so many Portfalls residents attended the funeral. It was as if, in the short time she and Keith had lived among them, they'd actually become part of the town, something she hadn't really felt until now. Friends from Seattle came, too, including several co-workers from Keith's former company, Chin Pacific, often called ChinPak for its abbreviation on the NYSE. Even Ethan and Diana Nance themselves came. Two women who had worked with Claire in the interior design and decoration firm had also driven in to pay their respects.

The small Protestant church was over half-full. The cars that lined the lane outside had purple and white funeral flags on their roofs, and were prepared to follow the hearse to the cemetery. There was no family, but then, Keith had none and Claire's father had to stay put in Southern California for his kidney dialysis.

She had talked to her father twice in the past few days, but had already turned down his invitation to come to California for a visit. She had to stay here and find out what had happened to Keith. Besides, once her mother died, her father hadn't seemed to want her around; Claire finally figured out she must remind him of her mother. She could not bear to relive all that agony right now.

Claire had considered taking Keith's body back to San Diego to bury him next to his parents. But this was the place he had chosen, the dream he'd pursued, so she would lay him here among others who had cherished this area.

She assessed the closed wooden casket with its simple spray of white calla lilies. She had selected them partly because they reminded her of their small wedding. They had hoped to have kids, but when Keith had finally agreed to be tested they'd learned he was not able to. Claire couldn't see upsetting him by insisting on the invasive and expensive procedures he'd need to undergo. A family had once been her dream, but she'd settled for decorating other people's homes and on Keith's fishing lodge, which was now all hers, whether she liked it or not.

On one side of the casket sat the big basket of carnations her father's family had sent. But all other flowers paled next to the stunning burst of exotic blooms from Chin Pacific. The birds-of-paradise, gold heliconia and Japanese orchids in a cobalt-blue-and-white porcelain oriental vase looked almost out of place in this simple setting. Claire had noted that the accompanying card included the name of Howard Chin, Diana Nance's father and the company's retired chairman of the board.

Several of the SAR team members were here, including Deputy Aaron Curtis and, of course, Nick. Both men wore full dress Portfalls County law enforcement uniforms befitting their ranks. She'd seen Nick in only casual civilian clothes and then a dark gray business suit. He looked almost austere in his gray-and-black sharply creased slacks, mirror-shined shoes and crisp jacket with brass buttons and gold braid, no less. Claire's college roommate Ginger had always been crazy about the guys in navy dress uniforms in San Diego. "Give me a man in a uniform, and I'll give—myself," she used to joke.

As Claire walked down the aisle to take her place, Nick remained at the rear of the church as if to keep an eye on things. The only others that far back were

DeeDee Duncan, who sat in the next-to-last row, fanning herself despite the brisk breeze outside, and Sam Twoclaws, who perched on the very end of the last row as if he would bolt for the door any moment. Anne Cunningham, dressed all in deep blue, sat with Claire in the first pew, just behind the wooden divider that separated the congregation from the altar area. Anne began to cry silently as the minister, Pastor Gene Snell, began the service.

His remarks were uplifting, but Claire could not bring herself to feel comforted.

"Let us turn to number 283 in our hymn books," Pastor Snell, a kindly man who had retired from a large church in Seattle, announced. "Perhaps the best-known and best-loved Bible passage, the twenty-third Psalm, is also a beautiful hymn."

They all stood and sang the slow, sonorous melody:

The Lord's my Shepherd, I'll not want,
He makes me down to lie
In pastures green, He leadeth me
The quiet waters by.

Claire had chosen the song herself. After the way Keith had been beaten and yanked around by the river he had loved, she liked the picture of the quiet waters where he could rest. Pastor Snell had planned to use that theme in his remarks, too. But one line of the hymn snagged in her thoughts:

My table thou hast furnished in presence of my
foes…

Did Keith have any foes? Someone who would harm him, after somehow luring him outside? It was a drastic, dreadful thought, but if he had neither killed himself nor had an accident, what option was left?

"I am reading from 2 Samuel, Chapter 17," Pastor Snell was saying, "the Psalmist David's song of praise, for in loss, we praise God for the life of the person who has gone on before us: *'He sent from above, He took me, He drew me out of many waters.'* So David said and such is true of our lives, if we learn to trust the Lord our God."

Claire took the Bible from the rack ahead of her and found the passage he'd referred to. But he had stopped the reading before it continued. *"He delivered me from my strong enemy, from those who hated me; for they were too strong for me. They confronted me in the day of my calamity."*

"That's it," Claire muttered, hitting her fist on her thigh. "Then he'll *have* to help me."

Anne looked at her out of the corner of her eye. "That's what the pastor means," she whispered, looking even more miserable.

Claire sat up straighter and nodded in return. But the *he* she referred to was not the Lord, but Sheriff Nick Braden.

Keith's grave was in the corner of the Sunset Cemetery outside town, where Claire had bought just one plot. The entire area was guarded by wind-worn Sitka spruce that drooped their heads and shoulders as if they were in mourning, too. She had noted that nearby tombstones bore the old local names Markwood, Collins, even Braden. Nick must have deep roots here, and she wondered fleetingly what relatives of his were buried beneath those stones.

After the casket was lowered and the final benediction given, she shook hands with, hugged and thanked as many mourners as she could. "Please come back to the fellowship hall at the church for sandwiches," she reminded everyone. "Thanks so much for coming. Keith would have been pleased."

Been pleased to have people attend his funeral? a voice in her head taunted. So she stopped mentioning what Keith would or would not have felt. She was starting to think—to fear—she didn't know what he would think at all.

"We'd love to see what you've done with the lodge, but today's not the day," her mentor Fran Kallile told Claire, giving her a hug. Fran had helped get Claire on her feet as a decorator in her firm, Kallile's Fine Interiors.

"I'll invite you all soon," Claire promised, "and there will be enough rooms for all six of you from Kallile's. But you'll have to remember, it's a rural fishing lodge, not a Seattle town house or Lake Washington mansion."

Claire did not try to explain the other reason she didn't ask anyone to the lodge today—she was starting to think of it as a crime scene. Though Keith had not left a suicide note, maybe he had left something behind to suggest he had enemies somehow, somewhere. Thank heavens, she felt safe and sure among these friends and neighbors.

Claire scanned the crowd as she made her way to the funeral home's black sedan. On the edge of the crowd, Noah Markwood was huddled with Anne, rather than with his own family, his brother Joel and his wife, Tess. Joel looked as uncomfortable here as he had the one time Claire had seen Tess drag him to church.

"Thank you both for coming, and Tess, for the wonderful array of food," Claire told them as Tess hugged her.

"It's the least we could do," Tess said, teary-eyed. "I hope you were able to share it with the search team like you wanted."

"Sheriff Braden sent his dispatcher to pick some of it up for them," Claire told her. DeeDee Duncan had been only too happy to stop by, and it had given Claire a chance to show her the ground floor of the lodge she'd admired the other day. DeeDee's gushing over the decor had made Claire almost homesick for her old job back in Seattle.

She started toward the Nances, but Joel called to her, "I'm really, really sorry about Keith. He was a good guy, but sometimes bad things just happen to good people." Claire turned back. She had heard Joel was clever and funny, but she'd never been around him enough to know and he'd never spoken to her before.

"I didn't realize you knew Keith," she said, though Joel didn't come any closer.

"I didn't, really," he admitted, shrugging. "Just said hey once in a while when I saw him or old Twoclaws fishing."

Claire could see the family Markwood traits this man shared with his brother, though Joel had a full head of hair while Noah was bald. Then she noticed Joel's hair looked too set in place with an abrupt hairline, and realized it was probably a toupee. She'd heard that the serious Noah's passion for art was day and night to the younger Joel's dedication to his cranberry farm and immediate family. She wondered what had estranged the Markwood brothers, however different their interests and personalities.

A thought hit her. "Joel," she called to him, "you weren't by any chance fishing on the river last Monday night, the night of Labor Day, were you?"

He looked startled, then puzzled. "I never fish at night. Too dangerous down there in the dark—I mean, slipping on rocks and all." Evidently embarrassed he'd put it that way, he hurried to catch up with his wife.

Claire spotted the Nances by their white Mercedes, several cars back from the funeral car and hearse. "Just one moment," she called to Karl Dortmund, the funeral director's son and her driver, and hurried toward the Nances.

Ethan and Diana Nance had been good to her and Keith. At Chin Pacific, Ethan had paid Keith generously and promoted him promptly. Keith had frequently traveled with him to China, for ChinPak imported Asian artifacts and art. Ethan had not held it against him when he left the company on rather quick notice to buy the lodge, but had generously continued to be supportive.

Diana Nance had also been kind, even requesting that Claire be on the team that redecorated their huge new home in Medina on Lake Washington, across the water from Microsoft mogul Bill Gates' palatial spread. She'd also consulted Claire about what to buy her father for a housewarming gift when he built his huge retirement home out by the Cascades. But all that belonged to the world Claire had left behind.

"My dear, we're so sorry and so shocked," Diana

Nance told Claire, squeezing her hands. A cloud of Diana's exotic scent enveloped Claire, then departed on the breeze.

Diana Chin Nance was of half-Chinese descent. Her father, Howard Chin, had married a Caucasian woman from a wealthy Seattle family. Diana's shoulder-length, straight black hair was like polished ebony, and accented her porcelain skin and dark, almond-shaped eyes. Starkly stylish, Diana dressed in monochromatic colors, and today she wore ecru silk slacks and a matching cashmere sweater set. A single strand of pearls as big as chickpeas graced her neck.

Although both the Nances must be in their mid-fifties, they looked decades younger, the result, Fran Kallile had told Claire once, of Botox injections that imparted youth but robbed one of the ability to frown or show facial emotions. It was true, Claire noted now; Diana looked perpetually calm, and her mouth barely moved when she spoke.

Ethan clasped Claire's hands and murmured his condolences. He was Diana's perfect match, trim and elegant, and tanned from the time he spent on the large sailing yacht he loved. Keith had greatly admired the man, and Claire was moved they had come.

"I can't thank you both enough for taking the time to remember Keith today," Claire told them.

"He was so promising, one of the best and brightest," Ethan said. His voice always surprised her, as it was rather high-pitched for such a distinguished-looking man. "I knew he felt stressed in Seattle," he went on, "but I had hoped he'd find a safety valve here, so that he didn't go overb—"

Ethan, not now, Diana mouthed, and he stopped in midthought.

As Ethan had suggested, Keith's tensions had dissipated when they came here to rural Washington. He'd been filled with endless energy, but that was surely just the excitement of living his dream, and not the result of being overextended. After all, he'd left behind so many of the pressures on him. But had he found new ones here?

"I just wanted to be certain you were coming to the church for a bite before you head back," Claire told them as they each held one of her hands.

"Regretfully, we can't," Diana said. "Previous commitments, you see. It's a very busy time for several charity benefits in which I'm involved."

"Then, I'll still hold you to that visit to the lodge—that is, if you still want to, now that Keith's gone."

"Yes, of course. We want to stay in touch," Diana said.

Claire squeezed their hands and turned away, then strode back to her car. Nick stood there, holding the door for her, while Aaron waited in his police car at the head of the line with his light bar blinking.

"I'll stay until they fill the grave, if you'd like," Nick told her. She could see her distorted reflection in the opaque, curved aviator sunglasses he wore. "My father always said someone from the family should stay until the grave was covered. I stayed for my grandfather's burial just over there, near Keith's grave."

So those were his people gathered around Keith, she thought as she got in the back seat of the sedan.

It made her feel as if his resting spot were protected in a way that, somehow, Keith himself had not been.

She jolted as Nick closed her door, and saw him motion to Aaron to start the procession back to town. The line of cars was getting ready to move.

"Are you coming back to the church?" she asked Nick, rolling down her window.

"I can't, Claire. Sheriff business."

"I was still hoping you could help me look around the bridge better than we did the other day. There could be evidence of foul pl—"

"Claire, let it go!" he commanded, leaning down to speak in her window. "I know this is terrible, and you're still in shock. Go home, grieve, rest—but concentrate on life. Okay, Karl," he told the funeral director's son. He knocked his knuckles twice on the trunk—dismissively, she thought—as the big black car pulled away.

Too bad Keith Malvern had to die, the watcher thought, keeping to the fringes of the other mourners. It would probably only lead to other complications that would have to be removed. If things got too bad, the grieving widow would have to be made to leave the lodge and the town. There was great danger in her getting in the way—danger to her.

6

Though annoyed at Sheriff Braden's advice that she drop her suspicions about Keith's death, Claire felt buoyed by the presence of friends on this difficult day. Still in her funeral suit, she stood for a long time, gazing through the windows of the lodge at the rushing river. In the background, always, she heard the falls as if they had something to whisper, some secrets to sing to her.

Surely decisive action would be the best remedy for her grief, she told herself—not just resting, as Nick had counseled. She might have buried Keith, but not her belief that whatever the reason he went outside that night, he had not intended to die.

She ran upstairs to shuck her clothes and to pull on a sweatsuit. Though Keith had been the runner in the family, she would jog to the site where the fisherman who saw Keith must have been—the place where Keith had met his death. She had to know and prove the why and how, police help or not.

From the path, she saw that the fishermen the SAR team had cleared from the river a few days ago were back. After all, it was a Saturday and the salmon were still in full run. Some men had waded out into the shallow rapids along the bank to cast their lines like silver threads into the runs and riffles, while others pointed their rods and reels outward from rocks or the bank.

Any bears lumbering out of the woods for claw-and-teeth fishing today would give people wide berth, so she felt safe. Besides, she knew what to do if she met a bear: stop and make a lot of noise, even wave her arms over her head to make herself look larger. She'd been told never to run. Some people who went into the deepest forests around here wore bear bells to warn the creatures away, for they preferred not to be seen. Only Sam seemed to actually go looking for them sometimes. She'd overheard him tell Keith that he sought to seize their strength.

She shuddered. Facing a fierce bear and trying to keep calm: that was how she felt holding her ground, when she just wanted to run away from probing Keith's death. Damn if she wasn't going to wave her arms and make a lot of noise, whether Sheriff Nick Braden liked it or not.

Out of breath from her run, Claire stopped to question fishermen as she followed the path toward the bridge and falls. "You weren't fishing here late last Monday, were you?" she asked. Most just shook their heads but a few asked why.

"My husband lost something that day. I'm just trying to see if someone found it—a big set of keys on a silver ring."

"If they fell in the river, lady, no one will ever find them," one man told her.

Claire was not surprised to see the number of fishermen dwindle as she approached the falls. Where the foaming frenzy spilled into the river, it was nearly impossible to snag a fish—so why, she wondered suddenly, were fishermen camped so close to the falls the night Keith died? Nick had said he'd fished around here for years, so why didn't he think of that? Perhaps the guy who called had just wanted a place to drink and was so blitzed he didn't know what he saw.

She found empty beers cans thrown in the bushes, but that proved nothing but littering. Still, the fines for littering were steep. Perhaps that was the reason for the anonymous call. Watchful for snakes, Claire poked a stick through the trash, even scattered the remnants of a campfire that may or may not have been the caller's.

She turned her attention to the bridge, edging toward it timidly as if Bloodroot Falls, several hundred feet beyond it, would do more than just roar at her. The falls were tall but narrow, which concentrated their force and sound. Water spilled in a series of cascades over protruding rocks into a churning foam that soon became the wild river. Here was the end of the road for the salmon, since they could never leap the falls themselves. The ones that didn't find the old salmon ladder needed to climb the heights spawned and died here in side pools at the foot of the falls. As for the bridge itself, the old concrete-and-iron supports proudly held its span high. It could easily be accessed by a path that curved upward through thick cedar and Douglas fir from where she stood.

As Claire began the twisting climb, she wavered and put out her hand to the smooth, olive-hued bark of a madrona to steady herself. She was obviously walking in Keith's fatal footsteps now.

Suddenly, she felt she was no longer alone. A frisson of fear raced up her spine to the nape of her neck. It did not feel as if a spirit were watching over her benignly, like Keith in heaven, but as if someone observed her with evil intent.

She tried to shed such foolish thoughts, but stopped to look back and below, scanning the woods and writhing river as far as she could see. Surely no one was watching, but this place was getting to her in a way it never had before.

Mesmerized, she stared up at the thunderous, towering falls. The rushing water made the bridge look like an etching, where each limb and joint stood out in stark contrast. She knew the structure well and had painted it numerous times. Only once had she walked it. Her reluctance to do so was not because she didn't like the height or the awesome view.

When she was up on the bridge that one time, with the falls flowing behind and the river running beneath, it seemed as if she was tumbling, sucked into a vortex of blankness. She had felt there was no top or bottom to the universe, only her small self plunging into oblivion.

Had Keith felt that way and simply been sucked to his death? Suicide, in a sense, but not intended?

The day they'd walked the bridge together, just after they'd bought the lodge, Keith had said she'd had a touch of vertigo, but that wasn't it. It was as if she had stepped inside a whiteout, a swirling snowstorm with no horizons and no sanity.

"But he said he never felt that way," she said aloud. "He was surefooted here."

Still, she admitted to herself, it had been night when he fell. Perhaps he had become disoriented. She assumed he hadn't been drinking. After the sheriff had asked about that, she'd checked his beer supply and the few bottles of hard stuff they had, and had found nothing gone or so much as moved.

She continued to climb the path toward the bridge then sat on the end of a railroad tie at the top. Putting her head in her hands, she fought tears, struggling with looming hysteria. After sitting there a very long time, holding to an iron support, she stood at the very end of the bridge and looked across.

Some ties were rotting; some looked sound. The rails themselves looked worn. If a train tried to cross these days, would the entire structure collapse? She was so tired that the bridge seemed to waver, to sway before her eyes. A trick of the water or the light? Her own mind?

Again she felt she was not alone, that she was being watched. But she could not bear to turn and look down. She could not face what that last freefall had been like for Keith, momentarily soaring...but then—

With a sob, Claire started down the path to the river, grabbing at limbs or trunks. She skidded and fell once. Nothing—she had found and proved nothing today.

Skirting the fishermen this time, she ran back along the river path. She was panting when she reached the lodge. Suddenly, she could not bear to go back inside, but went to one of the two outbuildings, not much more than cedar-shake sheds, which they had not attached to the main structure as they had the cabins.

The one closest to the lodge they'd been converting to a fishing gear shop with a fly-tying bench and a sink to clean fish. It was Keith's haven, and still had several boxes of his things that he had not un-packed, mostly books on fish and fishing. The farther one was her makeshift and as yet undecorated art studio, which she had not been out to for days.

To her utter amazement, the door to the studio stood ajar about a foot.

Claire stopped dead in her tracks. "Hello?" she called. "Hello!" Examining the padlock closely, she saw the lock was not cut or damaged but had simply been opened.

She realized, as she should have before—or Nick should have, because wasn't that his job?—that Keith's keys might not have been lost in the river, but could have been found or taken. If so, she'd be forced to have the entire lodge re-keyed.

Straining to listen, Claire edged closer and shoved the door all the way open. It creaked, then bumped the back wall. At least that indicated no one was behind it. No other space could hide someone, for the room was now mostly storage for her art supplies and her old interior design files, which she couldn't bear to part with.

Claire counted the stretched canvasses stacked against the wall. At least five were missing.

Claire stood on the deck with her cell phone two minutes later. "DeeDee, this is Claire Malvern." Her knees were shaking, and she hoped her voice wasn't. Since her studio had been opened, apparently with a key, she was afraid to go in the house.

"Oh, Mrs. Malvern, the funeral was lovely—well, you know what I mean."

"I thought you worked weekdays, DeeDee."

"Our weekend shift girl's sick, and the overtime's

great. Besides, what's a single gal in this little town gonna do on a Saturday night to find a date?''

"You might try fishing along the river," Claire said, amazed she was chatting like this. She was so tired it sometimes seemed as if another woman had taken over her body and brain.

"And get stood up by a fish? No, thanks. Listen, I just got here, but if you want the sheriff again, he's out right now. I'd be all business if you'd called 911.''

"I didn't call 911 because I don't want a fuss, but I do need some help. One of my outer buildings has been broken into—well, not broken, but gotten into, maybe with a key. Can you page Ni—the sheriff? I want someone to help me look around in the house, because Keith's set of keys were lost and— I'd just feel better here tonight if someone looked the place over first.''

"Sure, I'll get you some help right away. You know, there was a ring of thieves working out of Portland up and down the coast who would read obits in the paper, see when the funeral was, and rob houses when people weren't there. Is anything missing?''

"From the house, I'm not sure. From my shed, some of my paintings.''

"I'll take care of it, lickety-split. Now don't you worry about a thing.''

It was Aaron Curtis who pulled his cruiser into her driveway ten minutes later, when she had expected—wanted—Nick. Aaron seemed so young, so eager, compared to the more seasoned sheriff. He had freckles, no less, and his eyes were a guile-less blue.

"Someone broke into your art studio, Mrs. Mal-vern?" he asked as he sprang from his car. Feeling safer with him here, she walked him quickly through the house, down the deck and to the shed. She showed him where the missing paintings had been stacked in racks.

"Four or five, all of the river, falls and bridge," she told him.

"Forgive me for this question, ma'am, but first off, are you sure you had this shed locked? Can't tell you how many vehicles are taken 'cause they're not locked, some with the keys inside. One lady even left them in the door."

"Yes, we—I always locked it."

"When's the last time you were out here?"

"Several days ago. I'm sure you understand that things are a bit of a blur lately."

When he nodded knowingly, she realized she'd just weakened her case. When had she been out here last? "Oh, I remember," she said. "I searched here for my husband the night he disappeared. But even though I was distraught, I know I relocked it. Still, Keith's keys never turned up when— When he did."

"And other than your husband's missing keys and those in your possession, there are no other sets?"

"Keith took care of that, but he said he only made two, and I never saw any others."

"So one of you always had to be around, with all the workers you've had in and out of the lodge these past months?"

"Yes. That's what I'm saying. Besides, as you can see, no workers have done a thing to this messy studio, and I didn't get around to arranging or decorating it yet.''

He began to fill out what was labeled a B & E report, but she saw he scratched off the word *Breaking* and circled *Entering*. He asked a few more questions, then went carefully through the house with her, where, for the third time in four days, she was searching for someone.

''You know,'' he told her, writing on his report again, ''it could have been one of those fishermen on the river. We've had other complaints that turned out to be guys who are good with tackle and good at picking locks. Maybe someone looked up here and thought it was an old-fashioned outhouse, you know what I mean. When he saw it wasn't, maybe he got mad or curious, or even helped himself to a few paintings and became a thief. I can go down and ask what they've seen,'' he offered, nodding toward the river, ''but I doubt if the others noticed or would admit it, anyway.''

''Does Nick Braden train all of you to be the same sort of skeptic he is?'' she asked, hands on her hips.

''It comes with the territory after a while, ma'am,'' he said good-naturedly. ''But he's my idol in all this, in learning to do my job well. Ever since his wife died, he's been totally dedicated to his job.''

Nick's wife had died? Claire wondered how it had happened and how he'd coped with his loss. That meant they had something very deep and tragic in common. Though she was thoroughly frustrated with him right now, that knowledge made her sympathize with him. But she had to stay strong, not soft. As soon as Aaron left, she was going to phone Nick Braden and try to reason with him about helping her, although she did not feel reasonable about Keith's death at all.

"And I've learned a lot from the sheriff," Aaron went on, "even if it's been the hard way sometimes, when I made a mistake or two and he was tough on me. I'll sure get him up to speed on this when he gets back on Monday."

"Monday? But he was on duty this morning."

She instantly regretted the annoyed tone of her voice. Nick Braden, like anyone else, had the right to take a weekend off, but did it have to be the one when she needed him? And didn't he tell her he had sheriff's business?

"Right, Monday," Aaron said, putting his notebook back in his shirt pocket. "Tomorrow he's in the Bachelor Bid-Off at the Pacific Lights Yacht Club in Seattle."

"Bachelor Bid-Off?"

"Uh, yeah," he said, perhaps realizing he'd said too much. He quit ambling and stretched his strides out the back door toward his squad car. "It's tomorrow afternoon. The women who pay the most get dinner dates on yachts with the bachelors." He threw over his shoulder, "All for charity, you know what I mean."

She knew what he meant, all right. All for charity. Here she was desperate to feel safe and sane, while the county sheriff she'd voted for and relied on wouldn't help her, wouldn't even listen when she tried to tell him that foul play could be involved in a man's death. No, he was off in some studs-for-sale auction, while she couldn't buy his time to make him listen and help.

Or could she?

*   *   *

Claire couldn't have her locks re-keyed until Monday morning, so she could not decide what to do next. She felt immobilized by grief and frustration. If Nick Braden wouldn't help, she'd just find someone else right away, not Monday or whenever Nick returned to work and had time for her. She'd hire a private investigator to turn up information she could show Nick, to make him realize that something smelled about Keith's supposed suicide.

She marched upstairs to Keith's desk and rummaged for their checkbook and financial records. Yes, eight-hundred dollars in savings and about three hundred in checking after the funeral expenses, not counting money from their portfolio of ChinPak stocks. No one could say Keith had planned to go missing, or he'd surely have taken some money with him. Their assets had shrunk since they'd invested heavily in the lodge, so she looked at the records of their Certificates of Deposit Keith oversaw. They were also untouched, but unfortunately, she couldn't cash them in anytime soon, unless she wanted to pay a huge penalty. Still, it seemed everything was as it should be; nothing had been withdrawn suddenly.

But her financial status, especially after the funeral, was not exactly rosy. She hoped that a private eye would not charge more than eight-hundred dollars to do some sort of checking on Keith's possible enemies, looking for things or people she obviously didn't know about.

But there were no PIs in this rural area that she knew of. Actually, she knew of only one person who might be able to even recommend one.

Claire hurried to her phone and dialed Sam Twoclaws's number, and his phone rang endlessly. She recalled that Keith had said the old man refused to get an answering machine. Sam had not even wanted to put in a phone, despite his taxidermy business and the way he traded baseball cards. Keith had jokingly said that he would have been happy to use smoke signals or drums.

Still feeling trapped in the lodge and determined to at least leave Sam a message to call her, Claire changed into jeans and a sweater. She wrote a note to take to Sam's house and carefully locked hers. No one was going to scare her. In the remnants of the setting sun, she headed on foot for Sam's. At least outside she didn't feel so trapped, and the roar of the falls sounded softer as she walked away from them.

Claire had been in Sam's taxidermy shop, which fronted River Road only once. She'd never been inside his house. The shop alone gave her the creeps, with its mounted—Keith had told her never to say stuffed—glass-eyed animals, their fangs bared, frozen in half-stride or full leap, or coiled to strike, staring from walls or shelves.

Keith had said the house itself, a long, narrow, slant-ceilinged structure that resembled a tribal longhouse, was even more unusual than the shop. Though she'd been after Keith to describe it better—it was the interior decorator in her—he'd never said more than "It's all tied to his First Nation heritage," or "It's dingy and dark, and you'd hate it."

Now, as Claire peered through the trees, she felt relieved to see Sam on the river. He was catching salmon in long, wooden traps, then smoking them over a fire on the shore. Keith had said Sam never fished with hook and line, never touched a fish with a knife, and smoked and sun-dried his salmon rather than refrigerating them. Nearer Sam's house, she saw wooden racks of fish, each headless. How, she wondered, did he behead them if he refused to cut them?

She heard music on the breeze, raucous and synthesized with a pulsating, high-pitched female vocal. Could Sam Twoclaws be listening to rap or rock?

Despite the music, he evidently heard or sensed her before she could call out, and turned as she walked closer. He fumbled with the pocket of his jacket and the music stopped. As Claire got closer to him, she saw several long-slatted traps hidden in the shallows, where the fish swam in and were snared.

"Thanks for coming to the funeral," she said. Sam nodded, his mahogany eyes intent, as if waiting for her to say more.

"That's a lot of fish," she said, gesturing at those over the fire on green-wood racks, then beyond to those drying on larger ones.

"Even one man needs a lot in the winter."

She might as well just get to it, she thought. No use trying to make small talk with Sam Twoclaws. "Sam, I'm going to hire a private investigator to look into Keith's past. I just cannot accept that he killed himself, and I need to uncover any possibility that he met with foul play."

"I know."

"You know what?"

"I know he did not want to die, no more than you."

"Oh. Did he say— Do you know anything else?"

"I know I could not bring his spirit back. I know that no one should trust all the legal men."

"Legal men? You mean lawyers or police?"

"*All* of them will find ways to lie about you and your past, so be careful what you hear about Keith. When the few of us Sammamish Salish people in this area tried to prove the lands along the river were our heritage, they lied in court and we lost our case. I know where the sacred fishing and burial grounds are, but nothing was written down." Frowning, he gestured upriver, toward the falls and lodge, then turned back again to lift each trap with a stick to see if a salmon had swum in.

"Wouldn't Sheriff Braden help you, either?"

"All this was before his time."

"I heard you brought a lawsuit and hired a private investigator. That's what I wanted to ask you. Can you recommend one to me or did the one you hired lie to you too?"

"PIs are not the law," he told her with a sage nod. "They deal in facts. They work for you, not for the government. The PI we used is in Seattle. He is Jewish, so he always worked on Sundays."

Claire was so exhausted and strung out, she almost laughed despite her problems: a Jewish PI working for a Native American to prove land rights?

"I will give you his number," Sam said. "I liked him because he did not lie and has the name Sam, too."

"That's a real coincidence. Sam Two is close to Sam Twoclaws."

"No. Sam, *too*. His name is Sam Perlman."

Claire nearly laughed again, but she startled as a salmon thrashed into the long wooden trap at their feet. Sam lifted the trap and took the fish in both hands. To her amazement, he held it up, straight-armed as if to the sky. At first she thought he might chant something, maybe even to the staring, gasping fish, but he turned to her.

"Salmon's armor of scales deflects arrows, and he can leap far," he told her. "My people believed he could put a curse on other creatures, like the rattle-snake and even the wolf. But it cannot keep him from being caught and killed. Remember that."

The look he gave her was suddenly serious—it was intimidating at least, threatening at worst.

"Are you trying to tell me something else about K—"

"Keith once said that salmon have all the answers, that is all. Go home now," he ordered harshly. "Go before it gets dark on the river. I will phone you the number of the man."

She did as he said. Eventually, she heard the mu-sic, maybe his granddaughter's group, come back on, the shrill voice wailing wild lyrics. Claire darted a look back just in time to see Sam put a stick in the salmon's mouth and bend it back to break off the head. Then he placed a long, sharp stick inside the salmon and laid it across the roasting rack over his fire.

The salmon have all the answers, Keith said. It sounded like fisherman's talk to her. But she'd learned one thing just now: Sam's lawsuit to get land back had probably included that on which her lodge sat.

Claire ran back home, checked and locked each door, then braced each shut with her ladder-backed kitchen chairs. Sam called soon to give her the phone number of PI Perlman. But later that night, every time she tried to sleep, she kept seeing him rip that fish from the river like it was some sort of sacred sacrifice.

7

As dawn broke Sunday morning, Claire parked her car outside the still-locked gate of Sunset Cemetery and simply climbed the low stone fence. Though no one could disturb the residents anymore, she was glad the overseer kept at least the appearance of security here. Unfortunately, it was an age of voyeurs and vandals, partly created by the mass media, which tended to sensationalize everything, including Keith's death. At least no cameras had turned up at the funeral; it had been difficult enough with everyone watching her every gesture and expression.

She quickly walked the gravel driveway to the back corner where Keith's grave was, the earth brown and bare compared to the frame of turf around it. It looked like a still-life painting of strewn flowers, the remains of the lilies she'd selected and several from the ChinPak bouquet. She'd donated the rest of the arrangements to the church for the altar.

But who had scattered those yellow roses, twelve of them? She'd seen no yellow roses at the funeral or the burial.

Those flowers seemed quite fresh. She bent to move several aside, looking for a note. Nothing. There was no florist in town to check with, but she was grateful someone else cared about Keith, someone who must have come after his burial or sent them late. Perhaps she'd hear from the donor or figure it out.

Studying the plot, Claire realized she'd need to select a stone soon, but she wanted to think about what Keith would have liked. Staring down at the spot where he lay, she spoke aloud, almost before she knew she would.

"I know someone is to blame besides you, Keith. I swear to you, somehow I'll find out. I'll get help to prove it—" She sucked back a sob. "I'll be back," she whispered. As she turned away, tears blurred her view and she stubbed her toe on the next tombstone.

Claire headed south on I-5. She kept creeping up over the speed limit and had to watch the speedometer of the SUV. Cursing Nick Braden every time she saw a state trooper's cruiser—they were on duty today, so why wasn't he?—she turned east toward the town of Redmond and the private investigator Sam Twoclaws had recommended.

Redmond was a city in itself, though many thought of it as a suburb of Seattle, best known as the home of Microsoft and Nintendo Corporations. She got lost twice trying to locate Sam Perlman's address on Sammamish Lake, but pulled into his driveway at ten o'clock. She had phoned earlier to be certain he'd be in, and he'd told her he'd be walking his dog by the water. She spotted a portly man, tossing a stick for his golden Labrador to fetch from the lake.

"Sam Perlman?" she called as she hurried across a wide side lawn toward him.

"Sam's the name, and information's my game,"

he said, smiling as his dog emerged from the lake and shook water from his coat. "Mrs. Malvern, I presume?" he asked, and she nodded. "Atta boy, Mose," he told the Lab, wrestling the stick from his mouth to toss again before he shook hands with her. "His name is Moses, because he always thinks the sea will part for him—right, boy?"

Perlman chuckled as the dog dove in after his prize. Though man and dog made a charming scene, images of another canine sniffing for Keith's body on the river clung to Claire.

PI Perlman was probably in his late thirties, which surprised her, since she had expected someone older. He had a full head of unruly, curly black hair and wore jeans, a leather jacket and expensive running shoes he obviously never ran in. Shorter than her by half a head and shaped like a pear, he waddled when he walked.

She had envisioned Tom Selleck of *Magnum, P.I.* when she'd heard his voice on the phone. Claire hated to stereotype people, but Sam seemed the perfect picture of the jolly fat man, with a smile so broad it split his face. His head seemed balanced like a ball on his shoulders, which plunged to a barrel chest and big belly. Her hopes that Sam Perlman would be sharp enough to help her fell.

"Don't want Mose to overdo it—my life philosophy in general," Sam said, clapping as the dog swam to the stick, snatched it in his jaws and circled back. "Come on into the office, and Mose will catch up. So, a friend of old Sam Twoclaws from quaint little Portfalls, eh? Despite your name, I expected you to be Native American, but you look only native

Irish. Genealogy's a passion of mine. Now, what can I do for you?''

Claire took a deep breath and looked directly into Perlman's brown eyes. ''My husband died recently. Our local Portfalls police and the county coroner insist his death's a suicide, but I can't believe or accept that.''

There, she thought. She'd gotten that out without dissolving into sobs, as she had off and on all morning. She was suddenly glad she'd worn her navy-blue, tailored pantsuit. However casually Sam was dressed, she wanted him to know she meant business.

''I'm sorry for your loss,'' he said, frowning. ''Self-inflicted gunshot?''

''No. They say he jumped from a bridge, but—''

''That so-called suicide bridge up by Portfalls, right? Read it in the paper—if it was the most recent case.''

''I don't care what they call the bridge or what the evidence supposedly shows, Keith did not kill himself. And unless it was an accident, that means someone else may have.''

''Ah,'' he said.

Claire was grateful the PI didn't just dismiss her with a ''family always refuses to accept a suicide'' remark. He gestured her toward his office, which he'd explained over the phone was a back room in his home. Even before he held open the door of the rambling Cape Cod house for her, she heard the *thump-thump* beat of music within; as they entered, a passionate orchestral piece blasted them.

''One of the reasons I work from my home,'' he told her, raising his voice, ''is that I can enjoy my music. Mussorgsky, *Pictures at an Exhibition*,'' he added as the damp dog bounded between them into the room. Perlman gestured her toward a wingback chair and went behind his big desk to turn the music down. The panting dog raced once around the room, then loudly lapped water in his bowl by the door.

Claire scanned the office. The interior decorator in her always sized people up by the trappings of their chosen habitats, just as she'd seen Nick Braden study surroundings for his own reasons. In her direct line of vision, state-of-the-art electronics nearly obscured fine old oak-paneled walls. A stereo with massive speakers, a CD player, DVD machine, tape decks, and a large-screen TV took up one wall. File cabinets and a fax machine, printer, two computers and crammed bookshelves filled another. Corkboards stuck with maps, lists and photos covered the other two walls between windows overlooking the lake and side yard. Perlman's desk was littered with piles of papers, some six inches deep.

''I'll level with you, Mrs. Malvern,'' he said, tapping his fingers on the arms of his padded leather chair. ''I usually work with attorneys to background someone or with corporate entities on locates, not with private clients. But you sounded so determined on the phone, I figured I should hear you out.''

''I appreciate that. You usually do what? Locates?''

''Right, find someone who's skipped out on someone or something, or in the case of the Sammamish tribe, try to locate the historic boundaries of their lands.'' Sam used such sweeping gestures he might as well have been conducting the music. ''I never do surveils anymore,'' he added with a frown. ''Too tricky and dangerous. I mostly do paper or online work, you see. But when a really interesting case comes my way, like this disputed death case of yours..."

"Quite frankly, I'm desperate for help. The police seem unwilling to listen to my belief that my husband's death was either an accident or foul play."

"Now the latter possibility—that's where we may have a problem proceeding. Criminal cases are for the police, not a PI like me."

"The point is," she said, trying to keep control as her voice rose over the crescendo of the music, "because the police won't believe this is a criminal case, I have to find a way to prove it is. I assume you would want to follow up on Keith's financial status. I've brought information along to give you a head start with that," she said, digging a packet of papers from her big purse.

"I wish you had told me more over the phone about what you had in mind. Did your husband have any aka's?"

"Only a .38-caliber pistol which the sheriff took from me, but gave back after he unloaded it."

"Mrs. Malvern," he said, holding up his hands, "I meant, did your husband have any aliases?"

"Oh—you mean aka, *also known as.*" Suddenly, she felt overwhelmed again, a babe in the woods trying to track down Keith's past, but she was determined to do it.

"If I took the case," he went on, "I'd also need the names of the deceased's friends and associates, especially those he worked with recently, and his former POE—place of employment."

"You would check up on their backgrounds,

too?'' she asked, leaning forward on the edge of her chair, still gripping the financial records.

"I'd need to speak to them, find out if he had problems, if he borrowed money, if he was somehow unstable."

"I'd hate for you to upset some of them," she blurted, thinking especially of the Nances. Asking subtly about Keith was something she could do herself, without upsetting people as much as a private investigator would. Perhaps she could actually do some PI work herself, despite the time it would take. At least it would save her the money she could not really afford.

"Mrs. Malvern, I have a feeling you don't understand what a PI really does and doesn't do. It's not like that actor who plays Paul Drake on the old *Perry Mason* reruns. I don't carry a gun, and I'm not a detective. And unlike Kinsey Millhone—you know, the character from those Sue Grafton books, who always ends up getting into criminal stuff over her head—that's not how most PIs work, not how I work. I've got to admit, TV reruns and murder mystery novels are hobbies of mine, but those characters are not real-life PIs."

She could only nod. She had been certain this was the way to go if Nick would not help her. But it was starting to sound as if Sam Perlman had every hobby in the world except private investigation.

"Actually," he explained with a sweep of his hand around his office, "most days I don't leave this room except to fix myself a little something to eat. With the Internet today, I do ninety percent of my work online, with an occasional visit to a courthouse.

Right Mose?'' he added, patting the dog, which had flopped down beside his chair.

"I really thought you could help," she admitted, trying to cover her disappointment. "I came prepared to give you a retainer."

"It will be ninety dollars an hour you won't have to spend here, Mrs. Malvern."

That set her back in her seat. The eight-hundred dollars she'd mentally allocated for help to prove Keith could have been lured outside by someone and then intentionally harmed would buy just a little over one eight-hour day.

"I'm sorry," Perlman was repeating as the dolorous music depressed her even more, "but if you want someone to prove criminal intent and murder, you need the police. If they won't help, and if you have absolutely no proof of anything illegal your husband did—''

"Of course he didn't," she cut in, sitting up straight again. "I'm interested in something illegal someone did to *him!*''

"Listen, Mrs. Malvern," he said, leaning as close to his desk as he could with his big paunch, "let me help you the only way I can. Keep in mind that surveillance without a PI license is stalking, but you yourself are perfectly able to chat up friends, family and co-workers to see if you can discover a reason your husband was emotionally despondent."

"In other words, why he would kill himself. But I'm trying to establish just the opposite."

"Please hear me out. You could, of course, also turn up that outstanding debts had gotten him an enemy, and then you'd call the cops. But first, I'd check what are called incident reports. Those'll be

filed at police stations in counties where your husband lived, and recent ones could be especially helpful.''

"I'm sure Keith has never been arrested.''

"Incident reports don't document arrests or con-
victions. They are the daily record of every stop or
pullover a cop makes. The reports aren't online, so
you have to go to the police station and look through
the logs by hand,'' he said with a slight grimace, as
if having to leave this haven to do that would be the
worst thing to befall him.

"Incident reports. All right.''

"They're gold mines of data about who was
where, when, even though no arrest may have been
made, see? That way, anyone can track people's
whereabouts and companions.''

Companions, she thought. She'd been so certain
she knew personally, or knew about, everyone Keith
knew. But maybe not, because she couldn't fathom
anyone she was familiar with harming him. Since
such police records could be accessed by anyone,
and since DeeDee Duncan had asked if there was
any way she could help her...

"So incident reports are more or less police
notes,'' she said, wanting to be sure she understood
exactly what Perlman was telling her.

"Exactly. Which might tip you off to whether or
not your husband or someone he knew was seen doing something suspicious or at least unusual. It's just
one tool of discovery, but I've seen it work time and
again to put you on to another lead, to something or
someone else.''

"But I know Keith. He wouldn't do anything il-
leg—''

"Listen to yourself. You think someone wanted to kill him and you need a who and why. I know the guy just died, and there's that halo effect about him for you. But if someone killed him, Mrs. Malvern," he said, punching the air with his index finger, "unless it was pure random mishap, there must have been some reason, right? You may even have to use some pretext to shake the info loose, but you gotta go in with the idea that if there's wrongdoing on the part of a killer, the victim might not be lily white, either."

She just stared at him. Her mind went as blank as if she'd tumbled into the whiteout of the falls and the river. Perlman's words began to make sense— terrible, frightening sense.

"But," he went on, evidently surprised she didn't argue, "you better be damn careful where you poke around because it can get real dark and real dirty under some rocks you might have to turn over. The deceased might get smeared, and you, too. Like I said, if you think this is criminal, you'll need the police, but maybe you've gotta get something to attract them or force their hand first."

"Yes, I see. He— They," she murmured, picturing Nick Braden's stern face as she stuffed her records back in her purse and fumbled for her car keys, "will have to be tempted or forced to help."

"You got it. I'm sorry I can't commit to this, Mrs. Malvern, I really am, but what you want done is not like checking through old deeds and land records about where tribal fishing grounds and sacred shaman burial sites once were, so a lawsuit can be filed to get them back. And, sad to say, I failed to find enough in black-and-white for your friend so that the

Sammamish could get their land returned to them. Twoclaws told me, though, he'd find another way to reclaim it all at any cost. I just bet you'll find a way to ask around about your husband and then get the police to help you, too—if need be—or to let this whole thing rest in peace, with him.''

But Claire was hardly listening now. She was formulating a desperate plan she had thought of before, when Aaron Curtis told her where Sheriff Braden was today. Yes, she'd try to do some of the investigating on her own, but she wanted Nick to know she expected him to help. And right now, she could think of only one way to accomplish that.

Claire stood abruptly, startling the dog, which leaped to his feet as if it were playtime again. "I'm grateful for everything," she told Perlman. He came around the desk to open the door for her just as the music changed.

She grimaced as she left because she recognized this selection: "The Merry Widow Waltz."

The Pacific Lights Yacht Club was just north of the larger Elliott Bay Marina. Claire had helped to redecorate the latter's clubhouse several years before, when Kallile's Fine Interiors had landed the lucrative contract. The Pacific Lights looked vintage old-money with its docks sprawled among a forest of masts, though large power yachts were as common as sail-powered boats here. After driving directly from Sam Perlman's, she found a visitor parking place in a distant lot, and checked her appearance in the rearview mirror.

Disaster! She looked like a zombie, one with mascara streaks under her bloodshot eyes. And she should have stopped somewhere for lunch, because she was feeling light-headed. No way could she pull this off if she didn't look better before charging inside to try to see if she could talk to Nick before this so-called Bachelor Bid-Off. But if he wouldn't listen...

She pulled the packet of financial information from her purse and rechecked the bottom line of her scribbling. It would be worth the eight-hundred dollars to force him to listen to her. It wouldn't be a bribe, because the money would go to some charity, not to Nick.

Claire slipped inside to use the rest room and repair what she could of her makeup. As she emerged into the elegantly decorated lobby, the thick aquamarine carpet and mural of old racing ships almost calmed her thudding heart. Elegant glass cases displayed old ship's bells and regatta trophies.

"Are you here for the luncheon and auction?" the woman in the cloakroom asked as Claire tried to just walk past her station.

"Yes, that's right."

"In the Commodore Room right down the hall. I'm afraid it's under way, but you can just go in."

"Thanks."

Claire scanned the handwritten poster on an easel as she went down the hall. September events at the clubhouse included a Cruise & Snooze, Lobster Mania, Rigatoni Regatta, and Fishing Derby, as well as the Bachelor Bid-Off.

The volume of noise, chatter and clinking silver on china rose as Claire went down the hall and into the foyer of a larger room beyond. The delicious smell of food hit her so hard she began to salivate.

As the woman had said, the event was already under way. The two ladies who had evidently been greeters stood just inside the banquet room, listening to a woman speaker.

The well-modulated female voice floated to Claire over a microphone. "While you enjoy your salad, ladies and honored gentlemen, let me just remind you that our event today is in the best of Seattle traditions."

Claire's gaze dropped to the list of crossed-off names on the vacated greeters' table. The list was alphabetical, so Nick Braden's was near the top.

"After all, by 1865 our fair city was established, but the busy bachelors who had built it had no brides. Asa Mercer went east and returned with eleven brave and eligible young women and later brought back fifty-seven bold damsels from a second trip, including his wife-to-be."

Claire noted three names not crossed off the list of women, which must have run to at least one hundred names. Three corresponding name tags were left. With each was a table number, probably reservations so women could sit with their friends.

"And as you may know, ladies, a hundred years later that story of bachelors and their soon-to-be loves was made into the 1960s TV show *Here Come the Brides.*"

Claire grabbed forty dollars out of her purse to pay for her meal and shoved the bills under the list of names. Praying these women were no-shows and not just late, she took the name tag for Kaye Madden, but the table number for Anita Branin. That way, if Anita had friends waiting for her inside, they might not know Claire wasn't Kaye. Besides, she

could see from here that Anita's table, number four-
teen, was near the back, in case she needed to make
a hasty exit.

"Today, of course, ladies, we are turning the tables on traditions in more ways than one," the emcee
was saying as Claire edged behind the greeters'
backs and slipped into the empty seat at Table 14.
Six women and one bachelor, a tanned silver-haired
man, were already seated. Most nodded and smiled
at Claire, who responded as best she could, considering she was now doing exactly what Perlman had
said she might have to do—using pretext.

"Our twenty bachelors," the speaker went on,
"have been brought here today for this excellent
cause. Enjoy your main courses, because these gentlemen of various ages, interests and vocations will
be the dessert—uh, that is," she said coyly, when
the laughter quieted, "they will share an onboard
champagne and dessert with each of you who bids
the most for them for this afternoon."

Claire's stomach clenched as she responded to
greetings from the other women at her table, who
were, thankfully, already engaged in eating and chatting. She scanned the area for Nick and finally spotted him across the room, blessedly sitting with his
back to her. He was no doubt literally eating up the
flutter of female attention, as was the man at their
table, who turned out to be a manager for one of the
local TV affiliates. Under different circumstances,
Claire would have taken him to task for his net-
work's evident assumption that any death on the
Portfalls bridge was suicide.

She needed a steady head for what she was going
to do, so she forced herself to eat. She skipped the

wine and stuck with iced tea. Responding to polite inquiries when she had to, she prayed no one nearby knew Kaye Madden. And she prayed fervently that Nick Braden would not denounce—or kill—her for what she was about to do.

Nick kept telling himself this event was for a good cause—and penance for somehow failing Susan—but he felt like a stallion at a horse auction. If he didn't have his mouth full of food, these women would probably insist on inspecting his teeth. He already felt as if they'd visually probed through his best suit. He'd refused to wear his uniform today, despite how the woman who'd contacted him had hinted that a man in uniform would raise the stakes. Maybe he knew now how women felt when men ogled them or lifted one eyebrow as if to ask—

"Do you have to use your gun much on the job?" Sandi Santini, the chatty woman on his left, was asking.

"The point is to use it as little as possible," he told her.

"Even off the job—like now—are you wearing one hidden somewhere?" she went on with a wide-eyed look as she scooted her chair closer to his. "Like in a shoulder holster or leg strap?"

She stroked his upper arm lightly, sliding her hand up, around his shoulder and down to his ribs, where he did, indeed, have a gun. He shifted slightly away from her touch.

"It pays to be prepared," he said, "but I don't think I'm really prepared for this today. Shades of the old slave market days."

Sandi looked appalled. "Hardly," she insisted, as

the scent of her flowery powder or perfume hit him, making him want to sneeze. "Each of the luxury yachts will have a captain aboard to take them out and someone to serve the dessert and champagne, and it's for a good cause."

"That's why I'm here," Nick said to settle her down, but he was the one who felt unsettled. He took a sip of white wine and just managed to swallow it before he exploded in a sneeze from her powder. He'd much rather be arresting a drunk, even if he had to bring him back into the jail in a reeking police car. Hell, he'd rather take on Claire Malvern again.

"It's time, ladies!" the emcee cooed into the mike. "Take a bidding paddle with a number from the center of your table and loosen those purse strings!"

Nick blew his nose as the emcee introduced the auctioneer who would oversee the bidding. They were going alphabetically, so that meant he went first. He might as well get it over with so he could return to work. It was all for a dead woman, who must not have really loved or trusted him, no matter how much she'd said she did.

8

Claire's heart thudded and she felt herself flush. To calm down, she tried to think of things she was grateful for. That had always worked when she was scared or upset. Let's see, she was grateful that her table's bachelor, Paul Frederick, the TV station manager sitting across from her, had evidently not brought any cameras or reporters with him to cover this event. She was grateful she had a plan to aggressively probe Keith's death. And that Nick Braden already realized how dedicated she was toward that end. Thankfully, too, he was a man she knew she could trust, one who could comfort as well as confront, because she was scared to death about getting his undivided attention this way.

It was all Claire could do to keep from sinking under the table as Nick joined the emcee at her podium and scanned the audience with a tight smile. He seemed to look right at her, but was evidently taking in the entire scene. He probably thought she was the last person in the world who would suddenly turn up here.

"Now, ladies," the emcee said, "you can follow along in your programs as I mention highlights from Bachelor Number One's bio, before I turn the mike over for the bidding."

Suddenly, Claire had a dreadful vision of an old

TV show called *The Dating Game*, where a man or woman asked questions of three members of the opposite sex sitting behind a curtain, then chose the one he or she wanted to go out with. She shuddered. She should leave right now, sneak out and just go about her own sleuthing.

"Nick is a former LEO—that's law enforcement officer, ladies, and is currently sheriff of scenic Portfalls and several islands near the romantic San Juans. He's formerly of the marine military police who served in Operation Desert Storm, and you know they are *Semper Fi*," she added with a pert salute. "Nick loves to both fish and fly his own plane. We are all so grateful Nick Braden has taken time to be one of our bachelors for this important cause."

A swell of applause followed. Women who couldn't see well craned their necks or peeked over other heads. Claire noted the tips of Nick's ears had colored. Although she held one of the bidding paddles—number fifty-four—tightly in her lap, she felt frozen as the patter from the auctioneer began.

"An-a we will start the bidding for a lovely afternoon afloat with our bachelor sheriff at a one-hundred dollars. Do I hear, yes, over there, number eleven, one-hundred-fifty. An-a do I hear— Yes, two-hundred from number twenty-three, the lady in red..."

Despite how the food had stoked her strength and courage, Claire still felt she was going to be sick to her stomach.

"Bachelor Braden," the auctioneer went on in his staccato delivery, "is used to flying high with some gal in the sky, but today he's gonna take a slow boat to China with one of you lucky ladies— Yes, two-fifty, number eleven— Ah, three-hundred, number nine.''

Claire began to tremble. It was money she had intended to spend on the PI, and Nick could be so much more valuable to her quest than Sam Perlman, however helpful his free advice had been. After all, Nick knew the ropes around Portfalls. And, as much as they had argued, she trusted him.

She thrust her paddle in the air.

''Four-hundred, number fifty-four, back of the room. An-a four-hundred-fifty smackers—that's dollars, ladies, not kisses—from number eleven.''

Claire noted Nick was staring over the top of the women's heads instead of at them. That was a trick she'd learned in college when she had a required freshman speech class: don't look directly at people if you're nervous. Despite what she herself intended to do, her heart went out to him.

She lifted her paddle high.

''Number fifty-four, an-a five-hundred dollars! An-a five-hundred dollars going once, going twice... Five-fifty from number twenty-three!''

Claire wondered what charity this was for, but she dared not ask. Thank the Lord, no one here knew her. Imagine a new, grieving widow at such a thing, doing such a thing. ''The Merry Widow Waltz,'' indeed.

When the bidding went to six hundred, Claire told herself to quit. This was completely insane. Yet six-hundred dollars wouldn't have purchased even seven hours of PI help, when this would surely demonstrate to Nick that his ongoing assistance could be invaluable. Besides, she was supporting some charity he valued. So when the bleached blonde near the front—the ubiquitous number eleven—lifted her paddle again, Claire topped her once more and then again.

Women were standing along the back and sides now. Laughter and cheers swelled around Claire. It seemed an out-of-body experience to hold that paddle up one more time and hear, "Going once, going twice...a yacht ride with the sexy sheriff sold to number fifty-four for seven-hundred-and-fifty dollars!"

Applause, a few unladylike whoops. A woman came to her table to get the money right away, so Claire wrote a check to the Pacific Lights Yacht Club as the bidding on the second bachelor began. She hesitated a moment as she signed her own name, but she had no doubt they'd happily take the money, even if she had been masquerading as Kaye Madden.

When she looked up, Nick was glaring narrow-eyed and granite-jawed at her, not from the front of the room but from four feet away.

Surrounded by committee members, the two of them posed for a picture together, which Claire prayed was for the charity newsletter and not the newspaper. Actually, Nick held her up since her legs were like water; she was certain his fingers left permanent indentations in her upper arm and waist. When the camera strobe went off, she was stupidly staring right into it, so she went momentarily blind, but she could certainly hear what Nick whispered.

"What in hell do you think you're doing?"

"I needed to talk to you, and you weren't listening. I didn't buy your time for some date on a yacht, but so you'd help me search for—"

To her amazement and horror, more lights kicked

on and a mike was thrust their way. "Jennifer Crosby, *News Live at Six*. How does it feel, Sheriff Braden, to have the so-called weaker sex take charge?"

"It's starting to feel normal," Nick said, and turned Claire away from the camera. He thrust her purse at her as if he'd hiked a football into her midriff, and steered her down the hall the way she'd come in.

"By the way, if you think this was some big secret move on your part," he said, talking out of the corner of his mouth without looking at her, "Noah Markwood was in there, and you know how the Portfalls grapevine goes and grows. All I need is someone figuring one of us bumped Keith off so we could be together," he muttered as they went outside into bright sunlight.

"We didn't even know each other before he died. That's completely ridiculous!" she insisted as she fumbled for her sunglasses in her purse, though she kept seeing fuchsia dots before her eyes. But she realized she might have compromised Nick's position as disinterested law enforcement. If only she could get him away before anything else hap—

"Heavens, it *is* you, Claire," a well-modulated woman's voice said from behind them.

Claire turned back to see Diana Nance had followed them out of the clubhouse. She was certain the Pacific Lights Yacht Club wasn't the one the Nances belonged to, but Diana donated her support to many charities.

"I didn't see your name on the list," Diana went on, her hand fluttering gracefully to the pearl necklace at her throat, "and couldn't believe it could be you."

"I—I just came to support Sheriff Braden for all he's done—the help he gave when Keith died," Claire stammered.

"Well, in this instance a donation would have been entirely acceptable," Diana intoned, raising both sleek eyebrows.

Claire could have kicked herself. She could tell Nick would like to, too.

"I know how much your philanthropic work means to you, Diana, so I'm just grateful that I could help out," Claire replied, trying to appear calm in the midst of chaos. Maybe Diana would just figure she'd gone out of her mind with grief. For one moment, she considered lying even more than she already had: she could say that she had come to bid for her friend Kaye Madden. But she figured what she'd done today was enough "pretext," as Sam Perlman had called it, to suit any private investigation he could have concocted.

"Yes. Thank you for coming into town the day after Keith's funeral," Diana said icily with a narrow glance at Nick. "Ethan and I will be in touch, but you be sure to take some time off to get some rest." She turned and went back inside.

"I hope you're satisfied," Nick muttered. "Remind me never to hire you to work undercover."

"I'm sorry, but you made me feel as if I couldn't even buy your time, so I got desperate and did."

"Then, let's just see if the thoughtless, ruthless sheriff can make it worth your while," he said between gritted teeth as he propelled her toward the sprawling docks behind the clubhouse.

The watcher saw the sheriff escort Claire toward the docks. Unbelievable to find them together again, but it was hardly coincidence. Follow one, and eventually the other turned up. And that was not acceptable.

But now it was impossible to pursue them down the dock too closely without being spotted. Still, this camera worked well at a distance with its zoom lens. Hopefully, the constant clicking would not carry over the water. Darting from boat to boat on the parallel arm of dock would have to do. Maybe their voices would carry over the water, too.

The captain of a yacht was motioning to them and untying the mooring lines. They must be going out together. It was a very clever setup, one for which Claire Malvern would pay, in more ways than one.

Squinting into the afternoon sun, the watcher felt only helpless fury, but it wouldn't be the helpless kind for long.

"Wait," Claire insisted, balking as Nick led her down the dock. "We aren't actually going out on some yacht. I bought your time to help me search the area of the bridge and my house again, because I figured you'll know what to look for. And I'm going to go over incident reports at the station and—"

"Just shut up for once," he ordered as he marched her past power and sailing yachts rocking in their berths. Rope mooring lines creaked, and the grommets in canvas sails or flags dinged rhythmically against metal masts in the wind.

Claire noted several boats had numbers taped on their sterns, evidently to match the number of each bachelor. By boat number one, a smiling man waited dressed in a captain's cap, a navy, double-breasted jacket and white slacks. Standing with a thick mooring line in his hand, he appeared to have been sent from central casting. He held the line as if the massive, two-tiered power yacht was a pet on a huge leash. At least ninety feet long, the yacht sprawled the entire length of an arm off the main dock. Nick shook the man's hand, but Claire could only manage a mute nod and smile.

"Welcome to the *Lucky Lady*. Captain and host, John Patterson, at your service, with first mate and first wife, Ginny, to serve you champagne and dessert." An attractive brunette waved from the door of the large, furnished main cabin on board, but bobbed right back in. "However," Captain Patterson said as he reboarded, "you might want to hold off with the food until we find a quiet cove somewhere. It's a little rocky today."

"Tell me about it," Claire heard Nick mutter as he held her elbow tight and crowded her toward the edge of the dock until she had to step onto the yacht's ladder and climb onboard. Captain Patterson gave her a hand down, and Nick followed close behind.

"So, if you'll excuse me, I'll take the *Lucky Lady* out," the captain said with another smile. "Just give a holler if you want me or Ginny, but until then, we'll leave you to yourselves."

Not speaking, Claire and Nick stood at the lower-level stern rail of the yacht, watching the marina shrink into their churning white wake. The boat's powerful inboard motors seemed to vibrate through Claire's body. As they accelerated, the stern slanted into the water and the nose lifted as if to pin them in place with gravity and speed.

"I ought to toss you overboard," Nick said.

"Under the circumstances, that's not funny."

"I didn't mean for it to be."

They continued to stare at the changing coastline while the white-linen-covered table awaited behind them. Bracing themselves against the rock of the bay as they left the shelter of the marina, they gripped the polished teakwood rail, their knuckles white, their hands close but not touching.

"Did DeeDee tell you where I was?" he asked, finally putting his sunglasses on in the glare of sun on water.

"Aaron Curtis. My artist's studio was broken into and several paintings taken. When I phoned for help—not 911 this time—he came."

"How many paintings are missing?" he countered.

At least, she thought, he was thinking like a law enforcement officer instead of a man who'd somehow just been swindled—when she'd paid seven-hundred-and-fifty dollars for the privilege of being yanked around by him.

She hesitated. "I think about five."

"It's probably three, and Noah Markwood has them."

She turned to gape at him. "What? Noah Markwood took them?"

"Keith took them to Markwood a short time ago, hoping he'd like them enough to want to sell them in his Puget Treasures shop, even to take more on consignment or maybe sponsor a showing for you."

"Oh," she managed to say, gripping the rail even

harder. She felt shocked and foolish. The boat was bucking bigger swells now, and she had to spread her feet to keep her balance.

Nick took her arm, gently this time, and sat her on the cushioned bench that lined the sides of the enclosed aft deck where they had stood. The buffeting of the breeze was more muted here.

"I figured you didn't know he'd done that," he said.

"No, I didn't. In a way, it's really touching, but I wish he'd told me or that we had planned it together. I didn't think he believed my work was all that good."

"Maybe he thought you could use the extra money."

Loosening his tie with one finger, he sat down beside her. She smelled some crisp pine scent from him, though the sea air quickly snatched it away. The blue, opaque aviator sunglasses hid his eyes, but she felt those eyes boring into her anyway.

"I would like to think," she said, studying her clasped hands in her lap, "he did it to please me, for a nice surprise, and because he really believed my work was good, but I don't know. I guess there's so much I just don't know about him, but I'm going to find out. I didn't mean to pay for the boat ride and champagne, but for a couple of hours of help from you, even if it can't be in your official capacity. Maybe as a friend," she added, looking up at him again.

He raked his fingers though his short, crisp hair. "You do see that you've been jumping to conclusions again, don't you?" he asked, after a long, awkward silence. "You're accusing someone of theft when your paintings probably weren't stolen at all."

"And Keith probably met with no harm the night he died other than what he himself caused, you mean?"

He only shrugged, but his expression, even though she could not see his eyes, said it all. He still didn't believe her or want to help.

"I've also seen a private investigator for advice," she informed him, sitting up straight again. "I intend to ask around in Seattle and Portfalls—probably starting with Noah, now—about Keith's demeanor and activities. I intend to go through possible incident reports regarding him that your office has on file."

"It's a free country, and those are public records."

"Nick, won't you help me, at least with advice? If not, I've just miscalculated that I could trust you and spent a lot of money in the process for a charitable cause I don't have a clue about."

She was certain he was going to insist she didn't have a clue about much of anything, but his stern expression suddenly shifted, then softened. His lower lip tightened; he rose and stood at the stern rail again, leaning on it stiff-armed, his broad shoulders slightly slumped.

"What?" she asked, rising and going to stand by him. "What did I say now?"

"You really did crash that party back there without knowing one damn thing about it, didn't you? That's you, Claire, strong but headstrong, determined but dangerous."

"Don't you believe in women's intuition?" she demanded. "I have it about Keith's not killing himself. But there may have been something amiss in his life, and I've got to find out what. I'm going to search through everything he touched, because there have to be answers somewhere.''

''I'd start with that computer sitting on his desk.''

''I intend to.''

''Did he have a laptop, too?''

''It was stolen from him at the airport just before he resigned his job in Seattle. Actually, he took that as a sign.''

''Lots of those get taken. Don't forget to check for possible safety deposit boxes at your banks, or a home safe, if you have one.''

''We have none of those,'' she admitted, but her heart soared that he was already starting to help her again.

''Claire, I don't want to see you hurt,'' he blurted.

''I'm hurt now. I have to go ahead, to know the truth.''

He was silent for a few moments, and she kept still. They stared at each other, though all she saw was her image mirrored in his sunglasses. They stayed that way until the boat slowed and he looked away first. They watched the captain drop anchor in a rocky cove. The boat bobbed instead of rocking with each swell.

When neither of them moved from the rail, Ginny Patterson brought them flutes of champagne and disappeared inside the main cabin again, closing the sliding door behind her. They didn't drink, speak or move.

''The donations all go for the fight against breast cancer,'' Nick said, the words suddenly harsh amidst the sweet sounds of waves and wind. ''I'd rather just donate money, but they asked, and it's something I always support. My wife died of breast cancer five years ago, at age thirty-three.''

Claire was so startled she slopped champagne. "I'm sorry, Nick. I didn't know—how she died, I mean.''

"I realize that. Only those close to me do.''

Suddenly, she desperately wanted to be close to him, to comfort him. He seemed so alone and lonely. Who did he have, really? His staff admired him. The town relied on him. But she doubted if he even had a pet, like poor Sam Perlman had Moses. She stood a foot from Nick, yearning to be someone he could trust, someone she could help, though she was in dire need of all that herself.

"I'm sorry about what I said that first night Keith was missing,'' she told him, "that you could not possibly understand the sudden loss of a young spouse. But I suppose your wife's loss wasn't that sudden.''

"It was. It was over fairly fast once I found out about it,'' he said, his voice hard again, his stance stiff. "And yet it's never over. She kept her illness from me, held back. She said later she didn't want to hurt me.''

Claire could tell by the way he turned slightly away that he hadn't meant to confide all that to her.

"But she did hurt you,'' she whispered.

"I don't want to talk about it. It's water over the dam. I only told you that so you'll see that I can understand your frustration and pain that Keith might have held something back from you. And, since I'm off duty today, when we get back to Portfalls, I'll help you search your place or around the bridge. But you'll promise me in return,'' he said, leaning one elbow on the rail and clutching his goblet so hard she thought it might shatter, ''that if we turn up nothing strange there or in the incident reports, you will go back to painting and getting the lodge shipshape, so you can recoup the money you so generously donated today.''

''All right,'' she said, daring a tenuous but triumphant smile. ''Deal.''

She thought he might shake her hand, but he leaned close only to clink her glass with his, and they both drank to it.

9

By the time the *Lucky Lady* was back in her berth, Claire and Nick had agreed to cooperate. He would search the area around the bridge that afternoon, before more time or weather could destroy evidence. She would search her house after he gave her some suggestions she might not have thought of before. He would tell her how to look through incident reports, and she would ask people who knew Keith if they'd noticed anything unusual about his behavior.

If, after all that, they had turned up nothing suspicious, Claire would not challenge the coroner's ruling and would go on with her life. On the other hand, if something seemed askew, Nick would help her follow any promising lead and reopen the case if necessary.

"I don't want to get you in trouble," she had assured him as they sat across from each other at the elegant table on the yacht. "I don't expect you to spend taxpayers' money or unwarranted time on this cold case if you have others pending."

"It's not a cold case, Claire. That's a case that's old, one that's gone stale, maybe for years, with no new leads. The cause of Keith's death is technically closed but not cold."

His mirrored sunglasses in his pocket now, he'd looked at her intently. For the first time, she saw his eyes were an amazing color, one interior decorators called chicory or sage, green with the barest hint of brown. He had a rugged face and a slightly crooked nose that kept him just short of handsome. She had begun to see Nick as a man then, not just as a cop, the sheriff. He had losses, he had needs. That realization hit her with a force she'd never felt before, maybe not even with Keith.

"Actually—" he'd rushed on as if to keep from saying something else "—the department has a personnel policy prohibiting involvement in a case by an investigator where a personal relationship *preexisted* with a victim. That's obviously not the case here, though not long ago I did have to discipline and temporarily remove a deputy who got emotionally involved with a witness."

"Right—that's certainly not the case here," she'd put in, gazing out over the ruffled, blue-gray water of the cove. "Don't I wish I were a witness to what really happened, instead of having to rely on an anonymous fisherman I don't believe or trust. So we're not breaking any rules or regs for you, then?" she asked.

He shook his head abruptly. "Just so you understand that I may have to put this on the back burner if other things heat up more."

He'd looked uneasy, almost guilty, at the way he'd put that. It scared her that some sort of energy arced between them in what they said and didn't say. But it scared her even more that they might not find anything suspicious, and she'd have to do without his help again.

Late that afternoon, Nick followed Claire back into Portfalls, but turned off to his own place to change clothes before going to look around the site of Keith's death. At his small, shake-shingled house on the other side of town from the lodge, he donned jeans, a flannel shirt and a jacket.

As he gazed around his spartan, immaculately kept bedroom, he realized how tiny everything looked after being out on the water. And how impersonal, especially compared to the large rooms of The Falls Fishing Lodge, Claire's future B & B. He had to admit he could use an interior decorator around here, or a woman's touch. If they stayed friends, maybe he'd show her the place someday and ask her for some advice, just like she'd asked for his.

He'd advised Claire about how to really search her house: look for things possibly taped under drawers; go through every pocket of Keith's clothes, and even his shoes; spend time on his computer looking at sent mail or stored documents; check his toolbox and tackle box or any other male bastion where she seldom looked; fan through books and magazines.

Nick startled when his phone rang. No way could she have found something already, though he'd given her his unlisted number this afternoon. He grabbed the bedroom phone.

"Nick Braden here."

Silence. No one. Nothing on the line. But he was sure he heard someone breathing, someone there.

"Sheriff Braden," he clipped out. "I'm gonna trace this call—"

Click.

He swore and slammed the receiver down. He had an unlisted number for just that reason and hadn't needed caller-ID, but maybe someone had leaked his number.

He'd noted the night Keith disappeared that Claire didn't have either caller-ID or call-waiting. He'd tell her to carefully check the long-distance calls listed on her next bill; he could request a record of the lodge's incoming calls from an official database, but he'd wait on that. Just a quick site and house search, and let her look through incident reports and talk to a few people—that was all. That should satisfy her and clear his own conscience.

But could he just let her go, then? Sometimes when he was with her he felt he was in way over his head, swept along by a powerful compulsion to protect her.

Nick knocked on the back door of the lodge two hours later, just as twilight settled in. He scanned the rapids of the river below again. No fisherman right now, but then, it was a Sunday evening, so maybe weekend trips were over.

"Coming!" he heard Claire call. "I started in his office," she told him breathlessly, as she opened the deck door for him. "I looked under the drawers and just got into the computer. Did you find anything?"

He shook his head. "I even went partway out on the bridge itself, looking for his keys and shoes."

"His shoes? The river has probably dragged them clear to Puget Sound by now."

"Sometimes jumpers take them off before—"

Her hopes fell. "You're working from the opposite supposition I am about him," she protested. "You still believe he killed himself, not that he didn't."

"I'm just trying to cover all possible angles. So you've found nothing in his office so far?"

She closed and relocked the door and motioned him to follow her up the corkscrew stairs. "The computer will take a lot more time, but I might as well go through the stuff in the boxes I haven't un-packed since we've been here. By the way, I'm def-initely getting all the locks re-keyed tomorrow, since his keys haven't turned up, just in case."

"Good idea."

"Then, you realize someone dangerous could have taken his keys."

"I realize you need to have peace of mind any way we can get it for you. Claire," he said, standing in the office doorway as she slid the closet door open, "there is one more thing. I want you to confide in me about your search here. But you need to know that if you find something that, let's say, incriminates Keith, I will get an official search warrant. And I can't have you fight me on that."

"I hadn't let myself think anything like that," she admitted, wrapping her arms around herself.

"If it should happen, you need to realize I *will* get a warrant, that I couldn't just ignore some lead."

"I said I wanted answers—the truth. Finding something like that about him would make me wish I'd left well enough alone, but I want to know. No, I wouldn't fight you on it. Do you want me to sign something?"

"I just wanted us to be clear on that. It makes me a bit of a risk for you."

Their gazes snagged and held until she looked away.

"And just a few days ago," she said with a sigh,

"I thought my biggest risk was that I hated fishing, and Keith and our guests here would somehow find out."

He smiled grimly. "So you kept some things from him, too, like he didn't tell you about asking Noah Markwood to sell your paintings. Come on, let's go through these books, inside and out."

He stepped close to her to slide the cartons from the closet, the ones he'd noted marked X-tra Linens and Books the night Keith had disappeared.

"I packed these boxes myself in Seattle," she told him as she pulled open the tucked-in tops of the book box. "But, like you said, to be thorough..."

He watched her lift out two cookbooks, then, still staring in the box, gasp. She looked as if she'd seen a snake coiled there, and he bumped her shoulder as he stared down with her. The next two books were hardcovers that looked quite new. One was titled *Easing Depression Easily* and the other *Don't Let Life Get You Down.*

Claire felt sick to her stomach. "Nick, I packed this box, and these weren't in it. I've never seen them before. But Keith never read anything like this, I don't care how it looks!"

He picked up *Don't Let Life Get You Down*, looked inside both flyleafs, took the dust cover off to examine it, then riffled the pages. "I'm looking for a name of the owner or store receipt," he explained, so she searched the other book the same way.

"Nothing to identify owner or place obtained," Nick noted.

"It's not mine! And it wasn't his!"

She couldn't help her panic. She slammed the book back in the box and pressed both hands over her eyes. Exhausted, frustrated and frightened, she felt herself sway on her feet.

Nick's arm came around her like a solid band across her back, his hand clasping her waist. He led her to the chair and sat her down while he perched on the desk, leaning over her. She tried not to, but she began to cry, this time silently and unashamedly.

"Claire, once again there's a logical explanation, even though it's not the one you want to accept. These books look like they're not about stress, but depression. Keith was evidently aware he'd taken that next step into darkness, even if you weren't. But none of this is about accusing you of anything."

"Oh, really?" she said, her voice sharp and sarcastic. "I lived with him and didn't know him in the slightest. At best, that's the way it's starting to look, and you know it."

Grabbing a tissue from her jeans pocket, she wiped her eyes and blew her nose. She had to prove to Nick and herself that she had not been out of it, that she had not misunderstood or ignored Keith's problems. She had thought things could not get worse since he died, but she felt as if she were bucking her way up a roaring river and getting slammed back down by the fierce undercurrent of something she couldn't even fathom.

"He was not depressed, Nick, certainly not clinically depressed," she blurted out as he continued to study her. "That last day, he seemed consumed only by work. He talked to his old boss, Ethan Nance, in Seattle in a completely normal way. I heard him laugh once when he accidentally burped."

"You overheard their entire conversation?"

"No, just the beginning, but I could tell by the tone of his voice—serious, maybe at times, intense, but not depressed. People who are clinically depressed become lethargic and withdrawn," she argued. "They don't keep busy like Keith did."

She almost insisted that someone besides Keith could have put the books there, but she'd told Nick she'd packed the box and it hadn't been touched. Both Nick and his deputy probably believed she had merely left her art shed unlocked. She could claim that whoever had Keith's keys had broken into the house and planted the books, and had also broken into her little studio, but she didn't want to sound paranoid.

"We agreed," she told Nick, twisting the damp tissue, "that if we found proof one way or the other about him, I'd back off. But I'd like to check those incident reports and talk to Noah Markwood as well as look through the house and computer more, maybe talk to the Nances in Seattle."

"That's fine," Nick said, reaching out to steady her shaking shoulder with one big hand. "Give me your keys, and I'll go look around your studio, then we'll check to be certain no one's in the house. When I go, you can barricade yourself in like you said you did the other night. Then you'll promise to get some sleep and not take this up again until tomorrow—and you'll phone me on my cell phone if you find anything else. You didn't call me earlier at home, then decide to just hang up, did you?"

"What? No. Why—"

"Nothing. It just goes with my territory."

Her heart soared with the knowledge that he was

still going to help her. In silent gratitude, she gripped the wrist of his hand on her shoulder. He briefly squeezed her shoulder, then, as if she'd burned him, pulled away and moved quickly toward the door of the office. She heard him start downstairs ahead of her, and hurried to catch up.

It was time to act instead of just watch and photograph events. Whatever were they doing in the lodge this time, especially upstairs again? It didn't take much imagination to figure what could be going on. Now *those* would be some photos! Ah, the sheriff was coming down the stairs into view, but that didn't mean nothing had happened.

One of them must not only be warned but stopped, dispatched with, and Claire was obviously the most guilty one. The message to her must be unmistakably clear and memorable. Yes, it would be much easier and safer to deal with Claire Malvern than with the sheriff, even though he needed a cold bath in the river, too.

"Mrs. Malvern, whatever are you doing here so early on a Monday morning?" DeeDee Duncan greeted Claire when she entered the sheriff's office. The girl was in a bright yellow plaid suit with dangling pink-and-green pop-art earrings. It was unusual clear-sky weather, so perhaps, Claire thought, DeeDee had just dressed to suit the day, however out of place she seemed.

"Early?" Claire countered. "I've been up since dawn and have already had all my locks changed this morning."

"Oh, yeah, you said you would. Here, have one

of these doughnuts, and I'll get you some coffee. The sheriff's gone out to talk to a Chamber of Commerce breakfast meeting, but you can wait for him here with me. I'd love the company 'cause Mondays are usually slow, and I'd be grateful if you ate one of these doughnuts so I don't inhale them all.''

''You need that kind of help with Aaron and the other guys in and out of here all day?'' Claire said, forcing a little laugh. But the coffee did smell good. She let DeeDee sit her down by her dispatcher's desk, which looked like a secretary's cubicle, strewn with two big, stacked in/out boxes and piles of folders.

''By the way,'' DeeDee said, ''everybody really appreciated that food the other day.''

''You actually have the church ladies, especially Tess Markwood, to thank. Which reminds me—do you know what time Noah Markwood opens his shops on the square?''

''Ten o'clock prompt. He's very set in his ways.''

DeeDee handed Claire a foam cup of coffee and a glazed doughnut on a napkin, while she took another one for herself. ''And it's ten till ten right now,'' DeeDee continued. ''You shopping for scrimshaw or Puget Treasures? He's got some pretty but pricey stuff in there.'' She sighed so hard she could have deflated herself.

''Too bad the Markwoods, the town and farm branches, don't get along,'' DeeDee continued, lowering her voice, though no one else appeared to be in the office. ''Man, I hate it when family members don't get along.''

''Do you have a big family?'' Claire asked as she bit into her sticky doughnut.

"Dad dead, Mother remarried in Seattle and works at the Boeing plant," DeeDee recited with her mouth half-full. "Then I've got three older sisters, all married, who escaped this podunk place. Real pretty sisters, too," she added almost defensively. "One was a model for a while and even did Nordstrom TV ads. I live alone in an apartment just outside town, north of the airport."

There seemed to be so much said in that rush of words that sketched this girl's life. If her own life wasn't in such chaos right now, Claire thought, she'd love to take DeeDee under her wing, encourage her and give her a few hints about losing weight and dressing to suit her body. It appeared that the remarried mother and three pretty, married sisters had not bothered to bring DeeDee into their realm of looks or love.

And, Claire realized, DeeDee was probably a good source of information about anything or anyone in town. "I knew the sheriff wouldn't be in this morning," she told the girl, "but he said you could show me how to search through incident reports for the past year, ones dating from last autumn, since I've lived here in Portfalls."

"IRs? Sure. They're on file in back, not online. Most of them are scribbled and never retyped or anything, though, and you should see the way the deputies write! But I'm used to deciphering them. Anything to help. You don't mean IRs on yourself?"

"Actually, I want to know if there are any on my husband."

"Oh. Well, okay, we can do that. All we need is his complete name and date of birth. Here, fill this out when you get a chance."

"Great," Claire said, wiping her hands on her napkin before she took a ballpoint pen from her purse and began to fill in the simple form. "But I think I'll just pop next door to see if Noah Markwood's in before he gets any customers, and then be back to go through your files. And, DeeDee, thanks so much for your help."

Claire was bending to get her purse off the floor when she heard the door to the street open. Nick already? Her insides cartwheeled at the thought of seeing him again.

"Saint Nick back yet, DeeDee?" a man's voice asked.

As she sat back up, Claire saw Aaron Curtis had come in. "Oops," he said as he grinned at her, and DeeDee giggled.

"Saint Nick?" Claire said.

"He's a good guy, a straight arrow, that's where that nickname came from," Aaron explained hastily, looking like a kid caught at something.

"And he's generous," DeeDee added, pointing to a trailing ivy plant on her desk. "He brings little gifts, like that plant there." Claire saw it had a faded card on a plastic prong stuck in it, that said, in Nick's bold scrawl, *To the world's best SO sec./dispatcher.*

Claire had to smile. She realized she missed inside office jokes and the camaraderie she'd once enjoyed with her fellow workers—and once with Keith. When had that familiarity and solidarity, that intimacy, ended for the two of them? She was suddenly sure it had died before he did.

Claire entered Noah Markwood's realm through the door of the more distant The Scrimshaw Shop, mostly because she was interested in one particular Native American bone carving in the window. It reminded her of what Sam Twoclaws had used in his strange ritual on her back deck when he'd said he was trying to find Keith's spirit.

She was disappointed to hear men's voices coming from the rear room of the shop, which meant Noah already had a customer. While she waited, Claire scanned the glassed-in cases displaying beautiful if sometimes primitive sailors' carvings. In their spare time aboard whaling vessels, they'd carved nautical designs on everything from ivory-topped boxes to tusks and whale jawbones. But it was the men's rising, strident voices in the back room that really snagged her attention.

"If you think I'm independently wealthy, you're crazy."

"You wouldn't give a tinker's damn, would you, if our entire family heritage went under?"

"Of course I care, but I've invested heavily in this new Markwood heritage—these shops, and the art and culture which they preserve and share, not only at this location but through the Internet to reach the entire w—"

"Art and culture? Our grandfather and father busted their butts just trying to provide food—cranberries from the bogs, Noah. You know, sustenance, man's daily bread for his family? They'd roll over in their graves to hear you preaching art and culture. I'm telling you, if I don't get a loan, I'm gonna have to start taking all kinds of risks, more'n I already have."

"Such as? I am surely not going to risk my—"

Claire ducked out the front door. She didn't want

the Markwood brothers to know she'd heard them. Just like poor DeeDee had said, she too couldn't bear it when family members didn't get along.

Claire stared through the window of The Scrimshaw Shop, barely seeing the shaman's soul-catcher this time. In the precious northwest coast sunlight, the glass threw her reflection at her as if it were a polished mirror. She studied the image of her own face, but her expression and her eyes seemed whited out, empty in the glare. Her mother's gaze had looked like that as she sank deeper into her world of unreality, Claire recalled.

How had they missed that her mother was so ill? When her mother wanted to be left alone, had they deserted her when they should have stuck tight? And had Claire herself not been living in the real world with Keith? She must have missed something, must have tuned him out not to know there was something dire and dreadful going on in his life. When had she last looked deep, deep into Keith's eyes to read his feeling and thoughts the way she had Nick Braden's on the yacht, when they shared their fears?

Keith had taken the next step into darkness, Nick had said. From stress to depression to…

Had she known Keith—or thought she had—so long that everything just became routine, and she didn't even really see him anymore? Maybe she missed subtle signs he was depressed. The lodge had been his dream, and although she had tried hard to make it hers, perhaps she became too self-centered, too withdrawn from him. Did Keith have debts like Joel Markwood, or was he trying to protect himself like Noah? But from what, from whom?

Joel came storming out the front door, past Claire,

though she was sure he saw her and almost said something. He crossed the sidewalk to his truck parked several spaces down, yanked the door open, threw himself in, then slammed it shut. He took off with a squeal of tires. So that she didn't stare after him, Claire went back into the shop, affecting a calm she didn't feel.

"Good morning? Anyone in?" she called.

Patting perspiration from his bald, flushed head with a white handkerchief, Noah shouldered aside the back curtain. "Mrs. Malvern, this is a surprise— or did Sheriff Braden tell you about the paintings?"

"Yes, he did. And frankly, since you were at the bachelor auction yesterday, I wanted to explain to you that there was nothing personal in my bidding for Nick Braden. I just needed some advice from him—professional but *ex officio,* so to speak—and knew it was a good cause."

"So Nick said when he phoned this morning," he said as he walked toward her. "He owes me big time, not for my silence about who bought him, but because I went as a favor to him and got paired with a—well, a barracuda, or should I say a shark."

At least Noah managed a thin smile. She sensed he was glad to change the subject from what he'd just been through with his brother.

"I must tell you," he said, folding and pocketing the handkerchief, "I'd like to keep your paintings to display for a few weeks and, if they sell, perhaps take more on consignment."

"Really? And not because you enjoy helping out charitable causes?"

"Not at all. I'll draw up an informal contract, if that's all right with you, and we can negotiate prices and confer on possible matting and framing. I'm sure with your design and decorator background, you have definite opinions.''

''That's great, but Mr. Markwood—''

''Noah, please.''

''Noah, how did Keith seem to you when he brought the paintings in? I mean, did he seem at all upset or on edge? I realize you didn't really know him to compare, but...''

''He seemed intent and determined,'' he said, propping one fist on his cocked hip as he leaned against the longest glass showcase. ''Very set on the idea of my taking the paintings, which, I must admit, made me balk a bit—at his persistence, his urgency, not at the work. But with the regional interest in the falls and that infamous bridge...''

His voice trailed off and he looked embarrassed.

''I don't want people to think I'm cashing in on that,'' Claire said.

''No, me neither,'' he agreed.

''But I am pleased you like them, Noah, since I usually paint only to please myself. If they please anyone else, that will be at least something good to come from such a tragic place.''

''I'd be delighted to handle them, and I must tell you that nearly ninety percent of my clientele are out-of-towners anyway, and many aren't even from the northwest, so their interest in your rendition of the bridge will be for its evocative beauty, not any lurid sensationalism.''

As he talked, he fiddled with rearranging a pair of foot-high Chinese temple foo dogs in the case. It took a moment for Claire to register what they were.

''Those surely weren't carved by sailors, were

they?'' she asked. ''They look Chinese. You see, Keith used to work for Chin Pacific, a company that imports things like that.''

''Is that right? He didn't mention that, but we were over in the art store when we spoke, and I don't suppose he even knew that I dealt with antique ivory or bone Asian objets d'arte. These are just good re-pros, but I've a stunning antique ivory Tang Dynasty horse in the safe. Well, you hardly came to buy.''

''I do have a question about the Native American soul-catcher in the window,'' she said. ''Did Sam Twoclaws carve it, by any chance?''

''Sam does bone carvings for me upon occasion, but he'd never sell something like that,'' Noah explained, walking over and reaching into the sun-struck window to pick up the piece. ''Soul-catchers are strictly for shamans, and old Sam takes all that very seriously. He's Coastal Salish, you know, and his family owned, so to speak, the right to be sha-mans and to possess hereditary fishing and burial sites in this area.''

''I heard. He failed to get some of them back in the state courts a few years ago.''

''Fascinating, their beliefs,'' Noah went on, star-ing at the carved piece of bone he held in his hands. It was yellowed and cracked but beautifully carved with faces that looked part demonic, part animalistic.

''They believed the souls of hunters and fishermen could be reincarnated,'' Noah explained, ''that the boundaries between animals, humans and spirits could be crossed, especially by shamans. I imagine it's why Sam is a taxidermist. The Salish believed spirits resided in the bones, you see, the longest last-ing part of men and animals, so in preserving animal bodies, he thinks he's still in tune with their spirits or some such.''

Claire shivered. Sam might actually have believed he could recall Keith's spirit, resurrect it somehow. Suddenly, she needed to be back out in the sunlight instead of staring at things that spoke of the past and people long dead.

She moved away and put her hand on the door-knob.

''If it's all right with you,'' Noah said, looking up, startled, as if he'd emerged from some reverie, ''I'll put what I have of your work on display. I really think you've got a fine fix on the scenes you've done. They show subdued emotion tinged with a certain longing for the falls and river.''

''A longing?'' she whispered. ''Thanks. Just call me.''

She jerked open the door to his shop and rushed out as if she'd just escaped the darkness of Sam's spirit world.

Claire kept so busy searching the lodge that time and daylight slipped away. Nick phoned just after nine. She hadn't heard from him all day, and he sounded hurried and matter-of-fact.

''I'm on my way to the airport to fly to Cedar Island,'' he told her.

''Why not take the ferry instead of hiring a plane? Fog's set in here.''

''You mean you weren't listening intently to my Bachelor Bid-Off bio?'' he said, his voice almost teasing. ''I fly my own. A four-seat pontoon plane. The sky's clear here, so fog's probably only coming off the river.''

"Oh. You're flying in the dark?"

"I can fly by instruments, if need be. I've got an early-morning meeting there, so I'll be staying at a friend's house. It's a great night, only a fifteen-minute flight, and so clear you can count the stars." His voice caught. "It's great, soaring alone."

He sounded wistful, almost sad. "I'm sure it will be beautiful," she told him, her voice soft. "My dad used to take me flying when I was little, but I haven't been up for a long time."

"Claire," he went on, his voice all business again, "DeeDee says you two couldn't turn up any incident reports on Keith."

"Not a one, but she was a great help."

"That's DeeDee."

"When I get through all this, I'd like to be her friend, not that I'm not already. But I think she needs a more mature gal pal who can be a sounding board, give her some ideas."

"She'd like that, but she might just glom on to you. Her snooty sisters have written her off because she's not a size—whatever a slender size is. They think she's not willing to shape up so they can admit they know her. But she can drive you nuts trying to baby you at times.

"Listen, Claire," he said, "I'm trying one more thing I thought of when those depression books showed up. Toxicity reports from autopsies always take a little extra time, and in cases of a suicide ruling, sometimes they just get filed—so I've got a call in to the coroner to find out if Keith could have had any antidepressants in his body."

"I never saw him take anything, and never saw any bills or insurance claims for medicine like that.

Since we were no longer under our business medical coverage but took insurance out on our own, I would have noticed.''

"Yeah, but since you didn't know about the self-help books, maybe you didn't know about pills or a doctor we could trace from a prescription somewhere.''

"True. I appreciate that and anything else you can think of.''

"Gotta go. I'll be back tomorrow afternoon and call you when I shake this toxicity info loose.''

"Thanks. I'm still searching the house, though I'm scared what I might find.''

Scared what I might find. Those last words to him still echoed in her head when, a few minutes later, Claire clicked on the deck lights and saw the dreadful, dead thing staring in at her through the glass and fog.

10

As Claire glimpsed the horrid thing staring in her window, another scene flashed through her brain. Her mother dead in bed, staring, just staring. Blood, too much blood and white flesh against the sheet.

She blinked and shook her head to make it go away, but this scene remained. Because a pall of fog had crept up from the river, at first Claire wasn't even certain what it was. A skinned, bloody body— but animal or human? It hunched toward her, facing the windows as if trying to peer through them. Bones from some sort of creature stood around the base of it. In the shape of big X's. And the dreadful, staring eyes...

She didn't scream, but stared back, frozen in fascination and horror.

Then she scrambled for the inside lights, snapping them off one by one. She wanted that thing to stop staring at her.

Once in darkness, she fell to her knees behind the big leather couch, trembling so hard her teeth chattered. The damp, chill fog permeated the room, possessed her. Like a child, she peeked over the back of the couch at the terrible tableau.

It might be a skinned deer carcass, no ears, no hide, propped up by big bones—femur?—which were lashed together with something. And tied

around the neck of that thing was a piece of paper.
Some sort of note?

Cell phone in hand, Claire crawled closer to the
window, half expecting the thing to lunge at her,
even through the glass barrier. She squinted to make
out what the note said because the shadow from the
animal's muzzle fell on it:

DEER CLAIRE

That was what it said, just Deer Claire, in large
and clumsy printing. Beyond the arrangement of
body and bones, as far as she could see through the
fog, nothing on the fully lighted deck had been disturbed.

Was it vandalism by kids or drunken fishermen,
or the threat it seemed? Someone who knew her
name and wanted to scare or warn her—but of what?
Or someone with a perverted sense of humor...

She gasped as the full impact of the message hit
her. It was a subtle warning that something like
that—maiming, violation, death—could happen to
her too. It was proof Keith had been killed, perhaps
by whoever had left that horror at her back door,
wasn't it? Could the big bone X's allude to the sym-
bol for poison, or mean she could be crossed out, or
were they bizarre symbols of kisses to bolster the
mocking Deer Claire? Or were they simply the way
someone had hastily tied the big bones together to
support the carcass?

She punched in Nick's cell phone number before
she remembered he'd gone to Cedar Island. But what
if she could catch him first? Better him than a 911
call. She didn't want everyone to know. Nick needed

to see this proof that someone was out there with the intent to horrify and perhaps harm her. Maybe, like Keith, she had an enemy who would stop at nothing.

Nick's cell phone rang again and again but no one answered.

"Damn!" she muttered, hunkering back down behind the couch.

"Nick Braden."

He sounded so far away. His voice was scratchy, strange.

"Oh, Nick, thank God you haven't gone yet. Someone put a skinned deer and some human-looking bones on my back deck with a note that just says Deer Claire—*D-E-E-R.*"

"What? I'm already in the air, and you're breaking up!"

Yes, she thought, she was breaking up. She was so scared.

She shouted louder. "Can you come back? Nick?"

"Did you say a body and bones? Where?"

It hit Claire that she might know who had done this. The deck was the spot where Sam Twoclaws had performed his shaman ritual. Sam would certainly have access to animal bodies and bones. And he wanted his ancestral lands, including hers, back at any cost. She wanted to trust him, but could she?

"Animal body and bones here!" she shouted into the phone.

"Sit tight. I'll be back."

It seemed an eternity before Claire heard footsteps on the deck and peeked over the top of the couch to see Nick emerge from the fog with a big flashlight he played over the macabre scene, despite the fact she'd left the deck lights on. He was dressed in dark jeans and jacket and wore a baseball cap. For the first time since she'd seen the mess out there, she stood, then went to the back door.

"Open it carefully and slowly, but don't come out," he warned when he saw her.

She did as he said. "The note's facing the glass," she told him, pointing. He craned his neck to peer at it, focusing his bright beam on it, but touching nothing.

"Anything else weird happen since you spotted this?" he asked.

"No, but it's enough for one night. I'm thinking Sam Twoclaws had access to all of that."

"Yeah, me, too. And he's just a stone's throw away. Guess I'll have to go talk to him, but I want to photograph this first. And since I'm sure it's all animal remains, I can't see calling in forensics."

"It is a deer, isn't it?"

"A doe. The eyes look like glass, and that's definitely something a taxidermist would have. Stay put in there, okay?"

"Absolutely," she told him through the six-inch crack in the sliding door. "I may never come out again. Nick, it's a threat, a potentially lethal message. Well, don't you agree?" she challenged when he looked at her, frowning.

His flashlight beam lit his features from beneath his chin, making his face look like a carved mask with its rugged ridges contoured.

"I'm thinking," he said, "unless I can establish

this is kids' vandalism, that your theory about Keith's death just got a little stronger.''

"I was hoping you'd say that.''

"I'll bet you were.''

Nick's boots crunched through gravel as he approached Sam Twoclaws's sprawling house. Five wood rooms were built haphazardly onto an original stone cabin, one room leading to the next. The front two rooms nearest the driveway served as the taxidermy shop, and Sam worked and lived in the back four, which were closest to the river. Through the scrim of fog, Nick could see the back lights were on, but none near the front.

He had several reasons for not going in with a search warrant. It took a long time to get one, especially in rural Portfalls and in the middle of the night. Also, the carcass on Claire's deck could so obviously be linked to Sam, and the old man was sly, not stupid. Nick knew that local kids had occasionally stolen things from Sam, especially around Halloween time. However far away that holiday was on the calendar, Nick was getting real reminiscent about it right now, because the place was pretty creepy.

The gravel walkway to the house passed between two towering black bears on their hind legs, ever ready to lunge. They'd been stuffed and stuck here so many years ago their coats were mottled and mildewed. Other bizarre resurrected animals sat around the yard, not to mention the drying racks of salmon, which looked and smelled like flayed flesh. It usually took a stranger who didn't know any better, a local kid on a dare or a cop in the line of duty to call on Sam Twoclaws in the dead of night.

As if Sam had heard or seen him coming, his front

door, the one to the shop, opened. Darkness inside, no light and a mere silhouette in the doorway. Instinctively, Nick's hand went to his gun.

"That the police?" Sam called out.

Nick stepped behind the bigger of the two bears. Could that old Salish shaman see in the dark or what?

"It's Nick Braden, Sam. Sorry to bother you this late, but I need to talk to you."

"Figured you would, when I saw the stuff was gone," he called out. "I'll hit the lights. Come on in."

His hand still resting on his holstered gun, Nick followed his long-honed instincts to trust Sam. He could see Sam was in a tattered robe, not a bathrobe but a striped blanket type, with both hands visible as he pulled a cord for his ceiling light. Stark brightness bathed the outer room with its mounted heads of stags staring down from the walls.

"What's missing?" Nick asked him as he went in.

"A deer carcass, roadkill from this morning. Been looking for one without a bullet or knife tear in the fur to mount for a museum in Tacoma. Had just put the glass eyes in, and them things cost a bundle."

Now Nick knew Sam hadn't arranged that sick surprise for Claire. He took out his notebook and started to fill out a theft report. "Anything else gone, Sam?"

"Bear leg bones, at least eight. So where'd they end up this time? Not at the high school principal's house again?"

"On Claire Malvern's back deck," Nick said, looking up to see what Sam's reaction would be.

Sam did not so much as change expression. The old man merely nodded, which made Nick wonder if he could at least have had some knowledge of it, some part in it. He never could figure out what Sam was thinking, what he knew or didn't know.

"That doesn't surprise you?" Nick went on. "Sam?" he prodded after at least thirty more seconds of silence.

"Have you heard that speech Chief Seattle made when the whites wanted to take the last of the Indian lands in this state?"

"Yeah, I remember it from high school, local history," Nick acknowledged, though he didn't remember the specifics. Still, he'd learned Sam never said anything without a purpose, even if it was hard to decipher.

"He said that every part of the soil was sacred to the Native people. Even when the last red man will perish, and the memory of the tribes will become myth among the white men, the sacred shores will swarm with the invisible dead of the people and the animals. That is what he said, and what I say, too."

"Sam, do you know who took those things from your property or not?" Nick demanded when silence stretched between them again.

"I was not here. Before the fog, I was walking through the new night downriver. All this land to the falls was Salish once," he said, gesturing slowly, stiffly. "From where this place of mine stands to past the fishing lodge and the falls was my clan's ground, sacred for fishing and the shamans. So if animal spirits warn the whites away, if a dead deer moves and speaks a silent message—"

"Look," Nick interrupted, "there was a note

around the deer's neck which read Deer Claire, printed in English. *D-E-E-R*. Did the deer or the guardian spirits write that?''

Sam's eyes narrowed, as if he was deciding whether that was an insult or logic. He shrugged.

''I'd like to look at the place the carcass and bear bones were taken from,'' Nick said. ''And if you're still communing with the spirits—and I don't doubt you do, Sam—you just tell them to protect the woman who lives on their land and find out who could have possibly pushed her husband in the river at night.''

''I never did think he killed himself.''

''Really? Why's that?''

''He was still possessive of things, still interested in people—in men and women.''

''Women? You mean his wife.''

''I'll show you where the things were stored,'' Sam said with a decisive nod.

He started away so fast, Nick had to sprint to keep up with him.

Unfortunately, the screened porch area, between the house and river, where the bleached bear bones had been stacked and the newly skinned deer carcass left overnight, had a gravel floor. No footprints, no indentations, nothing unusual on the ground, though it did look as if the carcass had been dragged away in or on something and not carried. That theory was also supported by the lack of blood or flesh in the gravel. And Sam remembered that some twine had been taken, too. Nick figured it was the same twine that bound the bones.

''Tell you what,'' Nick said, more than ready to

leave. "You stay off Claire's property until we get this all settled."

Sam's nostrils flared and his eyes glistened like polished obsidian in the reflected beam of Nick's flashlight. He would have sworn Sam said, *It's not hers,* except he saw the old man's mouth did not move, and he didn't think Sam's shaman tricks included ventriloquism. He nodded again, but shrugged at the same time.

"You let me know if you figure out who took the things," Nick said as he turned away, "and I'll be back to talk more soon."

Any other investigation Nick intended went right out the window when another suicide jumped from the bridge the next morning, almost exactly a week after Keith.

"A woman from Portland, who evidently drove all the way here for that purpose, no less," Nick told the appalled Claire when he knocked on her door around noon to ask if the SAR team could use her driveway for their mobile command center again. And to suggest that she leave the lodge for a few days.

"I'll go to Seattle," she told him. "Thanks for the warning. I couldn't bear to be here with the team and dog up and down the river again. I've been wanting to talk to Ethan Nance about how he read Keith's mood, and that's better done in person. To tell the truth, I'm still real shaky about being in the house alone after that warped display on my deck you and Aaron cleared away. And I know this sounds crazy, but I'd swear that at night, the falls start sounding louder and louder, closer and closer."

"The time away will do you good," Nick said, taking both her hands in his, telling himself it was just a double handshake for good luck and goodbye. "Maybe it will help you decide what you want to do."

She nodded. "You may not believe this, but that dead deer, the bones, especially the note, only make me more determined to stay and find answers. But having to face a repeat of the day after Keith disappeared...for now I'm out of here."

When she stepped back, she looked surprised they held hands. He let go.

"A couple of other things," he said, crossing his arms over his chest quickly. "One, there were no fingerprints on the note, so it may have been handled with gloves. Two, in the toxicology report, Keith's blood tested negative for a range of substances, including antidepressants. Nor, evidently, was he taking medicine for those ulcers which surely must have bothered him, especially after the tomato sauce and spices you two had that last night on the pizza."

"I knew he wasn't on something like antidepressants, that he wasn't depressed."

"I don't have to tell you that ulcers indicate excess gastric juices, which could mean at least tension—"

"Tension is normal in life. I have it, you do—I mean, even when we haven't just been through all of this."

"Right. True." Hell, she was starting to make sense to him, starting to convince him. He had to keep his guard up against falling for everything she said, as well as falling for her.

"I'm telling you, Nick," she said, her voice passionate again, ''Keith didn't go off that bridge—or maybe even onto it—of his own accord, despite the fact he obviously did get out of bed and go outside himself.''

''I've got to get going, so just listen to me, please. Even though you're changing your environment for a few days, keep an eye out for anything strange. Just be aware of what's around you, okay? I don't even know how to go about figuring who arranged that stuff on your deck, except to talk to a few kids who've stolen gross things from Sam's before. And now, with this new jumper, I'm going to be really busy.''

''I understand. Just one more thing. I heard after someone dies on the bridge, especially if there's a lot of publicity like when Keith died—I mean, I know outsiders believe he committed suicide—there can be copycats. If the family of the dead woman's here, please tell them I'm sorry.''

''Whoa, don't start blaming Keith or yourself for what some Portland woman did. Besides, I heard she had a terminal disease and left a note, so it's a completely different thing.''

''I'm just sympathizing,'' she explained with a huge sigh, ''but maybe I'll find some of my own answers in Seattle.''

''Call if you need me,'' he added, as he backed away and opened his car door. He wished he hadn't put it quite like that. He was pretty sure they needed each other, just in different ways.

For Nick, it was a nightmare too frequently revisited. Dog tired again, dealing with distraught relatives of a suicide and with the media, and overseeing a SAR that stretched half a mile up the Bloodroot River were the last things he needed. As on the day they found Keith Malvern's body, reporters hung around, and Sam Twoclaws had materialized out of the trees to watch, standing just barely off Claire's property boundary. At least Nick's team and the dog people knew the drill by now.

"Why'd this one jump, chief?" Aaron Curtis asked Nick when he joined them to search over-hanging brush and protruding rocks on the riverbank. The two of them slogged through a shallow pool of foaming water, checking snags made by fallen limbs. Though they had a job to do, they tried not to disturb the salmon that temporarily rested here, fighting the current just to hold their places before lunging far-ther upstream.

"I hear she left her family a note," Aaron added when Nick didn't answer at first.

"I was first told it was terminal cancer," Nick said, for once refusing to wallow in guilt over Su-san's death, "but it turns out she was healthy—phys-ically at least."

"Screwed up mentally?"

"What her brother described to me sounds sort of like that Munchausen-by-Proxy disease, you know, where mothers crave attention, so they intentionally make their kids sick?"

"Oh yeah, I heard of that. So this jumper left be-hind a sick kid?"

"No. In her case, she kept doing things to draw attention to herself, big dramatic things, claiming someone was stalking her, insisting there were plots on her life, even concocting evidence to make it look like that could be the case."

"Isn't that paranoia or bipolar disorder?"

"They had her examined, and the psychiatrist said she was not psychotic, just desperately wanted attention from her family and friends, the police, too."

"You're kidding. Well, she got what she wanted, didn't she, only she's not around to enjoy it."

Nick shuddered and not from the chill of the water that occasionally sloshed down his thigh-high boots. He didn't want to think it, but each instance where Claire needed help—needed him—could have been set up. Not Keith's death, of course, surely not, but her insistence that someone had killed him. And showing up at the auction to buy his time. She could have just forgotten to lock her art studio, although he believed that she hadn't known Markwood had her paintings. She could have phoned his private number to shake him up on Sunday, then, when he was leaving town, rigged that mess on her back deck. Hell, she lived close to Sam and knew the territory, knew what Sam was like, and could have tried to set him up.

Nick shook his head and silently cursed himself. He wished like hell he hadn't seen so many bad things and screwed-up people over the years. For a cop, mistrust soon became like breathing, especially when he'd seen the same lack of trust in his own marriage. But even theorizing about Claire made him sick to his stomach. Leaning against a slick boulder, he hunched over his knees.

"You okay, chief?" Aaron asked. "You look kinda green at the gills."

"I'm okay. All this just gets to me sometimes."

"Maybe you're working too hard again, taking on too much."

"I hear you."

The tone of those last three words shut Aaron up. Nick almost regretted he'd come down so hard on him when he'd gotten emotionally involved with that witness a few months ago.

"I better get back to work, or you're going to be filling out an incident report on *me*," Nick kidded him.

"That reminds me," Aaron said as they shuffled ashore through shifting water, "I saw Mrs. Malvern at the office yesterday. She told me she was there to look at incident reports on her husband, and I didn't think a thing of it."

"Why should you?" Nick replied, trying not to sound annoyed or defensive. "She's got every right to them."

"Well, yeah, but I didn't remember until later that I'd filled out one on him for speeding, and I should have told her. It was strictly a code nine. He was kind of new in town then, trying to fix up the lodge and all, so I only gave him a warning. But I did write it up."

"On Keith Malvern? You sure?"

"Absolutely. It was late at night, and he was with Anne Cunningham."

"Anne? Yeah, she was their Realtor," Nick said, thinking aloud. "Where'd you stop them?"

"On River Road, heading east toward the falls, not far from the lodge. They were in her vehicle, but he was driving. Weird, huh?"

"What's weirder still, my man," Nick said, wearily clapping him on the shoulder, "is that you obviously forgot to file it."

"I filed it! I know I did, or at least put it in

DeeDee's folder so she could file it. It was like from last April or May, a real nice night with a full moon. As a matter of fact, I told DeeDee about it at the time.''

Nick frowned. DeeDee evidently didn't remember, and that wasn't like her. "Aaron," Nick said, "DeeDee did the search. But she evidently didn't recall talking to you and didn't find the IR.''

"Maybe it's misfiled.''

"Yeah, that's probably it," Nick conceded, but DeeDee had said she'd gone through the entire big batch of them. Yet Claire thought DeeDee was so helpful. River Road was known as a sort of lover's lane. Surely, the two of them hadn't found that IR, drawn some conclusions and concocted the no-can-find story. Could Claire have asked DeeDee to help cover up a possible romantic indiscretion of her dead husband? But if some romantic entanglement existed between Keith and Anne, it could be a factor in foul play, or at least in Keith's sneaking out at night. Claire had better not have kept that IR from him with the hopes of facing down Anne herself.

This opened up a whole new can of worms. Nick had heard rumors of Anne's fast-and-loose reputation in town, though she'd never come on to him. What if Claire had earlier discovered an affair between Keith and Anne and had been upset over it? In some cases, that was grounds for jealousy, rage— and murder.

No, hell, no way, he told himself. He refused to let that line of thought go any further. But what Aaron had told him needed looking into.

The cadaver dog's barks jolted Nick from his agonizing.

"Sheriff," one of the volunteers called from downriver, windmilling his arm, "we may have something here!"

Nick nodded and jogged toward them.

11

The next morning, Claire did not find herself facing Ethan Nance at the Nances' lakeside home or sitting across his desk at Chin Pacific Imports as she'd hoped, but driving to the Seattle Aquarium on the downtown waterfront.

It was raining hard enough that miniature waterfalls cascaded down her car windows. Though it was a Seattleite badge of pride to ignore rain, Claire finally acknowledged it by turning on her windshield wipers like the others in gridlock traffic around her. The wipers *whip-whip* whispers and the drops drumming on the car roof sounded disturbed, their voices urgent.

Claire had spent the night in an inexpensive chain hotel, because she couldn't bear answering the questions of friends with whom she could stay. It had been so strange to try to sleep with the sound of traffic from city streets; despite her exhaustion, it had been difficult even to nod off without the pervasive roar of the falls.

She found what appeared to be the last parking space in the aquarium lot. Perhaps that was a good omen, after the disappointment of learning from Ethan Nance's secretary that he'd be away for two days. She'd wanted desperately to see him. However, the secretary had set up a lunch date with Diana

Nance here at the aquarium, where she served as a docent once a week, helping in the gift shop.

Claire had nearly an hour before she was meeting Diana, so she bought a ticket and strolled through the exhibits. Principles of Survival was the first area. That was a good one, she thought, as she studied the lungfish and electric eels. Signs posted on the walls claimed these animals had developed particular coping mechanisms to adapt or protect themselves, and lately, she needed that too.

Claire realized she'd become newly suspicious and mistrustful. She'd become more aware of police- and private-detecting methods, more obsessed with every little thing that happened. As she moved on, she heard Nick's voice again, his face so intent as he told her to be careful in Seattle.

She glanced around warily but saw only mothers with kids in strollers and several classes of elementary students with their teachers being lectured to by museum staff. This was an educational and family haven, so surely she was safe here.

She marveled at the size of the giant Pacific octopus and watched seadragons and seahorses bobbing by in the Myth, Magic & Mystery exhibit. As mysterious as Sam Twoclaws could be, Nick did not believe he was the one who had put that dreadful display on her deck. Yet he'd admitted that Sam had said something about animal spirits on sacred lands, which included the lodge property. Still, Claire agreed with Nick about Sam. He had been a good friend to Keith, though she had to admit that if she hadn't really known her own husband, perhaps she should trust no one.

Claire spent the most time in the area called Salmon & People. It had a salmon ladder and a hatchery, but most fascinating was the glimpse it gave visitors into the salmon's instinctive drive to return to their spawning river to produce their own young.

Her mind drifted more quickly than the currents on the other side of the heavy glass barrier. How desperately she had once desired a child. She was only thirty-five now. Perhaps, when she learned what had happened to Keith and why, and once she decided whether to stay in Portfalls or return to Seattle, she could adopt.

Claire noted that a nervous-looking man with a map of the aquarium layout kept staring at her, so she went downstairs to the lower level to be certain he didn't follow her. No, he didn't come down the steps. She became entranced by the underwater tank with its sleek-furred sea otters, then moved to the dome where the wolf eels, rippling skates and sharks swam by, watching their watchers with lidless, gaping eyes.

"Claire, you came early," the woman's voice behind her said.

Claire jumped. It was Diana Nance, her long hair pulled up in a tight twist. She wore a pearl-gray leather skirt and jacket.

"Diana, I was so glad Ethan's secretary could reach you on short notice," Claire told her as they shared a quick, light hug and Diana bestowed an air kiss.

"I'm glad it's just us girls for once and you don't have that Mel Gibson sheriff in tow this time," Diana said, indicating they should go upstairs.

"I guess he does resemble good old 'Braveheart,' " Claire admitted. "He may not have the blue face paint, but he bleeds police blue. About the other day—he's been a big help, and I just wanted to support his favorite charity. His wife died young of cancer.''

"How dreadful! No wonder he was part of that crazy auction. Listen, I was just running an errand for the gift shop manager and saw the rain's let up. We can duck out of here for a while, maybe get a bite over by the market. Sometimes these heavy walls of water depress the hell out of me.''

"Lead the way,'' Claire said, and followed Diana to the gift shop to get her purse.

Walls of water depress the hell out of me. Damn, Claire thought. She needed Diana to buck her up, not discourage her. Despite the fact she'd had dreadful visions of Keith struggling for breath underwater, the aquarium had not depressed her. She'd thought of the huge windows of gray-green shifting water as an escape. But—was that how Keith had viewed the river and the falls?

"I know a shortcut,'' Diana said as they went outside. Like others around them, taking no umbrella, they ignored the continued sprinkles as they hurried toward Pike's Place Market. Claire startled at the boom of a ferry horn.

"You've been away too long in the peace and quiet of that place,'' Diana told her with a smile that moved only the edges of her mouth and left the rest of her face unfurrowed and flawless. "But I could use a little of that right now. Sometimes Ethan and I run ourselves ragged.''

"As I said before, you are both invited to the lodge at your earliest convenience—this weekend, if you want.''

"If you're sure," Diana said. "Since you wanted to talk to Ethan, perhaps we could drive up for one night."

"Great! Just let me know what day you're coming, after you talk to him."

"He drove up to spend a few days with my father, a working vacation, as Dad still heads the advisory board. His title is chairman of the board and chief executive officer instead of director now. Would you believe Dad's named his new retirement home in the Cascades Xanadu?" she asked, alluding to the Coleridge poem about the fantastical palace of the ancient Eastern emperor, Kubla Khan.

Yes, Claire thought, Howard Chin's wealth and power, even his Chinese heritage made that a perfect comparison. "It fits," she told Diana. "As for my humble fishing lodge, I'd love to show you both the area. There's a cranberry farm nearby, and it's nearly harvest time. They flood the fields and use big suction machines. Oh, and there's a scrimshaw shop on the square with Chinese dynastic reproductions and a real Tang horse for sale," she added, excited and grateful they would come to visit even after Keith's loss.

"I'll call," Diana promised. "Now how about some smoked salmon on Sicilian sourdough bread and fresh fruit for lunch? I'm starving, as I don't fix much when Ethan's gone."

"You should have gone with him. I'm sure it's beautiful in the Cascades."

"They don't need me around when they live and breathe ChinPak," she said with a rueful smile. "Besides, I have my commitments here, and, as I said, sometimes I crave the quiet."

As they climbed the stairs toward the market from the waterside, the smells and sounds of the familiar, bustling place embraced Claire. The frenzied banter of fishmongers rose above the buzz of shoppers and melodies of folk musicians. She could smell a blend of spices and was certain she scented Starbucks coffee from their original store.

"I've been laying off caffeine because it strings me out worse than usual lately, but I've got to have a latte today," Claire told her.

"After the wine," Diana threw back over her shoulder, then stopped right where she was in the press of people and gave Claire another, heartier hug. "Forgive me if I'm carrying on like everything's normal in your life, just because you're back here for a while," Diana told her. "I'm sure Keith's loss has been devastating."

"If I try to explain, I'll lose it right here."

With an understanding nod, Diana led the way through the throng toward a fish stall with hanging, hand-printed signs for smoked salmon, and they waited in a short line.

"You could come back here to live," Diana suggested. "I have a couple of friends who are building or moving, and I'd be only too happy to recommend you as their decorator, or recommend Kallile's, if you went back to work there.

"And," she said, becoming even more animated, "Dad has a neighbor—more or less a neighbor, given that the estates are so large there—who would love your work. Once I've seen what you've done with the lodge, I'll show this man some photos. You'd like him, too. He's newly divorced and—"

"Diana, you're not matchmaking already," Claire protested.

"Of course not," she insisted, raising a hand as if she were taking an oath. "It's just his ex had everything ultramodern. He's redecorating with a rustic flavor to frame his fabulous view of the mountains. It's rather, I suppose, the way you've framed your river."

Your river. Claire *did* think of it as her river, her home, despite the horrors of what had happened there. That was one thing she was discovering during this short stay in Seattle. She still thought she could hear the falls in her head sometimes, pulling her back, luring her to its strange peace in place of Seattle's noise.

"I haven't decided my future yet," Claire confided. "But I appreciate your offer and all the support you and Ethan have given me—given us, when there was an us..."

"Come on now," Diana coaxed as Claire's eyes teared up. "I know the perfect place we can eat and talk."

After they purchased food, Diana led Claire through a labyrinth of corridors and cubbyholes to a four-table restaurant on a tiny plaza where an awning kept the rain off. Diana bought a bottle of wine, though it cost more than Claire would have paid for a new dress. Diana knew the server; Claire saw her slip him ten dollars.

Halfway into their meal, hoping it would seem like an afterthought to Diana, Claire asked her what she'd originally come to find out. "Diana, did Ethan share any last impressions of that day Keith died—

you know, when Keith phoned him? I'm just storing up all the memories I can.''

The striking woman swirled the wine in her goblet, staring at it as if it would bestow some sort of tea-leaf answer. ''Though I shouldn't speak for Ethan,'' she said, ''I believe he said Keith sounded a bit manic.''

''Manic? In what way?''

''He hadn't been drinking, had he?''

''Just a couple of beers with our pizza. He was energetic, kind of flying high on getting our guest rooms done and really looking forward to opening the lodge. That's why a suicide doesn't make sense.''

''I'll let you talk to Ethan about their phone call and Keith's highs and lows.''

Claire was taken aback again. She felt as if she'd been slammed in her too-full stomach. ''Highs and lows?'' she echoed. She recalled the way her mother's psychiatrist had described her mood swings. After her father had remarried, Claire had come across a psychiatric report in her mother's things and kept it, though she hadn't read it for years.

''Claire,'' Diana said, interrupting her agonizing, ''you know, Keith was a very intense, ambitious person, a type A like Ethan, don't you think?''

Claire almost argued that a man who could walk away from a fast-track, well-paying job couldn't really be ambitious. But Keith had been absolutely determined to change his life, to get away, so he was ambitious in that sense. Claire decided not to argue, at least right now.

''It's strange how you sometimes don't really know the people you are most intimate with,'' she admitted, staring past Diana's shoulder at the parade of people. "I just hope you and Ethan can come this weekend. I know it will help me settle things in my head and heart to talk to Ethan, since he and Keith were so close."

"Did you mean earlier that you don't believe Keith killed himself?" Diana asked, pouring the two of them the last of the wine. "So you think it was some sort of...mishap?"

"A mishap? In the middle of the night on *that* bridge?" Claire cried. "When you come, I'll show it to you. He would never have gone out there of his own accord!"

At her outburst, people passing turned to look. One woman stopped in her tracks and stared before hurrying on.

"No," Diana said, her voice as controlled as her expression, "I—we couldn't bear to see that bridge, however magnetic it is for those who want to end it all." She stood and tucked her purse under her arm. "I didn't realize it had gotten so late, and I've got to head back. We'll be in touch soon. Claire, I'm—so sorry, so sorry," she whispered. She leaned forward to squeeze Claire's shoulder, then turned away to disappear into the market crowds.

Damn, Claire thought. After that sudden tirade, she'd probably never see either of the Nances again.

"DeeDee, I need to see you right now," Nick said as he approached her desk, heading into his office the next morning. His inner sanctum was in the middle of the building, with records storage, office supplies, two jail cells for temporary detainment, and a locked armory with equipment lockers at the back.

"Oh, sure," she said, looking pleased but also a bit wary. "If a call comes in, I can hear it from there. Are you feeling okay, Sheriff?"

"I'm fine," he told her brusquely. Another woman pretending to be concerned about him, he thought, when it was all too obvious that they were usually pursuing their own agendas. Susan had. And Claire? Had she been totally up-front with him?

DeeDee brought a pen and pad with her as if anticipating that he'd dictate a letter or give her some sort of important instructions. He tried to keep a lid on his seething temper. He was in a foul mood from the sad recovery of this latest suicide and its reminder of Keith Malvern's death. He was going to get that bridge torn down, come hell or high water.

"Close the door and sit down," Nick said, hanging his suit jacket on the back of his chair but still standing. He rolled up his shirt sleeves as he sat on the edge of his desk. Looking suddenly shy, DeeDee shuffled in, closed the door and sat. The chartreuse color of her skirt and blouse almost hurt his eyes, and he realized he was working on the start of a headache.

"I hear you helped Claire Malvern look through our IRs the other day—Monday, I think."

"Oh, right. It was on Monday, the morning you had the Chamber of Commerce breakfast. I feel sorry for her, and she's very nice. I didn't let my other work slide while she was here, honest, and—"

"That's not what I meant. It's fine that you helped her. But she said the two of you turned up nothing. Actually, that you did the entire search for her."

DeeDee's eyes opened a bit wider before they narrowed. "That's true. What's the matter?"

"The matter is that Aaron says he wrote Keith Malvern up for speeding and was certain the IR was filed by you. And that he'd mentioned it to you at the time. I know how careful you are with your office work, what a good memory you have, and I've never seen you make that kind of mistake before. DeeDee?" he prompted when she flushed and fidgeted under his steady gaze.

"Don't make me play good cop, bad cop with you," he plunged on, "because you've already seen good cop. Did she ask you not to divulge what was on the IR? Did you let her take it with her or destroy it for her?"

She looked surprised for a moment. "I don't want you to blame her," she blurted, clutching her notepad to her big breasts. "It's my fault, and she doesn't need more tragedy in her life."

"I'm sure she'd appreciate that, but just tell me what the hell happened."

"I did it."

"Did what?"

"Removed the IR Aaron wrote on Keith Malvern before she could see it, then told her none existed."

"Where is it?"

"I trashed it. Well, I figured some of them get lost anyway, and the man's dead."

Nick swore under his breath. He tried not to lose his temper. "Hell, it's precisely because he's dead that it's doubly important. I don't need my staff destroying evidence. It's tough enough when the criminals do it!"

Tears trembled on her lashes.

"Come on, DeeDee, you're a professional dispatcher and often my right hand around here, so I don't want tears, I want the truth, all of it.''

"After she filled out the form and told me what she was looking for, she went next door to see Noah Markwood. She was over there about a half hour, maybe a little longer.''

"And in that time, you went through the IRs from the entire time the Malverns have been in the area?''

"I filed them. I pretty much know what's there and where to find it, especially something that recent, and, yes, I remembered that Aaron mentioned it in passing. This place isn't exactly Sodom and Gomorrah with tons of big-deal IRs to file, you know.''

She was showing some mettle now. He much preferred that to the whipped puppy look.

"Go on," he ordered. "You lied to her that there was no IR because..."

"Because she would have figured out that her husband didn't love her!" DeeDee exploded. "Did Aaron tell you who he was found with and when? I'm sure it would be better for her to cherish his memory than to be turned against him, when—"

"We're focusing here on what *you* should do, or should not do, and that's tamper with police property and potential criminal case evidence," he shouted.

"What? It was just an IR on speeding.''

"The deduction you drew from the IR is that Anne Cunningham and Keith Malvern were having an affair, right?''

"Well—I guess they could have been. Mrs. Malvern might have thought that. I didn't tell her this, either, but I saw them coming out of the Bide-A-While Motel once.''

He raked his fingers through his hair and sat behind the desk. "So you made your deduction not only from the IR but from other corroborating evidence," he muttered.

"I guess you'd call it that. Then, too, there's Anne's reputation, but I guess that's hearsay."

"Tell me anyway."

"Well, I've heard she has a reputation, kind of a woman-about-town, to put it nicely. Has she—been flirting with you?" she asked, as if she'd call Anne on the carpet for it.

He couldn't believe it. DeeDee, whose red color had faded, blushed again as he glared at her. "Just answer my question," he ordered.

"I know she used to see Noah Markwood and several other men, a couple at the same time, I think. I actually saw her with Keith Malvern twice in town during the day and they looked pretty friendly, not counting when I saw them coming out of the hotel— but they weren't in the same car. Oh yeah, and one time I heard Noah Markwood tell her she was a whore for leading him on—Noah—and then stringing Keith along, and Noah sounded pretty mad at Keith and her."

Nick muttered another curse and raked his fingers through his hair again. His mind raced. He still couldn't quite believe that Keith had been murdered—surely he'd gone outside on his own that fateful, fatal night—but locals, including Anne and Noah, were possible suspects. And Claire?

Nick tried to sound calm and controlled. "And you didn't think," he said, "you should mention any of that to me, after the guy ended up dead? DeeDee, I rely on you around here, and I can't have this kind of thing going on among my people. I need to trust and believe every one of you. I'm going to suspend you without pay until further notice.''

She gulped air like a fish. ''I— Just for trying to help her? You're trying to help her, so I thought—''

''The point is, you *are* paid to think. And that little piece of paper you pulled and trashed and lied about could provide clues to a man's death—maybe lead to his killer or killers.''

''That's what you believe, after you signed off on the suicide ruling?'' she cried. ''You can't think that maybe Noah killed him, or that Mrs. Malvern found out about them and then she—''

''That's enough! You're not on staff to solve crimes or plead cases any more than you are to tamper with evidence.''

She'd begun to cry again, despite how angry she looked. He felt bad about this; he figured her job and the people here were a huge part of her life.

''For how long?'' she asked, hanging her head. ''Does indefinite leave mean I'm really fired?''

''Absolutely not. I would be twice as angry if you weren't so important and trusted around here. And as for how long, I'll let you know.''

''It's just like when you disciplined Aaron,'' she said, her face pouty but her voice petulant. ''You don't want your staff mixing in the personal lives of victims or witnesses, but all of us are human, all of us do that when we supposedly shouldn't!''

He heard the subtext she intended about him and Claire, but he refused to rise to that. He only prayed that if Keith and Anne were having an affair and if Claire knew, she hadn't used that gun he took from her pocket to force Keith out onto the bridge, shoved him in, then defiantly used the help of her friendly local sheriff to cover it all up.

For once, Nick didn't enjoy the flight to Cedar Island that afternoon, however beautiful the sea and sky. Still, he needed to spend some time on the island since he'd postponed the last trip, turning back instead to help Claire when that dead deer showed up on her porch.

All day he'd been striking out in anger, starting with having to reprimand and suspend DeeDee, then scrambling to get in a day replacement for her. He intended to recall DeeDee soon, but standards had to be upheld. He kept telling himself that it was absolutely nuts to get emotionally entangled with Claire right now, however much he wanted to, especially when he'd come down hard on Aaron and DeeDee for their personal involvements. But with this new lead about Anne and Keith—and Noah—he was absolutely right to continue trying to get to the bottom of all this, not for Claire, but for justice's sake.

But surely if Claire had known about Keith's apparent affair and decided to do something about it, she would never have insisted it be further investigated. He believed her, but he'd have to question her when she returned from Seattle.

He'd already tried to question Anne Cunningham, only to discover she was away at a Realtor's conference in Portland for two days. He seemed to be going nowhere fast—except to Cedar, an island so small and rugged it didn't even have a decent landing strip. If the winds were from the wrong direction, it wasn't worth trying to set down.

But the winds would favor setting down on the

sea today. He circled the small cove near the ferry pier once, then took the *Susan* in for a pontoon landing. He motored toward the dock through water that was choppy but nothing he couldn't handle.

Claire chose not to stay another night in Seattle. After her lunch with Diana, she'd heard on her car radio that a woman's body had been recovered from the Bloodroot River after her suicide from the Portfalls Bridge. Claire had almost thought she could hear the falls roaring in the background of the report, though the news reader was obviously in the studio, not on-site. She'd pictured the tons of crashing water, the spinning whiteout, and the fall of that poor woman. But the recovery of her body meant the SAR team would be gone and the lodge property would be her own again.

Arriving at the lodge just before dark, she was actually glad to be back as she went in and dropped her bag and purse in the kitchen. She didn't even change out of the loose-fitting, ankle-length skirt and jacket she'd worn all day. Although she had changed the locks, she made a circuit of the lodge, turning on lights, checking under beds, in closets. A gentle rain began to drum on the roof, a comforting sound not quite drowned by the falls. She gazed out at the river with the late salmon that struggled onward and upward, whatever the weather.

Suddenly, she wanted to go outside, to feel washed and cleaned by the rain. The rain on the cedars always scented the air. Seattle smells could be pungent and vital, but Portfalls aromas were more calming and uplifting. As she went out on the deck and turned her face to the gray heavens, she saw a single fisherman netting a salmon at the river's edge. Keith had always said fishing was good in the rain.

The fisherman had a full head of hair, but the set of the head—yes, it looked like Joel Markwood, with that toupee of his. She'd heard that when he'd first bought it to cover his balding head in his mid-thirties, he'd told a hundred hairpiece jokes. Despite getting even wetter, she went farther out onto the deck.

"Catching anything?" she called to him.

"Hey," he responded, looking surprised to see her. "Tess sent a casserole for you, but I knocked and you weren't home."

"I just got back from Seattle. You and Tess have been great through all this. I'm going to fix some coffee. Can I bring you a cup?"

"Thanks, anyway, but I've got my quota and need to be heading back. I shouldn't even have left, this close to harvest, but we can use the fish. I'll get that casserole from my car."

He left the river, and Claire waited for him on the deck. The rain was still gentle, though she was pretty much soaked now, and so was Joel.

"Here you go," he told her as he appeared around the back of the lodge with a paper sack taped closed. After he'd mentioned that they could use the fish and she'd overheard his argument about money with Noah, she felt almost guilty taking the food. She'd have to visit Tess soon with some sort of gift. Hopefully, once they got their cranberry crop harvested, they would have more money flowing in.

"Sorry I just stormed by the other day outside my brother's shop," he said, jamming his hands in his jeans pockets when she took the casserole. "We don't always see eye to eye."

"No need to apologize to me. I don't know many siblings who do. Joel, you said at the funeral you didn't know Keith well, but now that he's gone, I'm collecting people's memories of him. Can you recall any particular conversation you had with him?"

"We strictly talked fishing. And maybe weather, or how his lodge and my farm was going. Just everyday stuff. So, I'm late. Gotta go."

"By the way, I think I'm having guests from Seattle this weekend, and I'd like to bring them to see your farm," she called after him.

He turned partway back and spoke over his shoulder. "Most people just think the cranberries get picked off a damn bush. Sometimes, I think kids these days believe they just grow in plastic sacks in the grocery." He disappeared into the firs. He must have parked down the road a ways.

She put the casserole in the oven and turned it on low. Then, since she was wet anyway, she went back out on the deck as dusk descended. She vowed she would not be afraid anymore. She would eat well, sleep well and get exercise while she worked on finding out what had happened to Keith. Not even someone who dumped animal corpses and bones was going to scare her away. That odd sensation she had at times of being watched, which the deer carcass had made worse, was not doing to get her down. It had to be her own insecurity and imagination.

Feeling defiant, she walked to the river path and strode along it, back and forth between her property lines, to get some exercise and ease her frustration. The rain had finally stopped, though it dripped off boughs and branches. At the upriver edge of her property line, she stooped to gather some bright, rain-washed leaves to make a centerpiece for her table. Just beyond was a patch of the gray-green scalloped bloodroot plant for which the river was named. If their crisp stems broke, they bled an orange-red liquid, what Sam had evidently used to stain his nose and face that day he performed the soul-catcher ritual.

Since then, she'd done a little reading about bloodroot. Too much of the herb was toxic. It could depress the nervous system and prove fatal, but it would be pretty in this forest bouquet.

As she bent to pick some, she heard a rustling in the water-laden firs, or perhaps the river as it ruffled over the rapids nearby. The falls were a steady hissing roar, not as loud as they sometimes sounded at night despite the fact she was outside now. Perhaps she'd heard a deer walking through the leaves, even though the lodge lay in full view and they seldom came around people.

Picturing the dead, skinned doe again, Claire straightened and turned, squinting into the deepening shadows at the verge of the forest. She froze to look and listen even more intently. Nothing there. She'd best get back. The casserole would be ready.

As she started toward the lighted lodge, she was struck down by a searing, sudden agony that blacked out the world.

12

Wrenching pain obliterated the world. Claire crashed to the ground, writhing as her muscles contracted, screaming at her. In a tight fetal position, she fought for breath, for sanity and life.

Then something darker than night covered her. She tried to stay still until the pain stopped. Yet it ebbed slowly, chattering and nibbling at her. She felt lead-limbed and utterly exhausted. Each breath hurt. Certain she would black out again, she prayed the pain would not return.

Had she suffered a heart attack? Perhaps she'd been shot. Was that how a bullet would feel? Had it hit her spinal cord, paralyzing her legs?

If she could only get the breath to scream, would someone come? *Nick.* No, Nick didn't know she was back in Portfalls....

She was lifted and moved, or else she felt as if she were floating. Maybe she had screamed for help and someone came. Was it an EMR squad? They would take her to the hospital. It was dark in this place...wherever it was.

Or was she being swept away in the river, like a cat drowned in a sack? Is this what happened to Keith? Had he merely stepped outside, and someone hit him over the head, then put him in a sack and dragged him...the way Nick said the deer had been dragged. Keith dragged to the river...to the falls...but that's not what that eyewitness had said....

She struggled against the cocoon, like her mother must have ruffled the sheets of her bed that day she died, maybe trying at the last to get up, dreadfully sorry she'd tried to kill herself, but it was too late....

Drifting in and out of consciousness, Claire concentrated on breathing, on moving each limb, but she was encased in something tight. As in a nightmare, when she tried to scream for help, no sound came out. The falls got louder, louder, shrieking. Now she was being dragged, bumped along over something. Something like wooden railroad ties!

The roar came closer, deafening, trying to devour her. Just as when she painted, the falls seemed to take over the scene, grow larger, to actually move, to turn into the rumpled sheets of her mother's bed, to rock and swallow Keith....

She tried to struggle, but she was dizzy, so dizzy. Her muscles still felt encased in concrete. She feared she could not escape the darkness pressing in on her, drowning her, just like the sound of the white falls....

Claire regained consciousness slowly, breathing shallowly at first before she sucked in greedy breaths of clear, crisp air. It must have been a nightmare. Surely, she was home in bed in her dark room. But she could see stars overhead.

And then she felt the spray of water and heard its *hiss*. Though she was wet with rain and sweat, it wasn't that. Suddenly, she knew where she was.

With a half-strangled scream, she sat up. Yes...on

the suicide bridge, out in the middle of the span in the dark, where Keith had died, where others had jumped to their deaths.

Dizzy, she threw herself facedown, flat on the old trestles, gripping a rusted iron rail for support. And found herself staring straight down between two ties into the frothing river far below.

Dear God, how had she gotten out here? Crunching pain had seized and smothered her; she had blacked out. Someone must have drugged her or shot her or…she wasn't sure. She could not have walked here in her delirium. She felt rocky, as if the entire earth flowed under her.

Carefully, slowly, she turned her head. Though there was no moon, the falls seemed to reflect light within, as they bled into the rapids directly below. Claire flexed each limb, moved each leg muscle. Again, she stared at the white rush of water under her. It was not only terrifying but beautiful, mesmerizing and luring. If she tried to get up and walk off this bridge, would her muscles obey her brain? Or was she indeed having a nightmare? Worse, was she simply insane? Her mother must have been crazy to kill herself. And Keith? Perhaps some sudden, sick compulsion that had taken her loved ones' lives had rubbed off on her.

No. No, surely someone had put her here. She only prayed they were not waiting and watching, because somehow, she was going to get off this demonic bridge.

That's how she saw it now, as some giant ogre astride the river, a beast from a mythic tale that haunted children's dreams, and hers. Still gripping the iron rail, she shoved herself up to a kneeling position and looked around. Though it was dark, she sensed no one on the bridge. On her hands and knees, she went from rib to rib of the giant, praying she'd make it off and that the nightmare would end.

She scraped her hands and knees raw, splinters stuck in her skin. But finally Claire collapsed onto solid ground and, moments later, got to her feet. Shuffling, then stepping slowly, she clung to tree limbs and trunks as she made her way down to the river path, then limped along it toward the lodge. It was waiting for her, open and lighted, a beacon in the dark.

Once again, Nick found himself rushing to Claire. His answering machine had taken her phone message just after ten p.m. He was in the shower after flying back from Cedar Island, and he didn't hear his machine beeping until he was in his uniform. He'd told his deputy, Mike Woods, he'd go on duty for him, since Mike had caught some sort of stomach virus.

Nick called Peggy, his night dispatcher, to tell her he'd be a bit late covering for Mike. Then he drove like a bat out of hell to get to Claire's.

He and Claire were falling into a pattern: she needed help, he ran, or drove, or flew to her. Wanting to protect her, he kept falling for her. Though she'd said on the message that she was not in imminent danger, she'd sounded so upset that he couldn't just put her off until morning.

"Oh, Nick, thank God you're here!" Claire cried and hurled herself into his arms the moment she opened her back door.

He wrapped his arms around her and buried his face in her wild, damp hair, scented with forest and mist. Her face was smudged and scraped. Her skirt and jacket were a mess; she looked like she'd been through a battle. She was trembling and felt so delicate against his strength. He tried to force himself to sit her down and reclaim his control, but she was the one who pulled away first.

"Sorry," she whispered, stepping back from him. "I didn't mean to lose it." He let her go instantly but reluctantly.

"I understand. What happened?"

"I didn't expect you in your uniform."

"Never mind that. What *happened?*"

"I'm not sure. It's really weird, but then, so is everything that happens to me lately." She slumped into a kitchen chair. He took the nearest one, with only the corner of the table between them.

"I was walking outside on the river about dusk," she began, obviously groping for words, "but I was staying on my property. I was just getting a little exercise after my drive back from Seattle. I was gathering leaves, looking at bloodroot, when I had this terrible pain." She sighed but went silent.

"Pain? Where? From what?" he prompted, his stomach already churning with concern and anger.

"I don't know. Pain all over, devastating pain. I just dropped to the ground and then..." Her eyes filled with tears. She gripped her fingers together so hard they went white. He reached over to take her hands in his. When she flinched, he turned her palms up to find them scraped and full of splinters.

"Claire, what the hell happened?"

"My knees, too. From crawling off the bridge."

"The *bridge?* You said you couldn't stand to go out on it."

"The thing is, I'm not exactly sure what happened, except that I ended up in the middle of the bridge. I saw no one the whole time, just Joel Markwood fishing earlier, but he had already gone. He always says he doesn't like to fish after dark."

Nick wanted to protect her from the things that were happening to her—*if* they were happening to her. He desperately wanted to believe her, but could he trust what she said? He'd been so wrong about more than one woman he thought he knew well, better than he knew Claire.

"I'm sure it wasn't a heart attack or a ministroke," she went on. "I have no symptoms now, and those wouldn't have made all my muscles contract in agony. After Seattle, I was so sure I could come back here and face anything to get answers, but now, I swear I'm going crazy."

"What you just described," he told her, relieved there could be a logical if terrible explanation, "sounds like you might have been shot with a Taser gun."

Frowning, she said, "You mean a laser gun."

"No, that's *Star Wars* stuff. Tasers use a laser only to pinpoint their target. They're a step beyond stun guns, more debilitating and painful. The target is disabled, rather than just dazed and slowed. And stun guns need to touch a person to work, whereas Tasers shoot out tiny electrodes from a distance. You said Joel was gone by then. Was anybody around when this happened, another fisherman? Or Sam on one of his evening walks?"

"Not that I saw," she said, hugging herself hard. "But, now that I think of it, I maybe heard something. I thought it might be a deer. Oh damn, first that dead deer and now this!'' she cried, covering her face with both hands before she pulled them down to stare again at her bruised palms. ''Are Tasers legal?''

''In this state and most others. They can even be ordered online. But in an unprovoked attack, if we can establish who shot you, we can charge them with second-degree assault. I'll search the area thoroughly tomorrow in the light. Most Tasers shoot out little confetti pieces that identify the weapon and can be traced to the buyer. The Taser darts sometimes leave two tiny puncture marks in the skin, so let's look closer at you. Or I could drive you to your doctor.''

Nick knew it was the cop in him asking such calm questions. But the man in him was furious someone had hurt her.

''I don't need a doctor,'' she insisted. ''And, as you can see, this is what I was wearing. It's sleeveless under the jacket, so I can check my arms and legs myself, at least,'' she said, taking the jacket off gingerly. Her arms looked bruised. ''But the light's not good in here,'' she went on. ''Maybe I should go in the bathroom.''

''I could get those splinters out of your hands.''

''And knees?'' she asked, lifting her torn skirt hem to look at them.

Nick swallowed hard. Dirty, bruised, stuck with splinters.

''The light's the best in my bathroom upstairs,'' she said, ''but after being dragged in that sack, I'll bet there's no electrodes or confetti on me.''

''Dragged in a sack? You didn't say that before.''

''I didn't?'' She looked genuinely confused. ''I'm pretty sure someone wrapped me in something, and dumped me on the bridge, probably hoping I'd either get the scare of my life or end my life by tumbling off or jumping. Why are you looking at me like that?''

"Like what? I'm just trying to piece everything together to help you.''

"You were frowning. You looked like you didn't believe a word I said.''

"That's not true. I'm mad as hell at the bastard who shot you with that thing. You could never have made this one up.''

"*This one?* Then, you think I made up something else?''

"That's not what I said—or meant.''

"Then, I would appreciate it if you'd help me get these splinters out—of my hands, at least.''

Claire realized too late she'd made a big mistake in letting Nick come upstairs to help with the splinters, let alone look for tiny barb marks in her skin. The master bath had mirrored tiles, and just the sight—actually, the multiple view—of him from every angle in his uniform in this very private room didn't help her already shaky composure. She tried not to think, tried to just watch what he was doing in the mirror, but that didn't help either.

He was so much bigger than she was, so muscular. He ran his fingers along her arms as she held them both straight out. He bent near to scan her bare arms on all sides.

He was so close that she could see each crisp, separate dark hair on his head and his beard shadow. His nose was slightly crooked and his mustache barely silvered. His breath glided along her left arm to her shoulder.

The current of her emotions seemed to sweep her thoughts away, but she knew one thing: no way was Nick Braden going to search her bare, bruised legs for puncture marks.

The thought made her realize that she needed not only to find who had hurt Keith, and now her, but to face what had happened to their marriage. Friends from the first, both busy, they had just coasted through life. Had they coasted in different directions? Keith's impact on her as a woman—on her emotions and senses, her heart—seemed muted not only in memory but had seemed muted even during their most intimate moments. If their marriage died long before he did, it was partly her fault.

And it was being near Nick Braden that was making her realize her failure. She felt so attuned to Nick. It was not only because she needed his help, maybe his protection, too. Unlike with Keith, deep, jolting impulses coursed between them. What was that someone had said once, about the difference between lightning bugs and lightning?

Claire could not recall ever feeling swept away by Keith, but she hadn't fathomed such things possible. Maybe friendship, mutual interests and ambitions were not enough on which to build a marriage. After her mother died and her father shut her out, perhaps she'd turned to Keith for the wrong reasons.

"That's enough, Nick. Thanks," she blurted. "I can do the rest. The barbs were probably so small— mere pinpricks, right?"

"Actually," he said, clearing his throat, "with all the loose clothes you have on—I mean, you're fairly well covered—it's possible the electrodes initially hooked on to your clothes, though that wouldn't conduct the jolts as well as bare skin.''

Conduct the jolts. The words reverberated in her brain. Exhausted and scared, Claire suddenly felt boneless, as if she'd fall to the ground again. She turned away from Nick before he could read her thoughts, and headed through her bedroom out into the hall to the landing overlooking the first floor. She stood there, gripping the banister, breaking out in a sweat. But, as Nick caught up with her, one rational thought surfaced above her tumbled agony of fear and failure.

"Nick, I was wet!" she cried, swiping at her damp skin. "Outside tonight, I mean. I was walking in the rain, and the trees kept dripping, so I was wet when I was shot and water conducts electricity!"

"Anything else you forgot to tell me?" he demanded, sounding suddenly frustrated or angry.

"No," was all she managed to say, because there didn't seem to be any protection from this cascade of feelings. She felt both elated and depressed. Even if she had failed to fully love Keith, he had hardly fallen for her the way a man should a woman. They'd had more of a merger than a marriage. But, even though *until death do us part* had occurred for them, she would not let her quest go until she knew what had happened to him.

Luckily, Nick's night dispatcher called to tell him his deputy felt better and was back at work, so he didn't have to leave Claire alone. He paced the ground floor of the lodge while upstairs she took a shower and picked splinters out of her skin.

His growing desire for Claire aside, Nick knew he had big worries here. If she was telling the truth, she was up against someone with a real big, bad agenda. Someone who had evidently tried several tactics to scare her, then used a so-called "less-than-lethal" weapon on her. So was a lethal tactic next? Keith's potential—now probable—murder case must hold the key to who was out to hurt Claire.

Later, he went over her jacket and skirt and found no barbs or ID confetti there. Still, through all this, he'd been stalling over telling her about her husband and her best friend, Anne. And he'd been praying she hadn't already known of an affair and decided to do something to put a stop to it.

That was the ugly underside of possibilities here, that the clever Claire had staged all these things just to cover her trail of guilt. Spousal murder by a jealous or wronged mate was classic casebook. But he could not believe that of Claire. Besides, why would she insist then that the case wasn't suicide and that he look into it? He'd seen some pretty convincing liars in his day, but he was certain Claire could not be one of them.

After Claire finished showering, they returned to the kitchen. For over an hour, Nick continued his questioning, trying to make sure every base was covered.

"I said I saw no one around, Nick! The back door of the lodge stood open just as I left it, but now I'm afraid having the locks re-keyed will be for nothing."

"Are your new keys accounted for?"

"Yes. They were just where I left them. I did have

the presence of mind to check for them, after I called you.''

He stood and looked out her back door and the kitchen windows. He couldn't sit still. ''I can sleep on your couch tonight,'' he told her, ''and get the keys dusted for prints in the morning.''

''I can't ask you to do that. I'll just lock up and see if I can stay at Anne's for the night. I think I have guests coming for the weekend, so I'll be all right. The more I feel under attack here, the more determined I am to stay. Nick, what? You're not thinking some sort of Taser gun is Sam Twoclaws's MO, are you, despite the fact he wants this land—my land.''

''I'm counting no one out, but I am thinking two things,'' he said, sitting down again and leaning toward her across the corner of the table. ''One, the symptoms you've described sound like they were caused by a state-of-the-art Taser, an advanced M-Series. I thought I had the only two around locked up in the office's supply room.''

''Could someone have stolen them—well, not from the sheriff's office, I guess, but could someone have taken them out?''

''I'll check on that first thing tomorrow. But you can't go to Anne's. She's out of town at a Realtors' conference or convention for a couple of days.''

He watched her. Surely, she wouldn't have suggested she stay with Anne if she'd had any clue the woman had been having an affair with Keith.

''Oh,'' she said. ''Did Anne mention last week she was going, or have you seen her since the funeral?''

"I found out from her neighbor, when I tried to stop by to question Anne earlier this morning."

Her chin jerked up and her eyes widened.

"So," he plunged on, "how close were you and Keith to her, after the real estate deal for the lodge closed, I mean?"

She rose slowly, stiffly and went to the counter to fill the coffeepot. "We both liked her," she said, measuring coffee into the filter. "Of course, we didn't see her as much after a while, but she'd stop by, usually with some sort of gift." She started the coffeemaker; the low *hiss* of it was instantly muffled by the distant, pervasive hum of the falls. Was Claire unable to face him just now because she had known about Anne and Keith? But she turned to him again, leaning back against the counter.

"I had a couple of lattes in Seattle today," she explained, "and I guess I got the craving for caffeine again. I'm probably not going to sleep tonight, anyway, even though I feel like the walking dead."

"Claire, about Anne. There's no good time or easy way to say this, so I'm going to level with you, just as I always expect you to do with me. Unfortunately, what I have to say ties in with DeeDee, too."

An hour later, they still sat in the kitchen, Claire sticking to coffee, Nick demolishing a reheated plate of the macaroni-and-cheese casserole Joel had brought.

Claire was amazed—she knew Nick was, too— that she hadn't shed one tear or lost control when he'd explained DeeDee had lied about the IR to protect Claire from suspecting Keith's adultery. DeeDee had seen them uptown twice together, which alone meant nothing, but seeing them coming out of the motel sounded damning. Claire had felt so sick to her soul at the thought that Keith and Anne had both been cheating on her that it was too deep for tears.

Obviously, for Keith, their marriage had not been enough, either. He'd evidently been unfaithful, something Claire had never done, though she had deceived him in other ways. She'd let him think she was content and fulfilled. Only since he died had she come to face the fact that she had been none of those things. And that she had deceived herself into thinking they had a sound marriage, too.

Nor could Claire believe that poor DeeDee had been suspended for trying to help her. But worse, if Anne and Keith had been having an affair... Dear Lord in heaven, she'd made a mess of her marriage, but then, evidently so had Keith. Still, even if he was partly to blame for a bad marriage and, possibly, for his own death, she was determined to find his murderer and her attacker.

"You know," she told Nick, jumping to her feet, "I thought it was strange that Anne cried continually when Keith was missing and at the funeral. I even felt guilty. I had always thought she was rather hard-hearted."

Rage roared back into her. Despite how beaten she felt, she began to pace the kitchen, flinging gestures. "Even when she seems excited over something, she's very self-contained, like she's holding back. But *she* cried while she was holding *my* hand! If they were having an affair, and I didn't have a clue about it, what else could he have been doing I didn't know about? I've been such an idiot! It's like I've been in some sort of trance these past few years."

"Don't blame yourself."

"Of course I blame myself! You blamed yourself for not sensing that your wife was hiding her illness, didn't you?" she blurted before she realized she had no right to dissect his marriage, too.

"Yeah, I blame myself," he admitted. He tossed down his fork, which clattered against his empty plate. She could tell he was seething, either at her or himself, but then, she'd sensed frustration in him all evening.

"I was probably too damn busy, and I'd been away a lot during the Gulf War," he said, his voice cold and hard. "I guess, to use the old cliché, we just grew apart. But that doesn't excuse me—or her."

"Exactly. And I was trying so hard to fit in with Keith's dreams, to keep myself on task to get this place ready...when he was running around with her," she said with a sigh as she wilted into her chair at the table again and put her head in her hands. "That night they were stopped for speeding, he must have told me he was going out to run an errand or something. Or maybe he said he was going for a walk, and she picked him up on cue for some quick sex in her car, like a pair of teenagers before...before he came back and got in bed with me, damn the both of them. But," she added, lifting her head and emphasizing every word, "I intend to talk to Anne."

"Not until I say so. It's police business now, so I'm talking to her first. You don't need to be tipping her off or getting in some sort of argument or worse."

"Police business? Really?" she cried. "You're going to reopen Keith's case?"

"Maybe. Mostly because of what happened to you tonight. I'm going to question Anne, then decide. But you can just steer clear of her until I do."

"I suppose she could lie her way out of admitting to an affair. You'll need to find out where she was the night Keith disappeared. What if he sneaked out to meet her, and they argued? What if she wanted him to leave me, and he didn't want to do that, or was afraid he'd endanger his control of the lodge in a divorce? What if—"

"Cut!" he commanded and banged a fist on the table. "It's police business. You will sit tight. You will not think up a hundred possible scenarios, and you will not get in the way. You're retired from your unofficial capacity as sheriff's assistant, is that clear?"

"Of course it is. But I feel so bad about DeeDee."

"I'll get her back to work next week, but she needs to learn a lesson. I will not be lied to or crossed by those I have to trust," he said, punching the air with his index finger almost in her face.

"Believe me, I get the message," she told him.

"Good. Now go on upstairs and leave me down here to get some shut-eye on the couch."

Claire almost offered him one of the guest rooms, but she would much rather have him in the heart of her home instead of down the side hall. The great room seemed so open to the outside, where strange things kept peering in or pulling her away.

He hadn't said she couldn't visit poor DeeDee, she thought, and tell the young woman she was sorry she got in trouble with Nick for her sake.

Claire stopped at the top of the staircase and glanced down as Nick turned lights out, then arranged pillows the way he wanted them on the long, leather couch.

"I'm going to throw down a couple of blankets," she called to him, and hurried to get them from the box of extra linens in the closet. He looked up at her as she leaned over the balcony railing to drop them down to him.

Suddenly, it reminded her of the scene from *Romeo and Juliet* she and several other high school classmates had staged in British Literature for an extra credit project. She had sweated bullets all the way through it because she'd had a terrible crush on the guy playing Romeo to her Juliet. She should have known then not to start dating Keith Malvern, because he'd thought the entire play about dying for lost love was really stupid.

Claire turned quickly away, kicked off her shoes and got in bed, still in her jeans and shirt. If something else strange happened, she'd be ready to rush downstairs to help. Keith might have let her down, but, so far, Nick Braden never had.

Damn them! It couldn't be, the watcher thought, pacing, pacing, tree to tree, along the noisy river, hitting the trunks with both fists as the hours of the night dragged on. This time, the sheriff and Claire had turned the lights off. If only this camera had some infrared film. He had not come outside to leave. It was two a.m. Was his car going to sit in the whore's driveway all night? It had been hours ago they'd gone upstairs together, then come down, her clothes changed, and had coffee and food together, obviously after a bout in bed.

At least the can of spray paint was still in the backpack. It would serve Claire Malvern right if the word *whore* got graffitied all over her lodge. But if that bloody deer and those bones had not scared her away, what would? Besides, ridding this place of her was challenge enough without having to face the sheriff, if he heard a noise and glanced out. He'd looked out the kitchen windows earlier.

With the backpack upended, its insides scattered on the ground. The can of red paint rolled out, but where was the knife? The watcher gave the bag one more shake, and the knife fell out and stuck in the ground, shuddering as it hit. A few cuts on Claire Malvern's face would at least ease this agony. Nick Braden needed to be slashed, too, and it was going to feel so good to take care of it all.

13

By midmorning, Claire felt progress was finally being made. After she had fed Nick breakfast, he'd searched outside for Taser confetti. When he'd found nothing, he had gone to the office to check that his Tasers were untouched, which, apparently, they were. Later, he sent Mike Woods, his night deputy, who also did crime scene investigation, to fingerprint her and her new sets of keys. Claire gave Mike the name of the man who'd changed her locks so they could request his prints if needed. Near noon, Nick called to tell her that the only prints on the keys were hers, so she felt a bit better. At last, trained experts were looking into Keith's death, whether or not it was an official investigation yet.

Diana Nance also called to accept Claire's weekend invitation. The Nances planned to arrive about noon on Saturday and leave after lunch on Sunday. Diana was excited to see the cranberry farm and scrimshaw shop, while Ethan was exhausted and looking forward to just enjoying the lodge.

Grateful to have something normal to do, Claire planned her menus and ran to the grocery store. Each time she left the lodge, she looked all around until the coast seemed completely clear, at least as clear as it could be, with thick trees and the twisting river so close. She tried to mute the memory of the painful attack and the horror of being left on the bridge, but even at the grocery store it flashed back at her, as if she were suffering from posttraumatic stress syndrome, like a friend she'd had who'd fought in Vietnam.

Back at the lodge, deciding she owed both the Markwoods and DeeDee for their continued support, Claire fixed food for them. How good it felt to keep busy, to lessen her obsession with her grief and problems. Her so-called friend Anne Cunningham had now moved into the enemy camp, but Anne surely wasn't the type to haul a skinned deer around or shoot Taser guns. Besides, Nick had said she was out of town last night.

Claire made blueberry muffins and a pan of lasagna for the Markwoods and a pasta salad with artichoke, tomato and feta cheese for DeeDee. Partly because the lasagna was still warm, she decided to stop at the Markwoods' cranberry farm first.

Claire continually looked in her rearview mirror, taking a side road or pulling in driveways if someone seemed to be following her, even at a distance. But the lane to the Markwoods' house that ran along the dikes hemming in the cranberry bogs was deserted. She began to breathe a bit easier. It seemed amazingly quiet here without the roar of the falls; sometimes she imagined she still heard it, as if she carried it inside her head.

The berries in the bogs were turning from bright pink to red, so they were nearly ready to be harvested from their dense mats of vines. When she'd moved here, Claire had been surprised to learn that the bogs were not swamps, but were only flooded if the berries were to be wet-harvested. On the left side of the road, metal cars the size of small Dumpsters sat on rails, waiting for stacked crates of berries. Between the long, low storage shed and the peeling, white frame house sat two large harvesting machines that Tess had told her about the last time she'd bought berries from their stand.

During harvest time, both machines crept through the bogs, one for dry-harvesting that pruned with its sharp knives, the other one that literally beat the bushes for wet-harvesting. A single driver sat high above the rubber tires. Claire couldn't recall the name of the dry-harvest machine, but the wet one was "the eggbeater." Its big metal loops knocked fruit from the vines, shoving the berries down into the water so they would bob up to be caught in the large wooden corral before being suctioned out for sorting.

Claire saw no one around as she stopped her car and got out to remove Markwoods' casserole and the basket of muffins from the floor of the passenger side of her SUV. With the harvest near, it seemed someone should be working, but no one was in sight.

She walked up on the screened-in porch and placed the basket on a chair. A radio inside was tuned to some sort of call-in show, and the front window sashes were raised.

"Tess?" she called. "It's Claire!"

Slow footsteps inside. The screen door squeaked open, and Joel stood there. His eyes were bloodshot as if he'd been on an all-night binge. Had he looked that bad yesterday?

"You didn't need to bring that pan back."

"I'm returning it with something for both of you—a very small thank you for all you've done."

Strangely, he looked annoyed. "Tess's mother took sick down in Olympia," he said, coming out onto the porch and letting the screen door bang shut behind him. At least he took the aluminum-foil-covered pan from her.

"I'm sorry to hear that."

"Tess'll be driving back and forth."

"You can just pop the food in the fridge or even the oven if you want some of it. And here—muffins," she said, indicating the basket on the rocking chair when he said nothing else. "I'm sure you're busy with the harvest coming."

"Yeah, we'll be raking in the berries—if not much profit, this year. There's a big slump."

"Tess mentioned that—the push for white cranberries."

"Some farmers are even turning their bogs into ponds to farm fish, but damned if I will."

"Perhaps the market will turn around. I love them—cranberries."

"Used to be sixty bucks a barrel in boom times, then prices slumped to eleven. Now it's about twenty. You do the math. I got Stevens variety in, since they ripen earlier and are sweeter, but it's a risk. They're not durable and tend to break down quicker. Some of them got the black vine weevil, too. It's a big crapshoot, just like life. Look, I don't mean to unload all that on you, not with your...situation. Sorry, but I'm not in the best of moods."

"I can see why," she told him. Although she'd heard repeatedly that Joel Markwood had a great sense of humor, to her the man seemed as bitter as his berries without sugar. "By the way, I hope you don't mind if I bring a friend of mine by to see the bogs tomorrow. She's from Seattle—my husband's boss's wife.''

He looked annoyed again, so she accepted that he didn't have the time or inclination for her attempt at small talk. ''Drive her by if you want,'' he muttered, ''but there won't be much to see.''

''Well, I've got to run,'' she said, backing off the porch. ''Please have Tess call me if I can help in any way.''

She thought he'd say something kind, at least in parting, but he only nodded stiffly. As she drove away she looked in the rearview mirrora and saw him staring after her, past the big machines sitting silently, like metal monsters waiting to attack the bogs.

After several wrong turns, Claire finally found where DeeDee lived, in an area of town she hadn't known existed. It was a dead-end street of narrow, tightly spaced, 1950s-era duplexes near train tracks that were probably part of the same defunct railroad line that had once crossed the Bloodroot River Bridge.

Two boys playing on the street told her she should go around the back, where DeeDee's entrance was. She lived upstairs in a converted apartment. A back porch that was more like an old airing deck had a single plastic mesh lawn chair and a rusted TV table on it. Screened windows opened to the deck from what was probably, by the look of the different curtains, her kitchen and bedroom.

''DeeDee, are you home?'' Claire called through

the open back door, though she obviously was there. "It's Claire Malvern."

"Oh-oh, just a sec. I'm not dressed," DeeDee cried from inside. Claire heard scurrying about, and the curtains in the bedroom windows whooshed shut, evidently so she could get dressed. Claire sat on the sagging chair and put the Tupperware with the pasta salad on the TV table.

"Take your time," Claire called. "I just came to say thanks for trying to help—and bring you something to eat."

"Pizza or something chocolate, I hope," DeeDee said, opening and holding the door so Claire could step in.

Beyond the galley kitchen, Claire could see a small living room. The apartment's cramped quarters were done in pastel colors. On the TV by the door sat a big, framed black-and-white photo of Nick, Aaron, Mike, DeeDee and a few others who were probably sheriff office staff. No, Claire realized, the picture looked as if it had been cut from the newspaper. Being sent away from her working family must have pained this girl greatly.

"I'm in bad need of comfort food," DeeDee admitted.

"Aren't we all? This is a salad. It's not comfort food, but it's tasty and good if you want to eat healthy."

"To drop some of this lard, you mean," the girl said with a sigh. She wore a tent of a sleeveless dress in bright pink and lavender hues and was barefoot. Amazingly, she looked larger in the loose-fitting garment than she did in her too-tight work clothes. "That's what my family always says," DeeDee said, rolling her eyes. "My sister sent me this Hawaiian muumuu after her vacation just to make that very point."

"But that wasn't what I said. I just know you'd feel better if you were a little lighter."

"And brighter," DeeDee said, taking the salad from her and popping the top to pick out a few pasta bowties with her fingers. "You must've heard I did a really dumb thing."

"If misery loves company, you'll be glad I'm here. Yes, you made a mistake, but I've made a few of those myself. I just keep telling myself it's not the end of the world."

"Easy for you to say!" she blurted, choking on a piece of pasta she quickly washed down with a drink of water from the sink faucet. The sudden switch from confession to accusation surprised Claire. "Well," DeeDee said, when Claire just stared at her, "I didn't mean that, not with what's happened to you. How much did the sheriff tell you of why I tried to cover for you?"

"He told me about Keith and Anne."

"I figured you'd had enough heartache," she whispered, turning away. Her voice seemed deflated and her shoulders slumped. Claire noted her fingers, gripping the edge of the Formica kitchen counter, were as white as stuffed sausages.

"DeeDee, please don't take this the wrong way, but do you have enough money to get by if your suspension goes on for a few days?"

"Did he say a few days?" she cried, turning back and clasping her hands together. "Did he say when?"

"Not exactly. You do live alone, don't you?"

"Yes. I hate it, but I'd kill myself before I'd go live with my sisters. They all have kids and, as cute as they are, that hurts, you know, that they have kids and I don't. And they think I should lose weight, find a man, have a family—that I should do a lot of things I just can't seem to do."

"I always wanted kids," Claire said simply, reaching out to touch DeeDee's shoulder.

"Yeah, well," DeeDee said, turning away, "at least you had the father for them, even if you lost him. And you're pretty. Unlike some of us, you will have other chances."

"DeeDee, you don't have to give up those dreams for yourself. Maybe you have to work at them, as we all do, but don't give up. Are you sure you're okay alone right now?"

"Yeah, I'm sure," she insisted, swiping at tears under both eyes before turning back with a forced grin. "You aren't looking for a cook—or a food tester—for the lodge, are you? Just kidding. No, I'm fine, and I'll be more fine when I get back to work. I can only take so many soap operas before I start laughing at them. You know, laughing at how everybody cheats on and lies to everyone…"

The girl's face reddened and Claire was certain she would burst into tears, but she didn't. She was deeply touched by the fact DeeDee kept a sense of humor in distress, and thought of how Joel Markwood had not managed to.

"I'll call you later," she promised DeeDee, giving her a quick, light hug, though DeeDee stood rigid in the embrace. "I want to have you to the lodge for dinner soon."

"I'd like that," she said, but her voice sounded

listless again. Claire noted well her chameleonlike mood swings, especially because she must have missed something like that in Keith. She was going to tell Nick this girl needed to get back to work—soon.

Later that day, as Claire cleaned the lodge for the Nances' arrival, she couldn't get DeeDee out of her mind. She could invite her to stay here for a while. Perhaps the girl could sublet her apartment and make some extra money to get her over the gap in her salary this suspension might bring. A change of environment would do her good, and Claire could use the companionship, especially at night. She might even be able to help DeeDee with the exercise and diet she needed. And as soon as Nick reinstated her at work, she wouldn't be around in the daytime.

Besides, Claire couldn't forget the strange way DeeDee had talked about laughing at soap operas, because of the way "everyone cheats on and lies to everyone." Who could laugh at that? Worse, DeeDee had said she'd *kill* herself before she'd go to live with her sisters. It was a figure of speech, of course, but what if her problems had made her suicidal? Claire knew she'd evidently missed the warning signs when her mother was ill—and she'd surely missed them when Keith was depressed. But she was not going to miss them again with someone else who needed help and could be saved.

Her thoughts in turmoil, Claire furiously dusted the four wall plaques of salmon that Sam Twoclaws had mounted for Keith. "The salmon have all the answers, indeed," she said, repeating the supposed words of wisdom Sam had told her. "I ought to hang all four of you in a dark closet, for all the answers you have!''

She hated the things, with their glass eyes perpetually staring, but Keith had been adamant about them. For that reason, she couldn't bear to take them down yet, and her future B & B guests might love them. Claire had distressed the wood they were mounted on, rather than agreeing to the usual shiny finish, which would look too plastic for this wall of old barn siding.

One of the decorator's techniques Claire had specialized in during her interior design career was faux looks of various kinds. She'd recommended wallpaper with space-expanding vistas, and had personally painted more than one mural to trick the eye of the beholder in some stunning Seattle homes.

In her kitchen here, she'd installed molded plastic panels she painted to look like an expensive embossed tin ceiling. An interior decorator's deceptions, to extend a room or make something seem more antique or intimate, were her forte. She might have been the reputed master of all that at Kallile's Fine Interiors, but she still hadn't caught a clue that Keith was deceiving her—if he was. She'd like to give him the benefit of the doubt until she talked to Anne...but he sounded so guilty.

A shadow slashed across Claire. She let out an involuntary shriek and froze, then turned toward the riverside windows. A woman stood on her back deck, just where that deer had been, peering in. The late-morning sun glanced off them so that she could not see who it was at first. Tess, back from visiting her mother? Diana?

It was Anne.

Claire stared, astounded, as if just thinking about her former friend had conjured her up. It almost seemed as if Sam Twoclaws's soul-catcher ritual on the deck had snagged the wrong person at the wrong time. Anne wore a black pantsuit and held what appeared to be a bouquet of blown-glass flowers in yellow and blue. Yes, it was an expensive and tasteful bouquet of daffodils and Japanese iris made of colored glass.

Claire started toward the sliding doors before she recalled that Nick had made her promise not to talk to Anne until he did. Maybe Anne had seen Nick already. But surely Anne hadn't come to try to make amends?

"Claire, it's just me!" she called, sounding impatient. Anne could evidently see her through the sunstruck glass. She must not have talked to Nick or she wouldn't dare to so much as show her face here. "I've been looking for weeks for something that would look good on that big table in the great room," she went on as Claire unlocked the sliding doors. "Do you know how intimidating it is to buy something like this for an interior designer?"

Claire knew she should call Nick, but she was dying to confront Anne. This wasn't as if she sought the woman out, so he couldn't blame her for that. And if she told Anne she couldn't speak to her until she talked to Nick, she might bolt, especially if she was guilty of more than an affair.

Claire decided not to tell Anne all she knew, but to see if she could get the woman to give something away. Surely that's what Nick would do. She'd seen the way the police questioned suspects and so-called perps on TV, she assured herself.

But when she slid the door open, Claire couldn't bear to have Anne in her house. Rather than letting her enter and put the tall, glass flowers on the table to see how they looked, she stepped out.

Almost before she knew what she'd say, Claire blurted, "Are you the one who left the yellow roses on Keith's grave?"

"I—yes, I did. I meant to tell you."

"But why not just send them to the funeral home?"

"I was spending a lot of time with you, remember? Then I had to catch up on things I'd ignored at work. I ordered them late and felt terrible about that. But what do you think of these? I was at a conference in Seattle and found them in the cutest little shop."

As Anne held up the flowers for her perusal, Claire realized she was still blocking the door. "They're lovely," she admitted, then added, "but I can see right through them, just as I can see through you."

"What? Are you all right?" Anne asked, putting the arrangement down on the deck table. "The sheriff thought you should see a doctor before."

"I don't need tranquilizers to sleep."

"For counseling, Claire."

"Sheriff Braden told you that?"

"He only wants what's best for you. I'm sure your regular M.D. could recommend a psychiatrist."

"When did the sheriff tell you that?"

"After the funeral. Claire, it might do you good to just talk about your feelings and—"

"All right, I'll talk about my feelings. I'm feeling appalled and betrayed since I learned you and my

husband were seen together in town more than once,
and that he got a citation for speeding in your car
one night when he probably told me he was going
for a walk! Not to mention your little stay at the
Bide-A-While Motel!''

Anne's face drained of color. She took a step back
as if she'd been struck. So much, Claire thought, for
careful questioning. Nick would be furious with her,
but she just couldn't hold back.

''Claire,'' Anne said, lacing her fingers together
as if praying or begging, ''I'm so sorry.''

''Then, you admit you were seeing him?''

''Absolutely not. A motel? Someone is sadly mis-
taken. I mean I'm sorry you've been agonizing over
that at such a time. It's just not true. Yes, I ran into
him uptown once or twice—we even had lunch once,
I recall. Maybe he forgot to mention it.''

''Maybe you both did.''

''As for that citation from one of the local deputies, I was coming back at night along River Road,
from showing a house on the outskirts of Redmond,''
she said, smoothing down her sculpted white-blond
hair. ''On that night you refer to, my car started to
sputter.''

''Really? The River Road is hardly the route
you'd take from Redmond to your place.''

''I wanted to run by another property to be sure
my Realtor sign was still up, since some kids had
evidently taken the previous two. Anyway,'' she
went on without missing a beat, ''I was really scared
to think of being stranded out there alone, and I was
just about to use my cell phone to call the auto club
for help. Heaven knows, I pay enough for their extra
'anytime' service.''

"And Keith just happened to come to your rescue, instead?" Claire countered, her voice dripping sarcasm.

"Yes, as a matter of fact, he did. He said he'd been walking the river path near the falls and heard someone grinding the engine to start it. So he walked up to the road through the woods and did something to it under the hood. Then he told me to move over so he could test it before I continued home," she concluded with a dismissive little shrug, as if to emphasize that was all there was to it.

Her words were smooth. Her face had its natural color back, and then some. The explanation was plausible. It was no doubt what Anne would tell Nick. So had Anne and Keith betrayed her or not? And did Nick really believe she should see a counselor or psychiatrist?

"It's interesting that neither Keith nor you breathed a word to me about just happening to run into each other uptown—or of this fortuitous Sir Galahad rescue in the dead of night," Claire clipped out. "I would think one of you would have mentioned some of this, unless you had something to hide."

For a moment, Claire thought Anne might break the glass flowers over her head. "Look, Claire, you and the sheriff can damn well find me at home if you need me!" With that, she stormed around the side of the lodge to get in her car. From inside, Claire followed her window-to-window to be sure she was leaving. And why had she come around to the back deck, instead of just knocking on the kitchen door, anyway?

When Anne backed out of the driveway and roared onto River Road, Claire realized immediately that she must indeed have been lying. The falls had muffled the sound of Anne starting her car, let alone her gunning the engine. Anne had claimed Keith heard her car clear from the river path below, which was much nearer the falls. No way! Nor could he have cut his way through the thick forest near the falls to the road, unless he was out on the bridge itself and used the old railroad path, which just happened to be the local make-out spot.

Though she knew Nick would be angry at her for confronting Anne, she dialed his cell phone number.

"Eagle One, code four," he answered.

"Nick, it's Claire. Anne's back, and she stopped by on her way home. She says she's innocent, but I'm sure she's lying."

She heard a muffled curse. "You confronted her, Claire? Before I questioned her? Damn it. I'm heading to see you. One way or the other, your involvement could screw everything up!"

Once Claire related Anne's explanation to Nick, he got even angrier than he'd been when he arrived. He'd always seemed calm, under control even when he was upset, such as when she'd trapped him at the Bachelor Bid-Off. But now his big, square jaw was clenched, his dark eyes were narrowed, and his mustache actually seemed to lock down over his taut lips.

"I swear," he muttered, "if I open this case, I'm going to lock you up somewhere while my department works it. You did exactly what I told you not to!"

"I'm the one who should be upset," she insisted. "Anne says you think I need a shrink. Thanks for telling her that, and not me. You're starting to operate with her behind my back, just the way my husband did!''

He reached for her shoulder, then released her. She stepped back against the corner of the counter, where he blocked her in with both hands. ''You're the one,'' he said, slowly and distinctly, ''who keeps missing the boat in all this. There's nothing radical or accusatory in suggesting someone who's been through trauma see a counselor, doctor or minister, and I would have suggested it if you hadn't been handling the trauma yourself.''

''Don't bet on that. I evidently couldn't handle my own marriage.''

''Don't beat yourself up—especially since someone else is out to do that. You're a bright woman, Claire. But what you're saying is that you had no clue that Keith was seeing someone on the sly? Aren't there usually little hints?''

''Aren't there usually little hints someone is very sick?'' she countered. ''People don't go around with tattoos on their foreheads that say *adulterer* or *sick,* you know!''

''Let's leave my dead wife out of my investigation of your dead husband.''

''I was referring to my mother. We knew she was depressed but not that she'd kill herself! Actually, I'm starting to worry about DeeDee's state of mind. Can't you take her back soon?''

''You just let me worry about DeeDee, and take care of yourself,'' he said, lifting her chin to look steadily into her eyes. ''I'm gonna go try to pick up the pieces with Anne after you've jumped in again with both feet.''

''At least, untrained or not, I can tell when a

man's sudden drowning is really a case of wrongful death! You'd have let Keith just rest in peace as a sick suicide when he was probably murdered!''

Nick moved away, his jaw set even harder, before he headed for the door. ''Claire, just keep yourself in here and don't give me any excuses to lock you up somewhere else so I can do my job and you don't get hurt again!''

He banged out of the house, threw himself in his car, slammed the car door and roared away. Claire noted that the falls quickly drowned the sounds of his car, too.

Taking her cell phone with her in case Nick called, Claire left the lodge and made a quick trip into town to talk to DeeDee again. Nick had as good as told her to stay home and out of his way, but she was only trying to help. He was a typical type-A personality who wanted full control, but she had no intention of just sitting around the lodge waiting for something else dreadful to happen so she could phone him for help again. He was evidently one of those men who thought any woman acting emotionally—which was the natural state of any woman worth her salt, in Claire's opinion—was acting irrationally.

She pulled up in front of DeeDee's duplex just as a typical afternoon shower got under way. From low, clotted clouds, sprinkles blew sideways, but it was not a cold rain. She probably should have just phoned DeeDee, but she didn't want the girl making up some excuse to keep her away. Besides, Claire was feeling guilty that she hadn't done more to offer help.

Thunder rumbled in the distance as Claire hurried

up the back steps of the duplex again. Pale light shone through the windows. Good, DeeDee must be home, Claire thought. And even if the woman was depressed, Claire was happy that at least she had some lights on. She couldn't bear it if DeeDee was just sitting alone in the dark, the way her mother used to.

The back door was closed, but Claire could see through its screen and single, small window. She knocked. "DeeDee! It's Claire again."

She pictured Anne standing on her back deck earlier today, wanting in. Was she so brazen that she had lied to Claire's face about having an affair with Keith? Maybe Nick could get something out of her. Heaven knows, the man could be intimidating, as DeeDee must have learned all too well.

"DeeDee?" Claire called again, as a heavy feeling of foreboding washed over her. The small kitchen looked so dim and dismal through the old gray screens. Suddenly, the same ominous weight that she'd felt when she'd climbed the stairs to her mother's bedroom on that long-ago day sat on Claire's chest.

"DeeDee! Are you home?"

With great trepidation, Claire moved to the bedroom windows and stared through those screens. The curtains DeeDee had quickly closed earlier today were open just a crack. Though it was not as brightly lit as the kitchen, the bedroom lay open to her gaze.

She peered within, fearful she'd find DeeDee laid out on her bed after a pill overdose or something more dreadful. As her eyes focused, Claire almost felt as if she'd been slammed by another Taser. Her hands flew to her mouth. Not believing what she saw, she stared wide-eyed at the room through the screen.

14

Claire blinked and looked again. She still could not believe her eyes.

On cork bulletin boards lining the two walls of DeeDee's bedroom that she could glimpse through the crack in the curtains were tacked rows of photos, several taken at the fishing lodge or at the yacht club in Seattle. But most were close-ups, even blow-ups, of Nick—some cut from newspapers, a few glossies in black-and-white or color. More amazing, there were also several of Claire, some alone and a few with Nick. At least she *thought* the photos were of the two of them, since they'd been slashed and the words *Whore* and *I Hate You* had been sprayed in red paint across them.

She felt sick to her stomach, but her mind raced. Could DeeDee have a crush on Nick and be angry with him for reprimanding and suspending her? And did she blame Claire? Or was it much worse than that? DeeDee was obviously obsessed with her boss, a man she would never have. But the wild anger in the way these pictures—once, no doubt, dearly cherished—were hacked suggested something far sicker and more deadly than a crush.

Perhaps DeeDee had been stalking Nick or Claire, or both. If so, what else had she seen or done? Claire quickly glanced at her watch. It was nearly five-thirty. So where was DeeDee now?

Nick felt exhausted and frustrated as he left his office at half past five. He had questioned Anne Cunningham for over an hour, but she hadn't budged from the story she'd told Claire, so he had allowed her to go home. Anne *had* admitted readily, if privately, that she and Noah Markwood had had an affair. It had ended badly, she'd said. Noah had been overly possessive, and she didn't want her name linked with his. But she'd never had an affair with Keith, she insisted, though Noah had accused her of it.

Nick had tried to rattle her by using Claire's deduction that it was impossible for Keith to have heard Anne's car so close to the falls, but she'd claimed she was only repeating what Keith had told her. If that was a lie, she'd said defiantly, Nick might as well blame a dead man, one she mourned but had neither slept with nor harmed.

Nick felt so depressed as he got in his car to head home that he did the one thing that often lifted his spirits. He drove to see the only "she" who had never let him down: the twenty-year-old mistress he'd been in love with for years. She was expensive and high maintenance, but she was worth it.

As he pulled into the airport, he yearned to escape with her. After a hard day's work, his beloved Cessna 206 Amphib waited his arrival patiently, sitting quietly in her blocks for his key to turn in her door.

Nick ignored the gentle rain as he parked and strode across the tarmac toward her. Her body was sleek and shiny, her contrasting hues of burgundy and white as crisp and sharp as ever. Her cabin sat ten feet in the air. Though she'd been built in 1982, she was a real workhorse. His continued care and constant checkups had kept her healthy and ready for anything he needed.

He took his usual proprietary walk around her, thinking that, despite the cost of fuel, he might just take her up for a dance through the evening clouds and mist. He had named her *Susan* long ago, though his wife had not really liked flying and he was sometimes tempted to rename the plane something romantic, like *Sky Dancer* or *Wind Wings*.

He recalled that Claire had said she loved to fly, that her father had taken her up. He'd hardly known his own dad, a fighter pilot who'd died in the Korean War, and his grandfather had filled that hole in his life. Someday, after all this was over, maybe he could take Claire up for a ride. Still thinking of Claire, he patted the plane's tail.

Then he saw the huge graffiti painted—no, scratched—into her side.

He swore. Some jackass had scratched a huge, crude heart in the plane's finish and had drawn an arrow through that. No, it looked more like a dagger piercing the heart. Didn't they have any damn security around here? This didn't seem like the usual kid-vandalism stuff.

He made himself stand still and take several slow breaths, trying to compose himself. He decided that he was going to personally bust whoever was harassing and hurting Claire—even though he was too emotionally engrossed with the search, even though he had disciplined his staff for getting overly involved with civilians, and even though that always meant big trouble. Because if he could want to beat someone into the ground for simply defacing his plane, he finally grasped how desperate Claire must be to find who killed Keith.

The evening birthed mist, fog and night as Claire drove carefully into town to find Nick. She wasn't certain he'd take her call after their argument. He'd told her to stay put; over and over, he'd told her to keep out of things, but she hadn't. Now she had to explain to him about DeeDee, then have him look in her apartment. And he had to get the young woman some help, before DeeDee did something else with her knife.

Claire jerked so hard she almost steered off the street when she realized that DeeDee could be behind the terrors she had faced lately. DeeDee had seen her and Nick together, and could have misunderstood why. Thinking that DeeDee had left that deer carcass and bones was a stretch, but then, the girl had been full of surprises. She could have had access to Nick's Taser guns, too, even while on disciplinary leave.

Claire began to shake all over. She had actually intended to ask DeeDee to move in with her. Once again, she'd been an idiot at reading people—but then, Nick hadn't done too well with that, either. And why had DeeDee pulled that incident report of Keith's being caught with Anne? Surely, not to protect the feelings of the woman whose photos she'd slashed. That was one of the first questions Claire would ask her, except that she was going to do things right this time. She was going to let Nick handle it.

* * *

"If you're looking for the boss, he's been gone at least ten minutes," Aaron told Claire, meeting her coming into the sheriff's office as he was heading out. "Peggy can phone him for you if it's important," he offered, indicating the white-haired woman at the dispatcher desk DeeDee had used.

Claire figured she'd better not tell Nick's co-workers he'd given her his private cell phone number. And she didn't want to let anyone else know what was going on with DeeDee unless Nick okayed it first.

"No, thanks, Officer Curtis. That's all right," she told him, deciding to call Nick on her own. She headed back toward DeeDee's but stopped at the edge of her neighborhood. Turning on her map light in the car, she punched in his cell phone number. This is crazy, she thought, calling the sheriff's personal number for police backup.

"Eagle One here," Nick answered, sounding so angry she almost hung up.

"Nick, it's Claire. I know you told me to stay home, but you've got to meet me at DeeDee's apartment. I think she could be dangerous—for both of us."

"She didn't deface your car or the lodge, did she?"

"I don't think so, but you should see her bedroom. Wait—how did you know she defaced her things?"

"Her things? Someone's scratched up *my* plane, that's all I know, and I'm just trying to put two and two together. I've seen her doodle hearts like this one, though there's a dagger through it this time. I can't believe she's this mad at me. If she thinks I won't file charges for this, she's nuts.''

"She may be. She's got photos of both of us at her place, all cut up and covered with words in red paint, like blood, which—Nick, are you there?''

Not only had the line gone dead, but she was certain she'd heard a *thud* and a grunt before it did.

Claire drove to the airport so fast she didn't dare take her hands off the wheel to call 911. She burst into the D.B. Café because she didn't know where else to go.

"Does anyone know where Sheriff Braden keeps his plane?'' she shouted.

Several guys at the counter turned to stare at her. The counter man, who looked Native American, pointed out the window. "Third plane in that line of 'em,'' he said, and started singing "Come Fly With Me,'' evidently to tease her, as she tore back outside and around the building.

As she ran, she punched in 911, then cut it off before it rang. Nick would kill her for bringing his people here if they'd simply been cut off and he was fine. She vowed that if she found him safe, she would promise to never interfere in police business again.

For one moment, she actually thought she heard the roar of the falls, even here. But no, it was a small plane that pivoted to take the runway. Its headlights slashed across the wet tarmac, silhouetting two figures huddled under the parked plane that must be Nick's.

Claire skidded to a stop and hunkered down behind the tail of a nearby plane. Nick was sprawled out on the cement, and someone—DeeDee—sat holding his head and shoulders in her lap.

Claire froze, uncertain of what to do. What if DeeDee had hurt Nick? Stabbed or cut him? What if she'd been the one to use the Taser on Claire and now she'd shot Nick with it? The mere memory of that wrenching pain racked Claire with fear. But she had to help him. He was unconscious, drugged, hurt or worse. She could not underestimate the girl's explosive hatred.

She did not dare to try to accost her or talk her out of whatever she had in mind. How wrong she had been in thinking she could help DeeDee. But she hadn't then seen the depths of the young woman's sickness. Nick must not have had a clue that he'd been the object of his employee's warped affections, surely for longer than Claire had known her.

Feeling as if she were watching someone else in a movie, Claire pocketed her cell phone and took off her white jacket, leaving both in a little pile under the plane. Her dark jeans and sweater would provide camouflage.

Carefully, slowly, she edged away from her cover, then darted to the back of the closest pontoon under Nick's plane. She did not want to chance drawing DeeDee's attention if she glanced up from cuddling Nick. DeeDee weighed nearly twice as much as she, Claire judged; she needed the element of surprise.

As Claire tiptoed toward DeeDee, she could hear the woman humming. DeeDee swayed slightly, evidently rocking Nick in her arms, and she pressed a handkerchief to his forehead.

Claire saw DeeDee's camera behind her on the

pavement. It must have a flash. She shuffled closer, not breathing now, and reached for the camera, hoping she could handle it despite its unfamiliarity. It had a zoom lens and a strobe.

Just then, DeeDee turned her head and gasped.

"You! You turned him against me, but you can't have him!"

It took DeeDee a moment to lay Nick carefully down before she turned and lumbered to her feet. Claire found the button for the strobe and pressed it just as DeeDee lunged at her.

DeeDee was not only heavier but slower, too. The flash went off, partially blinding her. But she had a knife in her raised hand. She swung it blindly in an arc toward Claire, missing her, then advancing with it again.

"DeeDee, it isn't what you think between Nick and me."

"Nick this, Nick that! You're the reason he let me go from work!"

"He's ready to take you back."

"He didn't see what hit him just now. He was on the phone to you, saying I was nuts. I've been here other times, waiting for him. You were on the phone, turning him against me again," she cried. She leaned down, and Claire thought she was checking on Nick again. But then DeeDee came at her, swinging a triangular piece of wood on a chain.

One of the plane's wheel blocks! It whooshed so close to Claire's face it fanned her hair.

"Nick! Nick!" Claire screamed, risking a ploy. "Thank heavens you're all right."

Though he didn't budge, DeeDee turned around to look at him. Claire rushed her, shoving hard. She toppled over Nick's prone form and rolled. The wheel block hit the tarmac with a clap, its chain rattling. Screaming for help, Claire lifted it, awkwardly swinging the heavy thing back and forth to keep DeeDee at bay. One man came running from inside and then another.

"Hold her down!" Claire cried to them as she dropped the wheel block and ran to Nick. "She tried to hurt the sheriff. Call 911! My phone's over there under that next plane—in the white jacket."

"What…who's screaming?" Nick muttered when she pressed her fingers to the pulse on the side of his neck. His forehead was bloody under the handkerchief pressed to it. Surely DeeDee hadn't cut him? It looked more like he'd fallen against something. No, she must have hit him with the wheel block.

"Oh, thank God you're all right," Claire cried, though DeeDee was shouting loudly. "Just lie still and don't talk," Claire ordered. "I thought you weren't breathing at first."

"And you were going to give me mouth-to-mouth? Fine with me."

Was he delirious? Surely he wasn't kidding at a time like this. She saw him suddenly focus his gaze and take in his surroundings. He turned his head toward DeeDee and frowned.

He lifted his head and shoulders. "Nick, stay down," Claire ordered, but he struggled to sit, leaning heavily against her. Trying to help, Claire propped him against her knees. DeeDee shouted and shrieked, but one man held her while the other called for help on Claire's cell phone.

"Then, she didn't cut or stab you?" Claire asked,

running her hand down the ridges of his chest and stomach, over his shoulders and back, praying she wouldn't find blood. "She had a knife."

"No. I had no idea she was so...sick. I shouldn't have given you hell for not picking up on Keith and Anne, because I never picked up on DeeDee, either. Damn."

"Don't talk."

"She's got a lot to answer for," he went on, as if she hadn't spoken.

She recalled hearing that some victims of head injuries talked incessantly. At least he didn't have amnesia.

"And she might have seen something that will help us with whoever's after you," he said. "It can't just be her, and she couldn't have been the one who killed Keith, I think—or I would, if my head didn't hurt too much to think."

Who killed Keith. The words echoed in Claire's brain. Nick believed her and evidently knew she hadn't harmed Keith. They could work together on this now.

"Oh, my aching head," he said, his face distorted in a frown. "I'm gonna have to go get checked for a concussion and give DeeDee her Miranda rights. After all you've done here, I could let you make a citizen's arrest."

They could hear a single siren in the distance, getting loud enough to rival DeeDee's screams and sobs. Claire saw the man who'd made the call pick up her knife from the tarmac.

"Be careful not to get your prints on that," she told him.

"You tell them, Deputy," Nick muttered.

15

When Claire opened the door to welcome the Nances the next day, she couldn't believe that her phone started ringing at the very same moment. "I'm so glad you're here," she told them as she quickly hugged each in turn and gestured them in.

Though they were dressed casually, they looked chic. The power couple goes camping, Claire thought. Neither of them ever had a hair out of place, his silver, hers sleek ebony, and both were slender like matching bookends. Their black leather jackets were even coordinated, down to the oversize zippers. Looking as efficient as an airline attendant, Diana was wheeling a Vuitton overnighter, while Ethan walked in with just his laptop.

"Oh, no." Claire pretended to scold him. "You're going to relax while you're here, not keep checking the ChinPak stocks."

"Howard Chin and I don't ever intend to apologize for that," Ethan told her. "But you'd better answer your phone. You're running a business here now, too, you know."

"My answering machine should just pick it up," she said, but she dashed to the kitchen phone anyway.

It could be Nick. She'd already spoken with him once today. After he'd had stitches in the emergency room, he'd been up all night at home to be certain his concussion didn't lead to something worse. This morning, he'd obtained a search warrant and looked around DeeDee's apartment. It would be this afternoon, he'd said, before he could question her. He'd booked her on assault and kept her in jail overnight. She'd refused to call a lawyer and had waived her rights, though Nick was going to get a lawyer for her as soon as he questioned her. Meanwhile, he had called in a consulting psychologist who should be arriving soon from Seattle.

Though he'd told her all this in a calm voice, Claire could tell Nick was seething, at himself as much as at DeeDee. Though he hadn't quite said so, she figured he was trying to hide a crisis of confidence—she was now an expert at recognizing that—over being taken in by DeeDee.

"Hello."

"Claire, it's me. Just wanted to know how you're doing."

Her father. She gripped the phone, trying to focus. She badly wanted to be in the other room when Ethan and Diana first saw what they'd done with the lodge to showcase its view of the setting.

"Dad, thanks for calling again. I'm—I'm just fine."

"You don't sound like it."

"Fine under the circumstances."

"Decide to sell that place yet? You could move back to San Diego."

"No, I really don't think so. For the time being, I'm going to open the lodge and stay here. I can't wait to get back to my oil painting, and an art store here is carrying some of my work."

"You got art talent from your mother, just like your good looks."

Claire gripped the phone harder. It was exactly her resemblance to her mother, Claire used to think, that had made him not want her around, as if she reminded him of his failure, of both their failures. At least he mentioned her mother these days.

"Oh, Ethan, isn't it just breathtaking!" Diana cried from the other room.

"Now, I don't want you to get down," her father said.

"New widows get down, Dad, especially considering that some people believe Keith killed himself. But I can't accept that." She had no intention of listing the reasons right now, any more than she planned to burden the Nances with all her troubles during their visit.

"I understand that, Claire. Really. But don't you go doing something stupid like your mother did. Like Keith evidently did."

Wasn't he listening to her? The man had more or less quit looking at her and talking to her after her mother died. He'd never really known Keith, and had seen the two of them no more than five times in the ten years they'd been married. But he might be trying to make amends now.

"Dad, I'm not alone in this. The local sheriff is helping me look into things."

"I heard voices in the background. He there now?"

"It's a couple from Seattle, friends of ours."

"Don't want to keep you, then. Just remember what I said, that you can come home."

"Dad, no offense, but home is here now. Thanks

for the call, and the flowers at the funeral. Is your dialysis coming along all right?''

"It's working. I'll probably get on the kidney transplant list, pull a few strings with my cronies at the hospital if I have to. My young family would get me some points.''

"Give them my best. Maybe I can have the kids here for a summer vacation, fishing and seeing the area. There's a raw beauty here with the falls so close...."

When they'd said their goodbyes, she rushed to the Nances, who'd gone out on the deck. Ethan was pointing out salmon leaping over rocks.

"Sorry, but that was my father in San Diego,'' Claire explained. "He tried to pretend I didn't exist after my mother died. But he's remarried now and has two middle-school-aged kids, and I think he's trying to mend bridges.''

"That's right,'' Diana said, turning to put her hand on Claire's arm, "I remember. Your mother committed suicide, too, didn't she?''

Claire nodded, though, as she had with her father, she wanted to argue that Keith had not killed himself. She'd probably scare them away if she described skinned deer, bones, shamans and getting zapped with a Taser gun, let alone the mess with DeeDee. At least that was over now.

"I can't recall,'' Ethan said, still watching the river, "what business your father was in.''

"Charles B. White, M.D., is still a practicing pediatrician,'' she said, recalling how proud her father had always been of his medical degree. "He's taken two younger doctors into his practice now, since he's had kidney problems. He's good with kids, at least ones who aren't his,'' she added, trying to keep the bitterness from her voice. "His answer to problems when my mother got depressed or I acted up was to send us to a psychiatrist, a Dr. Clarence White—no relation. I used to think Dad chose the man for his name. Anyway, neither that Dr. White nor my father obviously helped my mother a bit, since she still took her life.'' Unshed tears soaked Claire's lashes and she looked away.

Diana gave Claire a hearty hug while Ethan patted her back. "Come on, now, why don't you show us the rest of the lodge,'' Diana suggested, "because what we've seen so far is absolutely gorgeous. I've brought my camera and I intend to take some photos to send to my father's friend who's remodeling in the Cascades. I know he'll want you to do his place with the same flair you've used here. And I'd love to get a photo of that old man I saw down by the river. He looked Native. He was there a moment ago, but it seems like he's just disappeared.''

Claire's head snapped around as she scanned the area. Several men in waders fished in the shallow rapids but no Sam. "That's a fishing friend of Keith's, Sam Twoclaws,'' she explained.

"A friend?'' Diana said. "Not to haul out a Hollywood Indian stereotype, but I thought he looked—well, hostile.''

"DeeDee, I've asked both Aaron and Dr. Miles to sit in while we talk about what happened last night—and why.''

Nick began the interrogation in his office just after lunchtime. He tried to keep his tone calm and conversational, although it was a battle. He was furious that DeeDee had conned him into thinking she was normal and helpful. Hell, when would he ever learn to psych out what women were really thinking? He was a lousy law enforcement officer if he couldn't read people better than that.

Dr. Lillian Miles was a young state psychologist with a perpetually worried look but unruffled demeanor. Both she and Aaron sat slightly behind DeeDee, so that unless DeeDee turned around, it would seem as if just the two of them were talking here, as they'd done in better times.

"I don't want them here any more than I do a lawyer," she said stubbornly, slouched in a chair across his desk with her arms crossed.

She still wore dark, scuffed jeans and a black T-shirt that she'd had on at the airport last night, though he'd had Mike Woods take her belt and shoelaces. Mike had kept her under a watch last night. People didn't need to jump off a bridge to kill themselves, and the real DeeDee had already shocked him once.

Nick was relieved she had not asked for a lawyer, though he was going to get her one after this initial interview. To safeguard his own rights, he'd not only Mirandized her verbally and in writing but had had her sign a statement saying she didn't want or need a lawyer. He was not going to make a mistake in proceeding to get her both prosecuted and treated. Besides, DeeDee might be able to throw some light on who'd been harassing Claire. He was starting to think that if DeeDee could slash and smear photos, carry a knife and clobber him with a wheel block, she also could have been the one after Claire. Could

there be some connection between DeeDee and what
had happened to Keith?

He pushed his chair from behind the desk to sit
facing her. He'd decided to go with the good-cop
approach, without a barrier: no sitting behind a desk
or perching on it to look down on her. Yet he wanted
her to understand how serious this was.

"I'll talk to you alone or not at all," DeeDee insisted with a toss of her head toward the doctor and
deputy.

"You're not making the rules here. I am."

"So what's new?" she muttered.

"You could have killed me last night, that's
what's new."

"I didn't mean to hurt you," she said, fidgeting
in her chair. She studied his bandaged forehead and
black-and-blue eyes. "But you've been spending too
much time talking to her and running to her—*et cetera*—at her lodge," she added, "and I finally lost
my temper."

"Let's just focus on you and your actions, not
Claire's," Nick said. "This morning I saw your
unique photo gallery, which proves you've been following me much longer than I've even known Claire
Malvern. You want to tell me why the collection
exists—and why it was sliced up and splattered with
what looked like blood?"

"It was spray paint, Sheriff. But you never knew,
did you?"

"That you were a party of one in my secret fan
club?"

"You're the sheriff, and you didn't know you had
a stalker," she goaded. "I mean, you might be good
at solving crimes, but you couldn't see the forest for

the trees on this one, could you? That's because it had to do with matters of the heart and you're blind to that. So—are you going to try to charge me with stalking and assault?''

''Yeah,'' he said in a clipped tone, ''I'm planning to charge my dispatcher and once-trusted staffer with stalking and multiple counts of assault—unless I can prove more.''

''Assault on you or on her?'' she demanded. ''She attacked me first last night.'' Shifting in her chair again, she added, ''What *more* are you talking about?''

''All those pictures of the lodge are proof you were more or less a Peeping Tom there. Since you obviously had it in for Claire when you pretended to be helping her, what strange events have you seen going on at the lodge? Or,'' he said, emphasizing each word, ''how much have you done yourself?''

DeeDee sat wide-eyed and silent for a moment, then shouted, ''I saw her go upstairs ahead of you, and you turn off all the downstairs lights so you could go spend Thursday night in her bed!''

''Stop trying to make this about me. You only saw her go upstairs and me turn off all the lights, and you imagined the rest, wanted to picture the rest, evidently wanted to be in on the rest. I slept on her couch. She needed the protection because someone had shot her with a Taser—maybe the one you have access to in our armory here.''

''One of ours?'' Aaron blurted. A look from Nick silenced him.

''So unless you want to be charged with second-degree assault and stalking two people,'' Nick plunged on, glaring at DeeDee again, ''and I'm sure

I could find a few other things to throw in—you'd better start giving me chapter and verse.''

''All right,'' she said, sniffling until the psychologist handed her a tissue, ''I'll tell you a few things, since *you* were so obsessed with her you couldn't pick them up yourself.''

Though that made his head throb more than it already had been, Nick nodded. He had to be careful that he, and not this screwed-up woman, was controlling the interview. He was shaken that he'd been led on and deceived, first by his wife and now DeeDee. And that he hadn't realized that either woman was sick, Susan physically and DeeDee emotionally.

But Claire was a woman he could trust, protect and help. He'd failed before, but he couldn't fail with Claire.

''Oh, how exciting!'' Diana cried as the two of them stood admiring one of Claire's oil paintings in the window of Noah Markwood's Puget Treasures. They'd had lunch and left Ethan behind to enjoy the lodge. ''I'm going to buy that,'' Diana added. ''I have the perfect place for it.''

''I'll do another one for you, compliments of the artist. After all you two have done for me, you don't need to pay for one of my paintings,'' Claire told her.

''No, I'm buying it, though I can't believe you did it of the bridge. It is *the* bridge, isn't it?''

''Yes, but it was done before Keith died. He's the one who took my work to Noah Markwood as a surprise for me.''

''Well, there's another thing you could do besides

running a fishing lodge where you'd have to put up with men day and night, ones who think they can order you around as if you're a short-order cook or a maid. You could travel to paint scenes of the coast or the Cascades. But I think your real talents lie in decorating. You've done a fantastic job with the lodge, but I believe I told you that before," Diana said, linking her arm in Claire's and drawing her toward the door of the shop.

Noah Markwood greeted them and showed them around. Claire's first instinct was to ask to speak to him in the back room and grill him about whether he'd had an affair with Anne. But she'd promised herself and Nick that she would let him do the police work, so she kept her mouth shut and let Diana take over.

"Claire mentioned you have a Tang dynasty horse," Diana said to Noah after she'd admired much of his scrimshaw and selected an ivory whale's tooth with a carving of a frigate for Ethan.

"Ah," Noah said, lighting up, "you must be connected with the Chinese art import company Claire's late husband worked for."

The two of them went off on a tangent, discussing emperors and dynasties, while Claire examined the newer items of Native American scrimshaw she hadn't seen before. A bone carving, marked with a card which said *Sammamish Artist, Sam Twoclaws,* portrayed a deer, staring straight ahead. Claire shuddered and moved on.

She joined the two of them as Diana was examining the ivory Tang dynasty horse. "Originally a drinking vessel," Noah was saying, looking as proud as if he'd carved it himself.

"Its legs have probably remained in such good shape because of this lovely square base it's on," Diana said. "The whole thing's such a combination of sturdiness and delicacy." She turned it over and studied the bottom of the base. "Would you measure this for me?" she asked Noah. "I'm thinking it's about four inches square."

"That's exactly its dimensions," he assured her. "They never signed them there, though," he added when she continued to hold the horse upside down.

"Oh, I know. I'll take it, as well as the scrimshaw and Claire's lovely painting. Our company has imported several bronze elephant drinking vessels, but never one with a base."

Nick wanted to cover all the bases with DeeDee. He raked his fingers through his hair, but yanked his hand back down when he hit his bandage. "You've always helped me before, DeeDee," he said, trying a less adversarial tone. She'd challenged him in "matters of the heart," so he'd just see if he could use that on her. "I need your help with this now."

"Until *she* came along, I helped you all the time. I practically killed myself doing a good job here."

"You did do a good job."

Her expression visibly softened. The emotional power he had over her amazed him.

"I do realize," she said, finally uncrossing her arms, "that by always keeping an eye on you, I was being overly protective."

"When you weren't able to personally keep an eye on me, did you ever phone my house?" Nick asked.

"Only once, because that's kiddie stuff. When you

went out on that yacht with her, I couldn't follow and I didn't know how long you'd be gone. I could hardly hang around the yacht club or sit out in front of your house waiting for you, because I figured you'd spot me. So I drove back home and just called your number every ten minutes until you answered. Then I knew you were back safe.''

"Okay. Let's switch topics for a minute. Did you ever go through Claire's garbage?''

"Her garbage? No way. Why would I? Looking for some love note you sent?''

"I never sent her a love note, DeeDee. See, I'm answering questions here today, too. So, did you ever take any oil paintings—art of the bridge and river—from a shed on her property?''

"I don't want her stuff, garbage or art! But I admit I saw some of her paintings when she showed me around the lodge. Those and a bunch of dead fish on the wall.''

Surely, she couldn't be making a joke, he thought. He decided to move on. "Why did you really pull and destroy that IR report of Aaron's code nine on Anne Cunningham's vehicle when Keith Malvern was with her?''

Though he thought he'd had her on a roll, DeeDee hesitated. "Because,'' she said, her voice low, "I didn't want her to think her husband was cheating on her.''

"Come on, now. You were hardly trying to help Claire in all this.''

"Your problem is you don't know how women think!'' DeeDee shouted so loud that Dr. Miles put a restraining hand on her shoulder. "I didn't want to give her any reason to resent her dead husband. If she knew he'd had an affair, she'd be more likely to turn to you for more than just help in solving his death. She needed to keep an idealized view of him, but she's a fool, just like I've been. And so are you! She's got you caught, just like—like that crazy old Sam Twoclaws traps those salmon on the river!''

Both Claire and Diana were excited to show Ethan the purchases when they got back to the lodge. They found him sitting at the desk in the upstairs office, his small laptop next to Keith's larger desktop, busy working rather than enjoying the lodge or scenery it overlooked.

''E-tha-ann!'' Diana drawled, hands on her hips. ''There's a beautiful world out those huge windows.''

''That's all right,'' Claire said. ''I'll serve drinks and appetizers on the table right by the windows so we can all enjoy the view.''

''Hey, I've been outside for a walk!'' Ethan protested, stretching his arms over his head. ''I've been watching some guys down the way hook big salmon.''

''Wait until you see this!'' Diana crowed when they all trooped back downstairs and Claire brought wine and goblets to the table. ''Ta-da!'' She produced the Tang horse, which Ethan unwrapped rather cautiously, as if he expected it to be bone china or crystal.

''It's fantastic!'' he said, admiring it from every angle. As Diana had done, he checked for signatures on the bottom of the base. ''What detail and proportions, and it's just the right size. Did the seller know when it was excavated?''

"Recently," Diana said. "The Chinese had sent it to Hong Kong, and it was originally purchased with permission of the Chinese government, just like at the company."

"But surely," Claire put in, "those delicate porcelain vases on lacquer stands that Chin Pacific deals in were not buried for centuries. This horse might last underground, but surely not the porcelain, at least not intact."

"True, but many of our artifacts were sealed in tombs," Ethan explained. "Our sources have made some major, fantastic finds lately, many decorated with the forms of beasts and grotesqueries. The ancient Chinese used to believe that items like these accompanied the souls of the prominent and powerful into the next world, you know."

"Like the ancient Egyptians," Claire commented. "In some cultures, death is the great preserver of what they loved in life."

She was fascinated and grateful Ethan was sharing such things, but felt annoyed at Keith. He had seldom talked about his work at Chin Pacific. Once, when she began to ask a lot of questions, he'd said that he just didn't like to take his work home with him. Even when he'd talked about his trips to China and Hong Kong with Ethan, he'd sounded like a generic tour director.

"Very similar to the Egyptians," Ethan was saying. "And like some local Native tribes, I understand."

Claire pictured Sam trying to preserve animals' bodies and spirits with his own beast and grotesquery carvings and mountings. Nick had questioned Sam a second time about the terrible tableau someone had left on her back deck, but he'd told Nick he had nothing new to add. Maybe she should talk to Sam again, at least about whether or not he thought Keith was depressed, which was exactly where she'd like to steer this conversation with Ethan.

"The northern Chinese peoples tended to bury objects for protection—figures of soldiers and weapons," Ethan went on, "while the southern people buried items for their afterlife pleasure. Protection or pleasure, quite a dichotomy, but both desperately needed and desired." An enigmatic smile played on his lips. "We Americans manage to have the best of both worlds today."

He lifted his wine in a toast, and Diana quickly clinked all their glasses.

"If people want to stay private, they should not live in glass houses, if you know what I mean," DeeDee insisted. "Yeah, I saw a couple of crazy things going on at her lodge. But the truth is, I was making sure you were okay, Nick, because you work too hard. I was never following her."

"Saw crazy things at the lodge? Such as?" Nick said, trying to cut through all the emotional stuff DeeDee larded into every answer.

"Sam Twoclaws. I saw him once walking by, and he scared me, but I just hid."

"Did he see you?"

"I don't think so. He kept going."

"When was this?"

"Uh, September 5, the night Keith Malvern turned up missing, when she phoned for help and you took the call yourself. I was sitting in the airport parking lot, watching your car, but got tired of waiting for you to come back. So I went home to monitor the dispatcher frequency and heard Peggy give you the information—and how you were only too happy to take the call. Are you sure you hadn't met her up-town and seen how pretty she was before that?''

That's right, he had taken that call on the fre-quency without switching to his cell phone that night. It would have been simple for DeeDee to mon-itor the calls; he knew others did it, too, but not for the same kind of thrill. He'd seen her radio monitor in her living room this morning, although since she was a dispatcher, he would not have found that un-usual.

"Was Sam watching the lodge that night, too?" he pursued.

"Just walking by it, I think. I—I saw the two of you through those windows like watching a big-screen TV. I pretended you'd come to help me, not her. All you wanted from me was your sunglasses you left at the office, but I brought you those during the search the next day, didn't I.''

"You did, and I appreciated it. You're really help-ing me right now, too. Were you possibly at the lodge just this last Monday? It was the day Claire visited the office to search our IRs. I was going to fly to Cedar Island that evening.''

"Yes, I was at the lodge then. Since I knew you were leaving the island, I went to spray-paint *whore* all over her place, as a matter of fact.''

Nick swallowed hard. That was the night someone put the bones and dead deer on Claire's deck.

"So why didn't you use the spray paint that night?''

"Two reasons. First, I hated to hurt the lodge,

since it is really pretty. But the real reason was I saw someone dragging something up onto her deck. It turned out to be the grossest thing—a skinned animal and some bones. After he took off, I looked through the zoom lens at the stuff and watched her find it. Then pretty soon you showed up—of course."

"Can you describe the person who put the things there?"

"Not really, and darned if I was getting closer to find out."

"You didn't happen to take a picture through your zoom?"

"Of that icky stuff? No way."

"Can you help me out at least by describing the person?"

"A man, not fat, not thin, wearing a baseball cap. In dark clothes, maybe jeans with a dark jacket."

"Cut, style?"

"It was dark—the night, too, I mean. Not a suit coat, or sport coat. You know, a flannel shirt or something like from L.L. Bean. I suppose it could even have been a woman. Maybe," she added, grinning and leaning forward, "she did it herself, just to get you to come running again, because it sure worked."

"Claire, you've simply got to consider taking this decorating assignment," Diana said as the afternoon stretched on and the three of them still sat at the table with the riverview. "You could stay a day or two at my father's place there and really relax."

"This is pretty relaxing, if you ask me," Ethan said.

"Keith found it so," Claire said, seizing the

chance to steer the conversation her way. "I was wondering," she went on, turning toward Ethan, "why you thought Keith was uptight before he died. Diana mentioned it the other day."

"He always had his ups and down," he said, swirling the last of the wine in his glass. "I think, actually, during the past year or so, he had bouts of malaise. He loved you, he loved his ChinPak job, but he wanted to change his lifestyle—yet he was torn about leaving Seattle and the life he'd built there. To draw the analogy to the ancient Chinese, he was torn about leaving the protection of a good job and the pleasures it afforded. Let's face it, your life here is much more iffy. A new, possibly in-the-red financial endeavor, being self-employed, you know what I mean," he said, encompassing the entire lodge with a sweeping gesture.

"I'm coming to, lately," Claire told him, and once again resisted sharing everything that had happened.

"Keith was like that river out there, Claire," Ethan went on, "deep and turbulent, not all on the surface, you know. He may have hidden it from you, but he could be volatile. Then again, aren't we all?"

"One more thing, DeeDee, and then we'll take a rest," Nick promised.

"How long are you going to keep me in that little holding cell here, anyway?" she asked.

"You'll be going with Dr. Miles to a place in Seattle for a few days."

"Don't tell my mom or sisters—not any of this."

"Your family has a right to know."

"They don't! I'm an adult, and they don't!"

"You've been such a big help here, and I know I can continue to depend on that."

"Don't patronize me. This isn't the Rotary Club or the PTA, Sheriff Nicholas Braden. I know you, remember?"

"Then I hope you realize how much I need your help here. Were you near the lodge on September 14, two days ago, about dusk?"

"That was the night you finally flew to Cedar Island, because you thought she wouldn't need you— but she did. No, I did not sneak into the armory here and get a Taser gun and shoot her. That's the next question, isn't it? I had no idea she'd been shot. I wasn't there. I was at the airport, waiting for you to show up in that plane you care about more than you do any woman—at least, before *she* came along. She's the first woman you've wanted since your wife died, isn't she?"

Before either Aaron or Dr. Miles could grab her, DeeDee thrust herself out of her chair and lunged at Nick. Her weight tilted his chair back. She clung to him, her hot face pressed against his neck, her knees pinning his legs down.

"You didn't even date, I know you didn't!" DeeDee cried. "You were all mine before she started calling for help."

Aaron started to pull the sobbing woman away, but she clung harder. Dr. Miles murmured, "Come on now. The deputy's going to drive us into Seattle. We want to help you, DeeDee. Come on now—"

"I'm sorry," Nick told DeeDee, awkwardly patting her back, though he, too, wanted to pry her loose and shove her away. Despite everything, he did feel sorry for her, and guilty he'd been so wrapped up in his own world that he hadn't realized how messed up she was. "We all—me, too—want you to go get some rest," he added.

The three of them moved DeeDee off him. Aaron went for his wrist cuffs, but Nick shook his head. The deputy and the doctor started to lead the sobbing girl out the door.

"Don't send me away," she pleaded, turning back to Nick, her red cheeks slick with tears. "I bet I can pick the man who left that deer on her deck out of a lineup, and maybe he's the same one who used the Taser gun on her. Just get the suspects lined up, or Mike Woods can take pictures of them, and I can look at them to help you."

He knew she was bluffing, just stalling. He nodded to Aaron who gently pulled DeeDee away. Nick could have cried himself as he closed the door behind them.

16

Claire was grateful she'd slept well the night Ethan and Diana stayed at the lodge, because she couldn't so much as get comfortable the next. She got up numerous times—for a drink of water, to look out the windows, to recheck the locks, to rearrange pillows on the big couch downstairs. What she wouldn't give to have Nick Braden sleeping on it again.

She tried thinking about what a good time she'd had with the Nances, hoping that would relax her. Over dinner, and again at breakfast, they'd talked about happier times. They'd encouraged her in so many ways. She'd enjoyed her solo time with Diana, shopping and sight-seeing. They'd done what amounted to a drive-by visit of the cranberry farm. Tess was evidently still at her mother's, and Joel had been nowhere in sight. Since Anne Cunningham had let Claire down, Diana filled some of that newest void in Claire's life.

One thing that didn't lull her to sleep anymore was the falls, she thought as she peered out her bedroom window. Frequently at night, like now, their noise seemed to swell, louder, louder, making them sound closer and angrier.

But how? Maybe, Claire theorized, it happened when the breeze shifted, or when some other strange quirk of the weather put more mist in the air, so sound carried more easily. It couldn't simply be that more leaves were falling from the trees, so that that noise barrier was lessening. But she was certain of one thing: she'd never heard the volume of the falls vary before Keith died.

She threw on jeans and a sweatshirt and went into the office just outside the bedroom. Yes, the light in here would do. She wasn't going to turn on the interior downstairs lights to paint because someone could look in, even though DeeDee was in Seattle being evaluated at a secure mental facility. Nick had said the girl denied having anything to do with leaving the *Deer Claire* message on her deck or shooting her with the Taser gun. And, though he hated to think that someone else was to blame, he'd said he believed her.

Claire went downstairs in the dark, padded barefoot to the guest rooms and retrieved her easel, paints and a newly stretched canvas. She'd brought them into the lodge in case her art shed was disturbed again, and so she wouldn't have to go outside to get them if the urge to paint hit. With Noah Markwood's request for more paintings to sell, she felt newly inspired.

Claire squeezed paint from the tubes onto her palette to provide an array of blues along with stark black and white. Another reason she couldn't sleep, she admitted to herself, was that she was excited about the offer Diana had phoned with, shortly after she'd returned to Seattle. Claire was invited to drive to the Cascades to consult on the home being redecorated from ultramodern to country casual, and she could spend the night nearby at Diana's father's Xanadu, which she'd always wanted to see.

Diana had said, too, "If you want to talk to someone who's very objective and good at assessing people, you could ask Dad about Keith's moods. Dad had more than one heart-to-heart with him to try to talk him out of leaving the company."

The offer to visit the Cascades was totally tempting. Claire would also earn a fat fee, which she could sink into opening the lodge this spring. Decorating was still dear to her. Nick had encouraged her to go, because he wanted her to get away for a while. He was thinking of setting some sort of trap here for whoever had attacked her with the Taser. Claire knew Nick was seething about that, and it thrilled her to realize he cared about her. But there was no way she would calm herself by thinking about Nick Braden, so instead she would paint until she was tired enough to go back to that mussed, lonely bed and sleep.

As so often happened, Claire felt mesmerized when she painted. Time slipped away; the only falls she heard were those she created on her canvas. Forms emerged from her brush strokes and her palette knife; colors birthed rushing water. She freed the falls to feed the river, creating cascades of water pouring into swirling pools with black depths. When this dried, she'd place the skeletal Bloodroot Bridge arched over them, clinging to bedrock, trying to stand steady.

Claire stepped back to see how the scene looked from a distance. She leaned against the edge of the desk, but jumped when her bottom bumped Keith's keyboard and the plastic keys clicked as if in protest.

Brush and palette still in her hands, she turned to stare down at it. The keyboard had been moved. Keith had never kept it off to the side like that, and she hadn't, either.

"Oh, Ethan moved it to use his laptop," she said aloud, but she wasn't sure why, since he'd had plenty of room for his machine beside this one.

Claire cleaned her brush and hands with a rag and turpentine. If she heard the falls even when she visited the Cascades, she told herself, she'd have Nick get her committed to that psychiatric hospital right along with poor DeeDee.

On Monday morning, as soon as he got into work, Nick called Claire. He had no qualms now about using his duty time to keep an eye on her. DeeDee had done him the favor of making Claire official business, even though he didn't yet have enough proof to open a case file on Keith's death.

"You sound like I woke you up," Nick said, when Claire picked up the phone on the sixth ring. "I was worried you weren't going to answer."

"I didn't get to sleep until about four a.m.," she explained. She sounded as if she were stretching, stifling a yawn. Maybe she was still in bed. He pictured her, tousled and sleepy-eyed amid rumpled sheets. As a jolt of desire shot through him, he sat up straighter at his desk.

"But I got a lot of thinking done," she went on. "I believe I will take Diana up on the invitation to spend a night at her dad's place so I can consult with that potential client."

"The change of scenery will do you good, and it will give me a chance to set up a bait-and-trap at the lodge, like we talked about. At least if I can arrest someone for breaking and entering, we can find out who it is, and get him locked up and out of our lives.''

He was surprised that he'd said *our lives*. Had that been a Freudian slip, and he actually meant their lives together? He wondered if she'd picked up on it.

''Sounds like you're planning to go salmon fishing,'' she said. ''What's the bait going to be if I'm not there?''

''I'm working on it, so I'll let you know. I may have to put it out via the town grapevine that you've found some proof Keith didn't kill himself, maybe something on his computer. By the way, with your permission, I'm going to have a techie who consults for the department search your hard drive for anything you might have missed. They can find some amazing stuff in there that was supposedly deleted or protected. Is that all right with you?''

''Anything to get to the bottom of this.''

''One more thing before I get to work here,'' he told her. Although his office door was closed, he switched the phone to his other ear and talked more quietly. ''I stopped by Noah Markwood's place last night to ask him, no holds barred, about his having had an affair with Anne. He admitted it, and agreed that it ended badly. But he was adamant that she dumped him for someone else she wouldn't name. He was real sure it was Keith. And Noah and Anne's relationship ended shortly after you two came to town.''

''Can we consider Noah as a suspect, or at least

someone hostile to Keith? Maybe he confronted
Keith, and they had words, then..."

"Then what? They agreed to duel over her at
twelve paces on Bloodroot Bridge in the middle of
the night, and Keith fell in? There are too many
missing pieces yet. And by the way, I heard that little
comment you slid in there. 'Can *we* consider him a
suspect?' Claire, I'm on this now, remember?"

"Of course. That's the way I want it."

"Good. Just so that's understood. Is it okay if I
come by around noon to take the desktop? I won't
need the monitor or keyboard. I'll give you a signed
form confirming you gave me consent to search your
property, so it will be official."

"Sure. I'll fix us some lunch—if that isn't too
unofficial."

After he hung up, he smiled at the way she could
still tease. At least lately she'd been willing to back
off from trying to take over the way she had at first.
Then he realized he hadn't warned her to let him
know if Sam came around—and not to be alone with
him. But he'd see her soon and tell her that Sam was
a suspect too.

He checked his e-mail messages and went out to
get his own snail mail from the front desk. DeeDee
had always sorted it and brought it to him. Now he
wondered if she'd ever tampered with it.

Meanwhile, he was out not only his daytime dispatcher, but a part-time secretary, so he'd have to get
an ad in the *Portfalls Portfolio* right away. Too bad
it would run in the same issue that would report an
assault on the sheriff by one of his employees, but
that was all public record now anyway.

In the main office, he saw that Peggy, whom he'd

moved to the day shift, was just signing for a courier delivery. "For you, Sheriff," she said, and handed the flat package to him. He took it to his desk, wary because he couldn't figure at first who the return-to-sender name was. He'd always been careful with his mail; it went with the territory. But now he'd become especially suspicious.

It was an overnight delivery from San Diego, from a Dr. Charles B. White. With all that had been going on, he wasn't taking any chances.

Holding it at arm's length, he ripped the cardboard pull-tab and tipped the package upside down so that the contents fell into his empty metal wastebasket while he moved quickly back behind his heavy desk. Nothing, no sound, beyond the soft curl of a paper settling. He stood over the wastebasket again and peered into it. The contents appeared to be only a single paper with a sticky note attached, so he retrieved them.

Sheriff, I understand you're helping Claire Malvern, the note read. *Hope this will help you and her. I'm trusting you not to let her know I sent this, as we've had a rocky relationship and I'm trying to make amends.*

It was signed *Dr. Charles B. White, M.D., Claire's father.*

Nick started to skim the single-spaced paper, but realized he'd have to read it more slowly. It wasn't the original, but a photocopy, because he could see dark edge lines where it had been put slightly unevenly on the copy machine. The top information was typed, but what followed were handwritten notes in a scrawl difficult to read. Nick perused the top text.

PATIENT DIAGNOSIS AND PROGNOSIS:
(MRS.) HELEN WHITE, AGE 38
Date: March 25, 1977
Next of kin: (Dr.) Charles B. White (husband)
Claire White, age 12 (daughter)
Address: 1800 Boca Ciega Dr., San Diego, CA
Diagnosis: Chronic Clinical Depression with periodic dysfunctionality and occasional psychotic delusions

This was about Claire's mother, Nick thought, as he read on, so fascinated and increasingly horrified that he soon began skimming again.

...is so egocentric in her depression, she refuses to accept such symptoms in others, such as in her only child... Patient wants attention from authority figure of husband and prevaricates to attain such...

Very creative and artistic—"Van Gogh" complex?—Outlets include painting whereby she reveals her inner turmoil and also her displacement of blame for her own apparent feelings of guilt or resentment...

Medications include valium, et al...

Final assessment: could become even more unstable if stressed, but husband refuses commitment to mental health facility, insisting outlets of patient's creative expression and love for her daughter keep her functioning at an acceptable level...

Interview with husband suggests he has put subtle pressure on patient to avoid social stigma of commitment to care facility...

Addenda: I theorize such a disease could be inherited, as patient's mother also demonstrated depression and delusions, though lived to age 80 in apparent good health... Possibility of grant monies to study this genetic link?

Nick put his head in his hands. What he read here was not only the tragedy of Claire's mother's mental illness, which must have led to her eventual suicide, but the suggestion Claire could be genetically inclined to be unstable—even suicidal.

Claire fixed Reuben sandwiches for lunch and set the table overlooking the deck. She stood, gazing out at the river as a fretful wind whipped the trees and clouds. One minute sun exploded to gild the scene, the next, clouds threw a dark scrim on everything. The churning river seemed to shift from cobalt blue to inky black as if it were a mirror of the threatening sky. That's what she'd been trying to capture in her latest painting; that was it, exactly.

While she waited for Nick to arrive, Claire checked to see if anything seemed strange on the deck, scanned the river, then darted outside to bring her oil painting back in. She'd put it there earlier, wanting the background to dry completely so she could paint the bridge today. People might think she was crazy for doing this scene repeatedly, but now it seemed more important than ever. It gave her control over the horror of what had happened there. It allowed her to make a potentially lurid place lovely.

But she gasped as she reached for the canvas, which she'd held in place with two bricks, wedging it in against the top step.

The bridge, which she hadn't painted yet, was already in place on the painting. And a man's figure sat on it, his feet dangling over the edge as he leaned forward to gaze into the rush of wild water far below.

"It can't be," she cried. "No!"

She blinked and touched the painting. The background blues were dry but the iron bridge and the figure smeared against her finger, downward, as if the sitter had jumped in a big, black blur.

"But I didn't...no!"

Claire ran inside and locked the sliding door behind her, then held the painting up to study it more closely. Yes, the background looked like hers, at least more or less what she'd painted last night. She knew for certain it was not one of the canvases Noah had displayed in his shop, nor the one Diana had bought, somehow doctored up. Could this be one of the paintings taken from her shed, with the added taunt of Keith—if it was supposed to be him—sitting on the bridge?

Claire dashed upstairs with the painting, uncertain whether or not to show it to Nick when he arrived. Surely, surely, she hadn't painted the bridge and man herself on that canvas, however exhausted and zoned out she'd been last night.

She checked the rag with which she'd wiped her brushes and found only small traces of dark paint. She had used it only to give depth to the river and its whirlpools, not for an entire bridge. If she had painted the bridge, there would surely be more black paint on this rag.

Her heart began to pound so hard it shook her body. This was no blatant assault with skinned deer or crossed bones. This was no high-tech Taser attack.

Its finesse was far more frightening because it struck at her very mind, heart and soul.

Claire's stomach was in knots as she let Nick in the front door. Even the way his taut mouth tilted into the hint of a smile didn't help. She was not sure whether to tell him about the altered painting. It seemed all she did was dump crazy crises on him. But if she was going to trust him, it had to be all the way.

He looked worried. Perhaps, after the shock and sadness of DeeDee's illness, he hadn't been sleeping either. His cheeks seemed shadowed and his eyes bloodshot, which hardly helped the black and blue around them and his bruised forehead, where a big, flesh-colored Band-Aid covered his stitches. She felt guilty that he'd been beaten up because he'd started helping her.

"Hey, I appreciate the lunch," he said.

She gestured toward the table, but he said, "Mind if I go up and get the desktop computer first? Here's the form to sign."

"Sure," she said, and followed him upstairs. He was going to see her painting now, anyway, as she'd left it on the easel.

"I see you're painting again," he said. "Did you inherit artistic talent?"

"My mother loved to paint still lifes of all kinds," she said. "As you can see, there's nothing still in mine. She claimed she wasn't good at doing faces or people, and I guess I'm not, either. Obviously, outdoor scenes are my thing, though I have been tempted to paint Sam."

"Not until we get all this solved," he insisted.

"Claire, Sam's technically a suspect, too. He's got motive, means, dead deer—the whole nine yards."

"And he's been lurking."

"I told him to stay off your property."

"I'm sure that where my friends and I have seen him is just off the property line, though it scare me to think he knows exactly where those lines are. But on the surface he's been nothing but helpful... I'm sorry to go off on a tangent. Here, I've unhooked the PC from the cables and surge protector."

"But what happened here?" he asked as he pointed to the smeared figure in her painting. He bent closer to it, frowning. "Claire, you painted a man on the bridge, then rubbed him out?" He straightened and stared down at her.

"I didn't do it, Nick. I didn't paint him there, but I did smear the picture when I realized some face-less, nameless enemy out there must have!"

She told him everything she could remember about it. At least, Nick thought, listening to the way she had reasoned it all out, she was observant, log-ical, and seemed totally candid. She had said she'd barely found any black paint on the rag she showed him and little was gone from the new tube of jet black she handed him. Surely it was not a risk—even though he'd failed to read some other women right— to let her help him try to solve this crime. And surely the implications in her mother's psychiatric report, that Claire might have inherited not only artistic abil-ity but instability, must be wrong.

"Claire, I hear you," Nick said, trying to calm her. "You didn't paint the figure in, even though you were exhausted and stressed. I believe you." He rested his hands on her shoulders. She reached up to clasp his wrists.

"I was actually tempted not to tell you, in case you'd think I needed to be hospitalized like DeeDee," she admitted.

He almost told her about the psychiatric report her father had sent him, but the man had trusted him not to, and he should honor that. If Dr. White was trying to make amends with his daughter, maybe he would tell her himself.

Yet one thing in it kept niggling at him: the psychiatrist had mentioned that Claire's mother might have a "Van Gogh" complex. Nick didn't know exactly what that entailed, but he did recall that Van Gogh was an artist of turbulent work. The guy also went off his rocker and killed himself.

"I'm looking forward to my visit to the Cascades while I consult about that decorating assignment," Claire told Nick over lunch. "I've always wanted to see Howard Chin's Xanadu. Do you know what the poem with that name says?"

"Nope. But I know Wordsworth wrote it. I always thought that was a great name for a poet," he said as he took another big bite of sandwich.

"It is, but the poem was written by Wordsworth's opium-addicted friend Coleridge," she said, looking out over the deck at the river as the sun disappeared to dim the scene again.

Despite the fact his mouth was full, Nick laughed. The sound of it was so strong and good, it heartened her, despite all they'd been through. She grinned, too. Their gazes met and held.

"Okay, so English poetry isn't my thing. Let's

hear it. Why did Howard Chin, the rich and powerful mogul of the east, name his place Xanadu?''

''Actually, his parents were Chinese, but he's native-born American,'' she corrected him. ''Anyhow, in the poem, Kubla Khan builds a pleasure dome, a fabulous place, and that's what Howard Chin's done with his retreat. In the poem, Xanadu was built, 'Where Alph, the sacred river, ran through caverns measureless to man down to a sunless sea.' ''

''The sacred river? Sounds like a poem Sam Two-claws could love,'' Nick said, and his expression sobered. ''But are you sure you're up to driving there alone? And venturing near 'measureless' caverns, considering everything that's been going on around here? It may be an escape for you, but if whoever's been rattling you is as dangerous as I'm starting to think, they might just take advantage of your being on your own.''

''But everything's happened in this area. I thought you said the trip was a good idea.''

''I thought it was at first, but I don't like someone lurking around here and repainting your work to show Keith's death. And ever since you got hit with that Taser, I've vowed to find the bastard behind all this.''

Her coffee cup clinked loudly as she set it down in its saucer. ''So you think I should turn down the invitation and the job?''

''No, I think you should let me fly you there and play pilot and bodyguard for you.''

That set her back. Her pulse started to pound.

''Nick, I can't ask you to do that.''

''I didn't hear you asking me. I volunteered. The

only thing is that I can't get away until Saturday. And I haven't been invited to stay there.''

"I'm sure Diana could arrange it. Or better yet, I'll just call Howard Chin directly. Diana gave me his number. I mean, they have six bedrooms, she said, and a separate guest house.''

She felt not only relieved but excited. She hadn't been up in a private plane for years. Her memories of flying were the last happy ones she had of being with her father, before everything went wrong in their lives. And to be away with Nick for two days, away from here, soaring...

"Xanadu, hopefully, here we come," Nick said.

Claire smiled at him as the sun came out again and slanted in the windows to bathe them in golden light. She shoved down any fears she'd had about going to the Cascades. Still, another line from the poem haunted her. However lovely the pleasures of Xanadu, "All who heard should see them there, And all should cry, Beware! Beware!''

"Mr. Chin, thanks for taking my call," Claire said later that day. She'd only met the "Emperor of ChinPak" once and was excited to talk to him.

"My pleasure, Claire. I haven't had the opportunity to offer in person my heartfelt condolences on Keith's loss. Sometimes we just can't understand why dreadful things happen to young, vibrant people like Keith, yes?''

"Yes, thank you so much.''

She'd forgotten that he spoke in clipped, quick phrases. Often his statements sounded like questions. His appearance sprang instantly back into her memory. Keith had introduced them at a dinner about three years ago, before the man had more or less retired.

Howard Chin looked pure Chinese with his narrow eyes, which, she recalled, he narrowed even more when listening to someone. Always impeccably dressed, he was very formal in his actions and manners. Years ago, he'd married Diana's mother, an heiress in San Francisco, but had moved to Seattle to found his art import business. Everyone said he was fabulously rich, though he'd give all his wealth away to have his son back. Tragically, their boy had died young in an accidental drowning at a beach, and Diana was their only heir. So Ethan had evidently become the co-heir apparent of the company when he married her.

"Diana tells me you will be making a visit here soon to help with a redecorating job she's arranged?" he inquired.

"Yes, that's right. At Chuck Matthews's house."

"Ah, our next neighbor, though it's hardly walking distance."

"I *was* going to drive up alone, but I have a friend who pilots his own plane, and he's offered to fly me there."

"Someone from Seattle?"

"No, a friend here. Actually, the county sheriff."

"Yes, fine, bring him along. We'll certainly all sleep better the night he's here, then, won't we?"

Claire forced a little laugh. "I'm hoping to talk to you about what you think Keith was feeling—how he was acting—the last few times you spoke to him, just to settle things in my own mind about what Ethan and Diana saw as his shifting moods. It's so hard to accept his suicide. I so desperately would like to get to the bottom of what happened to him.''

"I'd like to help in any way I can. Considering how sorry we were to lose Keith at ChinPak, I can't begin to fathom how devastated you must be that he's gone from your life. It is most unfortunate.''

There was a moment's silence, but then, indeed, he'd said it all. She wondered if Howard Chin was thinking of his lost son. Claire cleared her throat.

"If it's all right with you, we'll arrive about mid-morning on Saturday," she told him. "It's a pontoon plane, so we could land on a lake or large river, as well as at an airport.''

"Tell your sheriff friend we're overlooking Lake Hemlock, which he can no doubt find on a map of the area, yes? We're the sprawling house with the longest boat dock, and he can pull the plane right up to it.''

"I can't thank you enough. I hope to visit Mr. Matthews Saturday afternoon, and we'll head back on Sunday morning.''

"It will be lovely to see you, Claire. As they say in other cultures, 'My house is your house.' And just call this number if you change your plans or need more help in finding our Xanadu. I think, as an interior decorator, you'll be interested in some of the fantastical effects here.''

"I can't wait to see it. Thank you so much.''

"It's my pleasure. And take care until Saturday.''

17

———————

"I've done the preflight," Nick called to Claire as she walked across the tarmac with her overnight bag, briefcase and coat. "Are you ready to get going?"

"More than ready," she told him as he climbed up to stow her things in back. "It's a gorgeous day."

"Fog may set in around the mountains later, but we'll be there long before that," he told her as he jumped back down. "The *Susan*'s all set, and I've logged in our flight plan."

Claire looked up at the plane, sitting high on her floats and wheels so that the cabin stood at least ten feet off the ground. She watched as Nick removed the wheel blocks, one of which DeeDee had used to knock him out last week. Despite that dreadful memory, amidst so many others, Claire felt lifted above her troubles for the first time in ages.

As she recalled her phone conversation with Howard Chin only five days ago, his final words seemed prophetic. *Take care of yourself until Saturday.* She had done exactly that this week. Nothing out of the ordinary had occurred at the lodge, so she'd gotten back to business there. She had sold Keith's truck, had kept on with her painting and was beginning to sleep better. She had added some final touches to the lodge and had completed the complex and sad task of finishing the paperwork associated with Keith's death. And she had prayed every night that whoever had been tormenting her had now decided, for whatever reason, to lay off.

Claire felt Nick had made some progress this week on looking into Keith's past, though he called what he found negative evidence, or "no news is news," as he put it. A close examination of Keith's computer had turned up nothing suspicious, not even deleted e-mail correspondence with Anne, which was what Claire had been expecting at the least. Nick had called in a favor at the phone company so he wouldn't have to justify a subpoena to search Keith's long-distance phone calls from a database. That, too, had turned up nothing unusual. As for her, she'd called Sam Twoclaws four times to talk to him, but hadn't found him at home nor seen him on the river.

"Up you go," Nick said, and gave her a boost to the first step. "I usually have a box for guests to step on, but there's no one on the tarmac right now to take it away when we taxi out."

Claire felt very aware of the view she afforded Nick as she climbed up into her seat just ahead of him. His impact on her was always immediate and intense. She felt as if he'd hugged her hard instead of just touching her or looking at her.

Nick climbed up into his seat. All business now, he checked her seat belt, fastened his, and put on his radio earphones. He donned his reflective aviator sunglasses. As he turned the key to start the engine, she watched him scan the instrument panel. It looked like a scramble of dials and gauges to her.

The *Susan* began to move. Nick taxied them out onto the tarmac toward the single, short runway.

They would be taking off directly over the cove and Puget Sound.

"Cessna three-six-five-fiver," Nick said. "Port-falls Tower, taxi for a west?"

"Uh—roger, three-six-five-fiver" came the reply. "Cleared for takeoff west. Have a good day, Sher-iff."

"Throttle up," Nick whispered, whether to him-self or her she wasn't sure. The plane began to vi-brate, and the engine noise increased. At least, Claire told herself, stifling a smug grin, with the excitement of flying, Nick would not know his mere closeness made her jittery.

She held her breath a moment, wondering if she'd imagine she could hear the falls even up here. No, she decided, she was just fine. And she settled back to enjoy the flight.

Nick glanced at the instrument panel. Fuel flow and oil pressure looked good, but nothing could stop this baby. The roar of the engines increased. He pow-ered up and gathered speed. His heart soared as they lifted off; it was almost a sexual thrill.

His gaze slid over to Claire's legs, her thighs pressed together. Wearing a red, down-filled vest over a long-sleeved checked shirt and black jeans, she was leaning slightly forward, looking out. The revving RPMs vibrated through him as the plane soared over the water, then banked inland to head east.

"I've never seen Portfalls from the air," she cried, sounding as excited as a kid as she looked out her side window. "I'm trying to trace the river back, but I can't find the lodge."

"All that's visible is the driveway and part of the roof."

"Oh, I see! The falls stand out even from here."

"It's a short flight so we've got time to take the scenic route—which is anything under us, in this neck of the woods. It's always beautiful up here and seems even more so today."

She turned to smile at him. "I love flying. I guess your wife did, too, since you named the plane for her."

"I named the plane for her, but she didn't like flying. She merely tolerated it."

"Oh," she said, looking relieved—or was it pleased?—as she leaned away to look out her side window again. He recalled DeeDee's words that rankled him during her interrogation: she'd said he was blind to matters of the heart. If that was true, he'd like to change that in the future, maybe with this woman.

The engines wrapped their hum around them, and the view stunned them both to silence. A national forest blanketed the western slopes of Mount Baker-Snoqualmie. An occasional ski lift, logging trail or rural road zigzagged beneath them, and in the Alpine Wilderness area, little lakes blinked in the sun. Occasionally, they could make out rafters, kayakers, even fishermen on the larger waterways.

The deep greens of trackless hemlock and cedar seemed to spill from the bluish mountains. The Cascades had at last lost their shrinking cowls of snow, but in a few weeks would be covered again. It was that snowpack that became the swelling silver streams ribboning the rock face, foothills and valleys, including the Bloodroot River that flowed past the lodge.

"Mount Snoqualmie straight ahead, then we'll pass over I-5 before we start down," Nick told her, talking loudly enough so she could hear. "It probably would have taken us three hours to drive, since the last half hour of road is long and twisting, so you can't beat this as-the-crow-flies path."

"Oh, we're almost there? Can we just take a little longer?"

"Your wish is my command. I was thinking the same thing." Her smile lit up the cockpit more than the sun pouring in. He banked the plane slightly northeast and made a larger circle in. He'd studied maps of the area and was sure he could find Lake Hemlock simply by lining up roads and mountains, but he was qualified on instrument flying, too, and had the coordinates written down. At least in the plane, he always knew where he was going.

The drone of the engines, the sun and the thrill of being away from Portfalls with Nick lulled Claire into a reverie. It was almost as if they were running away today, flying around the entire globe. "Come Fly With Me," that man in the airport restaurant had sung to tease her the night DeeDee had attacked Nick. Up here, there seemed to be no fears or worries, no boundaries or property lines....

She watched Nick scan his monitors again. He jerked in his seat and bent closer to look at four indicators grouped right in front of her. *Left Fuel, Right Fuel, Oil Pressure* and *Oil Temp,* she read. He whipped his sunglasses off, his shoulders pressing hard against hers as he leaned over her for an even closer look.

"Impossible!"

"What?"

"How the hell could that empty out so fast? I checked it on the preflight."

"We're losing gas?"

"Oil. Gone."

She saw the oil pressure read zero and the oil temperature gauge plummeting.

"So we have to turn back?" she asked, her voice sounding shaky and small.

"We'd never make it that far. Listen to me," he ordered, shifting back heavily into his seat. "The engine's going to cut out in a few minutes, but I'll try to glide us down."

"Down to where?" she cried as she pulled her gaze from him to the heavily treed, uneven terrain under them.

"To an emergency landing on a lake, if we're lucky. We need to start looking for lakes—long ones, ones that run north-south, if possible." His voice was low and controlled but he looked furious.

She craned her neck to look out her window. "No, Claire, not behind us, way ahead of us!" he ordered, his voice nearly breaking.

She tried to do what he said, but she felt immobilized, blind. A thousand thoughts slashed at her. He had to be kidding; this had to be a nightmare. But she'd had so many of those lately, she'd recognize them. This was real and happening now.

Considering all she—they—had been through, was this just happenstance or some dreadful coincidence? Or was it another attempt to torment her? It was like the entire plane had been hit with a Taser this time.

As she had when she'd lost her mother and Keith, she felt fearful and frail. But she was not going to lose her own life.

"Don't panic on me now, Claire," Nick said, alternating between watching his other dials and leaning forward to search for a lake on which to land. Trying to steady herself, Claire also looked, squinting into the sun, and shading her eyes despite her sunglasses. The blues and greens below seemed to shimmer, to merge like one vast oil painting.

But she gasped and gripped her seat, stiff-armed, when the engine sputtered, then simply stopped, just as Nick had said it would. The silence, the whine of wind was deafening. Though the plane shifted downward, slowly, steadily, Claire's stomach went into free fall.

"I checked this thing," Nick muttered, gripping the wheel so tight his knuckles went white. "Hose, quick drain—can't be."

He cleared his throat and for one second Claire thought he might cry, just as she wanted to. She could hear her heart pounding so hard it almost drowned out his voice.

"I can glide one thousand feet for every mile up," he said, as if reciting something from rote. She saw him recheck the altimeter. "The lake where we land has to be within a mile and a half of our current position, less if possible. Help me look, Claire."

Suddenly, she felt very close to him. She needed him, and had to let him know that together they could do this.

"We can find a lake," she heard herself say, "a long one, north-south so you can put us down okay."

More terrified than she had ever been, she strained forward in her seat belt to peer out through the front windshield over the nose where the propeller no longer turned of its own accord, but spun silently. Nick, the man who held their chance of salvation, worked the pedals and flaps to keep them gliding smoothly down, down through this eternity of air.

"Can you swim?" he asked as the plane slid closer to earth.

"You said you could glide us down."

"Just in case."

"Yes, I can swim. There!" she cried triumphantly, pointing toward the front windshield. "See that fishhook-shaped lake? It runs mostly north-south, doesn't it?"

He leaned farther forward. "Looks like our best bet."

"Let's radio for help so they come for us almost as soon as we're down—I mean, when we land on the water."

"We're out of range of the tower frequency by now and probably too low to get radio signals. But someone in another plane may hear us and relay our Mayday. Take my headset and put it on. If you raise someone, I'll tell you what to say."

Her fingers brushed through his crisp hair as she took the headset with the attached mouthpiece. He didn't look it, but he was sweating; his forehead was soaking wet.

Claire heard nothing but white noise on the radio. She tried other channels as Nick told her, but when she looked out the windows again, they were almost down. Sheer terror racked her as treetops and the lake reached up for them. Her urge to relieve her bladder became almost unbearable.

"Mayday, Mayday," she cried into the mouthpiece. "Small plane—engine quit—going d-down for an emergency l-landing."

When she stopped talking, she heard only the whoosh of wind until Nick muttered, "Damn, the lake's calm."

"But that's good, right? We won't rock when—"

"I need waves or something on the water to judge distance. If we're too low, it will be too late not to hit hard."

Too late. Hit hard. She began to pray silently, fervently. For Nick, herself. At least she'd never had children to leave behind. It was the only time in her life she'd seen an advantage to being childless.

The headlines would literally make them an item now, in a way the lead article in the *Portfalls Portfolio* on DeeDee's stalking hadn't. This headline would read, County Sheriff and New Suicide Widow Crash Together. Or, Widow Dies in Plane Crash Just Eighteen Days After Husband's Strange Death. And this death would be strange, too, Claire thought. Though Nick was too busy trying to save them to speak, he must be thinking his plane—like her deck and her painting and her life—had been tampered with.

"Here we go," Nick whispered more to himself than to her. When he added, "Hang on, sweetheart," she didn't know if he meant her or the plane, but she hoped he meant her.

Claire squinted out the front window as he tried to make a low, even approach over treetops. His face showed the strain. She almost reached over to wipe his brow as he kept struggling to coordinate the rudders, wheel and flap switches. The lake, glaring at them in the sun, looked smaller the closer they got to it. An opaque gray-blue, it reflected sky and clumps of clouds as if the entire universe had turned upside down. The big blur of forest became individual cedars and pines rushing under them—at them.

Claire stared at the glassy surface of the water that would be their runway. Thick trees came right down to the water here, so there were no beaches visible. Nick was right. With the mirrorlike lake, she could not tell how tall the trees were or judge how high they were and—

She screamed and he swore as they brushed, then clipped treetops. They lurched as if they'd hit turbulence. Claire grabbed her seat, though she wanted to cling to Nick. They might not even make the lake. The belly of the plane thumped harder. Claire lifted her feet from the vibrating floor as if a treetop would poke through.

"Get your feet down to brace yourself in case we tip or nose in," Nick ordered, his voice steely now. "The floats might be broken or gone, and we'll have to ditch."

Claire could only tell how close they were to the water's surface when they skimmed it, at first like a skipped stone, then hit it. Wild wash flew up at their windshield, blinding them. Nick grunted as if someone had punched him in the belly. Claire held her breath as they smacked and twisted, turned and tipped endlessly.

Despite her seat belt, she nearly fell on top of him, then got jerked the other way. Her arms and legs flopped freely. Pain stabbed through her ankle. Her head snapped forward, then back. Suddenly the windows cleared, and sunlight shot at them, but only on her side of the plane, which was now above them.

"We have to get out," Nick cried. "We can't get trapped in here!"

For the first time he sounded panicked, and she saw why. The view out his side window was now churning green water and bubbles. He undid his belt, then hers. She fell into him again as if she had been thrown into his lap.

Her head spun. Disoriented. Sideways up. Had she jumped off the bridge with Keith? The water was trying to pull her under, the rocky bottom buffeted her. No, that was Nick under her in the plane.

"Out!" he cried. His face and voice were frenzied. He pointed up, pushed her away. "Go, go!"

He stood to reach beside—over—above—her and opened her door. He shoved it up. Fresh air slammed in and then a thin, bone-chilling wave of water slapped her face and soaked her. Nick's hands held her waist hard, then her hips, her thighs. He heaved her up, and she reached for sunlight. Her loafers fell off, but she dragged something after her.

She'd lost her sunglasses; brightness blinded her. The plane rocked in the water, waves reaching for her. She stood in her slippery sock feet on the side of the sleek fuselage, then fell to her knees to grab at the wing struts. Her ankle throbbed in agony. But they were down and alive—alive.

Panting, Nick hoisted himself up beside her. He looked dazed as if he were seeing some other place or scene. "Go," he gasped, "or it might—suck us down."

When she hesitated, he jumped, dragging her into the water with him.

The cold gray smacked her back to reality. Instantly, she relieved her bladder underwater. She kicked and sidestroked away from the rapidly filling plane, however much whatever she held—her purse—tried to drag her down. But she held to it as if it were a life vest.

When she stopped to look back, Nick's face was a mask of fear—no, raw fury. His expression was ravaged, his skin so slick it looked as if he'd sobbed a lake of tears.

"Get to shore," he ordered, treading water beside her. "The oil's gone but there's gas in the water. Keep it out of your eyes and mouth."

The lake lay long but narrow. They stroked and paddled toward the nearest thickly wooded shore. When at last Claire tried to stand in waist-high water, her ankle screamed at her. She cried out and stumbled. Fear, relief, shock. Shaking uncontrollably, she began to cry.

Nick sloshed over to her and lifted her in his arms, holding her tight to him. He staggered up on the narrow, stone-and-oyster-shell-littered shore, set her down, then threw himself beside her.

Forty feet out, the plane gave a loud gurgle. Side by side, silent, they just stared. One wing lifted forlornly as if to wave goodbye. Then the Cessna settled slowly into the lake to leave them alone in the vast wilderness.

18

To Claire's amazement, Nick, dripping wet, began to pace the ribbon of shore, stalking back and forth and glaring at the lake. He repeatedly shoved his hands through his short hair. Figuring he needed time to grieve the loss of the *Susan*, Claire let him go for a few minutes.

"Nick?"

"I'll be all right. *We'll* be all right," he told her, his voice gruff and angry. "I'll take care of things—of you."

He came over and slumped down beside her. He looked exhausted, yet tension and energy crackled from him. "How's that ankle?"

"Not broken, I think. Probably a bad sprain."

"I'll find something to wrap it tight." He touched it, and she winced. "It would be tough for you walking, anyway, since your shoes are gone along with—" his voice caught "—the rest of it."

"I'm so sorry about your plane. It wasn't your fault."

"I've been trying like hell to figure out how someone did it—partially cut the fuel line so it would drain after we'd been in the air awhile. I did the preflight check at the airport, and the oil hose was fine then. But before you came, I went back inside to hit the john. I got a cup of coffee inside, talked to a few guys at the counter—maybe ten, twelve minutes away from the plane. That must have been all it took.''

''You think someone sabotaged the plane?''

''I *know* someone did. I had no idea how serious this game that someone's playing with your life is, and now they're playing with mine, too.''

''You think...someone meant to kill me?'' she cried. But she knew he was right. DeeDee's obsessions aside, it was Claire, not Nick, who was the common denominator in all that had happened since Keith died.

''Then, Keith wasn't the only target,'' she reasoned aloud, ''but simply the first casualty?''

''Unless you've got some sort of skeleton in your closet, Keith was probably the prime target. But then, whoever got rid of him realized you weren't going to give up digging into it.''

''Maybe that's why someone went through my garbage can right after his body was found,'' she said, as jagged pieces of the recent past began to fall together. ''The murderer thought something of Keith's had been thrown out, something that would show how much I knew—or if I was searching through Keith's things.''

''Which you—we—have been.''

''I'm sorry to have gotten you involved in all this.''

''Thank God you did. It's where I need—I want— to be. Now all we have to do is figure out what Keith did or found out that was so important that someone needed to eliminate him. It must have been someone he knew—it's unlikely he sneaked out to meet a stranger the night he was killed. We just have to find the chink—the lies and motives—in someone's armor.''

"But first we have to find a way to get dry and then get rescued out here," she insisted with a shudder as her teeth began to chatter. She wasn't certain if it was from the excitement of having Nick finally, completely with her on this quest to solve Keith's murder, or the fear of how endangered they both were. Or the cool autumn breeze that bit into her skin through her sopped hair and garments.

"Right. First things first," he said, standing and helping her to her feet. "Speaking of which, I can't believe you managed to get your purse out of the plane."

"Female instinct. You better thank me for it," she said in an attempt to stay brave when she wanted to explode into tears again. "My cell phone got ruined, but I've got two small loaves of plastic-wrapped cranberry bread in here I intended for the Chins and some cough drops that may have to be our lunch until the rescue planes find us. At least when we don't arrive and Howard Chin checks with the airport, there should still be some hours of daylight left for a search."

"I don't want to spoil your picnic plans," Nick told her as he lifted her in his arms, "but our little sight-seeing jaunt took us ten or fifteen miles off the flight plan I filed in Portfalls. I'll leave an SOS with oyster shells, but there's no plane or wreckage visible. There won't even be a telltale oil slick because our oil was long gone. The radar was out of range, and the emergency transmitter won't work underwater. I grabbed you instead of the flare gun. It could take them days to find us."

"Days?"

"In short, we may be here a little longer than lunch."

Nick carried her away from the cool breeze on the lake into the shelter of the ragged line of Douglas firs edging the shore. She felt amazingly safe in his strong embrace. Putting one arm around his broad shoulders, she clutched her sodden purse against her chest.

"At least we have a source of water in that cold mountain lake," she said, trying to focus on something positive in this disaster.

"Not unless you want a high-octane cocktail. The *Susan* was loaded with gas for our round-trip flight. If we'd had any sort of rough crash landing, which is what the bastard who wanted to kill us was probably hoping, we'd have been literally toast. So we're going to have to find a better source of water, maybe a stream that feeds that lake. At least, except for loggers, there's no industry around here to cause pollution."

"Speaking of loggers, I think I saw a camp with some cutting areas up ahead. If no one finds us, we could try to walk to that."

"*We* can *walk* to that?" he challenged. "I don't think you're walking anywhere in the near future. I saw the camp, too, but distances are deceptive from the air. Our best bet may be to stay near the site where we went down. Except..."

"Except what?"

"Except there's no visible wreckage."

"You said that before, so what else were you going to say? Nick, if someone intentionally wanted us to crash, you don't think they'd come after us—to be sure?''

"It crossed my mind. But when word gets out that we're missing, the culprit will probably draw the conclusions he or she wants. There, up ahead, just what I've been looking for,'' he told her, and she craned her neck to look.

"Rocks? I thought we were looking for a stream."

"Sheltered rocks in the sun so we can get dried out away from even the meager lake breeze. I have a feeling my survival training from years ago and my duty during Operation Desert Storm is going to come in real handy.''

"If we have to go through a night here..." Her voice snagged. It was a terrible thought, yet at least they'd be together. Disturbed by the vision of them trying to keep warm at night, she shifted slightly in his arms. She had to stay brave and upbeat, however scared and distraught she was.

But she had to admit this small rocky area, open to the sky and fringed by protective alders, was as lovely a scene as the lake had been. The rocks were a mottled green in the sun, with long, sinuous grains and smooth contours. Nick put her down on one and walked away.

"Nick, where are you going?"

"To give you some privacy,'' he called back. "You need to strip completely and lay your clothes out on the rocks to dry before the sun shifts around and we're in shade. Lie on the rocks, as they've caught the morning sun's heat. I'll give you fair warning when I come back.''

"When you come back from just on the other side of these rocks, you mean?''

"Ah," he said, "it's nice to be wanted. Yes, from just over here. But remember that nonhumans like to warm themselves on rocks during the day, so keep an eye out for snakes."

She didn't like snakes, but somehow, after all she'd been through lately, they were the least of her worries. It was a human snake in the grass that terrified her.

Despite getting his skin so dirt-streaked it looked like he wore camouflage paint, Nick rubbed himself down with moss as he sat naked, not far from the presumably nude Claire Malvern. He had spread his clothes over the serpentine rock, wishing it were flint, so he could strike a spark for warmth and a signal fire.

The idiotic thing was, as chilled and shaken as he'd felt by the cunning attempt on their lives and loss of the plane, he still felt a warmth for Claire, a fire for her. It was going to take everything he had to stay calm and cool out here, to keep the danger of the wilds and his desire for her at bay.

"How are you doing over there?" he called to her.

"You're right that clothes dry faster off than on. You know, despite our predicament, it is beautiful here. I've been watching those graceful eagles soaring overhead."

Wishing he had his sunglasses, he squinted upward into the blaze of blue sky. "Those are vultures, Claire, and they're hungry, too."

He was close enough to hear her sharp intake of breath. Silently, he cursed himself. She might be one tough lady, but he needed to be tender with her out here. This wasn't like recon with a bunch of army grunts or marines.

"I checked the cranberry bread," she called to him. "Since I had the little loaves in plastic baggies they're not wet at all, though they did get pretty smashed."

"We'll have them later. We may end up eating fiddler ferns, cattail stalks and raw salmon before we get out of here. But if you've got any aspirin in that purse, you'd better chew some for that ankle."

"Good idea. It's really throbbing."

He put his head in his hands. Before this was over, he was afraid part of him would be throbbing, too.

In an hour and a half they were dressed and back together. He almost laughed. As well as brushing her wild hair, Claire had evidently put lipstick on. But just when he was congratulating himself that she wanted to look good for him even out here, she said, "I don't suppose you want some lipstick. My lips felt so chapped and I didn't have anything else."

"I'll pass on that. Let's go back to the lake, I'll lay out an SOS, and we'll eat some of your bread. This afternoon, you can sit near the SOS, and I'll scout the shore of the lake to see where a stream feeds in. I'll make us a camp on the lake for the night. But by tomorrow, we'll need to make a big decision."

Their gazes caught and held. Their eyes narrowed in the slant of sun as if they assessed each other anew.

"Which is?" she asked, her voice almost breathy.

"Whether to stay put on the lake or try to hike out, hoping to come across someone. This whole area's a patchwork of publicly and privately owned lands. We might find kayakers, rafters, hikers, campers. But I think our best bet is to head toward that logging camp. This is only Saturday, but if it's an active area, they could be in on Monday.''

"Or, even if not, there might be a phone."

He nodded, pleased and impressed she could keep a clear head with all that had happened.

"The only problem with plan B," she said, "is that you'd have to carry me there. Nick, you wouldn't leave me."

"No way," he promised, lifting her in his arms for the jaunt back to the lake. "I'll carry you piggyback if we have to hike out, but we're together all the way in this."

Her smile was brighter than the last remnants of noon sun.

On the narrow beach, using oyster shells, Nick laid out a large SOS, followed by N. B., his initials. They ate half of one of the two small loaves of her bread, then Nick hiked the circumference of the lake until he found a feeder stream.

"Water!" he shouted back, waving his arms from about one-fourth of the way around the lake. His voice echoed over the water. She breathed easier knowing he hadn't gone out of sight around the curve of the fishhook shape of the skinny shore.

Though she was so thirsty she was almost ready to guzzle lake water, she waited patiently as he walked back toward her.

"We'll make camp by that stream," he told her, "and I'll leave an identical SOS near there, in case the SAR planes come from another direction."

SAR, she thought. The search for Keith that she had hoped was a Search and Rescue had, tragically, been a Search and Recovery. With a shudder, she offered up a prayer it would not be so for them.

As he carried her toward the site he'd chosen, Nick's boots crunched shells in a rhythmic sound. With her right arm around his neck, the side of her right breast rubbed up and down his chest. It was almost as if she sat in his lap, cradled in his arms. She could imagine sitting with him in a swing on a breezy porch somewhere, rocking, so safe and content with their lives....

She jolted alert. She was so spent and exhausted she'd almost dozed off, even in this dire predicament.

"While you were looking for the stream, I made a mental list of suspects," she told him, desperate to keep her mind on business.

"Me, too. Let's hear yours."

"Obviously, not DeeDee."

"Stuff like the quick drain of the plane's oil is way beyond her, even if she weren't locked up. That is," he amended, "I think it is. She really taught me that I'm not as damn smart as I like to think."

Claire bit back the urge to comment on that. "Suspect number one, Noah Markwood," she suggested.

"Motive?"

"He may be hiding something, namely that he killed Keith because Anne dumped Noah for Keith."

"Okay, we can put him in our virtual lineup. He's definitely clever enough to pull everything off that's happened, but I can't believe he'd dirty his hands with the skinned deer."

"But he's really into symbols of Indian culture,

and he has a carving of Sam Twoclaws's on display in Puget Treasures that looks just like that deer.''

"Which leads us to Sam.''

"We can't escape the fact Sam wants the sacred Sammamish lands back for his people, and that includes the lodge property. Maybe Sam's been working for Noah in more ways than one. And Sam's often out in the woods at night.''

"Yeah, DeeDee said she saw him more than once. So we put strange Sam in the lineup, too. Who else, Sherlock?''

"Joel Markwood has turned into a bitter man. He acted really strange last time I visited his farm, and he was on the river just before the Taser attack. But I get the idea he never fishes at night, and doesn't even like to be out at night. Anyhow, he's hardly working with or for his brother, as I heard them arguing over Joel wanting money to keep the family cranberry bogs afloat—well, you know what I mean. Unless…''

"Unless what?''

"Unless they saw me coming that day and staged that argument for my benefit. No, that's getting too paranoid.''

"Being paranoid may be what keeps us safe until we can nail whoever's doing all this,'' he said with a frown as he scanned the sky.

"But Joel's a real long shot. Besides, Tess, like Diana, is getting to be a good friend.''

"Which proves what? In law enforcement, people are not always known by the company they keep. But I guess it does mean you could try sounding out Tess more about Joel.'' He shook his head.

"What now?'' she demanded.

"Maybe Tess knows her mate better than you and I evidently did. But how about the Nances, or Howard Chin, for that matter? They certainly have the dough to hire someone to do their dirty work. Would they take it as a personal insult when someone leaves their business?"

"You're making Howard Chin sound like a mafia godfather! Besides, the Nances are in Seattle, and Kubla Chin is where we're supposed to be right now. The only night I've felt safe in the lodge lately, besides the night you slept there, was when Ethan and Diana were visiting me. They've been nothing but understanding and supportive, just as they were when Keith left ChinPak."

"Tell me more about the company, like how they make their money, and what Keith did for them. They import Chinese art, right, like those beautiful vases you have at the lodge?"

"Yes, as well as other porcelain bowls, carved ivory figures of people and animals, Ch'ing Dynasty censers and many other valuable items. By the way, Diana bought an authentic Tang dynasty horse from Noah. And do you know that scrimshaw work, if it's on ivory, can be illegal today?"

"I see you've still got Noah at the top of your list. But humor me about ChinPak, since I'm a captive audience," he said, and bounced her. His expression was so intense she knew he wasn't kidding. "Since Keith went to Beijing and Hong Kong several times," he prompted, "did he speak Chinese?"

"He always went with Ethan, who's fluent. Of course, Diana is, too. I'd say Keith's use of the language was—serviceable."

"So his expertise with them was...?"

"Financial. He wasn't exactly an accountant, but oversaw the international and government rules and regs of imports."

"But he wasn't a lawyer?"

"He was a business major with an interest in what they used to call the Far East. Let's just say he was their chief troubleshooter," she insisted, before she realized she sounded angry. "And let's not forget in all this that there's one more suspect."

"Anne Cunningham."

"I can't fathom she'd kill Keith, but a few weeks ago I couldn't fathom any of this."

"That's why bright murderers sometimes get away with it. I'd include Anne simply because Keith evidently left your bed to go out into the chilly, foggy night, and I can't see doing that except for another woman, moron that he was for that."

He shifted her again in his grasp, and she tightened her arm around his neck. They were silent for a while as he trudged along.

"You don't think I had anything to do with Keith's loss, do you?" she asked.

"Only in the sense you might have missed the signs of his distress or guilt. But that you harmed him? No. Listen, I don't want you to be scared about anything!"

Beyond words for a moment, she nodded. What did scare her, though, was that even if they were back in civilization and life was normal, she would still want to hold him like this.

Claire and Nick were exhausted and edgy as night set in. The only planes they had seen overhead were silver streaks high in the heavens. Those were probably passenger jets on their way to Vancouver or Alaska, Nick had said.

And they were both ravenous. Ice-cold stream water, rationed cranberry bread and cough drops for dessert only went so far, especially when Claire had been looking forward to dining in style on Sechuan cuisine at Xanadu. But if she were honest, she admitted to herself, starving with Nick was better than most meals she'd eaten out elsewhere.

"In the old movies, after their Conestoga wagon's broken down, don't the stranded pioneers always find a patch of berries or hunt buffalo about now?" Claire asked as Nick brought back fresh fir boughs. Luckily, he'd had his pocketknife in his jacket when they ditched. He'd cut the boughs to cover the leaf-lined, hollowed-out beds he'd made side by side for them, just off the shore of what they were now calling Fishhook Lake.

"Whether or not we stay here or hike out tomorrow, I'll rig a way to catch fish," he promised. "Thank God for salmon and that it's still their running season."

Their running season. Claire felt as if she'd been running after or from someone or something since the night Keith disappeared. And she still didn't know what, who or why. But now she had to concentrate on simple survival.

"I think, despite my foot," she said, "we should try to hike out instead of waiting here. As you said, the flight plan you filed would put searchers off course from where we came down."

"If I carry you all the way out, you'll owe me big-time for portage fees."

"I already owe you big-time." When he lifted one

eyebrow suggestively as he stood over the makeshift beds he was building, she blurted, "It will take a lot of meals at the lodge for us to be even."

"Right," he said. "Well, lights out, campers. Big day tomorrow on the hike. Here's hoping Nature Nick will be able to get us to that logging site and not overshoot it in one direction or another."

As they settled into their nearly adjoining beds, the sun set in a blaze of orange and orchid. It was the most romantic scene. Silently watching it, Claire sat cross-legged with her sprained ankle on top, which Nick had wrapped tightly with cattail leaves tied on with vines. He sat with his hands clasped around his bent knees as the colors faded to grays. Someday, Claire told herself, she'd paint this sunset scene, for like the falls, it would be etched in her mind forever.

With a rustling of leaves, they lay down and both shifted to get comfortable. The boughs whispered in the dusk as they tugged them up for cover from the cold and any possible animal marauders. The forest scent seemed fresh and clean. If the nearby stream had not been so cold, she would have bathed in it. Tomorrow she'd find someplace to wash.

The water burbled pleasantly where it entered the lake—a far cry, she thought, from listening to the falls all night. And yet, in her head and heart, she could hear them yet, whispering, then roaring like the crash of the plane through the trees, a vision that leaped at her when she closed her eyes.

"Nick, I know I said this before, but I'm sorry for your loss of the *Susan* and that I insisted you get involved in all this. And that you have to carry me tomorrow."

"I lugged a buddy who weighs twice as much as you out of the desert in Kuwait once, while under fire. That was in a fireman's carry, slung over my shoulder, though. We may yet come to that."

His voice was husky, but he ended with a little chuckle. Like most men, she thought, he didn't take heartfelt compliments well and seemed to stifle or deflect deep emotions.

"But you're welcome," he whispered as if to prove her wrong. "Like I said before, we're in this together all the way. I should have renamed the plane a long time ago, anyway. Now that it's gone, the next one won't be *Susan II.*"

More awkward silence.

"Bears won't come down here to drink at night, will they?" she asked.

"More likely deer."

"I don't even want another one of those staring at me."

"Better than a wolf."

Even in the growing dusk, watching his profile, she saw him bite back a grin. His mustache actually twitched. Was he teasing her? She realized she'd never kissed a man with a mustache, but she decided she'd better not think about that right now. Besides, it somehow seemed a time for soul-searching, although not the kind Sam Twoclaws practiced.

"One thing I've learned—come to face up to—in all this," she said hesitantly, "is that I had no clue what marriage meant. Keith and I were partners but not really a team, if you know what I mean."

"Yeah, I do. The same for Susan and me. I thought I loved her, but how could I, if I didn't know the real her? She was a private person—at least with me. I guess she never really loved me deeply enough to have a real marriage. She didn't trust me to go through hard times with her, and that hurt.''

"Keith obviously kept so much from me, too. His fault or mine, I wonder. And deep feelings, shared passion...they just weren't there. I didn't even know it was missing, because I'd never felt that, or at least, I'd only experienced it in abstract ways, like in my art or seeing it in someone else's work or life.''

"I guess I was more married to my job some-times—and to the plane named *Susan*, instead of the flesh-and-blood woman who was my wife.''

She wanted to say more and sensed he did, too. Amazing, that she could sense things with Nick, when she'd evidently been so dense about Keith. And she knew Nick responded to her the same way. The failures of their marriages was surprisingly sim-ilar. They had both learned from the past and now yearned for something different—each other, she was sure of it!

"We'd better try to sleep," he said. "At first light, we're heading out.''

"Okay, Nature Nick," she managed to say, but she hardly felt in a light mood. An owl began to hoot nearby. It sounded exactly like *Who? Who?* and she began to agonize again about who could be tor-menting her and now threatening her life. She lifted her hands to cover her ears.

"You all right?" he asked when she rustled her bed and the boughs.

"Fine. Really.''

Neither of them slept for a long time after, she could tell by his breathing and his own movements. Despite the insulation Nick had built for them, a chill settled in quickly as the effects of the sunny day dissipated into a starry September night.

Some time later, groggy yet, Claire curled into a fetal position, but then had a nightmare about being shot with the Taser and falling into the bloodroot leaves, writhing, drowning in a lake....

"Claire? You cried out," someone said, and touched her shoulder.

Reality slammed into her. They'd crashed. She was stranded somewhere near the Cascades with Nick.

"Oh—a bad dream. I'm so cold."

"Me, too. Want to try sharing body heat? We'll use my foxhole, because it's bigger."

She noted he hadn't said *bed.* "All right."

They lay with her back against his chest, her bottom close to, but not quite in, his lap, her sore ankle stuck out, away from his. As his arms came around her and she settled her cheek against his hard biceps, her head under his chin, she thought this was definitely better.

Better but worse. Safer from wilderness dangers, but not from her growing feelings for Nick Braden.

As the sun climbed above the tree line, Claire woke with a start, alone in their little nest. Nick was gone, probably to do his morning duties behind a tree or to get a drink in the stream.

She rubbed her eyes and looked around. Getting carefully to her knees, she stood to test her ankle. It was incredibly stiff and sore but without that shooting pain—until she put weight on it.

When he didn't come back, she cried, "Nick? Nick!"

There was no sound but the lapping lake, the rippling stream, wind in the trees and birdcalls. Claire squinted down the stream to where it twisted into thicker spruce and firs. No Nick.

Keith had disappeared like this. She'd awakened to find him gone. Permanently. She'd run all over, looking for him, but he was already dead. She hadn't found her mother in time, either. Dead. Both dead.

It came flooding back over her like icy water, his loss, her terror. But Nick could not have fallen in this lake or stream like Keith had the river. Surely he hadn't decided to leave her here to strike out to the logger's camp on his own, even if it was to bring back help faster. Granted, she'd slow him down. Did he think she'd be better off here by the SOS, in case a plane found them? Or had whoever made them crash followed them here, and now they'd taken Nick?

No, no, she couldn't be alone, not here!

The sounds of moving water swamped her composure, her hard-won control and sanity.

''Nick!'' she screamed, then held her breath to listen. Only a faint echo resounded from somewhere. ''Niiick!''

19

Claire was on the verge of hysteria when she saw a slip of paper tucked in the single pocket of her down-filled vest. The paper was crinkled, and had obviously once been wet. On one side, she saw it was a blank speeding ticket. On the other side, in pencil, Nick's bold handwriting read, *Gone fishing. Couldn't bear to wake you.*

Both furious and relieved, she scanned the shore of the lake and looked upstream. He was nowhere in sight. Lurking panic began to niggle at her again.

She hobbled behind a Sitka spruce they'd decided was the "women's area" last night and relieved herself, then decided to stay undercover until Nick returned. Not far from their makeshift camp along the lake, a doe and a fawn drank, looking up nervously to keep an eye on her. Claire prayed the gasoline in the lake had dissipated by now. As the doe stared at her, she remembered the terrible tableau on her back deck and dedicated herself again to finding out who was behind all this—if she could just find Nick first.

He eventually emerged from upstream, wet to his knees but holding out a large salmon, as if someone were taking a photo of his prize.

"Breakfast is served, madame," he said, grinning at her, evidently oblivious to the emotional havoc he'd caused this morning. "Now I just hope I can start a fire by striking together these two flint rocks I found,'' he said, proudly producing them from his jeans pocket with his other hand. ''You and I are going to eat a hearty breakfast, because it's going to be a long day.''

Riding piggyback on Nick so he could see where he was going through the thick terrain, Claire soon learned there was a big problem. Once she had her arms and legs wrapped around him and his hands clasped under her, the rhythmic movement of his stride more than got her attention. His ribs and hips stroked the inside of her thighs as her breasts slid up and down the hard muscles of his back. Her heels bounced close to his crotch. She knew she was going to have to talk—to say something, anything.

''Another thing I've been thinking—'' she said. ''Despite what DeeDee did to both of us, we've got to help her.''

''Oh yeah, the state-appointed shrinks will love it if the object of her obsession and the woman she blamed for stealing him want to visit.''

''No, but we've got to get DeeDee's family to visit her. They're the ones who can help her, and they've been ignoring her needs and actually harming her.''

''So what's new? In my line of work, I see that all the time. It's usually family and friends that do people in.''

They both fell silent again. Claire wondered if Nick was thinking about his wife. She still regretted that she must have missed something big in Keith's world, and that she hadn't really helped her dad out much on the phone when he'd tried to make amends.

"My father called last week," she told him. "I should have invited him and his family to the lodge, however much he's tied to a kidney dialysis schedule."

"He's a doctor, right?"

"I didn't mention that, did I?"

"I wasn't going to tell you this, because he asked me not to, but—"

"You've been talking to my father?"

"Just hear me out," he said, bouncing her hard, either to get a better grip on her or to get her to be quiet. "I didn't talk to him, but he did contact me, via mail. He claims he wants to help you. You must have told him that I was trying to help you, too."

"Yes, though I don't think I used your name. And?"

"He sent me a copy of an old medical report on your mother, thinking, evidently, that if I knew what you'd been through I'd know what you might be facing."

"But if the report was on my mother? Like mother, like daughter, is that what he was trying to say? No way I'd ever end my life the way she did!"

"One thing in the report was how much she loved you and that your father, as well as her psychiatrist, evidently, thought that would carry her through her problems."

"Well, it didn't! My father's the one who should have seen the signs, not some child, however close Mother and I were. And I'm certainly not suicidal!"

"Would you settle down? I don't think that was his ultimate conclusion."

"I can't believe you're siding with him."

"Claire, loosen up on my neck! You're choking me, and it's hard enough going through here."

"Oh, sorry," she said, moving her arms farther down to his shoulders again.

"Don't be too hard on him. It was that report your dad sent me that partly made me decide to really stick with you, that and the diabolical way someone altered your painting with the man on the bridge. If I thought you were unstable, I would get you some help, just like I finally did DeeDee—and, okay, the way we can try to get her family's help for her, too. But I think you're reliable and trustworthy, so I'm sticking close, obviously," he added with another bounce of her bottom.

"I know you are," she said, hugging him from behind. "I didn't mean to explode, but years of my father's cold shoulder have turned me against him. Actually, I have a copy of the only report we ever got from my mother's doctor, since I think her psychiatrist destroyed his records when she killed herself. But, you know, it doesn't sound like the report you're describing—saying her love for me would help carry her through. Maybe there were really two reports, but Dad held one back—the one that mentioned me."

"Does the one you have speak about how the doctor thought your mother's art would be an outlet for her depression? Or that she might have had something called a Van Gogh complex?"

"Not at all. I can show you the report I have when we—when we get home." She couldn't help clinging to him. Besides, she suddenly thought she heard a waterfall again...but one never seemed to materialize and that scared her. What if she was really off balance, the way her mother had been?

"I wish," she whispered, "there was a yellow brick road to follow through all this, and we could ask the wizard for help, 'cause this sure isn't Kansas anymore."

Though she'd meant to be lighthearted, Nick nodded grimly. "Let's just keep our eyes peeled," he said, "for the Wicked Witch of the West."

It was midafternoon when they came to a second lake. It was a barrier to where they were headed, so they would have to go around it. Despite separate swims, they were soon hot again as they skirted it to keep heading south toward where they agreed they'd spotted the logging camp. And again they were hungry, although they'd roasted and eaten salmon at daybreak.

Storm clouds clotted overhead and thunder rumbled ominously. Across the lake, sheets of gray water slanted from the sky, obscuring the direction they wanted to go. At least the downpour passed on, heading for the mountains.

"They don't call them the Cascades for nothing," Claire said, still trying to keep their spirits up. They had talked less and less as the signs of a logging area or human life they were expecting failed to appear. They'd been following a stream due south that fed this lake.

"If it rains, it will make starting a fire with this flint an even longer shot," Nick muttered. "I could use another salmon deluxe dinner. I'm wearing down."

Especially with you on my back, she thought he

would say, but he didn't, and she silently blessed him for it.

"Let me try walking again," she said, shifting to change her stiff position.

"I'd wait until tomorrow. Maybe soaking it in a cold stream tonight will help."

They finally halted at a cliff-enclosed clearing where a feeder stream from the lake widened out to pools of deep blue water. A stony rapids frothed the water here, but Claire still saw no sign of the waterfall she had thought she'd heard. At least they could easily ford here.

"Look," she said, "all kinds of animal tracks, big ones, too. We can't stay here tonight if this is a watering place for bears."

He walked over to examine the small stretch of muddy bank where she'd collapsed on a fallen log as if she'd walked the whole way. "No," he said, bending over with a groan to flex his muscles by rotating both arms and shoulders, "the big tracks aren't bear, but moose or elk. Cloven hooves, see. Oh yeah, there's some bear, but too small to be a grizzly. At least it's not Sasquatch."

"Sasquatch?" she yelped, looking around, then back at him. "Surely you don't believe in those yeti or abominable snowman stories? Have you ever seen its tracks?"

"Just a plaster cast of one. It was hourglass-shaped and five-clawed," he said, overlapping and spreading his hands to indicate the size. "Really."

She shuddered. "As I said, we've got to push on."

"Easy for you to say. I'm going fishing, and I don't think you're leaving without me," he called back as he walked over the rocks, peering into the little spills of churning water.

They finally caught a single salmon together, Nick driving it into a net made from his shirt, which Claire held. The fish would no doubt taste like a feast fit for Howard Chin's table at Xanadu.

"Kubla Chin probably has planes looking for us by now," Claire said, as Nick managed to nurse a fire to life, then spitted the fish and began to roast it. With a shudder she recalled how Sam Twoclaws had broken the heads of his salmon with a stick, the day he'd told her how Keith had said, *The salmon have all the answers.* She was hungry enough today to know what he must have meant.

Thunder rumbled distantly again. Each time it did, Claire wished it were a plane looking for them. "We'll regret being under this forest canopy if a rescue plane flies over," she said.

"We're off track where they'd be looking, anyway."

"Howard Chin has his own helicopter," Claire said, fanning the flames as Nick had instructed. "If he's told Diana and Ethan we're missing, I'll bet they'll ask to personally join the search."

When the salmon was only partly cooked, the darkening skies dumped rain, first big, plopping drops, then a deluge. Claire and Nick wedged themselves under a low stone overhang that barely cleared their heads when they were sitting, and watched their precious fire drown.

"Oh well," Claire said. "The *chichi* thing to do these days in quality restaurants is to order salmon or tuna rare, anyway."

"It's nice to know we're in style."

But he gobbled the warm fish as fast as she did. They washed their hands by merely sticking them back out into the downpour.

"How handy," Claire said. "Don't tell me cavemen didn't have some advantages." When he continued to look grim, his dark beard shadow enhancing his caveman look, she punched his shoulder with her fist. "This will keep us dry, and the floor's slanted enough we won't have to sleep in puddles even in here."

"Ever the optimist," Nick muttered.

His mood had turned dark and that worried her. She felt so attuned to Nick's shifting emotions...so how had she missed something so troubled in Keith's life that he could be killed for it?

When Claire saw Nick rotate his head and press the back of his neck, she offered, "The least I can do is give you a neck or back rub."

"Your ankle's going to have to hold you tomorrow, Claire. I probably couldn't so much as lift you after that big dinner you just had, anyway." He glanced at her, and even in the deepening dusk, she saw he suddenly smiled, and her heart soared. "The massage—great," he whispered. "I could use it."

They scooted closer as he turned his back to her and took off his leather jacket. His shirt they'd used for a fishnet lay in a sodden pile, but he had his T-shirt on. She crouched behind him, leaning forward on her knees to give herself some leverage. Nick's neck and back muscles under the smooth stretch of thin cotton shirt seemed as stony as these rocks, until he began to relax under her hard, rotating touch. Despite the dank chill, his body heat radiated through her fingers and palm and up her arm to the inner depths of her belly.

"Yeah, that's really good," he said, his voice a throaty groan. "Haven't had a back rub for a long time."

She kept it up until her arms were ready to drop off, then sat back. An almost liquid warmth had seeped through her, making her so limp and languorous she wanted to lean into him, put her arms around his waist and curl against him as she had all day. She wanted his big body to shelter her against this storm like a second, rocky roof holding back an entire world of worries.

He slid slightly away and hunched down, pulling his jacket back on, then slouched to rest against the rough rocky wall. Suddenly he seemed tense again. He bent his long legs so his feet didn't stick out into the rain and gripped his arms around his knees. She could not see him studying her, but she could feel it.

"I'd better make you some shoes," he said, "because once you start to put weight on that ankle, you can't go barefoot."

"I still have my tennis socks on."

"Yeah, and after a couple of steps in these pine needles you'll need to be carried again. If you'd give your purse up, I could cut you a couple of makeshift shoes, hopefully held together with vines, or even that dental floss I saw you using."

"All right. I believe Mr. Blackwell's best- and worst-dressed list won't reach this far, anyway. It seems all the rules are out the window here."

"You can say that again."

She jammed the essential things from her purse

into her pockets, and he used his jackknife to slice the purse in two, using its natural curve to shape the crude slippers. "You're going to look like an elf with pointed toes," he told her, bent over his work in the dim light.

"Nick, I'm just thinking out loud now, but maybe someone at the Portfalls airport spotted someone hanging around your plane. I saw you had the cabin locked, but you can't lock the oil tank or the engine, can you?"

"The oil filler tube and oil sump are in the engine, and no, access to them is not locked. I've been over and over that in my mind—that I was stupid enough to be away from the plane after the preflight check, stupid enough not to spot that DeeDee was—"

"You told me not to blame myself about Keith. We've both got to realize that other adults are responsible for their own actions. Still, just to play devil's advocate about someone tampering with the plane, there must have been many other foolproof ways for our enemy to try to get rid of us. But—"

"But what?"

"Did you ever work with a police profiler?"

"Never had to, but I know law enforcement officers who have. You think we need one?"

"Maybe we can figure out who's behind this by how clever they are. They planned so well that they almost got away with Keith's murder, and they definitely could have gotten away with ours. Once the plane crashes, no one could find that an oil hose had been tampered with ahead of time, could they?"

"Not if the evidence is at the bottom of a mountain lake, or better yet, in the mind of a murderer, burned up in a fire with all that fuel we carried. But of the local suspects we listed before,'' Nick went on, ''only Joel Markwood or Sam are hands-on kinds of guys capable of tampering with an airplane's guts. Or it could be a professional job.''

''Like a hit man?''

''Like someone we don't even know, who knew how to carefully weaken the oil hose. Hell, I don't know. But I do know that right after we get back I'm going to have Aaron and Mike question anyone who was at the airport that day, about who they saw out on that tarmac besides you and me.''

''It will be a relief to have your staff in on this.''

As if he hadn't heard that, he went on. ''Probably Anne and Noah and definitely the Nances or Howard Chin have the money or means to plan a clever murder or hire someone to carry it off. But why? *Why?* We have no more proof that our killer's among our list of suspects than we know these shoes will stay on your feet.''

Although the rain had tapered off, deep darkness had descended. Still, her eyes slowly adjusting to the lack of light, Claire saw Nick extend the shoes. Their hands touched as she took them from him.

''When's your birthday?'' he whispered. ''Consider it an early gift.''

''No woman shopping at a posh shoe store ever had it better,'' she assured him, trying them on her feet. Even their warmth was welcome. ''You do know how to show a girl a good time, Nick Braden. Imagine, a gift after an exciting day with dinner out.''

He chuckled. And the mere sound of that was enough to hold the wet, chill night at bay.

* * *

"You awake?" Nick murmured. His breath stirred her hair and warmed her ear. When she shifted slightly in his arms, she felt strands of her hair snag on his beard stubble. "Rain's done, and it's at least an hour after dawn," he added. "We've got to get going."

"Yes. For sure."

Sore and stiff, she reluctantly rolled away from him and scuttled out from their overhang. Gray light suffused the area, pine needles dripped and the stream rattled on, but she could not see much through the fog. Everything seemed shrouded in shifting cellophane.

"I'm going to wash up," she told him, and gingerly put weight on her ankle as she walked. She limped and it hurt, but maybe it would loosen up. At least the stabbing pains had ebbed.

Claire didn't go far to get privacy, but then, she didn't have to in this thick soup. Still, as she washed in the stream she kept an eye out for the wild animals whose tracks they'd seen yesterday.

She remembered it was Monday. Hopefully, the loggers would be at work, and she and Nick would come upon their camp soon. They were both convinced it had to be nearby. Later, when they set out again, Nick walked slowly ahead, around brambles and sometimes through shallow brush.

"Let's eat the last of that cranberry bread here," he said, after only a short distance.

"I'm doing all right. I can go on."

"I know," he said, turning to her, concern etched on his face. "But we've got to take it easy with that ankle."

To her surprise, he reached out jerkily, almost reluctantly, and tucked a stray strand of hair behind her ear, then lightly rasped his knuckles down the slant of her cheekbone. She only realized her mouth was open when he slowly slid the pad of his thumb along her lower lip.

She nearly tilted into him. Even out here in the wilderness, Nick took up all the space, sucking everything toward him.

"You're a very brave woman, Claire. I admire you and—"

They came together in a hard hug, their arms tight around each other. His beard stubble scraped her cheek, but she didn't mind. Her breasts pressed flat against his chest; she almost couldn't breathe and didn't care, didn't want it to end.

"We'll make it out of here," he promised, "and we'll find out who's after you—us—I swear it."

"I can't thank you enough for—"

"Thank me later," he interrupted, his voice suddenly harsh as he set her back. "Thank me later when we're not stranded and shell-shocked, and you're not shaken and still grieving."

She nodded. It seemed she had known Nick forever. But a mere three weeks ago, she'd been that other woman: Keith's wife.

"Then I'll know," Nick added in a fierce whisper, "it's not because you just want police protection or help, but because you want me!"

They stared at each other. She nodded again, because she was sure her voice would fail her. It was as if an entire new world of possibilities had opened between them—a world she prayed they'd survive to see.

* * *

"Maybe we should go at this a different way," Claire said as they trudged along an hour later.

"You think we've gotten off track?" he challenged, pointing. "But that largest peak is still at about two o'clock, right where it should be to find the camp, and the fog's completely lifted."

"No, I mean, a different way to go about figuring out who tampered with your plane."

"Such as?"

"Such as who knew we were going to be flying together from the Portfalls airport in your plane on Saturday morning."

"I don't think that affects our initial list of suspects. You said you mentioned to Noah that you were flying to the Cascades when he asked if you had any more paintings for him."

"Right, but I didn't say you were taking me in your plane."

"Maybe he guessed it. You didn't tell Anne, did you? I thought you weren't talking to her."

"I didn't tell her, but what if Noah did?"

"Claire, my staff knew, so if we're going to wonder who told whom, let's suspect the entire town. In court testimony, who might have told whom is just hearsay."

"I suppose. When Tess called to thank me for the casserole, I did tell her, though she was en route back to her mother's."

"But she could have told Joel, and he could have told the butcher and the baker and the candlestick m—"

"Never mind! I thought I had a good idea."

"I'm going to talk to possible eyewitnesses at the airport first, and check your phone and maybe your entire place for bugs. I should have done that earlier, but even when you got shot with the Taser, I didn't think that meant someone had been inside your place. Now, I'm not sure.''

She trudged on, favoring her sore ankle. He still led the way, and she glared at his back, frustrated by his response, though she noticed and appreciated that he held bushes to the side so they wouldn't whip back in her face.

"Nick," she cried. "Do you hear that?"

"Hear what?"

"It might be a waterfall. Do you hear it?"

He tilted his head, and they both froze.

"It's not water, I think, but maybe machinery somewhere. We might be close to that logging camp."

She could tell he wanted to sprint ahead, but for the next few minutes he kept up the slow pace her ankle dictated. "Look!" he cried and pointed.

At first she saw nothing, until she peered around his big shoulder. Just ahead, nailed to the shaggy trunk of a big yellow pine were two faded signs. One read I Hate Tree Huggers and the other, Save a Logger—Eat an Owl.

"Bingo," Nick exulted with a little whoop. "Loggers! And where there are loggers there are national forest law enforcement agents. They usually watch for logging illegalities, but they'd do for a rescue."

Through the line of lodgepole pines below the ridge on which they stood, they could see a clearing with several metal-roofed buildings and huge pieces of timbering equipment.

They held hands like excited kids. "Even if no one's in that brush camp right now," Nick went on, "at the very least there will be a logging road leading out of it to a highway."

"But that hum I hear—someone has to be nearby."

As they came down from the ridge, the smells of pungent pine and sawdust assailed Claire's nostrils, and she sneezed. But in the silent clearing only the wind whining through the standing machines answered their calls.

"I'm going to check the buildings," Nick told her. "Be right back."

The moment he jogged away, she felt alone, dwarfed by the equipment, as if she were trapped among dinosaurs in some mechanical Jurassic Park. These behemoths made Joel Markwood's cranberry harvesting equipment look like midget machines. Humpbacked and vacant-eyed, a pair of rusted, clawed hulks blocked Claire's path. The muddy, black skin of one read Skidder 2 and it looked ready to drag entire trees away. Its jointed arm outstretched, the Slasher sprouted mammoth, bladelike rows of teeth set in a devouring maw, which reminded her of Josh's dry harvester-pruner. Claire could almost imagine how these monster machines would roar or growl.

She jumped as she heard it again—a distant droning. Not a waterfall, but a plane?

Despite the renewed throbbing in her ankle, she ran out from among the machines and cocked her head. Maybe a helicopter? Had one flown nearby, then circled away? Was that what she'd heard?

"Nick, Nick!" she screamed. "I hear a plane!"

He came running, scanning the sky. "No phone in there." He listened. "Sounds like a chopper. Get out here in the open. We don't have anything to flag them down, but maybe they'll see us. Even if it's one of those that carry logs out, they can radio for help.''

Claire hurried to stand with him by the long, open shed that sheltered a huge debarker. Piles of debris laid yards deep around the building. Nick took off his jacket and waved it. The increasingly distinctive *whup-whup* of chopper blades came closer. They still couldn't see anything, but it had to see them.

Then, just above the line of trees, the single black helicopter seemed to lift from the ridge. Delirious with relief, Claire began to scream, though she knew the pilot would never hear her.

To their utter dismay, the chopper flew over.

''Oh no,'' she cried.

The noise increased; it soon circled back again.

''They've seen us!'' Nick exclaimed.

Tears blurred Claire's vision as the chopper hovered, then lowered. Not only was there plenty of room for it to set down here, but there was even a spray-painted circle that was probably a makeshift landing pad. Maybe their rescuers would turn out to be loggers after all.

Claire could see men inside, two of them. She waved wildly while Nick semaphored the way airport staff do when a plane taxis up to the gate. The men inside opened the door before they landed, and one leaned out. He had on a helmet with a sun visor, the kind jet pilots wore.

Surely, Claire thought, surprised, they weren't just going to shout to them or drop something from fifteen feet off the ground and leave them here. Or was the man leaning out going to lower one of those

rescue ladders or baskets? Why didn't they just land?
She watched, fascinated, as if it were a movie in
slow motion, as the man leaning out lifted something
to his shoulder.

In the increasing turbulence from the blades, bark
and sawdust turned into a tornado around them. Nick
shouted something at her, but she couldn't hear his
words, couldn't hear herself think from the roar, as
if they would be devoured by the crash of the falls.

Suddenly, Nick bent low and tackled her. They
did not go down, but he half dragged, half carried
her and began to run from the chopper in a zigzag
pattern through the whirlwind.

She screamed as Nick lunged, then rolled them
under the long, clawed arm of the Slasher. She
sucked in dust and dirt, choking, her eyes gritty.

"What?" she shrieked.

"Gun!"

Claire's heart pounded so hard it drowned out the
sound of the chopper. She imagined the racking pain
of the Taser again, but surely a bullet would be
worse. On her belly, she huddled close to Nick.

"Should we run or stay put?" she screamed.

"My shoulder, I hit my shoulder."

"Shot?"

"Against the wheel of this machine. Broken, I
think. But we've got to run, in case they put down."

They *were* putting down. Squinting through flying
debris, Claire saw the chopper lower and land. She
helped Nick to his knees, clinging to his good left
arm. His face was distorted in a mask of agony. Unless they could get back into the trees, they would

be sitting ducks when the men got out of that chopper. At least, Claire thought through her panic, they were going to learn who was after them—if they didn't die first.

20

Claire was certain she was going crazy. Though the chopper had set down and its blades slowed, the roar had increased, like the sound of the falls.

But the flying debris had thickened, too.

"Another chopper!" Nick shouted. "Someone sent an army!"

Bent low, they ran out from under the belly of the Slasher, heading for the cover of the forest. Nick slowed and staggered, but she helped him, her shoulder under his good arm. They made it to the fringe of trees and threw themselves behind a big trunk.

Claire knew she'd never manage to get Nick even a few feet farther into the forest. His usual healthy color had gone ashen, his brow furrowed as he gasped for air. Sweat poured from him.

The men from the first chopper were out of it now, running after them.

Claire squinted to see if either of them had the gun Nick had spotted earlier. The one who had leaned out, his helmet was distinctive, had only a megaphone in his hands.

Still panting, Nick squinted back, too. "Second chopper—looks like Forestry Service," he gritted out over its subsiding roar as it set down next to the first chopper.

The men running after them halted about forty feet

away; the taller of the two lifted the megaphone to his mouth. "Sheriff? Mrs. Malvern?" came the tinny voice. "Howard Chin sent us to search for you. When we spotted you, we raised another chopper in the area. We're here to take you out."

"May I see Sheriff Braden now, nurse?" Claire asked again.

"I'm sorry, Mrs. Malvern. Not until they get his dislocated arm back into the shoulder socket. You know, the number of reporters downstairs is growing. It's up to you, though, if you want to face them or not."

"I need to see him first."

"I understand," the woman said, but only went back to her work at the triage desk.

Claire wished she understood how all this had happened so fast. It wasn't even noon yet of the morning they had been rescued. But ever since Nick's plane went down—actually, long before that—her life seemed to have crashed out of control.

Howard Chin's men had offered to take them to recuperate at Xanadu, but Nick needed a hospital. After an airlift in the Forestry Service chopper to the Skykomish Ranger Station, Nick and Claire had been brought to a Seattle hospital by ambulance. The paramedics had said they weren't sure if Nick had broken any bones; his agony came from a shoulder dislocation. But most surprising to Claire was that, somehow, in the two days they'd been gone, they'd become state-wide news.

"Maybe our instant fame will scare our enemies away," Nick had whispered to her in the E.R. when they'd heard about the waiting reporters. He'd spo-

ken between gritted teeth, though the paramedics had
given him something for the pain.

In the E.R. he had gripped her wrist so hard with
his good hand, she'd winced. "I don't want you staying at the lodge alone, Claire. We've got to plan
what to do next—"

"Next, you gotta go get fixed up, Sheriff Braden,"
a tall, thin orderly had said, and rolled Nick's gurney
out of the E.R., leaving Claire to her vigil.

Nick kept his eyes tight shut. Since the paramedics
had first arrived, they'd had a drip going in his good
arm to dull the pain, but it still surged back in his
shoulder when they examined him.

Had he told Claire to stay here at the hospital until
they could confer again? He hadn't been thinking
straight since, in the flying debris, he'd somehow
bounced off one of the big tire wheels of that logging
machine. He'd been trying to yank Claire away from
possible gunfire.

"Your shooting arm, isn't it, Sheriff Braden?" the
white-haired orthopedist, whose name he couldn't recall, said.

"Yeah," Nick managed to say, but his voice
sounded weak and breathy.

"With your help, we're going to put that humerus
bone back in the shoulder socket. But that will in-
crease your discomfort again, so we're going to give
you an injection of Versed to help with that."

Nick nodded and closed his eyes again. The jab
of the needle was nothing compared to the sheer,
gut-shaking agony of this damn shoulder. It was the
first time he'd been seriously hurt on the job, and
he'd done it himself. But had he been on the job?

Or was he on his own, trying to protect and help and love Claire?

His thoughts drifted. He couldn't catch them; they leaped and darted off like salmon fighting the upriver current. Maybe this was what it was like to be shot by a Taser. Damn it, he was certain the guy in that first chopper—Howard Chin's—had had a rifle. Instead, it turned out to be a megaphone. The air had been thick with flying debris, but rifles and megaphones didn't look alike. His old platoon would have laughed themselves sick over such a mistake. If he hadn't been so out of it, he'd have demanded to search their chopper.

"We'll wait just a few moments for that Versed to take full effect," the doctor said.

Nick nodded, then couldn't recall what had just been said. Claire had been the one who'd saved him, helped him. He'd opened up again to a woman, he'd fallen in love again…. Something about her used to remind him of Susan, but she wasn't like her. He was certain now he could trust Claire…trust her with his love…love her harder and better…

"Better now?" the doctor asked. "I'm going to carefully place your fingers of the injured arm into this device, Sheriff."

Nick opened his eyes a little. From a second IV pole hung a contraption that looked like a five-wire Chinese finger trap. When he was a kid he'd had one made of woven bamboo that was impossible to pull his finger out of.

"Chinese torture?" Nick grunted.

The guy dared to chuckle as he carefully lifted and maneuvered Nick's arm into the loops until his fingers were pointing straight up at the ceiling. His arm was at a right angle to the rest of his body on the gurney. Before he even realized another man was in the room, the doctor's assistant stepped forward to put steady pressure on his lower upper arm at the elbow.

Nick tried to keep his mind off what was happening as the two men rotated the arm to get it back in place.

It was getting even harder...to hang on to his thoughts. Who had been threatening Claire's life and then tried to kill them both? Of course, it was the same person who had murdered Keith.... Maybe on the river, under the lodge windows, Keith had spotted something illegal going down. Some random, accidental, off-the-wall event he hadn't told Claire about. Maybe he saw guys dealings drugs. Otherwise, why would a man who owned a fishing lodge in a rural area get himself killed, unless...

Again Nick tried to force his brain to go back over the possible suspects. But pain distracted him, derailing his thoughts. Anne's affair and lies... Joel's business in the red... Noah maybe smuggling illegal ivory scrimshaw...

He gasped and frowned at his fingers in that Chinese trap.

Through the *thud* of pain, possible pieces of the puzzle began to fall together.

"Are you okay, Sheriff? Don't faint on us now. Just a moment or two more, and the worst will be over."

"Aaugh!" Nick cried as he tried to yank his hand out of the finger trap. But the assistant and the trap held him firm; he heard and felt the arm go back in place. And in the pain and relief of that moment, he knew with sudden clarity who must have killed Keith Malvern.

He had to warn Claire before it was too late.

Claire jumped at the sound of a man's voice. She'd actually dozed off, perhaps from the large meal of cafeteria food she'd eaten as much as her utter physical and emotional exhaustion. Yet it was just noon and so much had already happened today.

"Sorry to startle you," Dr. Scherbarth, Nick's orthopedist, said as he stood over her in the family waiting room. A tall man, he leaned down to put a steadying hand on her shoulder. "I just wanted to tell you we got the sheriff's arm back in, and he's resting comfortably. I'm hopeful there will be no need for follow-up surgery."

"Thank God—and thank you, Doctor. I'd like to see him."

"Let me take you to his room, but I can't promise he'll be awake or lucid."

"Because of the painkillers?"

"Yes, he's sedated. The medics administered morphine earlier, and I gave him a push dose of Versed," he said as he led her down a hall, then turned twice before they went into an area called E.R. Recovery.

Nick was in one of several curtained areas. His eyes were closed, but his coloring was better than when she'd last seen him. He looked strange in that tie-on gown, as if he were a big child sleeping in a little bed—a child, that was, with the start of a thick, black beard. His injured arm was wrapped in a cushioned foam sling that bound it with Velcro to a wide foam strip on his chest.

"I must warn you, Mrs. Malvern," Dr. Scherbarth went on, not even bothering to talk quietly, "that Versed has amnesiac properties."

"Meaning he won't remember things?"

"Believe me, it's best that he not recall the agony of the shoulder dislocation or its repair. But yes, it blocks out what we did to him, including anything he was thinking at the time. Since there was trauma when his injury occurred, that part of his recall may be blocked, too, but there will be no long-range memory damage. If you'd like to sit here with him for a while, that's fine. He'll be moved to a room for observation for at least one night, especially considering how you two have been staging your own *Survivor* TV show in the wilds. I guess you've heard the media have been waiting for you downstairs."

"I'll give them a few comments on my way home. A friend of mine is coming to drive me back to Portfalls, but I'll be here to pick Nick up when he's released."

Diana had been told of their rescue by her father, who had kept her informed of their initial disappearance. She had traced Claire to the hospital to offer her services and should be here soon. Thank heavens Howard Chin had sent that helicopter, because they'd never even seen the other search planes, and the Forestry Service chopper had just happened to be in the area when the Chin plane contacted it. But she knew very well that this rescue hardly meant she and Nick were safe.

Dr. Scherbarth stepped out and left her standing over Nick, though she was still so shaken and exhausted that she soon collapsed in the single chair. When she faced the reporters, she could hardly accuse anyone of murder, Keith's or her and Nick's attempted ones, because she hadn't reasoned that out yet.

Nick's eyes opened. "Claire?" he murmured. He looked relaxed for the first time since his plane had crashed. She felt overwhelming relief that he remembered her, at least, but the doctor had said that the drug would only affect his recent memory. She stood, taking his good hand in both of hers as she bent over him.

"How are you feeling?"

"Good enough to tell you not to stay at the lodge tonight."

He'd forgotten he'd already said that, she thought.

"All right."

"I'd offer you my place, but whoever was after us might think of that. Get Aaron to meet you at the lodge while you get some things and stay with someone safe. And let him or someone else on my staff know where you are."

"Diana's driving me home."

He frowned. "But don't let her stay with you," he insisted. "Listen, Mike Woods will be on night shift, so tell my staff I said you should stay at Mike's tonight. That'll work. My place might be a target but not Mike's. Promise me!"

"Yes, I'll call Aaron or Peggy, and they can set it up with Mike. You get some rest now, and I'll be here tomorrow or whenever they release you to drive you back to Portfalls."

"It better be tomorrow. And Claire..."

"What?"

"Partners, in crime and out?" he whispered, raising one eyebrow.

Swamped with emotions, she couldn't speak. Only when she nodded and dropped a quick kiss on his stubbled cheek did he let her go.

"I don't know why you don't come stay with us in town," Diana said as she drove Claire north on I-5 toward Portfalls in the rain. "You described the accident and your ordeal in enough detail that those reporters probably won't bother you again. Besides, they'd never find you if you were with Ethan and me. We have plenty of room, you'd be with friends after that near disaster, and you'd be closer to Nick Braden at the hospital."

"I'm grateful but I want to pick up my SUV at the airport and get a few things from home," Claire said. She felt utterly exhausted.

"Don't you think we could loan you a car and get you some things for a brief stay? My father sends his own helicopter to search for you, and you think we can't loan you a car?"

She sounded hurt—no, more than hurt. Diana sounded insulted or angry, though it was almost hard to hear her with the drumming of rain on the car and the rumble of distant thunder.

"I appreciate everything, Diana, really."

"Better yet, I could stay at the lodge and drive back tomorrow with you to get Nick."

"Thanks, but no need. Besides, I've been in these clothes for almost three days."

Claire hesitated to say more. Her first instinct was to tell Diana that she was going to briefly check the lodge, collect a few things, then stay the night at one of Nick's deputies' homes. But she'd learned the hard way that she could trust no one right now, no one but Nick.

"I'll be fine," she assured Diana, wishing she could convince herself that was true. "I'm just sorry you had to drive me back here through this downpour."

"Storms are showing up midafternoon on a regular schedule lately," her friend muttered. "But the other thing about going back to the lodge is that the media may be lying in wait for you there."

"But you said you thought interviewing me should satisfy them, at least for now. I'm just hoping they don't bother your father."

"'At least for now'? You have some other bombshell coming?"

"I didn't mean that. I only hope your father, as kind and generous as he's been to Keith and me, doesn't mind the publicity." Claire stared intently at the road ahead, as if she herself were driving. "I know he's been trying to keep a low profile in his retirement. I'm just sorry I didn't get to see Xanadu."

"Of course, that can all be rescheduled. He's only relieved you're safe. He was horrified we'd lose you, especially after Keith's tragedy."

Did Claire's increasing paranoia make Diana's heartfelt comment sound hollow? Surely she could trust this woman....

But then, she'd been so certain she could trust Keith, too.

"So when can I get out of here?" Nick asked the nurse when she came in to check his blood pressure and temperature.

She announced that her name was Carolyn, but with her mannish face, short hair and military bearing she reminded Nick of a particular colonel he hadn't liked. Even her pale green scrubs looked ironed. All she needed was a colonel's bars on her chest, and Nick would have saluted. Though his vision was fuzzy, it hardly softened her impact. Those meds were still in his system, affecting his vision and thinking, and his head hurt like hell.

"You will be released when the doctor—or your insurance company—says so, Sheriff," Colonel Nurse said. She managed a tight smile as if she'd made a joke while she pumped up the blood-pressure cuff on his arm, then frowned, reading the meter as the air hissed out. "Immobility of that injured shoulder area is vital or you could actually pop it back out," she added ominously with raised brows.

"So how are my vitals?" he asked.

"Blood pressure up a bit, but after all that you've been through, it's not abnormal. Still, I'm going to tell Dr. Scherbarth."

If his blood pressure was high, he thought, it was from worrying about Claire. He should have told her not to budge from that chair by his bed; he should have called Aaron to insist he come here to get her and guard her with his life.

But it was Nick's own life he wanted to guard her with, give to her. He wished he could have driven back with her. Had she said Diana Nance was picking her up here?

His heart beat harder again. Some thought—some fear, among all his fears for Claire—lay buried just out of reach. There was something he had to remember; even if his head was splitting, he had to go back over everything to try to figure out who could have tampered with his plane and threatened their lives. If only Claire had not always stubbornly insisted on jumping into things with both feet. If only she'd not been so determined to get to the bottom of Keith's death by herself.

While Colonel Nurse filled in the chart that hung in a plastic container on the back of the door, Nick recalled Claire's painting of the suicide bridge. Around the periphery of the scene, the firs and spruce bowed their heads, moody, mourning. The falls crashed into deep, dark pools, and the arch of the iron bridge, which she insisted she had not painted on that particular canvas, looked as if it would throw itself into the torrents of oblivion. Yet he'd seen other such paintings by her: those scenes, those emotions had come from Claire's very depths, whether or not someone else added the person on the bridge, gazing over the edge, ready to jump.

And then, Claire had admitted, she'd smeared the figure downward as though he had fallen or had been pushed or—

The moment the nurse vacated the room, he threw the sheet off and slowly, carefully slid his feet to the edge of the bed, then reached with his good arm for the phone on the bedside table. Despite the fact Aaron was overseeing the county in the sheriff's absence, he had to call him, and call Mike Woods, too. He'd tell them to keep an eye on Claire the minute she got back in Portfalls. But would she go to the airport to get her van or go to the lodge first? He didn't want her alone or with anyone but someone he personally knew and trusted.

21

Though still fussing over wanting to help more, Diana dropped Claire off to get her car, and headed back to Seattle. Claire drove immediately from the airport to the sheriff's office. She needed Aaron to go with her so she could pick up a few things at the lodge, and she hoped to find out if Mike Woods would let her stay the night at his place while he was at work. She wasn't sure where she'd spend the rest of this afternoon before he reported for duty, but she was so exhausted she'd be willing to sleep in one of Nick's empty jail cells.

"Is Officer Curtis here?" she asked his dispatcher Peggy as she stood, dripping wet, inside the office door. Her umbrella and raincoat, along with the rest of the things in her overnight bag, were at the bottom of Lake Fishhook with Nick's plane. The sweet-faced, white-haired lady looked up from what Claire had come to think of as DeeDee's desk.

"My dear, come in," she cried, getting to her feet. "Everyone in town was so distraught about you and the sheriff being lost. We were cutting yellow ribbons to tie everywhere when you were found."

"We really appreciate how people pulled together for us. I can't stay. I've got to stop by my house, but I promised Sheriff Braden I'd get his deputy to go with me."

"Oh dear, Aaron's out at the scene of a car accident on the north edge of town. One of the Fencer twins skidded his car in this rain and went into a tree, but I'll just bet he was speeding. Those boys are both pretty wild, and I never could tell one from the other. High school seniors think they're invincible, you know."

"How is he?"

"I don't know yet, but the thing is, another call just came in from old Sam Twoclaws that someone broke into his place and assaulted him, so I've just called for another squad and was about to radio Aaron. I've called in Mike Woods, too, but he's off today, of course, and had gone to see a friend and—"

"I'll meet Aaron at Sam's!" Claire cried on her way out the door.

If his blood pressure was high before, it must be literally off the chart now, Nick thought when he hung up the phone after calling Peggy. She'd told him about Aaron's covering an accident scene, Sam's 911 call, and Claire darting back out into the rain to head for Sam's.

Nick decided to call Peggy right back to get Sam's number. If Sam had phoned for help, maybe he'd answer, and Nick could find out who'd attacked him and what was stolen. If Sam's assault could be tied to things that had happened to Claire on that stretch of river, it would eliminate him as a suspect and might help nail someone else. Or maybe Claire would answer Sam's phone, and he could tell her again to stay the hell put and not to pursue any of this on her own—as if a leopard could change its spots.

Nick knew his brain was starting to work again, yet he still seemed mired in memories he couldn't quite get hold of. And his words came out slow and slurred, no matter how hard he tried to talk normally. He redialed his office number.

"Peggy, it's me again. I need Sam Twoclaws's number," Nick told her the moment she answered. "And how did Claire look when she was there?"

"Exhausted, frazzled and soaking wet, as if she'd been dumped in the river," Peggy said, then read him the number.

"Thanks. You've got my number here, so keep in touch," Nick ordered and hung up.

Claire. Soaking wet...as if she'd been dumped in the river...

He dialed Sam's number, but the line was dead.

It was five after four in the afternoon when Claire drove past the lodge and pulled into Sam's driveway. The combination of dusk and storm made it nearly as dark as night. She stopped the van, noting Sam's sprawling place showed no lights.

It was possible the storm had knocked out the electricity; it happened out here along the river from time to time, even when the power was on in town. Or perhaps he'd had no lights on during the attack and could not reach the switches. She hated to think of that independent, hardy old man lying injured in the dark, however much he'd seemed to haunt the river at night—and however much he still could know something that he hadn't admitted about Keith's death.

Although Claire had felt dead on her feet earlier, adrenaline surged through her. She grabbed her big flashlight from the floor under her seat, got out and locked the doors. The moment she emerged from the metal shell of the car, the falls roared louder. She tried to ignore its voices.

Obviously, there was no rescue squad here yet, and it might take Aaron a while to arrive with that accident up north. She knew Nick would be furious he wasn't here, with all this going on.

Claire's feet crunched along the wet gravel walkway as she hurried past the stuffed bear sentinels that appeared to guard the place. Sam probably believed their spirits still did. A low rumble of thunder made it seem as if they growled at her.

Steeling herself for a bad scene, she touched the front door. It stood slightly ajar. Pushing it farther in, she called out, "Sam? It's Claire Malvern! The rescue squad's on the way, but I'm coming in to help."

No answer. No sound of any kind that she could hear over the rattle of rain on the roof, the distant thunder and the continual roar of the falls.

Claire had only been here once with Keith; more often, Sam came by their place. But she recalled the mounted stag's heads in this outer office of his taxidermy shop. The big horned beasts on the walls above seemed to shift and stare, watching her as she shone her beam around looking for a light switch.

No wall switches, but there was a pull cord for the ceiling light. She tugged it, but nothing happened.

"Sam? It's Claire Malvern!"

Recalling Keith had said that Sam's place was

built room on room, with no halls, she wasn't surprised to find herself immediately in the next room
when she walked through the door. From shelves on
two walls, amidst other birds of prey, an owl and a
falcon with spread wings seemed ready to swoop at
her. A big wooden worktable held a shallow sand-
box, where ghostly salmon made of white plaster
were laid out as if they'd been beached.

A mix of pungent smells made her stomach
cramp: shellac, bleach, vinegar, maybe turpentine
like the kind she used to clean her paint brushes.

A bowl of glinting glass eyes caught her flashlight,
winking at her. She skimmed the beam along the
walls: no light switches here either, but another pull
cord dangled from the single ceiling light. She
tugged it twice to no avail.

She felt a sense of foreboding. Where was Aaron
and that squad? But she knew, especially since the
local squads were volunteers, that it could take a
while. After all, she'd rushed here directly from the
sheriff's office. Perhaps the squad would be coming
from farther away, since rescue vehicles must be at
the scene of the teenager's accident. And what if
Aaron couldn't get away from that?

The doors linking the three outer rooms all stood
open. As she entered the third, Claire distinctly
smelled paint. On the worktable, she saw brushes
soaking in a peanut butter jar. Sam was a painter?

Then she remembered that the salmon skins lost
their hues and luster when they were stretched over
the molded plaster bodies and had to be repainted
and shellacked before they were mounted, just like
Keith's four fish hanging at the lodge.

"Sam? Where are you?"

Something crunched under her feet: she saw a sack of plaster had been broken, or maybe slit open. Ghostly footsteps, evidently from a struggle, showed in the mess of it on the floor. It was all evidence of whoever had attacked Sam, so she walked around it.

Searching for Sam, she shot her light around the room, along the floor, under the worktable, into corners. She pointed her beam at the walls and gasped. Dozens of leaping salmon, frozen in death but mimicking life, seemed to swim across these walls, as if Claire were underwater with them.

Her fears pressed in to smother her. Like Keith, these fish had been caught and killed. Outside and in her head, all through her, she heard thunder rumble as if the falls roared even closer. The walls were shifting, closing in, the waves of water bearing her down. So exhausted. So afraid. Light rippled on the surface of the river above. No—that was a strobe from outside bouncing off the ceiling.

The police, or at least the squad, were here! Sucking in a huge breath, Claire shouted toward the front of the house, "In here! Hurry!"

Her flashlight skipped past Sam, then back to him. In the far corner of the next room, wearing a striped robe, he was slumped on his knees. The pulsating lights from outside illuminated him as if he were in an old-time black-and-white movie where the frames jumped and flickered.

"He's in here! Help!" Claire called and ran to him through the fourth room. At one end sat another worktable and more shelves, this time filled with Sam's carvings.

She was stunned to see the old man's coppery skin had gone a pasty white, until she realized he was covered with the same plaster that gritted under her feet. He was bleeding from his nose and mouth, and she recalled that time on her back deck when he'd tried to summon Keith's soul and used the bloodroot juice streaming from his nostrils. But surely he hadn't done this to himself.

She saw his phone, an old black dial kind, next to him on the floor. The cord had been ripped from the wall. Had Sam done that after he'd called 911? If it had been disconnected earlier, had some one else called for him? But Peggy had said Sam himself phoned.

All around him were some sort of note cards, as if he'd dropped them or they'd been scattered in a struggle. No, they were baseball cards, each one in a perfectly fitted plastic envelope. So had the motive for all this been robbery of the baseball card collection Keith had told her about?

She heard the clatter of equipment and men. "Don't ruin those footsteps in the plaster in that third room!" she shouted to them.

"Sam. Sam, what happened?" she cried, afraid to touch him. Thank God he was alive; she saw his chest rise and fall. From under the blanket, slowly, he pulled out one of his mounted salmon and extended it to her, the wooden mounting block by which it would be hung on the wall facing her.

"Cursed, all cursed, until the land returns to the people," he said, his voice almost inaudible.

"Help's here now, Sam. Who did this to you?"

"Didn't see. Coverall. I came in from the river—he was here."

She tried to read his lips because she wasn't certain what he'd said. "Do you mean cover-ups, Sam?

Have you been covering up for someone you saw on the river?''

"On the river—I told you, the salmon have the answers,'' he whispered. "Keith knew that, Keith used that—''

Two medics knelt beside her, then shouldered her away so they could get to their metal cases. Claire took the mounted salmon from Sam's hands and stood back as they bent over him. She wondered if the old man had been delirious just now. As she shone her light to help them, she heard another car pull up on the gravel outside.

Aaron? Still, she stayed tight, hoping she'd get to ask Sam another question.

It wasn't Aaron, but Deputy Mike Woods who came in.

"Hey, Mike, you're on duty early,'' the older of the medics said to him, then turned back to tending Sam. "We just got here,'' he added. "Not much to report yet.''

Deputy Mike Woods was a thirty-something, husky six-footer she'd only met once before. "Ms. Malvern, did he say anything to you about who did this?'' he asked, motioning her into the next room, the one at the back of the house. Realizing she still clutched Sam's mounted salmon, she put it down on the table and followed Mike.

"No, and I asked him. He indicated his attacker must have been waiting for him when he came home. I can't imagine anyone sneaking up on him who wasn't pure spirit,'' Claire said with a shake of her head. "He also said the salmon have all the answers, that my husband knew that. And that there's a curse until the land comes back to his people.''

Frowning, Mike shrugged. Claire saw they were in Sam's living area now. A low pallet with blankets lay on the floor for a bed or couch; a wood-burning stove, sink, and hearth made this room, at least, look livable. She wondered where the bathroom was. Even the weirdest interior decorators she'd ever known could not have put this hodgepodge, bizarre place together.

"I'm going to check the back door," Mike said, "then ask you to go out that way so we don't all traipse back through the front. The sheriff's set up everything for you to go stay at my place. Plus, I just got radioed that he called back a third time to get Peggy to spend the night with you there. I'm going to be busy with this, anyway, and Aaron can't leave the scene of that accident right now."

"How is the young driver?"

"As smashed as his car, but early word is, he'll make it."

"Thank God for some good news."

"Back door's unlocked," Mike observed, not touching the knob.

"The front one was, too, but I doubt if Sam ever locked up. I didn't touch the knob in case you need to take prints. It wouldn't be hard for an intruder to walk right in. Over the years, I think Sam's best security has been that people are afraid of him."

"Someone wasn't."

"I don't know his baseball card collection's value, but maybe someone came to take it—only, if that's what the intruder was after, a lot of them are still scattered in there." Her voice faded, and she sighed.

"Sammamish Sam with his American baseball cards," Mike said and shook his head. "Look, Ms.

Malvern, I'd better scout around here more, but I've got a part-time cop, Jim Jeffers, out in front of this place in his own car. You been to the lodge to get your things yet?''

"The sheriff made me promise I wouldn't go there alone."

"Made me promise, too," he muttered, "so I'll have Deputy Jeffers go over there with you. When you head for my place, he can phone the sheriff to update him. Here's a key and the directions, though I gave the same to Peggy at the office."

"I can't thank all of you enough. I'm sure I'll be fine, but..."

"But whoever did this to the old guy could be the same river rat who's been harassing you and worse, with that plane crash."

Despite this tragedy for Sam, Claire felt better about her own situation. Though Nick was not here, like a guardian angel he'd called to update everyone and ask them to help her. She clutched the key and paper with directions in one hand and her flashlight in the other.

"Deputy, we're going to transport him," the younger medic told Mike as he stuck his head through the doorway. "I think we got him stabilized. Probably some internal bleeding, but he's a tough one. Ms. Malvern," he added, looking at her now, "the old guy said to tell you something that didn't make much sense. That if he dies, you're to tell the dark sky he likes music. 'Least, that's what I think he said," he added with a shrug and was gone.

He must have said, *Tell Dark Sky I like her music,* Claire thought. That rock song he had been listening to on the river—Keith had mentioned Sam's granddaughter was with a band. Maybe at least one good thing had come of this: stern, traditional Sam still loved his rebellious granddaughter. For the first time in years, Claire realized she desperately wanted to see her own father.

At least it sounded like Sam would pull through. Claire—hopefully, with Nick—could question him tomorrow. Perhaps the medics were taking Sam to the same hospital where Nick would spend the night.

While she waited for Mike Woods to confer with the medics in the other room, she noted Sam kept his dissecting knives, or maybe his fish-cleaning and cooking knives, too, in here, prominently displayed over the sink. Dangling through slits in a wooden rack, the blades glinted gray in the murky room, then shone silver as she turned her light on them. There on the top shelf, propped up behind the carved bone handles, was a painting of the falls and the Bloodroot River Bridge, one Claire had done, one she was quite sure had been taken from her shed.

Amazed, then horrified, she walked closer, shining her flashlight on the painting. Partly hidden behind the knife handles was a figure, one she was certain she'd never done. Unlike in her other picture that had been tampered with, this figure was not sitting on the bridge and was not a man.

A woman, with hair the color of hers, was either falling or jumping to her death from the bridge into the white-water river below.

Claire gasped. Had Sam added this figure and the one of the man in her other painting? Sam was behind it all?

Though she could hardly tear her gaze away from the figure, she saw something else on the shelf of knives: lying on its side was a square, space-age-looking pistol, unlike any she'd ever seen.

A Taser gun? *The* Taser gun?

"Deputy Woods," she called, shaking so hard her voice quavered, "could you come back in here for a second?"

22

Special Deputy Jim Jeffers turned out to be a silver-haired and silver-tongued retired LAPD officer who had volunteered to help out when the sheriff's office was shorthanded. He was bored by retirement here in Portfalls, he told her, especially when the weather was too rough for sailing, so the sheriff had given him and several other locals with law enforcement training a special on-call status.

Claire knew the man's entire life story by the time they had looked all around the lodge together and he pronounced everything "shipshape."

"If you don't mind just waiting down here while I get a few things together, I'd appreciate it," she told him as she started back upstairs. "There's some juice and soda in the fridge if you're thirsty."

"Thanks but don't worry about a thing. I got my orders to stay here till you lock up, then get back to the crime scene next door—if you can call Sammamish Sam's place *next* door, the way places are strung out on this river. It's a real surprise that he'll probably get arrested now for assaulting you with a Taser gun. The guy always looks like he should still be using bows and arrows. It's a crazy world, huh?"

Too crazy, she thought. Though she'd pointed out the evidence of her stolen painting and the Taser gun to Mike Woods, she'd also suggested the items might have been planted. As well as questioning Sam, Mike was going to get the gun and picture frame fingerprinted. Claire wanted to have someone to blame, but if Sam had been her adversary, why had he been attacked? Could he have simply surprised whoever planted them?

If Jeffers noticed she hadn't answered, he was too busy talking to let on. "You know," he called out to her as she reached the top of the stairs, "keeping an eye on you for the sheriff's office reminds me of the time I had to guard a murder-one jury witness, a young woman about your age."

"Oh, really?" Claire responded, hardly listening as she hurried into her bedroom.

"You won't believe it," he shouted, "but the mob had a contract out on her, and she eventually had to lose herself in WITSEC, you know, the witness protection program."

Claire tried to shut out his stream of talk to concentrate on what she needed to pack. She had to use Keith's carry-on bag because hers was in Nick's plane. This bag still had Keith's passport stuck in an inside pocket, one she knew bore the indecipherable stamps in Chinese from Hong Kong and Beijing airport security.

Putting the passport in a drawer, she tossed things into the bag, then saw the message light blinking on her bedside stand. Two messages. Both from Nick, no doubt. Wishing her timer for incoming calls wasn't malfunctioning so she'd know exactly when he'd phoned, she hit the play button.

"Claire, Nick. Call me as soon as you get to the safe house. I hear everything's set."

It felt so good, she thought, just to hear his voice,

though it sounded slow, his words slightly slurred as if his meds still had him a bit doped up. Nothing seemed to be wrong with his brain, though. Nick Braden was still on the case. She noted he didn't mention where she was going to stay. He probably feared someone could break into the lodge and listen to her messages. Considering what had happened to Sam—surely the old man could not have staged his own beating—Nick just might be right.

"They're bringing Sam to this hospital," Nick's voice went on. "I've got to figure out a way to escape from my nurse jailer and go check on him, hopefully talk to him. I got patched through to Deputy Woods. He said you got to Sam first, but he had no idea who assaulted him. I can't believe he had the painting and gun out in plain sight. It's like someone set him up, so we can't think we're out of the woods yet. By the way, Aaron's still on that accident scene. Take care now, and I mean it, because I don't want anything to hap—"

The machine cut him off, so that probably meant he called back and the second message was his, too. She listened intently.

"Claire, this is Tess Markwood." In total contrast to Nick's drawl, Tess talked very quickly, nervously. "It's a real answer to prayer that you and the sheriff were found safe. I hear the prayer chain at church was going 'round the clock for you. I'm so sorry I didn't know about it until it hit the papers. As you know, my mom's been ill, so I've been in and out of here, trying to nurse her and keep Joel from turning into a total stranger."

Claire's heart went out to her friend. Tess, who had been so kind to her, was caught up in her own trials. Claire heard a muffled sniffle, but Tess plunged on. "Anyhow, although I need to be back with Mother, I'm home for a while now. I feel so guilty about leaving poor Joel so much, as moody and depressed as he's been. He just left the house, or I wouldn't share this, especially with what you've been through, but he said he's going fishing with some guys tonight again, and that worries me—I mean, with the bridge's reputation and all. You know what I mean."

Claire's pulse pounded even harder. Tess was afraid her stressed and depressed husband might harm himself, and she was reaching out to Claire for help. Despite her own dilemma, she longed to be able to lend her support. But she'd said that Joel was going night fishing—again.

"I know," Tess continued, "others have seen Joel down on your stretch of the river at night, but he was always alone, they said. I can't call him because he didn't take his cell phone. Maybe he feels guilty he's been so moody, because he left me a beautiful piece of ivory carving. He must have gotten it from Noah, though I didn't think they were speaking. Sorry to unload on you like this. I hope to see you soon, and I thank the Lord you're home safe and so—"

The machine cut her off, too. Claire sat down on the bed so hard the small suitcase bounced against her hip. More than once, Joel had made a point of telling her that he never went night fishing, that he wasn't on the river the night Keith was killed. If he lied about that, why?

If he had been the one trying to scare her—although she wasn't sure why—he could be coming back to harm her again. But maybe she could turn the tables on him, and not just by keeping that blowhard downstairs as a bodyguard. She could get out of here fast, let Joel think she was inside, and go question Tess to learn more, so that she had some proof to get Joel arrested, at least for questioning.

But she could be dead wrong about Joel's guilt. She'd seen he was indeed depressed and moody. What if he was thinking about jumping off the bridge? She'd never forgive herself if she suspected such, then just ignored it. He could have purchased that ivory carving from his brother as a farewell gift for Tess. Whether Joel was Claire's tormentor or just tormented, she knew what she had to do.

She jammed a few other things in the suitcase and turned on all the lights in her bedroom. If Joel intended to harm her, let him think she was upstairs alone. Meanwhile, en route to Mike Woods's place, she was going to stop by the cranberry farm to question Tess. After the plane crashed, Nick had even suggested that.

Claire zipped the suitcase shut, wishing desperately that she had been able to help her mother and DeeDee before they self-destructed. Despite her current dangerous situation, she had no intention of letting Tess, or maybe even Joel, down.

"Ready to go?" Jim Jeffers asked when she joined him.

"All set."

Nick knew he was better when he could stomach the entire, bland hospital meal the peppy little volunteer brought him. It was awkward as hell eating with his left hand, and he couldn't imagine trying to do most other things this way. He probably couldn't drive for days, couldn't shave this three-day stubble off without cutting himself, couldn't shoot his gun for weeks. Even getting dressed on his own would be a real challenge.

Just when he was going to phone Peggy to get an update on things, he got the damn hiccups. His belly had been too empty too long before he stuffed himself.

He turned on his call-nurse light to get more water because he'd drained his pitcher. Slow breathing and slow drinking was the only way he ever got over the hiccups. Only a few drops came out when he tipped the plastic pitcher to his lips.

Drip by drip water fell on his tongue, like Chinese water torture, he thought.

He slammed the pitcher on his table as something flitted through his mind, something he must have forgotten but still couldn't quite grasp. He hadn't been able to come up with a reason that someone would kill Keith, someone Keith had dealings with so he would sneak out at night to meet him or her. Despite all his years in security and law enforcement, he hadn't been thinking big enough. Sure, Keith's murder could be a crime of passion involving a love triangle with Anne or Noah Markwood. But Nick knew he'd more likely figure things out by following some sort of money trail.

How many times had he seen money as literally as the root of all evil? Claire had known so little about what her husband actually did for a career, but she had known it was "finances." Given how bright and bold Claire was, her lack of knowledge about Keith's job had not been because she didn't care, but because Keith, for some reason, had stonewalled her on it.

Perhaps Keith hadn't picked Portfalls just because he fell in love with a derelict fishing lodge, but because Noah Markwood was one of his contacts to distribute the imported Chinese art. Keith's taking Claire's paintings to Noah could be a cover, a ruse to keep in touch with him or to hand things off.

What if Noah were importing illegal Chinese ivory carvings for big bucks from Keith? On his trips overseas, Keith could have set it up, then left that arena so he couldn't be traced. Maybe Keith demanded a bigger cut to help fund the lodge, or Anne really did desert Noah for Keith. Something must have been the straw that broke the camel's back for Noah. So Noah Markwood, a man he'd never suspect of it—educated, cultured, well-off, evidently fulfilled in life other than not getting along with his brother— became a murderer. The only question then was, did his brother Joel, who seemed to be at odds with him, suspect something? Had Joel blackmailed Noah, or was the down-and-out cranberry farmer actually aiding and abetting?

As Claire drove to the cranberry farm, she kept an eye out for someone on her tail and for Joel coming toward her, just in case she passed him. She saw no car that could have been his.

She noted in the gloom of thickening dusk that the two cranberry bogs closest to the house, where Joel had told her he'd planted that early-harvest berry, were flooded. At least he was working his farm and getting some bogs ready for harvest. He had not sunk so deep into the depths of despair that he had withdrawn from the family business he once loved. Perhaps, if she looked at it another way, the gift to his wife of the ivory carving, which he'd no doubt got from his brother's store, could be a good sign. It might mean he had not withdrawn from Tess, either, and that he had made some sort of truce with his brother.

In the slanted rays of setting sun that shot out from clumps of glowering clouds, the crimson harvest of the two flooded bogs looked like floating rubies. Some of the berries had bobbed to the surface, though many, no doubt, still clung to their vines underwater. As Claire got out of her car, she could see that Joel or his workers already had the corral of floating boards in place. When the eggbeater harvester freed the rest of the berries from the vines, the boards would pen them in so they could be sucked out a big pipe into the hopper, which sat just outside the dike. But the hopper was dwarfed by the big machine that would beat the berries into the water.

Claire saw no vehicles around, so Tess must have parked her car in the nearby warehouse that doubled as their garage. Several lights were on in the house and the storm door was open, so at least Tess hadn't gone out like she'd said Joel had.

Claire instinctively locked the SUV, then jammed her keys in her jeans pocket. Hurrying up onto the porch, she knocked on the old screen door. It rattled so hard in its frame that it sounded like a double knock.

As Claire glanced in, she saw the ivory carving Tess had mentioned, sitting incongruously on the Formica-topped kitchen table. It was of a carved fish, ornate and stunning. Unlike Sam's mounted salmon, it did not have a plaque behind it but appeared to jump from a pedestal of teak or some other wood. Its base, Claire judged, was similar in size to the base of the Tang horse about which Diana had been so particular.

"Four inches square," Claire whispered. The imported Chinese porcelain pieces she owned sat on the same-sized bases, ones ChinPak had specially made in China to display their valuable items. It was almost as if Joel had gotten the vase from ChinPak, instead of Noah.

"Tess?" Claire cried, cupping her hands to her mouth. "It's Claire. I need to talk to you!"

"And I need to talk to you," the deep voice behind her said.

Claire gasped and spun to face Joel. He stood at the bottom of the porch steps, his arms crossed over his chest, his coveralls stained red. It took her a moment to assure herself it was cranberry juice, not blood.

But what if it was blood—Sam's blood? Could Sam have tried to tell her that his attacker wore coveralls, not that something was being covered up? Unfortunately, she was putting the pieces together too late.

"Where's Tess?" she demanded, her voice shaking. "She just called me."

"She called you over an hour ago," he told her, not moving, blocking her way down the steps. Claire again cursed her broken timer on her answering machine.

"She said you'd left to go night fishing," Claire said, "when *you* told me you never fished at night."

He grinned grimly. "Something sounds fishy, doesn't it?"

"What's the point, Joel? Where is she?"

"Maybe when she made that call to you, I came back to tell her something and overheard her. And then," he said, as his eyes narrowed ominously, "maybe when I figured you might come calling, I decided it would be better if I were here and not Tess."

"But where is she?" Claire repeated, her voice rising.

"You know, she thought she'd be here for a while, but I told her that my gift to her, besides that ivory fish you've been gawking at, was that she should go back to see her mother. I was really sorry, I said, that I'd complained about the time she'd been spending there. Great guy that I am, I sent her packing."

"Then, I'll be leaving, too," she said, edging toward the steps, though he still didn't retreat. "As I said, I just came to see Tess."

She wanted to accuse him of so much, but where to start? Of night fishing? Of lying? Of being on the river when Keith was killed? Maybe even of being that anonymous caller who said Keith had jumped to his death. She was not crazy enough to accuse him of murder when they were evidently alone out here, and he'd deliberately set her and even Tess up, but she could think of one thing to possibly make him give himself away.

"Someone beat up Sam Twoclaws at his place tonight," she told him, trying not to stare at his stained work clothes. "The police are looking for his attacker, and they're expecting me to drive to see Sam at the hospital in Seattle where the squad took him. As I said, since Tess isn't here, I'll just be leav—"

"You never let up, do you?" Joel interrupted. "Nothing warns you to so much as shut up and back off. You've had your chances."

Even standing a good ten feet from him, she was certain she scented liquor on his breath. Yet he seemed steady and stubbornly sure of himself.

Her heart beat so hard in her chest it shook her. However much she wanted to scream at him, to throw herself at him and kick and scratch, she knew flight was her best tactic. In her desire to help Tess, she'd overstepped, and badly.

Their eyes met and held. She still could not imagine why Joel would want to scare and harm her. Perhaps he'd done it strictly for money, like a hit man working for someone else, as Nick had theorized. Or for his own flesh and blood, Noah, who had much to hide and didn't want to dirty his hands.

Claire saw two possibilities for escape. She could run into the house and try to lock him out, then call 911. But she had nothing on him. It would be his word against hers, even if she could get the police here. Besides, he might grab her before she closed the door or get in his house another way. And if he'd hurt Sam, perhaps he'd ripped the phone out here, too.

Or she could try to vault the rickety-looking railing on this porch and make an attempt to get to her SUV, lock herself in and drive away. But she'd have to back out near the flooded bogs and turn around. If she could only keep him talking, make him think the police knew where she was or that they were on their way...

But in her moment of hesitation, Joel, maybe thinking fear had immobilized her like a deer in the headlights, decided for her.

Nick was furious that Colonel Nurse had refused to give him so much as an update on Sam's admission to the hospital or to get him Sam's room number, though he fully understood that they didn't want him bothering a new patient. But when she marched out, saying she was going to get permission from the doctor to see he was sedated at night because he'd been acting as if this private room were his office, that was it for him around here.

Though dizziness assailed him, Nick got out of bed and shuffled over to close the door to the hall. He got his filthy and torn wilderness clothes out of the tiny closet. Suddenly, he felt he was needed desperately in Portfalls, whatever condition he was in.

Besides, he couldn't stand it that everything was happening in Portfalls without him. And he couldn't keep Claire safe from here, either. If anything happened to her, he'd just as soon take a header off the Bloodroot suicide bridge, just the way those other poor damn fools had done.

Joel dug a pistol from his coveralls and leveled it at Claire. No, it was a Taser.

Instinctively, she screamed and ducked. The tiny darts hissed past her. She ran toward the porch railing, put one hand on it and vaulted.

She hit hard, off balance. Her previously sprained ankle, which had done so well today, wrenched. Yet she ran, limping, lead-footed toward her car.

She heard him behind her and knew she'd never

get inside and lock the door in time. Panicked, she ran toward the flooded bogs.

He'd catch her on the road, she reasoned. But if she could jump in here and swim, at least lighten her weight on that ankle, it might even the odds. Across the bog, she could climb out and try to hide in the surrounding woods. It was the edge of dusk and the forest would be darker still. Then someone would come looking for her—if they could figure where she was when she didn't show up at Mike Woods's.

She leaped into the bog with a crimson splash. The chilly water jolted her, and the vines, like a spongy web beneath her feet, were like nothing she'd ever felt. As if she were the harvester, loosened berries popped to the surface and slowed her.

Claire didn't dare look back at first, but she didn't hear Joel jump in. Perhaps she'd caught him off guard, or else he'd gone to reload that terrible Taser gun again. If he hit her with that in here, she'd drown for sure. She had to get farther away.

She fought through the bog in thigh-deep water, slogging on as if in a nightmare where she couldn't make any progress. It was more shallow here than she had envisioned. If she tried to swim, she'd get caught in the woody vines.

She saw she was trapped by the floating boards of the corral that penned in the berries. If she just ducked under it, could she escape, or could it go under the water to halt her flight?

And then, she heard an engine sputter to life. At first she thought maybe Joel had gone to start a car or truck to drive around the bog to fish her out when she reached the dike closest to the forest.

She glanced back. He had started the eggbeater

and was driving it on its big balloon tires, with its sharp beaters flailing, into the bog.

Ducking out of the main door of the hospital after walking down the emergency staircase, Nick figured he looked so bad he might even get arrested.

He had managed to get his shirt on his good arm and buttoned at his neck, but, of course, his arm and sling made such a bulge under it that his bare chest and stomach showed. He wore his leather jacket draped over his shoulder.

But he had his billfold, as sodden as it still was, jammed in the pocket of the jeans he'd finally fastened with difficulty. He needed a public phone booth to call his office, but when he saw the hospital security guy standing near the pay phones and noticed an empty cab on the curb outside the glassed-in reception area, he opted for a clean getaway.

"You sure you been released, man?" the cabbie asked him as he got gingerly into the back seat and reached way over, slowly, with his left hand to close the door.

"Special circumstances," Nick muttered.

"Okay by me. Where to?"

"Portfalls, thirty miles north."

"I won't get no return fares from there, so it'll cost you round trip."

"I know I look like hell but I'm the sheriff there."

"Ri—ight," the man drawled.

"Really. Here, I'll show you my shield."

He pried his billfold out of his back pocket and flipped it open.

"Don't look real to me."

"This is real!" Nick said, and fought, one-handed,

to dig some twenties from his folding money. They were still wet and flopped out in a pile of at least four or five stuck together onto the cab's front seat.

"Portfalls it is, man. Don't matter none if good money gets wet in all this rain we been havin' anyway, know what I mean? We all oughta just grow us gills and fins round here."

Nick nodded as the cab pulled away. He couldn't wait, not only to get back in his own bed but to be certain Claire was safe in hers.

23

Claire tried to scramble faster through the berries and vines, not paddling but clawing away from the big machine Joel drove into the bog. He sat high above the water, leaning forward over its steering wheel. The harvester was wider than it was high, with big arms supporting rotating metal thrashers used to beat the berries from the vines. Its forward wash rocked the surface of the bog, almost swamping Claire. The woody vines grabbed her feet and she swallowed water. Her sinuses burned. She began to cough and choke as she fought to right herself, to get her bearings.

All the things Joel must have done in the past were nothing next to this. He meant to drown her. Kill her. But why?

Out of breath. Out of strength. No hope...

In that split second when the machine bore down on her, she pictured salmon fighting upriver. With the last remnants of her strength, she wiped water from her eyes and shoved her sopping hair back. Joel loomed over her in his lofty seat. The revolving metal beaters sucked her closer, throwing water and berries at her. She was trapped against the connected floating boards of the corral.

Claire sucked in a big breath, then thrust herself into the shallow water between the surface of bobbing berries and the vines. She fought her way under the boards of the corral, pushing away from the maw of the machine.

Yet the current yanked her back. The revolving arms reached for her, dragging the boards underwater.

No, she thought. She was not going to die like this, drowned like Keith. No!

She threw herself sideways to escape the riptide of the machine. The current was not so strong here, though eddies swirled around her. She half crawled, half pulled herself from the bog.

But the dike was too high here to climb out. She saw her escape had to be where Joel had driven the harvester in. Lunging through the water, trying to ignore her throbbing ankle, she fought her way back under the floating corral and made for the lower side of the dike.

Realizing the roar of the machine had muted, she glanced back. Joel was turning it, but it was balking. He climbed down on one of the big arms and tried to free the snagged boards from the beaters. Now she might make it to her car.

But he saw her intent and ran across the long metal arm to leap onto the dike and run around the edge.

"Why?" she screamed at him as he cut her off again. "Who's paying you? Noah finally loaned you the money?"

He looked as frenzied as she felt, but he didn't answer.

"You beat up Sam tonight to warn him to keep his mouth shut because he saw something," she shouted over the rumble of the machine's motor. She felt so furious that a new jolt of energy coursed through her. "A little beating of an old man's nothing, since you killed Keith!"

"I handled Sam, yeah, but not Keith," he insisted. "I just called Braden's office to say he killed himself. They're gonna find you drowned tomorrow, Claire, not here, but in the river. I'm sorry, but that's the way it's gonna be. I got orders."

"From Noah. And you rigged Nick's plane so we'd crash, didn't you."

"We have to get this over!" he cried, and leaped into the bog after her.

Claire knew she'd never scramble up the bank of the dike away from him, but she felt her salvation pressing against her. Yes, one of the boards that the machine had torn loose from the corral. As Joel closed the gap in the sea of blood-red berries, she put both hands around it as if to hold on to something in the swaying water.

When he was a few feet away, she lifted it and swung it, the board heavy, flinging water. She imagined how DeeDee must have hit Nick with that wheel block at the airport, and put all her strength into the only chance she might get to use it.

The board cracked across the side of Joel's head, sending him off-kilter and his toupee flying. He looked stunned yet enraged. She hit him a second time, then dropped the board and staggered away from him. She crawled up on the bank of the dike. Joel had righted himself but, standing stupefied in the water, he didn't look at her or chase her.

Claire ran for her SUV, then panicked that she didn't have her keys. But yes, they were still stuck in the pocket of her sopping jeans. She dug them out, staggered to her car, unlocked it and threw herself in. The engine roared to life; she forced herself to back up carefully near the bog. When she hit her headlights, they illuminated Joel's bald head as he stood, evidently still dazed, in the middle of the red sea of his harvest. She could only pray he'd still be there when she got Mike or Aaron out here.

Claire drove like a madwoman until she left the farm lane, then forced herself to slow. The roar of the machine in the water had sounded like the falls; she was certain she still heard them. No, it was the car engine racing. She had to keep calm, to think.

Wishing her cell phone had not been ruined when Nick's plane crashed in the lake, she stopped at the public pay phone at the gas station. As she dialed 911, she realized this was the booth Nick had said the anonymous fisherman had called from to say he'd seen Keith jump off the bridge.

Joel must have made that call on his way home from the river that night. But had he seen someone kill Keith or had he done it himself?

"Peggy," Claire cried when the familiar voice came on the line, "it's Claire Malvern. Joel Markwood just tried to drown me in his cranberry bog, and he's there now, if you can get an officer out there. Tell Nick that Joel either was Keith's killer or worked for the killer. I'll see you at Mike's place soon."

"Listen, Claire—" Peggy said, but, soaking wet and still thoroughly spooked, Claire hung up and ran to her car.

She didn't have a change of clothes with her, but that wasn't the reason she was going back to the lodge. Joel was out of the way for now, so she wasn't afraid to go there alone. And even if Sam had had anything to do with trying to harass and harm her earlier, he was in the hospital. Surely no one was following her, or she'd not only see but sense it. She would be in and out of the lodge fast, but she had to check on something that could solve the crime.

Because Sam had said, *The fish have the answers, the salmon have the answers. Keith knew it, Keith used it.*

Maybe Sam was trying to help, not hurt her. The old man might not know what Keith had meant, any more than she did, but now she had a place to look. She'd missed so much, starting with the fact that Keith—Diana, too—had cared that the bases of their imported Chinese art must be a certain size. It was Keith, not Sam, who had reworked the bases for those four mounted salmon before he hung them on the great room wall. He'd said something about wanting them a particular size, and she'd paid no attention. How many times had she dusted those, how often had she told Keith she didn't like them, but he had insisted they stay?

Claire pulled into the driveway, then killed the light and the engine. She fumbled with her key in the kitchen door. She was glad she had left her bedroom lights on upstairs, because the lodge looked welcoming and safe after all she'd been through.

Careful to lock and latch the door behind her, Claire tore into the living area and turned on more lights. Ignoring the fact she was shaking with wetness and cold, she lifted the first mounted salmon off the wall and turned it over.

The wooden piece that Keith had adapted to

mount the fish on the wall was slightly larger than four inches square, the standard ChinPak size for its bases. That had to mean something, but what? She carefully lifted one of her two big Ming vases off the mantel and brought its display base over to the couch. Yes, it was very similar in shape and size to those that held the fish to the wall, but so what?

She flipped both the vase stand and the fish plaque over. Under the vase stand, she saw a four-inch square indentation where something flat could have been hidden. When she pulled the plaque loose from the piece of wood screwed to the fish, a computer diskette fell onto the couch.

She examined the unmarked diskette and jumped up to check the other three mounted salmon. Each plaque hid a diskette between the wooden wall fastener and the fish.

Claire gathered the four diskettes and ran upstairs, turning on more lights. She booted up Keith's computer, which Nick had returned after his expert found nothing unusual on it, then placed one diskette in the disk drive.

When she clicked the mouse, the machine whirred; vertical rows of Chinese calligraphy appeared, line after line of it as she scrolled down. Her mind raced. This could be nothing, or everything. But as she bumped Keith's keyboard to take the first diskette out to check the next one, she realized what Ethan Nance must have been doing here the day he claimed he just wanted to stay at the lodge, that day Diana bought him the Tang horse at Noah's Puget Treasures. Ethan must have been searching Keith's computer for the information on these diskettes. But what was it?

Had Keith been smuggling additional art pieces Ethan or Diana or Howard Chin didn't know about, but they'd eventually caught on somehow? Or had they been smuggling in art on the side, and Keith had caught them, and this was the proof?

No, she reasoned, feeling sick to her stomach, because it seemed the diskettes themselves were the hidden treasures. But what was this information? The second diskette, then the third filled the screen with more rows of Chinese characters. She couldn't trust the Nances now, but she'd have to find someone to read what was on these. She'd take them and head for Mike Woods's place to get some sleep until she could show them to Nick tomorrow.

Then she had another thought. That single psychiatric report she had on her mother—she knew right where it was.

She pulled open the only drawer in this desk that had not been Keith's. Yes, in this file, that's where it would be. But it was gone—no, just misfiled one folder back. Ethan must have read it that day she and Diana found him here at the desk, then perhaps put it back hastily when they returned. And with a reading of that and what she had told him about her mother's suicide, he forged the fake report he sent Nick.

A shadow fell across the desk. A silhouette of a man blocked the door to her bedroom. For one crazed moment, she thought of Keith, Keith come back from the dead.

When the man stepped forward from the hall into the room, she cried out as if someone had punched her in the stomach.

"So you didn't know where they were until now,"

he said. "I actually thought I was going to have to take this lodge apart board by board, evidently over your dead body."

Nick was so relieved when he pulled up at Mike Woods's house. He couldn't wait to see Claire, to hold her. Peggy would never be enough protection for her tonight, even if no one knew where to look for her. He was going to spend the night here to be certain she stayed safe.

"Three of those twenties should cover this," he told the cabbie.

"And then some, man. You want me to wait till you get in your house?"

"Yeah, just until I give you the high sign," Nick said and carefully, painfully edged out of the back seat. The meds they'd given him through the IV he'd pulled out of his arm were starting to wear off, and he was hurting all over. His shoulder had begun throbbing again, though his blurred vision had cleared a bit. He still spoke slowly and deliberately, as if he had a mouth full of peanut butter.

Then he realized Mike's place was totally dark. The doorbell and banging on the door with his good hand brought no one.

"You sure this is the address, man?" the cabbie called to him.

Swearing under his breath, Nick got stiffly into the cab. "Back out and turn right," he said. "Head for the police station uptown."

"You mean you really are the sheriff? Or you gonna turn yourself in for something? Look, I could drive you back outta here."

"Get going," Nick muttered. "And you have my permission to speed."

But the cabbie's last words brought something else to mind. Nick was still haunted by the way the guy in Howard Chin's chopper had said, "We're here to take you out." He'd obviously meant to fly them out of the area, but he could have meant to kill them. Nick knew he'd spotted a gun in the guy's hands at first, pointed at him and Claire.

"I kept telling Howard," the man said to Claire, "if he'd just give you enough time before we scared you off or eliminated you, bright little broad that you are, you'd find those disks for us."

Ethan. Once friend and protector. It was Ethan Nance. She'd had the place re-keyed and locked, but he could have had her extra set of keys copied that day he'd spent here.

"What's on the disks?" she asked, managing to keep her voice under control, though she shook as if she were chilled again. Her hair prickled on her arms and the nape of her neck while gooseflesh glided over her skin. Her instincts were to do anything to stall until she could get a weapon, even if it was a ballpoint pen or scissors from the desk drawer. It must have been Ethan—and Diana or Howard Chin, too?—behind all this. And this man certainly hadn't come here now to simply fill her in or chat.

"In a nutshell," Ethan said, taking one step into the room, "the disks hold information about American intelligence software for which my father-in-law paid a lot of money and which he then had translated into his native language. We didn't dare send it to

Beijing over the Internet. I believe the feds' current term for it is 'illegally trafficked technology.'"

Though she had demanded he tell her, she was dumbfounded that he had. She was not relieved by that; his open confession of spying and treason showed he definitely meant to eliminate her, now that she'd found what he wanted.

"It's nice to know you're surprised, Claire," he went on. "I told Howard the fact you were hot on our trail didn't mean that Keith had told you. You see, if the feds find those disks, they will want to charge ChinPak—and me—with conspiracy."

"And not with treason?"

"The point is, such charges would mean up to five years in prison and a $250,000 fine for conspiracy, as well as another $500,000 in fines and five additional years in the slammer for each count of trafficking, and we're talking lots of counts here."

"But the pieces of art were coming *from* Chinese-held territories, not going *to* them. So why worry about hiding information for the Chinese in the hollowed-out bases. I don't get it."

"Oh, I think you do. Or will."

His voice was so ominous, she shuddered. He was dressed all in black—jeans, T-shirt, a fanny pack he wore in front of him, loose flannel shirt, shoes and gloves. What appeared to be a knitted, black ski mask protruded from his shirt pocket. Her pulse pounded harder and faster. She had to keep calm, keep him talking.

He shrugged as if he couldn't be bothered to explain more, but went on. "Keith and I took the— contraband, shall we call it?—into Hong Kong and Beijing secreted in our custom-made briefcases, but

Keith didn't know he was a courier for a long time. Unfortunately, he figured it out, then made the very big mistake of copying four disks before he delivered them, so he could blackmail us.''

"You're trying to put the blame on him.''

"He's guilty of complicity, at least, since he decided to make a profit from it, too. It's Keith who went around me to arrange the four-inch bases, so he could smuggle copies of the disks *out* of China that he couldn't get his hands on until he was *in* China. To cover his tracks, he had most of our new bases for the art made to those specs, but was only able to smuggle out four of the disks—those four I've been looking for—before I caught on and suggested he take early retirement. I had to get him out of the company before I got him out of our hair permanently.''

"How do you know there were only four disks? I just might know where others are, and we can make a bargain for them, if—''

He laughed harshly. "Nice try. You are such a clever girl. Too clever, and that's been as much of a problem for me as Keith was. He was good at secrets, wasn't he, including Anne Cunningham?''

Claire had been convinced she couldn't feel worse, but, despite her horror at his other admissions, Keith's adultery and her stupidity about it still hurt. Yet, why should she believe this liar and murderer?

"Anne wasn't involved in this, too?'' she asked.

"I wouldn't even know about her if Keith hadn't mentioned her. Her only involvement was her fling with him. Joel says she's evidently not talking about any of it, which is fortunate for her. Now, sadly, I'm going to have to arrange it so you don't do any talking, either.''

Claire felt numb. Keith had taken the wrong path and paid for it. She'd like to believe he'd intended to tell the American authorities, but it sounded as if he only intended to blackmail ChinPak for profit. If so, he must have hidden money somewhere.

"No more questions?" Ethan asked. "I thought you'd rant and rave at me for trying to manipulate you, for being a traitor to the red, white and blue, or something."

"You killed Keith, of course."

"You should have let it just be another suicide off the bridge, Claire. You should have just moved away, gone back to Seattle, or better yet, San Diego or—''

"You sent that fake psychiatrist's report about my mother to Nick Braden, didn't you? Were you trying to make him think I was as unstable as she'd been? Or make me think so when you altered my paintings? Does Diana know?"

For the first time, the bastard actually looked upset. "I swear she doesn't," he whispered, ignoring her other questions.

Strangely, Claire believed him. She hadn't known what Keith was up to, either, and would bet that Tess had no clue about Joel's involvement in all this.

"Maybe I know where the blackmail money is," she said.

"You never cease to amaze me, Claire. It's your brains and tenacity—and your dragging the sheriff of this podunk place into this—that have caused all your trouble. Yeah, I paid Keith a lot of money at first, just to buy myself time to decide how to handle him. But that's all water over the—over the falls now, so let's quit the chatter and get going.''

Defiantly, Claire faced Ethan and sat back against the edge of the desk, leaning her hands behind her. The scissors weren't out on the desk. She wasn't sure she could open the drawer and reach them, but she did manage to cover a ballpoint pen with her right hand. Paltry protection, she thought, against a man who'd paid for Tasers and threw those who crossed him off bridges.

"I said, we've got to be going, but you know that. I can't trust that your police friends won't come looking for you here."

"They've arrested Joel," she said, hoping she wasn't bluffing. "And I have no doubt he's ready to plea bargain about being your hey-boy in all this."

"You know, I wondered why you're soaked," Ethan said, coming toward her, "and have those bright red stains all over your clothes. Been rolling in the berries with poor Joel? He called but failed to fill me in on all the details, as he was in a bit of a hurry to get out of town."

Claire moved slowly around the desk as Ethan came closer. He picked up the disks, including popping out the one still in the computer. She slowly opened the desk drawer, wishing she could lunge for the scissors, but like Joel earlier, Ethan pulled a Taser gun on her.

"These are so much neater than bullets and blood," he said. "And after a body's been knocked around in the river, there's absolutely no sign the Taser's been used. Shall I use this now, and wrap you up to carry you, or will you come along with me like a good girl?"

''You shot me with the Taser before.''

''Joel did, but he was acting for me, as he has been since you and Keith moved here. I found him and proposed our working relationship, a lucrative one on his part—to keep the farm afloat, as he put it—because I needed someone on site to watch Keith. When I started to pay Joel, I told him to carry on as if the farm were on the brink of ruin.''

''How did you find him at first?'' she asked, sliding her hand slowly into the drawer. The scissors were cold to the touch.

''I'd read in a newspaper a very angry and bitter op-ed piece he'd written about the plight of small, family cranberry farms, and being in a family business myself, really felt for him.''

''You bastard. You don't feel for anyone but yourself. You not only killed Keith but tried to kill Nick Braden and me by partially severing the oil hose in his plane!''

''I plead guilty to helping Keith off the bridge, but Joel, master mechanic with those harvesting machines, handled the oil hose. And now, I'll have to tend to Joel somehow. But he's scared and on the run. He called me on my cell phone about fifteen minutes ago as he was hitting the road out of Portfalls, and he warned me you were loose again.''

''Now you're bluffing!'' she accused, closing her hand around the scissors.

''Am I? Keith erroneously thought the same thing. That he could control and outsmart me. That he could deceive and deny me. He was so cocksure he was in the driver's seat that he sneaked out of your bed in there,'' he went on, pointing toward their bedroom, ''where I've been resting just now, hoping you'd stop by before going to the 'safe house' the sheriff mentioned on the answering machine. That night he died, Keith sneaked out to inform me the quarter million I'd already paid him in cold cash would only get me one of the four disks back. But now I've got all four—and you. Let's go, Claire.''

''Go where?'' she countered, shifting the scissors behind her hip.

''Don't you know?'' he asked, his voice almost mesmerizing now. ''Don't you know you've heard the falls beckoning, getting louder and louder at night?''

''You arranged *that?*''

''Joel, with a tape in a boom box. I hoped you would tell the sheriff or someone else, because any sane, stable person would know it was all in your head.''

But it *had* been in her head, she thought. Sometimes she had actually thought she heard the falls when she was nowhere near them, when Joel could not have been hiding nearby with a tape in a boom box. Damn this man for doing that to her!

''Those books on depression were yours, not Keith's,'' Ethan went on, his tone calm and coaxing. ''At least, the sheriff will think so after the rash, desperate act you're going to commit tonight. He'll accept that you altered your paintings to show your death wish. Why, that one painting might suggest *you* actually killed Keith. At any rate, you've decided to follow in your dead husband's and your sick mother's footsteps and end your life.''

24

———————

"No!" Claire screamed and lunged at Ethan with a ballpoint pen in one hand and the scissors in the other. She was certain that Ethan would try to shoot her with the Taser gun, but she evidently took him by surprise. With a downward thrust of the scissors, she stabbed his wrist, making him drop the gun.

He seized her from the back. In the struggle, one of them kicked the gun, and it slid into the hall. If she could only get past Ethan, get the gun or make it downstairs to run.

Claire lunged for the hallway and tried to pick up the gun, but he, too, scrambled for it on the polished wood floor. The four disks scattered. Again the Taser skidded away, sailed between two spokes of the banister and clattered to the floor in the room below.

"No," she cried again. "I won't go outside the way he did that night!"

Claire clawed and kicked but Ethan was bigger, stronger. He shoved her facedown on the floor and wrenched her right arm up behind her back. Her cheek was pressed up to one of the diskettes that had caused all the chaos.

"Stop struggling, damn you," he ordered. He spoke through gritted teeth. "Once you're in that river, no previous bruises or broken bones are going to matter, anyway, so don't give me the excuse to beat you first!''

The vision of Keith or herself in the river sobered her. She'd never outfight this man physically. Perhaps she should pretend to go along, look for her chance to throw him off guard somehow. Even if he took her out on the bridge she dreaded, maybe she could find a way to break free. If only she could convince him she was weaker than she was.

Claire pretended to accidentally bang her forehead on the floor. She lay very still.

''Claire?''

She could hear him gathering the disks from the floor. He pulled out the one from under her cheek. Should she pretend she was unconscious, or try to make him think she was just dazed, perhaps that she didn't remember some of the things he'd said? Hopefully then, he wouldn't use the Taser on her. But her ruse was for nothing. He yanked her to her feet. Dragging her back into the room, with one hand still bending her arm, he managed to put the disks into the fanny pack he wore.

''I forgot to bring some rope, so Keith's neckties from your closet will have to do,'' he muttered, pulling three of them knotted together from the sleeve of his flannel shirt. He tied her tightly, wrapping his makeshift rope around her wrists behind her back, then encircling her entire body, talking nervously all the while.

''If the cops find and identify these ties, maybe they'll think you went out on the bridge to hang yourself, but fell in instead,'' he muttered as if reasoning aloud. He shoved her toward the steps, then, when she balked, dragged her downstairs, stopping only to locate the Taser gun on the floor. Making sure the safety was on, he jammed the gun in his jeans pocket.

"You know," he told her, "after they find your body, your suicide may actually be enough to get that lovely old bridge you paint so well torn down."

"You had Joel take my paintings from the shed."

"And had him drag that dead deer display onto your back porch when he suggested it might make you mistrust that old Indian more, dear, *deer Claire.*" He laughed at his own bizarre joke. "I even spotted that Indian hanging around the river the day I spent here searching the lodge. I was furious I didn't find the disks or the money I paid Keith."

"You should have kept him alive to tell you."

"No, he had to go. He was a loose cannon. I couldn't control who else he'd tell, maybe even the feds."

As Ethan marched her toward the glass doors of the lodge, their reflection leaped at her. She could almost see again the image of that dead deer looking in at her.

The minute Ethan opened the back door to her deck, she heard the chatter of the river rapids and, as always, above and beyond that, the beckoning voices of the falls. They sounded strangely comforting, almost luring. She should never have hit her head; she was so dizzy.

But *was* she crazy? Did she want to escape all this through the dreadful fall Ethan would force her to take? Did she want to follow in the footsteps of her mother and Keith? It would be so much easier than fearing and fighting....

No, she refused to give up or give in. Ethan was

demented, not her. She wanted to live, to have time
to discover if she could have a life with Nick. And
she wanted that life to be here along the river she
had grown to love, which, even now, leaped to life
with sturdy salmon.

"What do you mean, you don't know where she
is?" Nick roared.

Peggy flinched as if he'd struck her. "I mean,"
she said, wringing her hands, "she phoned to tell me
what I just explained about Joel and said she'd see
me at Mike Woods's place soon."

"But she's not there!"

"Maybe she's still on her way—no, it's been too
long. Well, she certainly wouldn't go back to the
lodge. I can't send Mike there, because he's out at
the cranberry farm. Claire said Joel would be there,
but he's apparently left."

Nick sank into the wooden chair next to Peggy's
dispatcher desk. He hurt all over, and was running
on pure adrenaline. He wasn't even sure if he was
thinking straight. He only knew he loved Claire Malvern, and he was scared to death he was going to
lose her.

"I let the cab go, so you'll have to drive," he told
Peggy. He knew he was risking his entire career on
that order. If a 911 call came in, and he'd pulled the
dispatcher away and left an office empty of help...
But the part-time night-shift dispatcher should be in
here soon. He was certain Claire needed him, and he
couldn't drive himself. It would be worse than DUI
in a car with these sedatives and painkillers still fog-
ging his brain and his sight.

"You mean, I'll drive a cruiser?" Peggy asked, perking up a bit. "I always wanted to do that."

"No, your car. Now."

He got to his feet again while Peggy grabbed her purse. If Joel was after Claire, or there was someone else more clever and powerful involved, Nick figured he'd have one chance, one guess, where to look for her before it was too late.

Claire had no choice but to walk along the river path with Ethan, hoping he'd drop his guard. At least he didn't have the Taser out now. It was raining, but the water felt good to her, cleansing, even rousing, as her mind raced for a way out.

She could try screaming, but she saw no fishermen, maybe because of the rain all day. Even Sam would not come drifting along the river like a wandering spirit tonight. The falls would probably drown her voice, but she would not let them drown her.

"You paid Joel to phone the sheriff's office to say Keith jumped when you actually pushed him," she accused, as Ethan forced her up the path that led to the bridge. She had to get him talking again. Things were spinning by too fast; the bridge and falls were coming too close.

The wet leaves lay slick and slippery underfoot. Perhaps she could stage a fall and shove him off balance down the slope. But when she tried going to her knees, he merely hoisted her to her feet again and shoved her on.

"That helicopter crew of Howard Chin's that supposedly came to rescue us were intended to kill us, weren't they?" she demanded. "Nick Braden spotted a rifle, which they then switched with a megaphone when that other chopper landed near them. That will tip Nick off to pursuing Howard Chin and you.''

"Don't bet on it. Howard's money can make most things go away, but he put me personally in charge of handling Keith, then you. But yeah, when they saw the other chopper, they had to pretend they'd been trying to radio for help and change their tactics,'' he said.

"You seemed to be upset that I asked if Diana was in on this. Noah Markwood will testify that she was in on everything when it comes out about those four-inch bases on that Tang dynasty horse and the smuggled disks. You may lie to me she wasn't involved, but she'll go to prison, too, when—''

Ethan jerked her so hard that Claire almost passed out from the pain.

"She only knew we'd switched to bases that size, not why. And as I said, Keith was behind that. I'm protecting Diana. She can't know this about her father and me. The night Keith died, she thought I was at her father's place. He covered for me, and that's what's going to happen tonight, too.''

"Howard Chin's guilt will make international headlines,'' Claire taunted, so desperate she wasn't sure what she was saying anymore, only that she had to hurt—to stop—this man. "I can see it now,'' she said. "Howard Chin Ruins His Daughter's Future and His Proud Family Heritage and Fortune by Betraying the Country That Took Him In and—''

"And as good as drowned his only son, that's how he sees it!'' Ethan shouted to be heard over the crash of the falls as they emerged from the foliage near the bridge itself. "His only son was with a U.S. senator's son at the beach when the senator saw the two boys caught in a riptide. He rescued his own son first. When he supposedly turned to help Howard's son, he'd gone under. A man like that represents a country where there is no honor, no sacrifice like in China—that's Howard Chin's opinion!''

She had no time to argue as Ethan shoved her out on the first of the rotted railroad ties. When she balked, he dragged her, straddling the bad ones.

That night she'd wakened on the bridge after being shot by the Taser had been terrifying, but now she felt frozen in abject horror. This man would kill her, throw her off into that boiling, brutal water just as he had Keith. The agony of the Taser gun first or not wouldn't matter in that dreadful death.

Claire let her knees buckle, taking all her weight off her feet. Her ankle wrenched again; her terror had made her forget the pain from each step she'd taken to get here.

Ethan pitched off balance, but not enough for her to shove him from the bridge. Again, he hauled her back to her feet and pushed her farther out on the old iron span. At least he'd have to untie her arms before he threw her off, she thought, and then...

"You know, Claire, I'm really sorry about this. Keith was a traitor—''

"You ought to know.''

"—but you were only being a good wife to try to find out what happened to him. A good wife to a man who didn't deserve you. You're smart and brave, and I swear I'm sorry it has to end like this. So you won't have to suffer in the river, I'm just going to shoot you with this Taser the way I did him, so it's over faster. You know, he thought he got me out on this bridge because he lied to me about hiding my money and the disks out here, when in fact I wanted to come out here to kill him.''

''Won't you be surprised when those disks merely list sales of artifacts you've as good as stolen from Chinese graves?'' she cried. It was the last thing she could think of to try to stop him. ''And what if he wasn't lying and the money is out here? What if I know where it is? I didn't want to share it with you, but now I'm willing to bargain.''

''Once again,'' Ethan shouted, ''you never cease to amaze me.''

He turned her away, pressing her against a rusted bridge support while he loosed Keith's ties from around her wrists and torso. Did he believe her about the money? Was he going to free her to show him where it was? But no, he dragged her a step away from the girder, facing outward. She knew then that he would push her.

Though she wanted to shut out the scene below, she studied the raging river's depths. Fallen stars swam in swirling white pools of inky water. She wished she could capture this in a painting, the blurred dark colors, each momentous movement, the power of it all. As if there were no top or bottom to the earth and universe, she felt off balance. Yet, beyond the trees, she imagined she could see the lighted lodge, awaiting her return.

It would be so easy to give in, but she wanted desperately to live, to see this scene in sunlight again. And to see it with Nick Braden.

Nick became crazed with panic. The lodge was locked up tight, except for the back deck door, which had been left unlocked. With one of the wrought-iron deck chairs and his good arm, he broke a window to get in.

The four mounted salmon had been torn off the wall and their wooden plaques pulled off. Each had a place for something the size of a computer disk to fit in, and the computer in the office upstairs was on. The office showed signs of a struggle. Worse, there were drops of blood in the hallway.

And, as if Keith's ghost had come calling, a necktie with the words *Made in Hong Kong* and the initials *K. M.* on it dribbled down the steps of the back deck—the steps that went toward the falls.

"But why would a dead man's tie be here?" Peggy asked as Nick read the words aloud from its label.

"Claire may be leaving a trail for us to follow her, or whoever took her. Go back inside and call Mike Woods, even Aaron if you can raise him, to meet me at the bridge."

"The suicide bridge?"

"And make it code eight!"

Gripping the tie, he thudded down the stairs. Each step jarred his shoulder so painfully he clenched his teeth.

He cursed himself for not bringing a flashlight from the lodge, but his eyes soon adjusted to the dark. Squinting to look for another tie along the river path, he tried to hold his arm in its sling to his body as he ran.

He had, he realized, not only no flashlight, but no gun. No backup, no stamina, no strength. Only desperation and his love for Claire. And a mounting fear he would lose her as he had loved and lost before.

*   *   *

Despite the roar of the falls, Claire squinted into the darkness, certain she'd heard someone call her. It must be the voices in the falls again. Or Keith's spirit, which Sam had tried so hard to summon. Had Ethan said something else, in the moment before he planned to shoot her with the Taser or shove her off into the abyss?

But it had sounded in her head and heart like Nick. Along the path below, running...yes, Nick.

"The police are here!" she shouted to Ethan. He either didn't care or didn't believe her. She did not believe it herself, but must have dreamed Nick, imagining him like a figure she could paint on a canvas.

But the man on the river path below kept running, running.

It all happened so fast, but like slow-motion, too.

Ethan lifted the Taser to her neck, and she could feel how cold the muzzle was. She tried to thrust it away and saw as she did that he was in such a rush she had two of Keith's neckties still knotted around her wrist.

Standing sideways, she tried to knee Ethan in the groin. He grunted and the gun spun away into darkness. She was shocked to see he'd donned his knitted ski mask. Only his eyes and mouth showed, as if some faceless form had emerged from the night. He cursed, half righted himself and shoved her hard. She tried to cling to the metal girder and to embrace it.

But she fell free.

Claire's captor didn't seem to have a face. No, Nick thought, the man wore a black mask, but he still knew who it must be. It had all come together earlier, despite the still-missing pieces. Behind everything was Ethan Nance, a man he had never seen, like a river phantom in the dark mists on the bridge.

In that instant he charged up the slippery path toward the bridge, Claire seemed to lunge, to fall.

A cry wrenched from Nick's gut.

But she didn't fall into the river. She jerked to a halt and swung several feet below the bridge, above the ranging torrent, suspended by some sort of rope connecting her wrists.

Nick blocked out his pain. With his good arm he clawed his way up, up the twisting path to the bridge, then started across the gap-toothed span toward the man who meant to kill her. If Nance had a gun, Nick and Claire were both dead, but he ran like hell, anyway.

Evidently, the man had not seen him until he charged onto the bridge. Still masked, he was trying to cut Claire's ropes, which must be her own tether.

As Nance saw Nick and finally stood to run, Nick put his good shoulder into him.

The impact jarred Nick to his teeth, but Nance went down. He had to incapacitate him quickly, and get to Claire before she dropped. He'd kill the man if he had to, anything to save her.

Claire could not believe Nick was here, fighting Ethan on the broken span of railroad ties above while she clung to the neckties below. She wasn't certain how she had managed to wrap the silk strips around the girder before Ethan shoved her. It was Keith's last gift to her, despite all he'd done.

One tie was still knotted taut around her right wrist; the other she held wrapped around her left hand. If only she could swing on them to get closer to the web of iron supports under the bridge...but the material could tear or slip. The rain and mist from the falls was soaking her hands, making everything slippery. The whiteout of nearby roaring water reached out to her. Still, she had not come this far to die in the depths of the river she loved.

She felt the ties cutting off the circulation in her wrists. Her hands, cold and prickly, were going numb. How dreadful that her mother had cut her wrists. Despite their similar looks and their artistic talent, she was not like her mother. Claire Malvern fought against tough times and did not give in.

She screamed as a body hurtled past her and was lost in the churning depths below. Who? Which one of them?

She looked up, terrified that Nick's injuries had hampered him against that madman. If Ethan leaned over that bridge to cut her loose again, she might just let go.

But it was Nick's face, Nick's arm.

"I don't think I can pull you up," he shouted, "but I'm going to lower my arm sling for you to get into. I can wedge myself in up here somehow and hold the sling with my one hand—hold you until help comes."

She wondered how he had managed to get out of that sling; he was obviously in so much pain. But he lowered it to her. She rigged it under her arms so it helped take her weight off the ties.

Yes, she thought, staring up into his steady, strong gaze as he kept her suspended there, he could hold her forever and she'd never be afraid of anything again. Besides, he needed her to take care of him.

"I know we've only known each other for about three weeks," Nick said between clenched teeth, "but I'd like to have that dinner at the lodge you promised me. The hospital food wasn't the best."

"Don't I know. Are you busy tomorrow?"

"Tomorrow's good."

"Done! What else?"

"I'd like to tell you how you've changed my life, how much I love you."

At that, she almost felt she could fly. "I think I'll hang around to hear more of that," she managed to say.

"I know it's all so fast—"

"After all that we've been through?" she interrupted. "Three lifetimes in three weeks!"

"I'll help with the lodge, and you can help me with my work. You've been telling me how to do it from the first, anyway."

"I like the compliments much better, Nick Braden!"

"That *was* a compliment!"

They were both crying, but they kept talking, shouting. Some of their conversation was bravado, some teasing, but all of it full of courage and love.

Yet it seemed an eternity before flashlight beams illuminated them and they heard shouts. Soon, Aaron and Mike had a rope under her armpits, and she was up and in Nick's arms—his good one, anyway— where they held tight in fierce defiance of the fury of the falls.

Epilogue

Claire could not believe it had been a year to the day since she had hung by neckties, and a shoulder sling, and the strength of Nick's love from the Bloodroot River Bridge. Now, men in harnesses hung there as their blowtorches cut its iron and steel beams apart. Other workers winched the beams down on big cables and cut them into smaller pieces to be hauled away.

As they had for several days, Aaron and Nick held the crowd back from the demolition company's safety ropes. This afternoon, they kept the increased number of people who had come to see the grand finale behind the neon-yellow police tape, too.

Those terrible times a year ago paled, she thought, compared to the past two weeks since the Twin Towers across the continent had been toppled by terrorists. Today, for far different reasons, the Bloodroot Bridge was also coming down, and she'd had a taunting nursery rhyme in her head all day:

London Bridge is falling down, falling down, falling down...London Bridge is falling down, my fair lady...

It was enough to drive her crazy.

Except she didn't let herself think that way anymore. She was not crazy, and those who had tried to make her think so were dead or in prison. Claire did not blame the widowed Diana, who had also lost her disgraced father when he went to jail for the rest of his life. Claire felt sorry for Tess, too, who had sold their place to a farmer who wanted to turn it into a salmon-breeding farm, and had gone to live with her mother after Joel was indicted, convicted and incarcerated.

At least all that, Claire thought, had brought her closer to her own father.

"It won't be long now," her dad said. Standing next to her on the riverbank, he put his arm around her shoulders and gave her a quick hug. Unlike the others here, he was not looking at the remains of the bridge, but at her—really looking at her. "That baby's history, and your bad times with it, honey," he went on, pointing upward. "It's a good thing the kids have school in San Diego. If they were visiting with me this time, we'd have to tie them down out here to keep them from getting too near those beams and girders these guys have been chopping up this week."

"It will take all of us to watch the two of them this summer when they learn how to fish here," Claire said. She was grateful her dad's wife and kids loved the lodge, and she carefully scheduled the paying guests to vacate rooms for visits from family and friends.

Today, Claire was surprised to see Tess Markwood back in town, standing like many Portfalls people along the riverbank, watching the bridge's death throes. Claire hadn't spoken to her since the last day of Joel's trial. She had evidently been watching Claire, too, and waved forlornly.

"I'll be right back, Dad," Claire said, and made her way to Tess.

"How's your mother?" Claire asked to avoid an awkward opening.

"Better, actually. She says I cheer her up," Tess answered without meeting Claire's eyes. They both watched the men working on the remnants of the iron skeleton.

"And you, Tess?"

She frowned. "It's a real adjustment, my living with her after so many years here. Even though Noah offered me a job in the shops, I thought it best to pull up stakes."

"As far as I'm concerned, you can come back to visit any day, including at the lodge," Claire told her, touching her arm and turning to face her. "As I told you, I don't blame you for anything Joel did. I can't, considering my own situation."

Tess started to nod, then leaned forward to give Claire a hard hug. They clung to each other for a moment, then stepped apart. Tess's eyes widened as she looked at Claire's hand.

"Claire, that's a gorgeous blue sapphire ring, but you're wearing it on your left hand. Is it what I think? Nick Braden?"

Claire smiled down at her ring. It caught a slice of sun and glittered brighter than the river.

"We decided we wanted to do things very differently this time, but yes, it's an engagement ring.

We'll be married next month, and the reception's at the lodge. Then we're flying in our new plane to Santa Fe for a honeymoon while my dad and stepmother stay at the lodge for two weeks.''

"Is Nick going to help you run it?''

"Only in his spare time. He's going to continue to be the best sheriff this county's ever had. Actually, he's been really busy with security details, even out here in the boonies, since the September 11th tragedies. You know, sometimes I feel guilty being happy right now, with all the nation's losses.''

"Don't ever be sorry for happiness, Claire. But, you know, having lost a husband, even if mine's in prison, makes me feel more for all those other losses—even this bad, old bridge.''

Bloodroot Bridge is falling down, my fair lady...

Today the demolition crew from Seattle had cut through its very spine, until just two beams were left on this side. Safety cables snaked from beam to beam to hold them up until the last moment. No other sad or sick souls, Claire thought, would jump from the bridge into the foaming river below.

Claire saw Anne Cunningham standing on the other side of the river, where fewer people waited since that bank was harder to get to.

"Well, would you look at that,'' Tess said, as she, too, evidently spotted Anne.

Claire was going to ask her if she knew anything about Anne and Keith, but she soon saw that wasn't what her friend meant. Tess's brother-in-law Noah was walking toward Anne. Even from here they could see Anne smile at him before they huddled, whispering or perhaps shouting over the noise of the water. Noah and Anne suddenly seemed to Claire to look, maybe not exactly happy, but hopeful.

Claire sensed Sam's presence almost before she saw him. She excused herself from Tess and went to stand with him, not along the path where most people waited, but in a clump of sharp-scented cedars on the bank.

"I suppose you're glad to see the bridge go," she said to Sam as they gazed out over the scene together.

"The bridge itself is not to blame," he said solemnly. "It is only man who can ruin the salmon's river."

"Sam, I've been wanting to ask you something. When you told me the salmon had all the answers and that Keith knew that and used that, you didn't mean you were aware he'd hidden something behind his four mounted salmon on the lodge wall, did you?"

"No, I didn't know. I meant he was wily like the salmon. Now I know you are the one who has their strength."

As Claire studied him, he turned his head slowly to look at her. Something like a smile lifted the old man's lips just as a loud cracking sound made them all jump.

From the rock face that had long held the bridge, the next-to-last beam came loose and was lowered to the ground.

"I want to be with Nick when the last one comes down," she told Sam, and hurried along the river path.

With the addition of his construction hard hat, Nick was wearing his dress uniform, just as he had

that day he'd presided over Keith's funeral. Instead,
this ceremony was for the bridge. All morning, he'd
been worrying about and watching the crowds—the
way, Claire thought, DeeDee used to watch him.

At least that poor girl was better now after being
under the care of physicians who specialized in both
medical and mental needs. This summer, DeeDee
had sent both her and Nick letters of apology. She'd
written that she'd lost forty pounds *so far,* and was
hoping to work for her sister after she served her
prison sentence.

Her sentence had been greatly shortened by time
in a psychiatric ward, because both Nick and Claire
had testified on her behalf at her trial. *I can't thank
you enough for that,* she'd written, *because the doctors can help me get my head on straight before I
have to serve any time. After I'm paroled, I'll be
working as a nanny for my sister's kids. They write
me cute little notes, and I couldn't do without them.
Well, I want you to know I'm trying to change, and
I realize both of you tried to help me when I was so
messed up....*

Nick and Aaron kept moving people even farther
back as the last cabled beam was lowered. But
Nick's gaze caught Claire's, and his dark eyes lit to
see her. When he was sure that people were standing
completely clear, he headed toward her, put his arm
around her waist and pinned her to his side. Like
everyone, they stood silent, craning their necks to
look up.

"I'll still see it there whenever I paint the falls,"
she said.

"I'll still see it in my worst nightmares and best

dreams,'' he said, his breath warm in her ear. ''In a way, it gave me you.''

They turned to gaze into each other's eyes and they kissed. It was a mere peck at first that turned to a devouring roar of its own that made all other sounds go utterly silent.

Finally, a gasp in the crowd made them pull apart. It echoed the way Claire felt with this man when he so much as looked at her: suspended, breathless, dizzy and awed. She couldn't wait for their wedding and the family they had planned.

But again, everyone was looking up. She saw that one of the three cables on this final big beam had snapped. As the I-beam twisted, then tipped, it was obvious why people had reacted.

From one end of the beam poured money—hundreds of green-and-white bills, catching in the trees, littering the banks and fluttering into the river in a steady stream of their own.

Despite the rope and police tape, people ducked and darted out, scooping up money like confetti. Nick ran to push people back again, yelling at them not to get under the rotating beam.

''Fifties and hundreds!'' someone shouted.

Another voice announced, ''It's not old money— crisp bills!''

''Pennies from heaven!'' a woman screamed.

Nick and Aaron held the crowd back, but the shower of riches continued, thicker than salmon in the river. Claire pushed her way closer to the tape, to Nick.

''It's got to be Ethan Nance's blackmail money!'' she shouted to him as the bills became a blizzard. ''Keith really did hide it there!''

She didn't know whether to laugh or cry. It was hardly needed for evidence in a case that had already been tried and settled. It could go back neither to Ethan nor to Keith. People would never want it to go to Diana, who had inherited what little was left of her father's estate, and Claire would certainly never want it. Blackmail and blood money, all of it.

"It's like the suicide bridge is trying to say it's sorry, to pay us back!" someone yelled.

"Manna from heaven, to add to the survivors' funds for 9/11!" Aaron shouted, as he, too, began to gather bills as fast as he could.

Soon, as far as they could see, people harvested money, wet and dry, and ran up to hand it over to Aaron and Nick. "This will go to those people who jumped, who fell or were lost in the Twin Towers," Claire overheard someone say. "Hand the money in here, and we'll donate all of it from the people of Portfalls!"

Soon Claire also had her hands, then her arms, full of fifty-and hundred-dollar bills, though she'd rather still be holding Nick. But together or apart, they were the inheritors of riches in each other, and were survivors of tough times. In this precious place, they would build bridges anew that no one could ever tear down.

Author Note

I would like to thank the following experts in their fields for information and advice which helped me write this story:

Aaron Kurtz, police officer, Sharon Township, Franklin county, Ohio.

Sheriff Mike Hawley, Island County Sheriff's Office Coupeville, Washington. Mike's online course about a county sheriff's duties was invaluable, although I did not pattern my sheriff or Portfalls after Sheriff Hawley or his jurisdiction.

Linnea Sinclair-Bernadino, former private investigator, on information about how PIs work.

Beth Anne Daye for information about flora and fauna in the Whidbey Island area and for a fine description of the beautiful Deception Pass Bridge on which the Bloodroot River Bridge is very loosely based.

Earl Redmond, pilot, for his detailed help on Cessnas and flying.

Susan Wiggs for wise words about the Seattle area and its yacht clubs.

Laurie Miller, R.N., for advice about setting a dislocated shoulder.

Loewendick Demolition Contractors, Columbus, Ohio, for information about demolishing an old iron railroad bridge.

Several experts who work with Search and Rescue dogs, including Marian Hardy whose fine National Water Search Report was invaluable.

Any mistakes or misinterpretations made in presenting facts are the author's and not those of my generous informants.

My fascination with salmon runs was inspired by my trip to Alaska, where my husband and I followed a salmon river and were awed by the determination and stamina of the battered fish. I thought it would be a perfect extended metaphor for a heroine like Claire. My visit to an Ocean Spray cranberry farm in Massachusetts was of much help, as was visiting the downtown Seattle sites I used.

Karen Harper
July, 2002